# Angels of War

LANA KORTCHIK



HQ

ONE PLACE. MANY STORIES

HQ
An imprint of HarperCollins*Publishers* Ltd
1 London Bridge Street
London SE1 9GF

www.harpercollins.co.uk

HarperCollins*Publishers*
Macken House, 39/40 Mayor Street Upper,
Dublin 1 D01 C9W8
This edition 2025

2
First published in Great Britain by HQ,
an imprint of HarperCollins*Publishers* Ltd 2025


A catalogue record for this book is available from the British Library.

ISBN: 9780008656775



Printed and bound in the United States

**LANA KORTCHIK** grew up in two opposite corners of the former Soviet Union – a snow-white Siberian town and the golden-domed capital of Ukraine. At the age of sixteen, she moved to Australia with her mother. Lana and her family live on the Central Coast of New South Wales, where it never snows and is always summer-warm. She loves books, martial arts, the ocean and Napoleonic history. Her short stories have appeared in many magazines and anthologies. She is the author of the *USA Today* bestselling *Sisters of War* and *Daughters of the Resistance*.

Also by Lana Kortchik

*Sisters of War*
*Daughters of the Resistance*
*The Countess of the Revolution*
*Sisters of the Sky*

*For Christopher and Sophie. You are my everything.*

*War broke: and now the winter of the world*
*With perishing great darkness closes in.*

*Wilfred Owen*

# Part I

# Manila

# Chapter 1

## October 1941

As she stood on board US Army Transport *Willard A. Holbrook* bound for Manila, her dark hair blowing in the wind, Rose Williams waited for the mist to part so she could catch a glimpse of her future. When she was a little girl, growing up in the sleepy town of Brownville in Maine, she often longed for a bit of magic in her life, for the pages of her favourite books to come alive and whisk her away. And here she was, finally, on the brink of the greatest adventure of all! Somewhere behind her, she heard excited voices and the sound of stomping feet. 'Land, land!' And yet, all she could see in front of her was the twirling grey fog and the silver expanse of the sea, the view she had become accustomed to during the long and uncomfortable passage. She rose to her tiptoes, trying to make herself taller, and pressed the palm of her hand to her heart. With the first rays of tropical morning, the fog dispersed. The water was no longer silver but shimmering blue. Out of nowhere, it seemed, a ragged outline of land appeared, as if someone had pulled the curtains open. Even though she was expecting it, it took Rose completely by surprise. It was like a magic trick, and Rose blinked, wondering if the land was a mirage that would soon melt away in the blazing sun.

But it didn't melt away. Rose watched as, little by little, pale sand and white residences rose from the sea. It looked nothing like Brownville, rainy and grey at this time of year. At the thought of home, she felt a stab of loneliness. Her mother had been horrified when Rose told her she was going to the Philippines to be a nurse. But then, she had been horrified when she applied to the nursing school all those years ago. She didn't want her around sick people at Eastern Maine General Hospital, where Rose had spent the most exhausting but also exhilarating twelve months of her life. Her mother wanted her to live the same life she herself had lived – quiet, safe, uneventful. 'There's a war on. If you leave, how can I keep you safe? What if something bad happens?' she repeated, holding her daughter tight one wet morning in San Francisco as they waited for the train that would take her away.

Rose wanted to tell her mother that the whole world was out there for her to explore. She wanted to say that she had never seen a tropical sunset before, that she had never swum with the dolphins or sipped a cocktail on the beach. Like all young people, she didn't believe anything bad could happen to her. What she said instead was, 'Maybe it's my turn to take care of you for a change. It's good money, Mama.'

Arriving in Manila on her twenty-second birthday seemed like a good omen to Rose. It was a fresh start and she embraced it with all her heart, even though her heart ached a little. She had never been anywhere other than Brownville, Bangor, Boston and, briefly, San Francisco three weeks ago. There had been a short stop in Hawaii, a warm breeze on her face that carried with it the unknown, a sense of otherness, a hint of excitement. Now, 8,000 miles away from home, part of the Army Nurse Corps and ready to start her two-year tour of duty in the Philippines, Rose found herself teetering on the edge of her new life, trembling from fear and anticipation.

The other four nurses on board the *Holbrook* didn't teeter or tremble. Their loud voices rose above the sound of the waves and the screeching of the seagulls.

'The sky is a different colour here,' said Kate, a beauty from New York, her long blonde hair neatly brushed off her face, her small feet tap dancing with excitement. 'And look at the jungle. It's dark green, like emeralds.' She clapped her hands, looking delighted.

'You should be a poet, not a nurse,' said Rose, admiring the greenery that sprawled over the hills all the way down to the sand that was so white, it looked like a bridal gown. Rose wondered what it would feel like to walk on it with her bare feet. Like treading on a cloud, perhaps. The sand on Carson Beach in Boston was a murky yellow, almost brown, and looked nothing like this. In the far distance, she could see rugged mountains reaching for the sun, as if they were raising their hand in greeting, beckoning her closer, imploring her not to be afraid. 'I've never seen anything like it,' she whispered.

'It smells of seaweed and dead fish,' said Anne, a tall redhead with a face of a fairy-tale princess and an expression that was sour like bad grapes. 'And my dress feels damp. This heat, it makes me sweat too much.' Even though they had all made an effort for the landing, putting on their best gowns, hats and gloves, no one looked as elegant or well dressed as Anne. She would be so beautiful, thought Rose, if only she learnt how to smile.

'Look at the fishing boats bobbing on the water. And the houses, glowing in the sun like pearls. We are going to have the best time here,' said a bubbly fair-haired nurse called Tess, grinning from ear to ear, her eyes sparkling with mischief.

Ida, a shy brunette who seemed to prefer listening to speaking, nodded and turned towards the shore.

The land was close but the ship wasn't moving. Rose looked at the quivering shoreline in silence, wondering how much longer it would take and whether she would remember this day for the rest of her life. Suddenly, something white flew past, nearly hitting her on the head, twirling and dancing and looping through the air like a gull diving for fish, and finally landing in the water. 'My hat,' cried Kate, running across the deck and leaning over the railing to see better.

The girls fell quiet, watching the hat as it jumped on the waves. When Rose looked up, she saw Kate slipping her shoes off. 'What are you doing?' she asked.

'Going in to get my hat.'

'Ladies don't jump in the ocean from ships to retrieve hats,' said Anne, squinting, surveying Kate's dress, her gloves, her neat hair, her bare stockinged feet. 'Can you even swim?'

'I can't lose this hat. And yes, I can swim perfectly well. Back home, we used to race each other on the Hudson. No one could swim as fast as me or stay underwater longer.'

'This is not the Hudson, Kate,' said Tess. 'There could be sharks. Deadly jellyfish. You have no idea what's in that water.'

'My hat is in that water and I'm not getting off this ship without it.'

But before Kate had a chance to prove how well she could swim, they heard a loud splash. The girls turned around. One of the soldiers of the 19th Bombardment Group was in the water, waving. He was a few feet away from the hat, and a moment later he was holding it in his hands, pumping his fist in the air in triumph.

'Beware of the sharks,' cried Tess.

'That hat is ruined now,' said Anne with disdain. 'All that salt water.'

But judging by Kate's elated face, she didn't care whether the hat was ruined.

'Would you really jump in there?' Rose asked Kate while the soldier climbed back on board.

'Of course.'

'You are fearless, Kate. I wish I could be more like you.'

'Not fearless. Just … My brother gave me that hat before we said goodbye. He is the only family I have.'

When the soldier approached them, dripping water and grinning at Kate, the girls surrounded him, clucking like hens, wanting to know if the water was cold, where he had learnt to swim like that and whether he could make it all the way to the shore. Kate thanked him and clasped the wet hat to her chest like it were a baby.

Another ship passed them and everyone onboard waved at the nurses and the soldiers gathered on deck. Smiling, Rose waved back. 'Who are these people? Where are they going?' she asked the dripping wet soldier who had fetched the hat. He told her they were families of the officers stationed in the Philippines, evacuating back to the States. When she heard the word *evacuating*, Rose's hands began to tremble. It seemed menacing, filled with danger. She wanted to ask the soldier what it meant but didn't dare. On a day like today, when she could close her eyes and almost touch the joy and anticipation in the air, she couldn't bear to think of war. Instead, she wanted to run on the sand with frangipani flowers in her hair and feel the tropical sea beneath her bare feet. She wanted to hold on to this feeling of happiness with not a care in the world, but as she stood on deck staring at the big ship in the distance, filled with smiling, waving people, a cold fear gripped her. Nervously, she twisted the ring on her finger, a present from her mother for her eighteenth birthday.

The *Holbrook* slipped into Manila Harbour, past Corregidor Island, while the girls stared in wonder at great battleships and tiny fishing boats anchored side by side. On shore, people lined the harbour and greeted the newcomers like they knew them, like they were welcoming their families. The aroma of flowers, the sea breeze, the excitement of it all – Rose couldn't find the words to describe it but, as she gulped for air, taking it all in, her heart was racing.

A band in white uniform struck up a lively tune, the sun reflecting off their brass instruments. Everything seemed brighter here, the sky a vivid blue, the houses a striking white, the trees and the grass a deep green. In Brownville, Rose had seen postcards from tropical paradise and had always thought it couldn't possibly look like this in real life, intense and filled with colour, it must be exaggerated for effect by the artist's brush or the photographer's lens. But now, as she was ready to step ashore, she could see that the colours really were that intense. Everything she looked at made her gasp in wonder.

As they docked at pier seven, Rose caught her breath. She had been anticipating this moment for so long, she thought the earth would move the moment she stepped on firm land. But the earth didn't move, although her head was spinning a little from hunger.

It wasn't the hard work she was afraid of. The year she had spent at Eastern Maine General Hospital had prepared her for anything. And it wasn't the whispers of war, coming from half a world away. The Philippines was a spec in the ocean, away from *everything*. Rose was certain she would be safer here than anywhere else. As she stepped off the gangplank into the rest of her life, as she listened to speeches welcoming the new nurses to the Philippines, as she received a corsage from their new leader, Miss E. Valine Messner, the Chief Nurse of the Philippine Command, she wondered if she had what it took to make her new life a success.

Two chauffeur-driven cars waited to take the nurses to their quarters. As the drivers started the engines and they began to move slowly through the busy streets of Manila, Tess exclaimed, 'Look at those trees. What are they?'

'Palm trees, silly,' said Anne. 'Haven't you seen them before?'

Tess shook her head. 'I grew up in Boston.'

'So did I. But we holidayed in Florida every year.'

'Lucky you. We had no time or money for fancy holidays. My parents were too busy working and putting food on the table.'

Rose was barely listening, too busy gaping at purple bougainvillea and yellow plumeria that adorned the city walls, splodges of colour so striking, they took her breath away. They passed

Fort Santiago, the defence fortress that rose from Manila's colonial walled city, the Intramuros, built by the Spanish in the sixteenth century, according to the driver. Buildings flew past and soon expensive residences gave way to shantytowns, lopsided huts made of bamboo sticks and mud. Finally, they made it to downtown Manila, a settlement of shaded porticoes, white like alabaster. They drove around a grey building, which Rose assumed was the US Army Sternberg General Hospital, and stopped outside a row of bungalows.

The nurses spilled out of the cars, gathering under the canopy of acacia. A housekeeper greeted them, directing them to their quarters. Rose was to share a bungalow with Kate and Tess, while Anne and Ida were to live with another nurse who had arrived a few weeks earlier. Rose was thrilled to learn that she would have her own room. She had never had a room all to herself before. In the past, she had slept behind a partition, her bed inches away from her mother's.

There was a shared bathroom, dining facilities and a porch with a swing. Outside, a swimming pool sparkled in the sun. When Rose saw it, she wanted to jump up and down with delight, throw off her gown and dive in. Instead, she had to listen to the housekeeper, who was showing them their beds, the mahogany fans that cooled the rooms, the wicker furniture.

'Excuse me,' Kate said to the man, who introduced himself as Fernando and was perspiring in the midday heat in his heavy suit. 'We are a little bit hungry.'

Standing by Kate's side, Rose nodded.

'You girls should have eaten the scones and biscuits onboard the ship before we docked,' Tess whispered, pinching Kate. 'They were delicious.'

'I was too excited to eat,' said Kate.

'And I was feeling seasick,' said Rose.

'Dinner will be served in the dining hall promptly at six,' replied Fernando.

'We get dinner cooked for us?' Rose looked around the small bungalow. There was no kitchen, no stove or oven, only a small fridge in the corner by the settee.

'You will be served three meals a day. The cleaners come every morning at eleven. Kindly leave your dirty laundry in this basket and our staff will take care of it.'

Rose could hardly believe her ears. She had grown up watching her mother clean and cook for other people. Now these simple tasks would be taken care of by someone else. The other girls looked as amazed as Rose. Everyone but Anne, who seemed bored and unimpressed.

Fernando told them they were to report for their first four-hour shift at the hospital in the morning and left. Kate cried out with glee and fell on the bed. 'We're going to live like queens! Everything done for us. We won't have to lift a finger.'

They found their uniforms laid out on their beds – white dresses and caps, similar to Rose's former civilian uniform except for the small military badge on the collar. She touched the badge, contemplating what it meant. The moment she put on her new uniform and reported for her first shift at the hospital, she would become a military nurse. She felt her hands tremble with fear and anticipation.

After a short rest and dinner fit for royalty, the girls gathered in the living room. Rose felt her eyelids grow heavy, like someone had filled them with sand. When she closed her eyes, it still felt like everything was spinning a little, like she was still on board the ship, heading into the great unknown. She needed a good night's sleep in her comfortable bed that stood on firm ground and didn't bob up and down on waves. But she knew she wouldn't be able to sleep. She was too excited.

Kate jumped up on the spot, clasping her hands together. 'Why don't we go out and explore?'

'We start work tomorrow,' said Anne. 'We need our rest.'

'I once worked two eight-hour shifts back-to-back at home,' said Tess. 'I can do a four-hour shift in my sleep.'

'We should recover from the journey. It's important to make a good first impression,' said Anne.

'What are you, 90?' cried Tess, her eyes sparkling. 'Live a little. How many times have you been away from home before?'

'Plenty,' muttered Anne.

'How many times have you been away from home alone, with no one to tell you what to do?'

Rose nodded. 'We'll be fine tomorrow. We won't stay out late.'

'Do what you want,' said Anne, turning her back to them. 'I'm going straight to bed.'

They put on their bathing suits underneath their summer frocks and slipped out of the bungalow, giggling like schoolgirls, leaving Anne to catch up on her beauty sleep.

The balmy air was perfumed with flowers, as if someone had sprinkled expensive perfume as a special welcome for the new nurses. A slight breeze played with Rose's hair. Suddenly she felt free like the wind and just as fearless. She could go anywhere. She could do anything. Her mother wasn't there to tell her how to behave, how to wear her hair or what time to go to bed. When she was away from home during her internship at Eastern Maine General, she had no time to enjoy her freedom. They studied hard and worked even harder. But here in Manila, she had all the time in the world.

'It's so warm here. Isn't it divine? I'm not living anywhere cold again,' said Kate. 'Or anywhere where I have to do my own laundry or cook my own meals.' She stretched her arms out and spun down the road in a dreamy waltz. 'I don't want to see snow ever again.'

'What about Christmas? You can't have Christmas without snow,' said Rose, who felt a little sick in her stomach at the thought of the streets of her hometown dressed in white.

Kate shrugged. 'A warm Christmas will be wonderful this

year. A Christmas when I can swim in the ocean. That's where we should go. We should go swimming.'

'Now, in the dark?' asked Tess.

'What are you afraid of?' Kate demanded.

'Sharks. Drunk sailors. Enemy ships.'

'What enemy ships?' Ida's eyes became round.

'I've never touched the ocean before,' said Rose, who, until she got on the ship in San Francisco, had only seen the ocean once, on a cold winter afternoon in Boston. But it wasn't the same ocean. It had looked foreboding, heavy and frightening, not warm and inviting like the waters of the Philippines.

'We're going swimming!' Kate cried, twirling with joy in the near darkness.

They caught a cab to Manila Bay Beach, feeling like teenagers playing hooky from school, and stood by the water that was the colour of the plums Rose's mama used to bring back from her employer's garden in autumn. The stars and the moon reflected off its shimmering surface like pearls, while the palm trees whispered of dreams and adventure. The sand felt like a soft quilt under their feet.

Kate jumped in the sea. 'It's like a warm bath,' she cried. 'Like warm milk.'

Moments later, everyone was in the water except Tess, who stood timidly on the sand and watched them.

'Get in! What are you waiting for?' Kate called out to her. 'Don't be afraid. Can you see any sharks?'

'I can't see much of anything. It's too dark.'

The girls looked at each other, Kate winked and the three of them ran out, grabbed Tess by the hands and dragged her to the water, while she kicked and shouted, begging them to let go. But they didn't let go. They were laughing, and soon Tess was laughing too, splashing in the water, saying how good it felt on her body, on her parched skin, on her hot face after almost three weeks onboard the ship.

Rose glided on her back. She could see the girls' silhouettes in the moonlight, could hear them chatting excitedly nearby. She closed her eyes, feeling like she was floating on a cloud, and experienced a strange sense of displacement, like it was all happening to someone else, like it couldn't possibly be her, a galaxy away from home, swimming in the tropical sea under the gleaming moon. The water sparkled in the dark, hypnotising her. 'It was my mother's dream to travel to Hawaii one day,' she said. 'Every time she spoke about it, her eyes would light up. She always wanted to live somewhere warm. She had a special jar at home where she would put her spare change, hoping one day she would have enough for a trip. But inevitably something happened; the roof leaked, one of us got sick, she lost another job, and the jar would be opened and the money would disappear. She never got to travel somewhere warm.'

'But *you* did,' said Tess. 'You are living your mother's dream.'

Rose nodded. 'And maybe one day I can save enough money to take her to Hawaii. That's one of the reasons I'm here. I could never make this much money back home, working at a civilian hospital.'

Tess said, 'I'm here to find a husband. You know how many American servicemen are stationed here? And hardly any American women. Where else will you find odds like that?'

Kate said, 'I have a friend in the army at Fort McPherson in Atlanta and he told me all a nurse in Manila needs is a uniform, a bathing suit and an evening gown. I can't wait to go to all the parties.'

'You have your priorities all wrong,' said Ida. 'I came here to become a nurse. To help people.'

'We can help people and have a little fun in the process,' said Kate, splashing water at Ida, making her cry out. 'Maybe we can even meet someone.'

Ida said, 'I don't want to meet anyone. I came here to join my sweetheart. His family has a business in Manila. We met in Texas but then his mother got sick and he had to come back. I thought if I could get a post as a nurse, we could still be together.'

They spoke about nothing and everything, but no one mentioned the spectre of war that hung over them, even here in tropical paradise, an ocean away from Europe where Hitler and his troops trampled over countries at the cost of millions of lives. They didn't return home until midnight because the water was warm silk upon their skin and the stars sparkled like diamonds above their heads.

The sun was bright in the sky, streaking golden light across the room. Slowly, Rose opened one eye and then another, sat up in bed, rubbed her face and stretched, wondering if she should go back to sleep. Her new bed was so comfortable and her body was still aching from the journey, and all she wanted to do was hide her head in her pillows, close her eyes and …

The journey! Suddenly, it all came back to her. She remembered where she was and shot up in bed. Today was her first day of work. She glanced at the clock on the wall and gasped. It was nine in the morning. She catapulted herself out from under her cover, pulling on her brand-new military nurse's uniform as fast as she could, getting entangled in sleeves and stockings. She found Ida, Kate and Tess in the living room, looking frantic.

'Our shift started an hour ago,' said Kate. 'And Anne is already gone.'

'Nice of her to wake us up,' grumbled Tess.

'I'm surprised she didn't,' said Rose. 'She could have said I told you so. And she would have been right. We should have listened to her last night.'

There was no time for breakfast, even though Rose was starving. And there was no time to put on make-up, even though she would have liked to make a good impression on her first day and look professional and put together.

'Don't worry,' Kate said. 'No amount of make-up could hide

the fact that you're over an hour late.'

'Is that supposed to make me feel better?' Rose muttered.

The girls ran out of the bungalow, crossed the car park in large strides and galloped through the main entrance and down the long corridor. Rose was so flustered and out of breath, she didn't pay any attention to her surroundings, concentrating only on moving her feet as fast as she could and keeping up with the others. 'The ambulances must have come from the Spanish-American War,' Tess joked. Rose paused long enough to note that the hospital equipment looked outdated compared to what she was used to at Eastern Maine General.

At quarter past nine, the girls stood with their heads held low in front of Elsie Andrews, the chief nurse at Sternberg Hospital. A petite woman with dark hair and lips like thin pencils on her chubby face, she seemed bigger than she actually was because her eyes flashed with anger and her voice was loud. With her red face and her foot tapping with impatience, she looked like a miniature bull ready to charge. 'We're here to fulfil our calling,' she said to the four girls who seemed ready to burst into tears. 'To take care of others. Our patients need us every moment of every day.'

Rose glanced around her. A 450-bed facility, Sternberg General Hospital appeared almost empty. She didn't say anything.

'It seems you are not taking this job seriously. There are many nurses back in the States who would give their right arm to take your place.' Elsie raised her eyebrows, as if daring them to argue.

Rose stood straight, trying to appear taller, hiding her trembling hands behind her back. 'We are sorry, ma'am. We were tired after the long journey and overslept.' Elsie's eyes bore into Rose as if waiting for her to say more. Rose cleared her throat, fidgeting under the older woman's glare. She wasn't used to lying. Her mother always said she could tell Rose was lying even before she started to speak. Her whole body betrayed her. Even now, she felt her cheeks burning.

Elsie shook her head. She no longer looked angry, only deeply disappointed. 'Anne here tells me you girls snuck out after dark and didn't return until midnight.'

The girls glared at Anne, who was in the corner cleaning surgical instruments and didn't look in their direction, as if the conversation didn't concern her.

'The most important thing for a military nurse is discipline, which you clearly lack,' said Elsie. 'The four of you will be dismissed, effective immediately.'

Rose blinked away the sudden tears. She didn't want to cry in front of the chief nurse on her first day. She had travelled across oceans for her dream job. She had been looking forward to it for months as she lay in her bunk bed at Eastern Maine General after a twelve-hour shift. It was an opportunity of a lifetime and now it was over before it even started. 'Please, ma'am. Give us another chance. It will never happen again.'

'You've had your chance. My decision is final. You will return home on the next ship. In the meantime, please leave the ward and let the rest of us get on with our work.'

Elsie turned away to check on a patient, while the girls shuffled across the ward towards Anne.

'What were you thinking? Why did you tell on us?' Kate whispered, clasping her fists.

'Yes, Anne, what's wrong with you? I thought we were friends,' said Tess.

Rose didn't speak. She was trying very hard not to cry.

Anne scoffed. 'Friends? I just met you girls. There are rules that must be followed. If you can't face the consequences, you shouldn't misbehave. Now, if you excuse me, I have work to do. Not everyone is going back home.'

The girls watched mutely as Anne walked away, her heels clicking on the timber floor.

When Elsie returned, she didn't say a word, just waved at the girls and pointed towards the exit. They followed the chief nurse in silence, their faces red with embarrassment.

'Mama was so proud of me when I got accepted. Even though she didn't want me to go, she bragged to all her friends about it,' Rose whispered to Ida, who was walking by her side, her eyes to the floor. 'What will she say when I come back in disgrace?'

'At least she cares. I don't think my dad was sober long enough to even notice I was gone. I came here to escape him. Where will I go now? If they send me back, I will have to leave Karl behind and I can't bear it.'

'Your sweetheart?'

Ida nodded, her eyes sparkling with tears.

As they made their way through the paediatric ward, Rose heard a piercing scream. A small boy of seven or eight was shouting hysterically, his little fists flying out, trying to push a Filipina nurse away. The nurse had a kind face and troubled eyes. In her hands she held a vial of medicine. The boy tried with all his might to hit the liquid out of the nurse's hands. His hair was pointing in all directions, making him look like an enraged blond porcupine. His arms and legs were slightly too long for him, as if they had shot out overnight and his body hadn't had a chance to catch up yet. 'I want Mama!' The boy sobbed. 'Leave me alone! I don't want to be here.'

The nurse looked like she was about to burst into tears herself. When she saw Elsie, she took a deep breath and said, 'He's been like this all day. We've tried everything. He's not taking his medicine. We don't know what to do with him.'

Rose crouched next to the boy, so she could be the same height as him. At the sight of a new face, he stopped shouting and hiccupped sadly. 'What's your name?' she asked softly.

The boy glared at her suspiciously from under his blond eyebrows. 'I'm not telling you.'

'My name is Rose and I miss my mama too. Do you want to know what makes me feel better sometimes?'

'No, what?' The tears were gone. The boy watched Rose with curiosity.

'Chocolate. You like it too, don't you? I don't know anyone who doesn't.'

The boy nodded.

Rose reached inside her pocket. 'Here, have some.' While the boy was busy unwrapping the chocolate and shoving it inside his mouth, she asked, 'Is your mama here, in Manila?'

He nodded.

'Then you'll see her soon.' She touched his forehead. 'You're burning up. How about some medicine to take care of that fever?'

The boy shook his head, wiping chocolate over his shirt.

'The quicker you get better, the quicker you can go back to your family,' said Rose. 'I bet your mama misses you as much as you miss her. If you take your medicine and do what the nurses tell you, you'll be home before you even know it.'

'All right,' he said uncertainly, his eyes darting from Rose to the nurse with the medicine and back to Rose again, as if he was uncertain of what to expect from either of them.

The nurse sprang into action, bringing the medicine closer. The boy put his hand over his mouth. 'No. I want *her* to give it.' He pointed at Rose.

'Of course,' said Rose, taking the medicine from the nurse and feeding it to the boy. 'Now, you need to be a good boy and do everything you can to get better, so that your family can take you home.'

'Will you be here to give me my medicine?'

Rose hesitated. 'I'm on my way home but the other nurses …'

The boy's eyes filled with tears. 'Don't want the other nurses.'

'I wish I could help but—'

Elsie interrupted. 'She'll be here,' she said.

The boy smiled happily. As the girls shuffled after Elsie towards the exit, he cried out, 'It's Tommy, by the way. My name is Tommy.'

Rose turned around. 'Nice to meet you, Tommy.' She saluted him.

Tommy waved, smiling happily. In his hands he held what was

left of Rose's chocolate.

'You have a way with children,' said Elsie when they were outside. 'I must admit, I'm impressed.'

'Before I graduated from nursing school, I did some work at Boston Children's Hospital.'

'You surprised me. You possess patience, kindness and compassion. Great qualities in a nurse.'

'I love helping people, ma'am. That's why I'm here. I want to make a difference.'

Elsie looked Rose up and down, as if considering something. 'I think you will fit in here just fine. We need that kind of attitude at this hospital. It might not look busy now, but we expect it to change soon. We are going to need all the help we can get.'

Rose felt her heart jump all the way to her throat. 'Does that mean I can stay?'

'You can stay.'

The girls cheered. They jumped on the spot and hugged one another. 'Thank you, ma'am,' said Kate.

Elsie smiled. She no longer looked scary and intimidating. 'I didn't mean you could all stay, but all right. Consider this your final warning.'

'You won't regret it,' said Rose, overjoyed.

'Don't think you're getting away with it. Your punishment is two shifts back-to-back, starting now.'

'Two four-hour shifts?' asked Kate. The girls exchanged smiles when Elsie wasn't looking.

'Do you think you can handle it?'

The nurses nodded.

Before ordering them to return to the surgical ward to help Anne clean the instruments and prepare IV drips, Elsie asked if any of them knew how to drive. Rose lifted her hand, like she was at school answering to a teacher. 'I do, ma'am,' she said.

'My regular driver is off sick. After work, I need you to drive to a warehouse near Fort Stotsenberg Station Hospital to pick up supplies. It's fifty miles north of Manila. Are you all right with that?'

'Yes, ma'am,' said Rose, even though her driving experience consisted of a few lessons in a friend's old car, stalling the engine time and time again and fearing for her life. Elsie nodded as if it was settled, turned around and walked away down the long corridor. Rose wanted to run after her and tell her she wasn't the right person for the job after all. She lifted her hand in protest and opened her mouth but it was too late. The chief nurse was gone.

The day went by in a blur of sorting out plasma, saline solution, IV equipment, suture material, adhesive, bandages, scissors and blankets as Rose assembled countless surgical trays and cleaned the operating rooms.

'That's it. That's a thousand dressings,' said Ida, observing the pile of white fabric that occupied the corner of the surgical ward, ready to be stored away for future use.

'Why do we need so many?' wondered Rose. Other than a few children with fever and sore throats, an old man who was having his appendix out and a young girl with tonsilitis, the three wards under their care were empty. The hospital catered to the families of military personnel stationed in the Philippines, who for the most part were young and healthy and didn't require medical attention. Rose heard there were wards for the locals at Sternberg General somewhere, but she hadn't seen them yet.

'I don't know. I can't think straight,' said Kate. 'Who would have thought that two four-hour shifts in this heat would be so hard? I would rather work eighteen hours back home.'

'I'm ready to fall into bed and sleep for a hundred years,' said Tess.

'I'm ready for dinner,' said Ida. 'I was so busy, I missed lunch. The roast beef they served yesterday was to die for. And the desserts were heaven.'

Rose thought with longing of the food that would soon be

served in the dining hall and of her soft and comfortable bed. She wished she had kept quiet, instead of trying to impress the chief nurse and volunteering for a terrifying mission. The girls would return to their quarters and enjoy their evening, while Rose had to navigate the dark maze of Manila on her own, having had nothing to eat all day. To make matters worse, dark clouds gathered in the sky, obscuring the setting sun, and the distant din of thunder could be heard overhead.

Kate must have noticed her mournful face. 'Would you like us to come with you?' she asked. 'We'll go together. We can keep you company in the truck, make sure you find the place all right.'

'It will be an adventure,' said Ida, nodding.

'You know how to drive, right?' asked Tess. 'We'll be safe in the truck with you?'

Rose didn't want to admit how limited her driving experience was. She faked a smile. 'Thank you, girls, but there's no need. I'll be fine on my own. Go home and relax.'

The girls tried to argue but Rose wouldn't have any of it. She got herself into this mess, she should be the only one to suffer. The girls said goodbye and disappeared with excited chatter, while Rose walked out into the hospital car park, lifting her face and enjoying the timid rays of late afternoon sun peeking through the clouds. Pink and purple flowers filled the park behind the hospital, and Rose felt her heart soar from the beauty and wonder of it all.

But then she saw the truck she was to drive and forgot all about the sun and flowers. The vehicle was the size of a tank, a tall and impregnable mountain, and Rose felt small next to it, like a helpless mouse in front of a cat. Placing both hands on the hood of the truck, she tried to smile. 'Let's be friends, shall we?' she whispered, opening the door with trepidation, climbing into the driver's seat and sitting there for a while, looking out the window at the fast-moving clouds, studying a map in her lap, too nervous to put the key in the ignition and start the engine.

'Come on, it's not going to bite,' she told herself. 'It's like riding a bicycle. I've done it before. I can do it again.' She knew she had to hurry or soon it would get dark.

When she tried to put the truck in motion, she realised that no, driving wasn't like riding a bicycle at all. She spent the next ten minutes turning the key in the ignition this way and that, screeching gears and stalling, while she sweated and swore under her breath. Thankfully, the hospital car park was deserted. No one was around to witness her humiliation.

The wind had picked up and the first drops of rain fell on the pavement in front of her. The palm trees trembled in the breeze, looking pitiful and sad. When Rose was about to admit defeat and give up, imagining Elsie's disappointed face and shuddering in trepidation, a miracle happened. She must have done something right because the engine murmured happily and the truck started to move. 'Here we go,' she whispered, steering the vehicle out of the car park and towards the road. A stream of cars, bicycles, rickshaws, even horse- and carabao-drawn carriages moved at a high tempo, like dancers on stage. She waited for a break in traffic and slowly pulled out onto the busy road to the screeching of brakes and blaring of horns. The sun went down and she could barely see the road ahead. Her hands grasped the steering wheel so hard, her fingers ached.

'It's all right,' she said to herself. 'I'm doing it. It's going to be fine. Slow and steady now.' She spoke to the truck like it was a horse, a living and breathing creature that could hear her.

A few minutes of frantic and nervous driving later, Rose came to a crossroads. She tried to remember what she had seen on the map. Both roads ran off into the darkness without so much as a sign. Did she turn left or right? How did she know which way was correct? She pulled over and stared at the map under the quivering light of her torch, while angry clouds shifted overhead like ghosts. She told herself she was lucky she had found the map by the passenger seat, but the problem was, she had never been good at reading maps. She knew where she had to go and where she had come from, but she had no idea where she was *right now*.

Rose sighed, folded the map away and started the engine. At least she was getting the hang of it. Encouraged, she turned the steering wheel and followed the road going left. She had a fifty-fifty chance of getting it right, so she crossed her fingers for luck and continued to drive.

Finally relaxed in the driver's seat, she was taking her time moving slowly past paddies and bamboo huts when she heard a bang in the dark – sharp and startling like a gunshot. The truck careened to one side. Crying out in shock, Rose gripped the steering wheel tighter and hit the brakes. The truck stopped abruptly, nearly throwing her out of the seat. For a few seconds, she sat still, breathing heavily, then she stepped out of the truck and bent down to examine the tyre that looked torn and, even to her untrained eye, irreparably damaged.

She walked around the truck and looked in the back, wondering if it had come with a spare tyre. But even if it did, she had no idea what to do with it. Dejected, she stood on the side of the road with her hand raised in the universal I-need-help gesture, hoping someone would take pity on her and stop. No one did. The cars continued to zoom past like she was invisible. Everyone had somewhere to be and no one seemed to care about Rose and her broken-down truck.

She was all alone in the middle of nowhere in downtown Manila, with no way of getting back to Sternberg Hospital. As she watched the indifferent river of traffic drifting past with no beginning and no end, she thought it couldn't possibly get any worse. But a moment later, it did. The skies opened up and a flood came down on her, drenching her instantly. Her hair clung to her face and even her undergarments under her uniform were instantly wet. She remained in one spot for a moment, stunned. Then, trembling, Rose climbed inside the truck and considered her options. There was only one. She would wait for morning and hope someone would help her. Then she would return to the hospital and tell Elsie she had failed in the first mission she had entrusted her with.

Berating herself for raising her hand and speaking out when she should have kept quiet, Rose leaned back in her seat and closed her eyes. If she was stuck here for the foreseeable future, at least she would get some sleep. Everything would seem brighter and more hopeful once the sun was up. She wished she had a piece of bread or a slice of chocolate to take away the ache inside her stomach. But she had given her chocolate to Tommy and hadn't thought of packing any food, so eager had she been to complete her task quickly and efficiently.

As she was drifting off to sleep, exhausted after her eventful day, she heard a strange sound, like pebbles hitting glass. Someone was knocking on the window. Sitting up in her seat, she looked into the rear-view mirror and saw a pair of headlights behind the truck. She wound down the window.

'Are you all right? Need help?' she heard. She couldn't see the man behind the wall of water in the dark but he sounded friendly and American.

Rose perked up, all thoughts of sleep forgotten. 'I'm all right. I do need help.'

She shone her torch straight at the stranger, who covered his eyes. 'Sorry,' she muttered, pointing the light away.

The man was tall and broad-shouldered, his smile wide on his face, teeth sparkling. He wore a military uniform of MacArthur's US Armed Forces in the Far East. 'First lieutenant David Taylor at your service,' he said.

He extended his hand to Rose through the window of her truck. She shook it, taking a deep breath of relief. 'Rose Williams,' she said, sitting up straight, pushing wet hair off her face.

'How can I help you, Rose Williams?' When she told him about her quest across Manila and the torn tyre, he shook his head in amazement. 'Who would send a young girl out in this?'

'What can I say? Our chief nurse is not my biggest fan. And

if I don't do what she says, I'll be in trouble.'

'We don't want that.' He grinned. 'Not to worry. We'll get that truck running in no time.'

'I wouldn't want to impose. I don't want you to get soaking wet on my account.'

'It's no trouble at all. And I'm already soaking wet.'

Lieutenant Taylor was true to his word. While Rose remained inside the truck, he found the spare tyre, which had been in the back all along, hidden under some cardboard boxes, brought a toolbox from his car, which was some kind of a military vehicle Rose had never seen before, and got to work. Rose was impressed. 'You've done this before.'

'Once or twice,' he replied. 'Never in the rain.'

'I don't know how to thank you.' She rubbed her hands together, suddenly nervous.

'No thanks necessary. I'm an officer. It's my job to help those in need.'

'I thought your job was to kill the enemy and protect the borders?' she asked teasingly, her eyes twinkling.

'We haven't had a chance to do any of that. Yet.' His eyes twinkled back. 'The truck is good to go. Now you can be on your way.'

The thought of driving in heavy rain through manic streets of Manila made Rose shudder. Looking at the pavement, stammering slightly, she said, 'I have no idea where I'm going. I'm looking for Stotsenberg Station Hospital. I have a map but …'

'You'll never find it in this weather,' he replied, nodding at the rain. Rose didn't know how it was possible but in the last ten minutes the storm had become stronger. Even in the light of her torch, she couldn't see the road in front of her. She could barely see his face and he was standing next to her.

'Could you perhaps tell me which way to go?' she asked. 'I would be very grateful.'

'I'll do better than that. I'll drive you there.'

Rose wanted to protest and tell him that she had already wasted enough of his time, that he probably had other things to do and should be on his way, that she couldn't possibly delay him any longer. But she didn't. If this kind officer got into his vehicle and drove away, she would never find Stotsenberg Station Hospital and would have to return to Sternberg empty-handed and face Elsie's anger. Besides, she had a feeling that no matter what she said, this man would not leave her alone in the storm at night until he knew she was safe.

She moved to the passenger side, while David climbed into the driver's seat. She thanked him quietly but didn't think he could hear her over the howling of the wind and the pounding of the rain.

'Once again, no thanks necessary,' he said. 'Just doing my job.'

The truck obeyed David in a way it wouldn't obey Rose. The dark streets flashed by in a blur of squalid buildings and trees. Rose found it fascinating. Manila was a new experience and she couldn't get enough of it. But it wasn't as interesting as the man sitting next to her. She turned away from the window and faced him. 'Where are you stationed, Lieutenant Taylor?' she asked.

His hands on the steering wheel, he replied, 'Fort William McKinley. Do you know where it is?'

Rose shook her head. 'I don't know anything. I arrived yesterday afternoon.'

'And now here you are, lost in the rain.' Taking his eyes off the road, he appraised her. 'Fort McKinley is seven miles south of Manila.'

'You know the streets of Manila so well. Have you been here long?'

'Six months and yes, I'm an expert by now. All we do is drive around all day, patrolling the streets.'

'And what do you do when you're not on duty?'

'When I'm not on duty, I read.'

She tried not to sound too teasing when she said, 'You came all the way to the Philippines to read?'

'I like exploring, too. This place is incredible. But wherever I go, I always bring a book with me. My comrades give me a hard time about it.'

'What's your favourite book?'

'Anything by Fitzgerald. *The Great Gatsby* especially. It makes one think about what's important in life. Money can't buy happiness.'

'I don't know about that. If we had some money, maybe my mama wouldn't have to work so much and she would be happier.'

'My parents have money. They are the most miserable people I know. What about you? What's your favourite book?'

'*Twenty Thousand Leagues Under the Sea*. It takes my breath away every time I read it, the adventure, the suspense, the excitement of it all.'

'And that's why you are here, in Manila? For the adventure?'

'That's why I'm here.'

'How do you like the Philippines so far?'

Rose shrugged. 'We docked on my birthday. I thought it was a good sign. So far, I've swum in the ocean, been told off by my supervisor and gotten lost in the rain. I'm here to be a nurse, to help people, but the wards are almost empty. There is hardly anything for us nurses to do.'

'The wards are empty because they have evacuated most US families from the islands.'

'Evacuated them? Why?'

She didn't want to know and wished she hadn't asked. For a moment, he looked like he didn't want to tell her. 'Because there is every chance the Philippines could fall to the Japanese.'

Rose fell quiet, staring out the window. The truck was moving fast and behind the thick wall of rain she could make out colours, the whites of the houses, the darker shades of trees. Around them, the roads of Manila were alive with sound, engines screeching, horns blaring, people shouting. Rose tried not to think of his words, of what they meant for her, for all of them. Instead, she thought of the breathtaking moments in the tropical waters with her new friends, of treading water and chasing each other under the northern stars. She had arrived here so full of hope and excitement but now that feeling was gone, replaced with dread and exhaustion. Twenty-four hours later, everything seemed different. There was no sign of the stars, the rain was coming down hard and the soldier next to her was talking about war like it was inevitable.

She didn't even notice when they arrived at Stotsenberg Station Hospital and David pulled into the car park. He opened the door for her and helped her out. Huddling close together under a small umbrella that did next to nothing to protect them from the torrential rain, they walked around the main building, located the warehouse and knocked. No one answered. Rose knocked again and pulled the handle. The door was locked.

'No one's here,' she said dejectedly. Her drenched uniform clung to her body and her wet hair covered her face. She shivered. 'We're too late.' Frustrated, she knocked one more time and gave the door a push. Silence. 'Our chief nurse will kill me.' Discouraged, she leaned on the wall and closed her eyes.

'I bet they'll be back first thing in the morning. All we need to do is wait in the truck.'

'We?' She glanced at her watch. It was almost ten in the evening. 'David, it's a long time till morning. You can't possibly stay here with me.'

'You think I would leave you here by yourself in the middle of the night?'

He helped her into the truck and she leaned back in her seat. She could barely keep her eyes open but forced herself to stay awake. She didn't want to go to sleep just yet. The window steamed up and she couldn't see anything anymore, not that there was anything to see outside beyond the darkness. She could hear the rain unabatingly hitting the roof of the truck, on and on like horses' hooves galloping over their heads. David shared a loaf of bread with her and some cheese. Gratefully, she took the food.

'I've never seen rain like this before,' she said. 'It rains in Brownville, of course. It drizzles for days and days. But nothing like this torrent of water.' It was a deluge straight from heaven, flooding everything in sight.

'I love this climate. Everything is extreme, everything is spectacular. The sun, the rain, the stars over your head. On a clear night, you can see thousands of them. I love the heat. It hits you like a wave and it feels wonderful. I never enjoyed winters in Boston. Wait 'til you see the volcano, the waterfalls and the national parks. Everything here takes your breath away.'

'What do you like the most about the Philippines?' she asked, watching his dim silhouette in the dark. She couldn't make out the details of his face but she saw that he turned around and smiled.

'The people,' he said. 'They are so polite and welcoming. No matter how little money they have and how much they are struggling, they seem happy, like they don't have a care in the world. I find it incredible.'

And then they slept, their heads close together. She woke up with the first rays of sun. As if by magic, the rain was gone and dawn tinted the trees a dark shade of purple and made the mountains in the far distance light up from the inside. For a moment, she sat still, contemplating it, then she watched David as he slept, watched his chest rise and fall under his uniform. For some reason, she felt her cheeks grow warm. The tips of her ears were burning. She touched his shoulder. 'Shall we try again?'

They climbed out of the truck and knocked on the door. This time they heard a noise and a cranky voice, complaining about early morning visitors and never having any time to rest. The door opened a crack. On the doorstep stood a dishevelled man hidden behind a matted beard. He looked at them with suspicion, not saying a word. Rose smiled. He didn't smile back. When she explained who she was, he said, 'You are late. I was expecting you yesterday evening. Stayed up past my bedtime.'

'I'm sorry I made you wait. The storm … And the tyre on my truck blew up. If it wasn't for Lieutenant Taylor, I would never have made it.'

'Save your excuses for someone who cares,' grumbled the man, shuffling away.

There were ten boxes of supplies that had to be lifted onto the truck. Rose was grateful David was there because the boxes were heavy and the grouchy man with the beard didn't offer to help. It didn't take long to load the boxes and soon they were driving back to the hospital. Rose realised with relief that she would make it back just in time for breakfast.

Outside her quarters, she thanked David for everything he had done. 'How will you get back to your car?'

'I'll walk. It's not too far.'

'You can't walk all the way there. It will take forever.'

'I'm not in a rush.' He grinned and she grinned back.

'I feel bad. I should have dropped you off on the way.'

'Yes, but then I wouldn't know where to find you.'

'Oh,' she said, blushing.

'And I needed to know where to find you because I want to see you again.'

Before she had a chance to respond, he saluted her and walked away. She remained in the doorway, watching him, and when he came to a bend in the road, he turned around and waved. Smiling, she waved back.

At work that morning, Elsie brushed past Rose without so much as a greeting, not mentioning the supplies or acknowledging her help. All she said was a gruff, 'There's a patient waiting for you.'

The patient turned out to be a young woman called Bess, with a long pale face, elfish ears and the saddest smile Rose had ever seen. As Rose picked up her chart, Bess said, 'What's wrong with me, Nurse? They won't tell me anything and I'm tired of asking.'

'Acute anaemia,' Rose read aloud and instantly bit her lip. She didn't know if Elsie allowed the notes to be freely discussed with the patients. Back at Eastern Maine General, the nurses were told to smile politely and reveal nothing. It achieved little to upset the patients unnecessarily. But she was absent-minded this morning and couldn't focus. 'Don't worry, a couple of iron injections and you'll be good as new.'

'Acute anaemia,' Bess repeated in wonder. 'I'll tell my mother-in-law. She thinks I'm faking it just to get out of the house and force her to look after the children. Is it my fault the only time she babysits her own grandkids is when I'm in hospital?'

'How many children do you have?' asked Rose, preparing the injection.

'Seven. The youngest is six months old.' The woman's face spread into a smile. 'I miss them terribly. Isn't it funny? When I'm with them all I want is a minute to myself. And the moment I'm alone all I want is to hold them in my arms.'

'That's part of being a mother, I suppose.'

'Do you have children?'

'Not yet. I want to, one day.' Rose administered the injection, helped Bess get comfortable on her bed and smoothed the sheet over her legs. 'You'll be home with your little ones before you know it, don't you worry.'

'Not too soon, I hope,' said Bess, shaking her head, her ginger hair shaking around her face like a ring of fire. 'This morning was the first time in months I was able to read a chapter of my book. No one interrupted me. No one shouted for me. No one pulled me by the skirt or asked for anything. A nurse brought me a cup of tea and a biscuit. It was divine.' She scratched the tip of her nose. 'I hope the doctor isn't planning on discharging me today?'

The small Filipina nurse who had been looking after Tommy the day before laughed from across the ward, waving her hands at Bess. 'Even if they discharge you, you'll come back. You always do. This place is like a holiday for you.'

Bess smiled. 'If you had seven children, Nurse Carmelita, you'd be the same. And my husband wants another one. The man is mad.' She sighed. 'But no, it's my last time here. We are returning to the States next week.'

'You're leaving Manila?' asked Rose.

'All military families are being advised to leave. We had a good life here. But the children, you see. We want to make sure they are safe.'

Rose remembered David's words. She remembered the ship filled with smiling, waving families passing the *Holbrook* as it sailed into Manila Harbour. She shivered.

She spent the rest of her shift unpacking the supplies she had delivered that morning, sterilising instruments and checking on a few patients in the ward. Tommy followed her like a shadow. He wanted to know everything and help her with every task, and she let him, even though preparing the dressings took twice as long and the pillowcases got put on the pillows inside out. After lunch, Tommy's mother arrived to take him home. The little boy skipped to her side, throwing his little arms around her. The woman thanked Rose with tears in her eyes. 'When his fever spiked, we didn't know what to do. You helped him so much. He won't stop talking about you.'

'Just doing my job.' Rose turned to Tommy. 'We enjoyed having you here. You are welcome to come and see us any time you like. I'll make sure I have lots of chocolate for you.'

Tommy shook his head, suddenly looking grown-up, his little face serious. 'We are going home to Los Angeles. The ship is coming for us tomorrow.'

As they were leaving, Rose whispered to Ida, who worked on the same ward as her, 'Soon we'll have no patients left. It will be just us in an empty ward.'

'Us and a thousand dressings.'

After their four-hour shift was over at one that afternoon, the girls spilled out of the hospital, chatting excitedly. Rose didn't think she would ever get used to the feeling of the tropical air enveloping her like a hug. She squinted in the sun. 'We have the whole afternoon ahead of us,' she said. 'What should we do?'

Kate suggested going for another swim. Tess said she wanted to play golf, even though none of them had ever done it before or knew anything about it. Ida told them a couple of nurses were going to the Officers' Club for a drink and a dip in the pool. Rose heard that a retired colonel was giving free tennis lessons at his villa and everyone was welcome. She had always wanted to learn, having watched other children chase the ball with their rackets on the courts around the corner from her house. Rose never told her mother how desperate she was to play tennis. If her mama had known, she would have worked three shifts to make it happen. However much Rose wanted to hold the racket in her hands and hit the ball as hard as she could, watching it bounce across the court, she didn't want her mother to be more tired than she already was.

Rose wanted to say yes to all of it – a dip in the pool, golf, a glass of wine at the Officers' Club, a tennis lesson. All these options sounded wonderful to her as she thought of the months to come and the fun they would have in Manila, when suddenly, across the road, she saw the familiar military vehicle. David was standing next to it with the biggest smile on his face, a bouquet of flowers and a box wrapped in pink paper.

'I have to go,' she muttered and, before the girls had a chance to ask questions, ran to him as fast as she could, her heart thumping. He looked even more handsome than she remembered. 'What are you doing here?' she wanted to know, out of breath and laughing with joy.

'I told you I was going to see you again.' He grinned. 'We officers always keep our word.'

'Are these for me?' She blushed and hid behind the flowers, hoping he wouldn't notice. 'What are they? I've never seen flowers like this before.' She wanted to tell him no one had ever given her flowers before but didn't.

'Jade vine,' he said. 'I like them because they remind me of home. Mother grows exotic flowers in her greenhouse. I have a present for you too. You mentioned it was your birthday.'

She took the box, shaking it, wondering what was inside. He helped her into his car and then sat watching her while she unwrapped the present. 'You wrapped it so nicely,' she said. Carefully she untied the red ribbon and removed the paper. Inside was a musical instrument. 'What is it? World's smallest guitar?' She ran her fingers over the strings and they made a soft sound, like a kitten meowing.

'A ukulele. It's easier to learn than the guitar and although it only has four strings, I prefer the way it sounds.'

She was touched. Unexpectedly and perplexingly, she felt close to tears. It was the first birthday she had spent without her mother by her side. She had felt sad and homesick on the day and hadn't even told anyone it was her birthday. David's simple gesture made her feel warm inside and a little less lonely. 'Thank you. I wish I knew how to play.'

'I will teach you. Music always makes everything better. If you're having a bad day, all you need to do is pick up your ukulele and it will cheer you right up.'

She stroked the smooth wooden surface of the instrument. 'So it has magical powers?'

'Absolutely.'

David took her to his favourite restaurant for dinner, where she sampled spicy lamb cooked in garlic and vinegar and grilled chicken marinated in lemongrass, announcing she had never tasted anything so delicious. Afterwards, when they walked side by side through the manic streets of Manila, he took her hand and her heart nearly burst out of her chest. For a moment, she forgot what she was saying. They strolled through the park and sat on the grass watching the ships dock and grey-clad fishermen shout to one another as they unloaded their boats, while seagulls dived in the water with a hungry yelp, hunting for their dinner.

The harbour was poetry in motion. Everything was harmonious and pleasing, the song of the birds, the murmur of the waves, the warm breeze on her face.

'Let me show you how it's done,' David said, placing his hand on hers and positioning her fingers on the four strings of the ukulele. 'Relax and hold the instrument close to your chest, like this. It's more comfortable this way.'

She did as he said.

'Now gently stroke the strings with your thumb, one at a time. Perfect. It creates a nice, soft sound.'

He told her about the chords and the frets, showing her how to strum. He played his favourite melodies and sang 'Happy Birthday to You' and 'God Save America', while she lay on her back and stared at the sky, shielding her eyes from the setting sun. His voice was strong and deep, unlike any Rose had ever heard before, as he serenaded her with Wayne King, Guy Lombardo and Al Jolson.

*California I've been blue*
*Since I've been away from you.*

He sang about love and joy and being young, while the sky lit up in a kaleidoscope of pink and purple and red, making her gasp.

'The famous Manila sunset,' said David. 'It's quite something, isn't it?'

'You were right, you know? Everything in the Philippines takes my breath away.'

As the colours faded and his voice fell quiet, the tiny clouds in the sky above their heads looked like the cotton candy that she used to buy as a child at the fair in Brownville. The palms swayed in the breeze, the man by her side strummed the ukulele just for her, and suddenly she wanted to dance with joy, wanted to jump to her feet and spin and twirl in a breathless waltz. She knew that for as long as she lived, she would never forget this magical evening.

# Chapter 2

## November–December 1941

The next day at work, the girls surrounded Rose, hurling questions like hand grenades. 'Who was the handsome officer you ran off with yesterday?' Kate demanded. 'Last night we returned early from the Officers' Club, expecting answers, but you were already asleep.'

'We almost woke you up,' said Tess. 'We were desperate to know.'

'In the dining room, we saw flowers and a card,' said Kate. 'You never told us it was your birthday.'

Rose had slept like a baby the night before and felt refreshed, rested and content. This morning, she left for the hospital early, before the other girls were up because she hoped to reverse the unfavourable first impression she had made on Elsie. The chief nurse was in the ward, her eyes following Rose's every move, but instead of concentrating on her work, Rose was backed into a corner by the girls and subjected to an interrogation. She looked around nervously, hoping Elsie wouldn't notice she was idly chatting to her friends instead of tending to her patients. 'I went to bed early last night because I was exhausted. I was asleep in seconds.'

'You're not answering our questions. Who is your secret admirer? And when do we get to meet him?'

Rose was saved by a shrill voice from across the ward. 'Nurse!' shouted a grey-haired, pointy-faced woman with yellow skin and dull eyes. 'I've been waiting twenty minutes for someone to help me.'

'Excuse me,' said Rose to the girls, rushing to the woman's side, fetching a glass of water and checking her temperature.

After her shift ended, she didn't wait for the other girls but ran out of the hospital, taking shallow nervous breaths of the perfumed air, her hair a mess, cheeks burning, lips red with lipstick she had hastily applied, eyes searching for him. He hadn't mentioned their next meeting when they said goodbye the previous evening. What if he had no intention of seeing her again? She hesitated, her hands trembling, and then she spotted him across the car park, waiting for her. He had no flowers and no presents but his face lit up with joy at the sight of her.

'I'm taking you somewhere special today,' he announced. 'I want you to fall in love with the Philippines, just like I did.'

'You don't have to try very hard. I'm already in love with it.'

Twenty miles from Manila, in the province of Rizal, Rose and David sat by Marikina River as it rustled quietly past, whispering of times long gone. Mounts Pamitinan and Binacayan rose like green-haired giants above them, guarding the precious stream that glistened like a diamond in the blazing sun. There was no one else around, just Rose and David, the rugged mountains and the swirling river. It felt to Rose like she had left her life behind, the hospital, the patients, the murmurs of war. None of it existed here, in tranquil paradise. 'How do you know about this place?' she asked.

'Sometimes on our days off we go hiking here.'

'And here I was, thinking all you do is read and play the ukulele.'

He smiled and took her hand. 'According to the legend, a man called Bernardo Carpio is trapped here between the two rocks.

Some say he split the rock in two out of anger. Others, that he is still here, trying to break free. Every time he shrugs, the earth moves. This area is famous for its earthquakes.'

'I hope he doesn't shrug while we're here.'

David spread a picnic blanket on the grass. As if by magic, meats of different types appeared out of a hamper, followed by bread and cheese, fruit and a bottle of wine. Rose clapped her hands when she saw it all. 'I thought you might be hungry after a day of work,' he said.

'I work four-hour shifts. It's like a holiday compared to what we did at home. Although I have to admit, I am a little hungry.'

'It can't be easy, what you do. What made you become a nurse?'

'I wanted to help people. It's an amazing feeling, knowing you made a difference in someone's life. But also, the only tuition we could afford was the nursing programme at Eastern Maine General. It was only two hundred dollars a year and we didn't have to pay for room and board.' At the thought of home and her mother, Rose felt a little lost, displaced like a ship without direction. To hide her emotion, she reached for a slice of watermelon and looked at the river running fast towards lands faraway. She wondered where it was flowing to and if its destination was as stunning as the spot where they were sitting side by side, enjoying their picnic. No, she decided. Nothing could be this beautiful. The vivid colours of the jungle and the mountains against the topaz backdrop of the sky took her breath away every time she looked up. She wished she was an artist, so she could capture the rustling river and the giant mountains and the flawless sky on her canvas but she suspected she would never be able to do it justice, even if she knew how to paint.

'Two hundred dollars a year. That sounds almost too good to be true.'

'Believe me, it wasn't. In return, we were required to work on the wards. Ten-hour shifts, seven nights a week, for six-week stints without pay. Nursing school was the first time I've ever left home. It was a big adjustment. I didn't have my mama by my side, I was exhausted all the time and there were all these strange rules we had to follow.'

'What kind of rules?'

'Oh, you know, the usual. We were not allowed to sweep dirt from our rooms into the corridors.'

'Of course not.' David chuckled.

'We were required to make our beds and only use twenty-five-watt lightbulbs.'

'Yes, I can see how that might be important.'

'We were not allowed to call out of our windows to anyone walking past.'

'Not allowed to call out of your windows? That's barbaric.' He was laughing even harder, the glass dancing in his hand, spilling red wine.

Laughing herself, she poked him in the ribs with her small fist. 'It's a serious matter. You shouldn't be making fun of it,' she said.

'Any other serious rules I should know about?'

'We weren't allowed to listen to the radio during the day or leave our room after 10.30 p.m. unless we were on duty. We were required to select our social contacts wisely.'

'Did you select your social contacts wisely?'

'I had no time for socialising. After a year at Eastern Maine General, the hours here in Manila are a piece of cake.'

Something in his face shifted. He was no longer smiling. 'That might all change one day,' he said quietly.

'What do you mean?'

He hesitated. 'All I'm saying is enjoy the easy hours while they last.'

She felt there was something he didn't want to tell her. And on this carefree day in the most beautiful place in the world, she didn't want to hear it. 'I am.' She grinned and reached for a glass of wine. 'I'm making the most of them.'

In the weeks that followed, David took Rose horse riding and dancing. They played tennis and strummed ukulele to each other in the park. They dined at some of the best restaurants in Manila and even gambled at a casino. Having never been to one before and not having a clue what to do, Rose watched David play blackjack and roulette with her hand on her mouth and her heart in her throat, cheering when he won and stamping her feet when he lost. It was all so new to her, so tantalisingly exciting, she looked forward to every outing, wondering what he had in store for her next.

'Where are we going today?' she asked when she was seated next to him in his car and it moved swiftly through downtown Manila. It was early morning on her day off. She had a whole day alone with him and she couldn't wait.

'I am taking you to the most beautiful place on earth. I am taking you to Hulugan Falls. It's a bit of a trek but I promise it will be worth it.'

The three-hour car journey flew by in an instant as they talked about their childhoods, the things they had done and the places they had been to. Rose had never been anywhere, while David was a world traveller. He told her all about the gondoliers of Venice crooning Puccini and Verdi, the northern lights illuminating the sky in a kaleidoscope of colours in Sweden, the foggy fjords of Norway and the tulip fields in the Netherlands.

'I can't believe you've seen all this with your own eyes. What's your favourite place in the world?' she asked.

'Paris, without a doubt. It breaks my heart thinking of it destroyed and ravaged by war. King Francis I once said that Paris is not a city, it's a world. And he was right. Everywhere you go, everywhere you turn, you see history. And the crepes are good too.'

'I'd love to visit it one day. I've read too many novels set in Paris not to.'

'When the war is over, I'll take you to Paris. I will show you everything.'

The walk to the waterfall was shorter than the drive, but not by much. She was exhausted by the end of it, but as they made their way through the lush jungle, she didn't think of her aching feet at all. Instead, she took everything in, barely able to believe her eyes. Brownville and its wintry hues were half a world away. Everything was alien and therefore fascinating. She heard the murmur of the water long before she saw it cascading down its bed of rocks, and when she finally laid eyes on it, for a moment she forgot how to breathe. At 230 feet, the Hulugan Falls was the tallest waterfall near Manila. It stunned Rose into silence and she watched without a word as, shrouded in mist, the majestic stream fell from its great height.

'Race you to the water,' David cried, pulling her by the hand.

'Can you swim here?'

His response was letting go of her hand, stripping to his skivvies and catapulting himself into the green basin. 'What are you waiting for? It feels like heaven after the long walk.'

She undressed to her bathing suit and jumped in, crying out in shock. 'Are you serious? It's freezing. Why is it so cold? I thought we were in the tropics.'

'We are in the tropics. But it's a waterfall. Waterfalls are always cold. Even here, in the Philippines. Feels good though, doesn't it?'

'Sure, if you like being submerged in ice-cold water and getting frostbite.'

'You won't get frostbite. Let's swim to the falls.'

'I don't think I can swim in water this cold. I'll get a cramp.'

But he was already halfway to the waterfall and she had no choice but to follow. Thankfully, it wasn't deep and she soon caught up to him under the raging water that hit her from above and made her shriek with delight. Even though she continued to complain about the cold, she had never felt more alive.

He picked her up gently, like she were a doll and weighed nothing, and threw her in the water. She squealed, her breath catching with excitement. He caught her again and brought her close to him. 'They say if you make a wish under a waterfall, it's sure to come true.'

'Have you made a wish?'

'I have.' His face was close to hers, his lips in her wet hair.

'What did you wish for?'

'I wished to kiss you under the waterfall so you would never forget me.'

'Like I ever could,' she started to say but stopped suddenly because his lips were on hers and he was kissing her with such passion, such tenderness, her chest hurt. She couldn't believe she was here with him, underneath a waterfall in December, with the rest of her life stretching before her like a joy-filled ride.

When they were on firm land and dry, relaxing side by side on a rock, his hands behind his head, her feet touching his feet, she asked, 'Did you make it all up? About making wishes under waterfalls?'

He laughed and stroked her hand gently. 'My wish came true, didn't it?'

She blushed and turned away from him, towards the crashing, churning water. To change the subject, she said, 'What brings you to Manila?'

'Just like you, I wanted to make a difference, I suppose. Change the world.' He shrugged. 'But most of all, I came here to get away from my father.'

'What is he like?'

He thought about it for a moment. 'Controlling. Never satisfied. Nothing my sister and I do is ever good enough for him.'

'That must have been tough growing up.' Her mother could be a little bit like that. She wanted Rose to have a life that was more pleasant and less difficult than her own had turned out to be. To achieve this objective, she believed Rose had to work twice as hard as her peers. Her childhood had not been easy but it had been filled with warmth, laughter, kindness and unconditional love.

David said, 'I know that deep down he cares about us. He

expects a lot from us but he expects a lot from everyone, himself included.'

'He's a perfectionist. A terrible trait in a parent,' Rose said, smiling.

'I had a best friend growing up called Celia.'

'A childhood sweetheart?' she teased, pinching him.

'No, just a mate. Our fathers were in business together. I remember going to her house on the weekends and finally being able to relax. Her parents were the opposite of mine. They were always joking and laughing and trying to spoil her. Being at her house was the only time I didn't have to walk on eggshells and watch every word I said and every move I made.'

Rose shuddered despite the hot breeze on her skin. 'What was it like at home?'

'A bit like a military academy. Do you see this?' David pointed at a long scar running down his wrist. 'My father did that to me one day after school because I couldn't understand the concept of gravitational waves.'

'Oh, no,' she whispered, tracing the scar with her finger, bringing his hand to her face, kissing his wrist. 'I'm so sorry. How old were you?'

'Ten, I think. The moment I arrived home from school, I was forced to sit down at my desk and study. If I was too slow to solve an algebra equation or couldn't understand Newton's Third Law of Motion, I got punished. As soon as I was old enough, I left home. Being in the army is a breeze compared to growing up with my dad. For the first time in my life, I could breathe freely, but it never truly leaves you, does it? It always stays with you. Do you know what I mean?'

She nodded.

'My sister tells me I moved halfway around the world to escape our father, but I never will because he'll always be inside my head, telling me I'm useless at everything I do. At least I get to do some good while trying to find my own way.' He was quiet for a moment, lost in thought. 'I've never told anyone about this before.'

'I'm glad you told me,' she whispered, her eyes scanning his face.

'Me too. It feels good to finally talk about it. For a long while I thought it was all my fault. Perhaps if I was smarter, quicker to grasp things, not as dumb, my dad wouldn't be so angry with me all the time.'

'None of it was your fault,' she said, her heart aching. 'You were just a child.'

He shrugged, the expression on his face suggesting that none of it mattered, that it was all in the past, when she could see clearly in his eyes that it mattered very much. 'Anyway, enough about me. Tell me something about yourself. You could go anywhere in the world to be a nurse. Why did you choose Manila?'

'You came here to get away from your father. I came here to feel closer to mine.'

'Is he here, in the Philippines?'

'He died,' she said in her smallest voice.

His arms tightened around her. 'I'm sorry to hear that.'

'Before he died, he was a doctor here, in the Philippines. That's one of the reasons I became a nurse. I wanted to understand him better, to feel like we had something in common. I don't know much about him at all because he left when I was little. Mama told me he left because he wasn't ready to be a father. I try not to think about it because every time I do, I feel guilty. Maybe if I hadn't been born, he would still be around and Mama wouldn't be so lonely.'

'How can she be lonely? She has you.'

Rose closed her eyes and thought of her childhood, of the little girl who was lonely and afraid but tried very hard not to show it because she didn't want to upset her mother. 'I don't have many memories of my father. I remember feelings rather than events. The giddiness, my heart racing because he was spinning me around the room. The joy at being close to him. The emptiness after he left, like there was a hole inside my heart that could never be filled. I have so many questions and I'm afraid I will never find answers.'

'Does your mother ever talk about him?'

'Never. Every time I brought him up in the past, she looked like she was about to cry, so I stopped asking. Sometimes I dream of a tall man walking towards me and I'm about to see his face but before I do, I always wake up. I tell myself he was a good person, selfless and kind. If he wasn't, he wouldn't be a doctor. Sometimes I make up stories about him, made-up memories to replace the ones I lost. Does it make me crazy?'

'No, not at all,' David whispered, kissing her. 'It makes you human.'

Every time she thought of her father, Rose felt a longing she couldn't understand or put into words. It was like reaching for the remnants of a morning fog, trying to grasp it with the tips of her fingers and watching it slip away and disperse without a trace. For a long time, it made her feel incomplete, like a part of her was missing because her father was no longer in her life. But she didn't feel like that here, at the majestic Hulugan Falls, with David by her side. Her father had brought her to the Philippines, where she found David, and for the first time that she could remember, she felt she was living the life she was truly meant for.

# Chapter 3

## December 1941

One evening after work, on the beautiful island of Corregidor, only a short boat trip across the harbour, David was teaching Rose to play chess. She enjoyed chess, the complexity of it, the challenge, how the pieces felt in her hand as she made her move and the way David frowned when he tried to concentrate. When she played chess, she felt smart, like she should be wearing glasses and a business suit. In chess, unlike life, everything was black and white. There were no shades of grey. She preferred it to reality because lately she had been filled with nothing but doubt.

When she was with David, she felt giddy and light-hearted but when he wasn't around, she was lost and heartsick. The feeling was new and all-encompassing, one that had taken her completely by surprise. Nothing in her past had prepared her for it. At school, she had been aware of boys glancing her way, of their shaking, nervous hands as they spoke to her. But her heart had never fluttered like a frightened butterfly before, her thoughts had never run from her like a getaway train, leaving her confused and questioning herself. Until now. And all she could think of was, *what if he doesn't feel the same?* When she saw him, her breath caught in her throat. When she thought of him, she found it hard to breathe. But what if he never thought of her at all? As he moved pieces around the chessboard, she searched his face for signs, finding it hard to think straight and making the most obvious mistakes.

On the hill behind them, a fortress like a lone guard rose above the ragged landscape, watching over them, silent and imposing. 'What is this place?' she asked.

'Corregidor is nicknamed the Rock, and with good reason,' he replied. 'It's a fortified tunnel built underneath three hundred feet of rock and soil, a shell- and bombproof self-sufficient shelter that can withstand a siege of many months.'

'Who built it?'

'Americans, as part of War Plan Orange.'

'War Plan Orange?'

'A series of plans the United States made in the '20s and '30s to prepare for war with Japan. Back then, it was a distant possibility. Now it has become a reality. Which is exactly what I wanted to talk to you about.' For a few moments, he didn't speak, as if searching for the right words and unable to find them. His fingers were fidgeting with the knight, like he was considering his next move. But Rose knew by the expression on his face that he was no longer paying any attention to their game of chess. 'I think you should leave the Philippines and return to America.'

A few moments earlier, she had been looking at the peaceful sky over Corregidor, counting down the minutes until another perfect sunset. She was thinking about inviting David for dinner and introducing him to her friends. She was wondering what her first hot Christmas would be like. Her first Christmas with him. And here he was, saying he wanted her to go back home. It wasn't what she was expecting. 'I don't want to leave,' she said softly.

'You'll be safe back in Brownville.'

'You don't think I'm safe here?' Since the day she had stepped ashore, her time in Manila had been nothing but magical. She didn't believe anything could break the spell, not even war. 'I'm not afraid. Japan is barely the size of California. They're no match for the US Army. We have the navy, we have the air power, what could we possibly have to worry about?' She fell quiet. The truth was, she knew close to nothing about any of it. David knew more and his grim face was making her shiver.

'Just like you, many people are underestimating the Japanese. They shouldn't. The Imperial Army is one of the best trained and equipped in the world. And they have something we don't. They are fearless. They fight to the death.'

'General MacArthur won't let them come here. He said so himself.'

'He might not have much choice. President Roosevelt's main focus is on the war in Europe. Unfortunately, the Philippines are not his priority. And tensions are rising.'

'How many US troops are stationed here?' she asked in a weak voice.

'31,000 soldiers.'

'Sounds like a lot. I always see them around town. How many Filipino men?'

'I don't know.'

'Roughly, how many?'

'120,000.'

'Thank you for telling me. I feel much safer now.' She squeezed her tense fingers together, looking at the tranquil sea, while the fortress of Corregidor loomed behind them like the spectre of war.

'I know it sounds like a lot but 120,000 badly trained and poorly equipped men are no match for what's to come. We are facing a relentless enemy with technology superior to anything we've ever seen. Their Mitsubishi Zero fighter planes alone are quite something.' For a moment he was quiet, staring at the sea stretching in front of them as far as the eye could see. 'If there is no danger, why did Britain order the evacuation of all its citizens from Hong Kong six months ago?'

'We are not in Hong Kong,' she whispered.

'Why have they been evacuating military families from the Philippines? And if your wards are empty, like you tell me, why are you preparing thousands of dressings?'

'In case of more patients?'

A cloud ran over the sun and for a moment the day was not as sparkling, not as dazzling as before. David's eyes dimmed. 'Yes, Rose. In case of war.'

Before he brought her here, David had told her the sunsets were even more spectacular on the island, and she had been holding her breath, waiting for the sun to slip away and light up the sky. But now, she couldn't even look at the red and purple display on the horizon. For weeks in Manila, she had busied herself with work, with cinema and golf and dancing and chess, with waterfalls and tennis and swimming in the ocean, anything not to be afraid, anything not to think of the threat that was hanging over them, unknown and therefore terrifying. She was afraid now, while the birds sang with joy and the sun threw its last rays on the flawless sea.

David said, 'Before the year is over, they'll be here.' He pushed a strand of hair off her face. 'I don't want you to go. I want you here with me. But more than anything I want you to be safe. I can speak to my commander. They are still evacuating people. Perhaps you could go home on one of the ships.'

Rose thought of arriving in Manila only weeks before, of the military band welcoming them like they were conquerors coming home in triumph. Back then, she had thought she was ready for anything. But she wasn't ready for this. 'Are you trying to get rid of me, Lieutenant Taylor?' she asked teasingly.

'On the contrary. I am trying to save you for myself.'

Rose didn't want to believe David's grim words. Why would the Japanese come here? What did they want with the Philippines, a speck in the ocean, a tiny dot on the map? The sheer vastness of the Pacific created a false sense of security, and she convinced herself that nothing bad was going to happen, that David was mistaken, that he was overcautious, that he wanted to protect her *just in case*.

But when she returned that evening, her heart heavy with fear, she found the hospital and their quarters plunged into darkness. She stumbled around the room when she heard Kate whistling softly under her breath. 'What's happening?' asked Rose, desperately trying not to panic. 'Why is it so dark?'

'It's the blackout. All the lights have been turned off.'

'Why?' Rose whispered.

Kate must have heard the fear in Rose's voice. 'Don't worry. I think it's just a practice run. The lights will come on soon.'

And a moment later, they did. Rose breathed out in relief, as if the electricity coming back pushed the possibility of war further back and they could go on as before, dancing and enjoying long lazy afternoons without a care in the world. But David's terrifying prediction haunted Rose. Contemplating her pale face in the mirror, she splashed her forehead with cold water. It made no difference. Her cheeks were burning.

Kate seemed unconcerned. She continued to hum to herself and then asked, 'Are you coming to the ball on Sunday? Or are you going to abandon us for your mystery man like you always do?'

Rose could barely hear Kate over the dark thoughts inside her head. 'Which ball?'

'Only the most important event of the year. Christmas ball at the Officers' Club. Everyone is going to be there. Everyone is talking about it.'

'I'd love to come but I have nothing to wear.'

'Why don't you borrow my blue dress? I've never worn it. Would you like to try it on?'

Kate opened her wardrobe, pulled out the dress and placed it on the bed. Rose ran her fingers over the fabric. It was the purest silk she had ever seen. 'How can you afford something like this?'

'Present from my dad. He left us, you see. Divorced my mother and married a woman half his age. Before he died, he gave me guilt money and bought me anything I wanted. I guess he was hoping to buy my love back.'

'Did it work?'

Kate shrugged. 'He didn't need to do any of it. I never stopped loving him, not for a moment.' She waved her hand in the air, as if chasing away a ghost. Then she looked at Rose, at the dress and back again. 'The colour will go perfectly with your eyes.'

When Rose tried the dress on, it hung on her like a tent. She blinked, trying to hide her disappointment. 'It's too big.'

'Shame,' said Kate. 'You would be the belle of the ball in it.' She pulled the dress back and admired Rose's reflection in the mirror. 'Perhaps we can adjust it.'

'You know how to sew?'

'I don't. But Tess does. She's the domestic goddess in our tribe.'

'Where *is* Tess?'

'She's off on her weekly shopping trip. Haven't you noticed? She's been buying canned goods for weeks.'

As if on cue, Tess appeared, bending under the weight of two bags. She nodded to the girls, who watched her with curiosity, and proceeded to unload her purchases. Rose counted ten cans of spam and eleven cans of pickled vegetables.

'What do you need these for?' asked Rose, wrinkling her nose. 'They feed us like royalty. You can get fresh meat and vegetables any time you like.'

'Yes, and you don't even have to pay for it,' said Kate. 'Why would you waste your money on canned goods?'

Tess blushed. 'The spam and the pickles are cheap. I can afford them.'

'Do you even have space for them in your room? I looked under your bed and there are cans everywhere,' said Kate. 'What are you hoarding them for?'

'Just in case.'

'In case of what?' Rose whispered, her voice trembling.

'If the Japanese come here, food will be hard to get. Everyone says so. I want to be prepared, that's all.'

'You shouldn't listen to silly rumours,' said Kate. 'Better get your sewing machine out and help Rose with this dress.'

As Rose watched Tess perform miracles with the dress, dread spread through her like poison and she felt like she were falling through the air without anyone there to catch her. Perhaps, instead of teasing Tess about her hoarding, they should be rushing to the stores, buying up all the canned goods they could find because war was coming to the Philippines.

The next evening, Rose returned from dinner with David to find Kate and Tess in the shared living room, dressed in evening gowns with their hair up and their faces made-up, like two princesses heading to a ball. 'Where have you two been, dressed like this? A party?' she asked, smiling.

'We went to the cinema,' said Kate. 'We watched *I Met My Love Again*.' She closed her eyes with an expression of sheer joy on her face.

'You went to the cinema in evening gowns?'

'We wanted it to be special,' said Tess. 'The film was beautiful. Henry Fonda was perfection. It was about love.' She stretched the last word, making it sound like a song. 'Speaking of which, we are still to meet your secret admirer. You never tell us anything.'

But before Rose had a chance to tell them, they heard a scratch at the door. A moment later, Ida walked in, her hair and make-up a mess, her eyes red with tears. Without a word, she sat down on the settee, put her head in her hands and began to cry. The girls gathered around her, patting her on her back. 'Darling, what's wrong?' asked Rose.

It took a few moments for Ida to speak. 'They're dismissing me.' Her lips trembled. She rubbed mascara into her cheeks with her fists and glanced at the girls, looking like a distraught panda.

'I have to leave by the end of the day tomorrow.'

'Why would they dismiss you?' Kate demanded. 'What have you done wrong?'

Ida shrugged. 'Elsie asked me to stay behind after work. She made me wait an hour and then lectured me about loyalty and commitment and what it means to be a military nurse, and how my allegiance should be to my country first. Apparently, I'm not taking it seriously enough and they can't have me working for them anymore.' Ida hiccupped and fell quiet, her lips trembling.

Rose said, 'You're an excellent nurse, caring and hardworking. You always volunteer for extra shifts. Your patients love you. You are an example to us all.'

'Someone told them about my relationship with Karl,' Ida said softly, not looking at the girls.

Kate gasped, like she knew something. But Rose still didn't understand. 'Your sweetheart you met in the US? So what? What we do in our personal time is our business. If they dismiss every single nurse for having a sweetheart, they'll soon have no nurses left.'

Ida didn't reply. It was Kate who said, 'Karl is German, Rose.'

'Oh,' said Rose. Her hand flew to her mouth.

Ida said, 'He's the sweetest man I've ever met. He asked me to marry him and I said yes.' She stretched her left hand out and Rose saw a stunning diamond sparkling on her finger. 'He doesn't believe in this war. He doesn't support Hitler. He's horrified by everything that is going on. But none of that matters because he happens to be German.'

'Of course it matters,' said Rose. 'Karl sounds wonderful.'

'Elsie didn't even give me a chance to explain. She refused to listen.' Fresh tears filled Ida's eyes. 'I can't go back home. My father drinks too much. And every time he drinks, he looks for someone to take his bad mood out on. Usually that someone is me.'

'Where will you go?' Rose asked quietly.

'Karl said I could stay with him and his parents for a while.

It's a busy household. He has four younger siblings living there too. He says I don't need to work. He will look after me and once we are married, we can find our own place.' Ida looked at the girls with sad eyes. 'I want to work. All I've ever wanted was to be a nurse. It's when I'm happiest. What am I going to do with myself all day?'

'Do you love Karl?'

'More than anything.'

Rose hugged her friend. 'I'm happy for you, Ida. You found love. You are getting married soon. Everything else will work out. You'll see.'

Ida nodded but continued to cry in Rose's arms. Rose shook her head. 'Who would do such a thing? Who would tell them about you and Karl?'

Set on three acres of land overlooking the sea, the Officers' Club was surrounded by palm and flame trees and everywhere Rose glanced, she saw splodges of red and purple of the bougainvillea. The gorgeous grounds had been transformed into a winter wonderland for the most important event of the social calendar. Crystal snowflakes were trembling in the wind, the light of the myriad stars reflecting off them. Fairy lights were strung over every surface, making Rose feel like she was caught up in a fairy tale.

Champagne flutes clinked, smiles lit up the room and eyes sparkled. A deep baritone sang about love and loss and sadness, while in every face Rose saw nothing but joy. It seemed to her that she had imagined David's horrifying words a few days before. But only at first glance. When she sashayed through the crowd in her stunning dress, looking for her friends, she couldn't help but overhear the conversations. As they danced and laughed, as they sipped expensive champagne and sampled lobster and crab, as they enjoyed the breathtaking views and the warm breeze, all they spoke about was the possibility of an attack.

Rose saw Tess and Kate waving at her. She waved back and made her way across the festive gardens, relieved to be out of the crowd. But her friends, too, were talking about war.

'See,' Kate was saying to Tess. 'You don't need to worry. If there was any danger, would the army officials be throwing a party? They would have more important things to worry about, like defence and evacuation.'

'They have been evacuating,' replied Tess. 'Look around you. It's just us nurses and the officers. All military families are long gone.'

'They wouldn't be dancing. They would be preparing for war.'

They talked about home and their time in the Philippines. Kate told them about the young man from the *Holbrook* who had retrieved her hat from the sea. One day, he had found her at the hospital and invited her for a drink. They had been seeing each other ever since. Finally, after all this time, Rose told the girls about David. After a glass and a half of champagne, everything was swaying a little in front of her dazzled eyes, the palm trees, the festive lights, the merry dancers. She wasn't used to drinking, and now her head was light and her heart was filled with happiness. There was magic in everything she looked at.

Kate and Tess spent the whole night on the dance floor, waltzing and foxtrotting and even attempting a tango. There was no shortage of handsome officers willing to dance with the nurses. They laughed and flirted and drank champagne. They dined on roast beef and seafood and had the most amazing chocolate fondue, frozen yoghurt and fruit for dessert. Half a dozen young men invited Rose to dance but she said no to all of them. One told her she was the most beautiful girl at the party, the most beautiful girl in all of Manila. 'It's the dress,' she told him.

'No, it's just you,' he replied.

And still she refused to join him on the dance floor. David was on duty that evening and couldn't make it to the ball. He was the only one she wanted to dance with. If he wasn't there, she was content to just sit, sip her champagne and watch the others have the best night of their lives.

They walked home holding hands and chatting excitedly, like a flock of noisy cockatoos. It was no longer pitch-black outside but not quite light either, the moment between night and dawn that Rose loved so much. The world seemed to hold its breath in anticipation of another day. It was peaceful and quiet, and there was a sense of expectation in the air, a new beginning.

At home, they sat side by side at the round table in their living room, like the knights of King Arthur, sipping tea and talking in low voices.

'Can you believe it's less than three weeks till Christmas?' exclaimed Rose. A sudden wave of homesickness washed over her, making it hard to breathe. Despite the lights draped over houses and trees, despite the festive music and decorations, it didn't feel like Christmas here in tropical Manila. Back home, hardwood trees would turn silver with frost, there would be snow on the mountains and the streets would be icy. Her mother would be searching for just the right tree, adorning it with homemade baubles and putting up their stockings, like Rose was still a child and believed in the magic of Christmas – as if she were still home.

Kate said, 'My brother and I always went ice skating on the pond outside of my grandparents' house at Christmas. It was the happiest time.'

'I love ice skating,' said Rose. 'When I was nine, my mama worked extra shifts for a month so she could buy me a pair of ice skates. I spent every free moment skating that winter. It was magical. The next year, I grew out of my skates and Mama couldn't afford to buy another pair.'

'I miss home so much,' said Tess. 'I bet we'll miss this place too when we go back. You always want what you can't have. We will be sitting around a table with cups of tea, just like we are now, looking at the snow falling outside, and reminiscing about the tropical sunsets. I know I will never forget this place, for as long as I live.'

‘I would stay here,’ said Rose. ‘If it wasn’t for my mother all alone back home, I could live here for the rest of my life.’

They were finishing their tea and biscuits when they heard a loud knock. The girls sat up straight, looking at one another with surprise. It came as a shock in the quiet of the morning when most people were still asleep.

‘Who could it be at this time?’ muttered Rose. She pulled on a robe and made her way to the door. Behind it stood Fernando the housekeeper, grim-faced and dark-eyed, as if he hadn’t slept either, but instead of dancing he had spent the night worrying. ‘Can I help you?’ asked Rose, shivering despite the heat.

‘Good morning,’ Fernando said, hesitating, looking at Rose and the other girls who waited behind her in silence. Rose knew right away Fernando was the bearer of bad news. There was something in his face, in the way he wrung his hands, in the way his eyes darted this way and that, in the moment’s delay before he spoke, like he was putting off an unpleasant task. Finally, he said, ‘Please forgive me for disturbing you so early. I’m here to let you know that all nurses are required to report to the hospital immediately.’

‘It’s six in the morning,’ said Tess.

‘We are not supposed to work today. It’s our day off,’ said Kate.

Rose stayed quiet, waiting for an explanation.

‘All time off has been cancelled as of this morning,’ said Fernando.

‘We can’t work today,’ said Tess. ‘We were out all night, dancing. We had the best time.’ She twirled in their hallway, as if in her mind she was still on the dance floor of the Officers’ Club, lost in the music, in the twinkling lights, in a handsome officer’s arms.

The sun rose behind Fernando, making him look like he was glowing from the inside. But his eyes remained dim and when he spoke again, his voice quivered. ‘There will be no more dancing, I’m afraid. A few hours ago, the Japanese attacked Pearl Harbor.’

# Chapter 4

## December 1941

A knock on the door, a few ill-fated seconds, a dozen terrible words, and Rose knew her life would never be the same again. She knew she would remember this moment forever, would remember Fernando's pained face as he waited for the girls to say something, anything, before he turned around and continued on his terrible quest of delivering bad news. Rose couldn't look at the others because she didn't want to see the panic in their eyes. After the door closed behind Fernando, a dark silence fell.

Rose and Tess glanced at Kate, whose brother was stationed in Hawaii. As if in slow motion, she slid to the floor and covered her eyes with her hands. Her shoulders shook as she sobbed, while Rose and Tess dropped to her side, kneeling next to her and stroking her back in silence. Faced with such distress, Rose felt helpless and didn't know what to say. And Kate was not talking. Curled up in a small ball, she was crying silently.

'Honey, listen to me. Your brother will be fine. I'm sure of it,' said Tess.

Kate lifted her eyes to the girls. She looked haunted. 'What if, while I was dancing and laughing and drinking champagne, my brother was killed?'

'Nonsense,' said Rose, hugging Kate. Her small body felt like that of a frightened kitten in her arms, small and trembling. 'We don't know anything yet. Don't jump to conclusions.'

'Let's go to the hospital,' said Kate, suddenly pulling herself together, wriggling out of Rose's embrace and wiping her eyes. 'Let's find out what happened.'

At the hospital, no one seemed to know anything. Some said it was misinformation, that it couldn't be. Others believed the Pacific Fleet in its entirety had been destroyed in one sneaky early-morning attack. Everywhere she looked, Rose saw fear and heartbreak. Five minutes after the girls arrived, they heard a deafening sound that made them jump.

'What's that noise?' Kate shouted, putting her hands over her ears and grimacing as if in pain.

Tess said something that Rose couldn't make out over the wailing of the alarm. *What?* she mouthed to her, wanting to cover her own ears but knowing it would make no difference.

The furious shrieking stopped as abruptly as it had begun. The tense silence that followed seemed even louder to Rose. It screamed of uncertainty, of things to come that she couldn't fathom but was afraid of anyway. 'An air-raid siren,' Tess repeated.

'Are we in danger? Do we need to evacuate?' Rose felt her hands begin to shake.

'It's stopped,' Kate said. 'Perhaps it was a practice run, just to make sure it's working fine.'

No one seemed to have any answers, so Rose and the other nurses started their shifts, partly to make themselves useful and partly to take their minds off the unspeakable horror that was taking place across the ocean. When Rose was doing her rounds, her patients didn't seem to care about their treatment or prognosis. They wanted to know what was happening.

'I know as much as you do,' she would say, checking temperatures, measuring blood pressure, making notes on charts as if it was just an ordinary day. And the question on everybody's mind was, *what does it mean for us?* The Philippines relied on the Pacific Fleet for protection. If it had been destroyed like everybody said, who would stand between them and the Imperial Army of Japan?

At eleven, Elsie called all the nurses to the staff room. She didn't confirm nor deny the reports but told them in a grave voice that their immediate orders were to discharge all naval officers and sailors who were mobile so that they could return to active service.

'Discharge them?' exclaimed Rose. 'But Jack in bed fifteen has a fever that won't go down. And Brendan can't walk without a stick.'

'It's war. If they can stand, they can fight,' said Elsie.

Most sailors welcomed the news. Jack seemed to forget all about his fever. Brendan jumped to his feet and hobbled around his bed without his walking stick, gesturing with his hands and declaring that he was ready. Japan had attacked the United States. It was not the time to lie in a hospital bed, doing nothing. When Brendan completed his victory lap around his bed, he came to Rose's side and took her hand, winking and grinning. 'If I leave, who is going to look after me? Who is going to make me tea?'

'Don't worry about tea, soldier. War has started,' Rose replied, helping him to bed. Ideally, he needed a few more weeks to recuperate or his leg would never recover and he would limp for the rest of his life. Unfortunately, he didn't have a few more weeks.

'What about my marriage proposal? I'm yet to hear your answer.'

'Defeat the Japanese first. We can talk about marriage later,' she said, trying to sound hopeful and optimistic, even though she felt like crying. She couldn't stop thinking about Hawaii. When the *Holbrook* had been stationed there for a brief period of time before embarking on its long journey to Manila, the sailors stationed there welcomed the nurses with open arms. They brought them onboard their ships and fed them scones and biscuits. Rose would never forget their hospitality, nor would she forget the tears on Kate's brother's face as he said goodbye to his sister, as if he knew he would never see her again.

By 11.30 a.m., all able-bodied men had their discharge orders. Her heart hurting, Rose wondered what their future held and what horrors awaited them at the front. By midday, the hospital fell quiet. Rose walked through the empty wards, feeling lost without her patients, unsure what to do next, fighting a dark foreboding, a feeling that something terrible was about to happen.

She was helping set up saline drips for a few remaining patients inside the paediatric ward when Ida came to see her. She followed Rose, moving from bed to bed, talking fast. 'We were supposed to leave today. Karl thought it would be safer for us back in the US. He wants to start a family, somewhere we don't have to worry about the war. But we couldn't get on the ship. We already paid for our passage but they told us the ship wasn't leaving.' She was flushed, her neck red, her usually impeccable hair was all out of place, with not a trace of make-up on her face.

'I didn't know you were leaving.' Rose felt flushed herself. Her hands trembled as she fiddled with the drips.

'Not anymore. Everything seems to have changed overnight.' Ida looked lost and afraid. Unable to face her terror, Rose turned away, nodding in agreement. Her blood ran cold at the thought of her motherland under threat, of bombs falling on the tranquil Hawaii, the place of her mother's dreams.

'I have *some* good news,' said Ida. 'Look!' She stretched her hand out.

Rose saw a simple golden band next to her diamond engagement ring. She squealed with delight. 'Ida! You did it! I can't believe it.'

'We went to the registry office yesterday. It was just us, his parents and brothers, but we had a wonderful day. We decided not to put it off any longer. We figured, with the war looming, there is no point in waiting.'

'You did the right thing. I'm so happy for you.'

Rose hugged her friend. At the sight of Ida's joy, she felt warm inside and for a moment forgot all about her fears.

'Ida Burns! What are you doing here?' The girls jumped when they heard the cranky voice behind them. They span around and saw Elsie moving towards them at great speed, her hair flying around her face like a grey ring.

'It's Ida Freimann now, thank you very much,' said Ida. Turning to Rose, she whispered, 'I'd better run before Elsie burns me on a stake.'

Ignoring Ida, who waved to both of them with a smile on her face and was shuffling towards the exit, Elsie said to Rose, 'We don't have time for idle chatter. We have work to do. Those dressings won't make themselves.'

'We just discharged all our patients. What do we need more dressings for?' asked Rose.

Elsie's face changed. One moment, she looked irritated and upset, the next, the anger was gone and her mouth twisted in fear, like she knew something and wasn't telling. Even though Rose knew nothing, Elsie's panic was contagious. She felt her knees begin to shake.

After her lunch break that was spent not eating but speculating and discussing the current events with her colleagues, Rose was walking back to the ward when she saw David. He was leaning on the wall with his hands in his pockets and his eyes on the ground. She looked around, making sure Elsie wasn't on the warpath, searching for nurses who were chatting and not doing their job. When she was certain the coast was clear, Rose rushed to his side. At the sight of her he stood up straight and smiled but his smile didn't quite reach his eyes. He took a few steps in her direction and she ran into his arms, feeling breathless and hot around her neck. 'What are you doing here?' she asked. 'I wasn't expecting to see you till the evening.'

'I had to make sure you were all right after the news.'

Rose let go of him and sighed. 'It's hard to believe that while we danced and enjoyed ourselves, the Japanese were bombing

Pearl Harbor.'

'Yes, the attack took many people by surprise.'

'Are there many casualties?'

He looked like he didn't want to tell her. 'Yes, unfortunately.'

'Oh, no,' she whispered. 'Kate's brother is stationed in Hawaii. She is going out of her mind with worry.'

'I'm sorry to hear that.'

Rose trembled a little. 'This bombing … what does it mean for us?'

'The war in the Pacific has started. We can no longer rely on the navy to come to our rescue when the Japanese attack the Philippines.'

'*When* they attack? You think it's inevitable?'

'It's only a matter of time.' He took her hand and squeezed it, as if trying to emphasise the importance of what he was about to say. 'Which is why you can't stay here any longer. I talked to my commander. He will let me know tomorrow if there is a spot on a ship going back home.'

She hesitated. 'What about you?'

'I'm an officer. I have no choice. It's my job to stay behind and fight. But you need to go.'

Rose struggled not to cry. The thought of David standing in the path of the invading Imperial Army was too much to bear. 'I'll stay too. I'll stay so I can be there for you. You'll need me.'

'I need you to be safe. If I know you are here, I will worry about you. I won't be able to focus on my job. I will make mistakes. Promise me you will get on that boat.' *No*, she wanted to say. *No*. But she knew it wasn't what he wanted to hear. His eyes were pleading with her, imploring her to say yes. She nodded, suddenly unable to speak. He hugged her. 'I know,' he said. 'I don't want to be apart either. I love you, Rose. Your safety is all that matters right now.'

'All right,' she whispered. Elsie appeared in the corridor, glaring at Rose, who stood close to David, lost in his arms. 'I'd better go,' she said reluctantly, moving away from him, wanting nothing more than to stay in his arms where she felt protected. 'Elsie is here.'

'Go,' he said, kissing the tips of her fingers. 'I'll see you this afternoon.'

When she was at the end of the corridor, she turned around. 'David?' she called out. *I love you too*, she wanted to say. But it was too late. He was already gone.

Rose did her best to concentrate on her work, to think of nothing but her patients' needs but all she imagined when she closed her eyes were the soldiers of the Imperial Army trampling the Philippines under their boots. In her mind she saw the place she had grown to love, the place that felt a little bit like home, destroyed by war. She didn't want to stay and see that. She wanted to go home and be with her mother, who always knew just the right words to say when Rose felt scared or upset. One look at her mother's loving face and all her troubles would disappear like snow in spring. But if she left, she might never see David again.

In the afternoon she worked on the paediatric ward. Only five patients remained, four of them almost well enough to go home. The two older girls entertained everyone by telling stories and singing their favourite songs, while two younger patients listened, fascinated. Seeing their innocent little faces, untouched by worry, warmed Rose's heart. It almost made her forget about the spectre of war that hung over them. But then a terrible thought occurred to her. If the Japanese came to the Philippines, what would happen to these children? She continued to smile as she sang their songs and praised their stories, while on the inside she wanted to scream.

The fifth child, a small boy called Andy, had the dreaded diphtheria. He didn't sing or tell stories, nor did he sit on the floor with his legs crossed, listening to Rose and the other children. Two days previously, he had been put in isolation. The grey membrane over his throat and tonsils continued to spread and the intravenous serum was no longer helping.

Rose put up a steam tent around Andy in the hope that it would help him breathe easier. Still, he was struggling, his little face red, his eyes screaming in mute horror. Every time Rose approached him, he grabbed her hand in desperation, squeezing her fingers until she cried out. She knew she had to do something fast or it might be too late.

Telling the other children she would be right back, Rose ran out of the ward and down the corridor, looking for the chief surgeon, Dr Stephenson. She found him in the staff room and begged him to come with her. Andy needed a tracheotomy. There was no time to lose. It would have to be performed on the ward because the child was too ill to be moved.

Dr Stephenson, a kind giant who was respected and loved by patients and staff alike, told her he would be right there. While she waited for the doctor, she wrapped the boy in a blanket tucked below his shoulders, securing it with safety pins. Lifting him gently, she placed him on the operating table and adjusted a sandbag under his shoulders so that his neck was fully extended. His breathing became louder and more laboured. He couldn't talk but his eyes spoke volumes. Rose stroked his head, moved his long hair out of his face, repeating, 'It will be all right. Everything will be all right.'

The boy's eyes became calmer, as if he believed her.

'The doctor is on his way. He is a wizard who can do anything. He will fix this. He'll make you feel better. Then you can see your family. You can go back to your mama and daddy and little brother.'

Andy's eyes filled with tears. Rose felt sorry for him and all the other sick children at the hospital. It was tough for the little ones without their families nearby.

When the surgeon arrived, he praised her for her quick actions. 'You might have saved this child's life by coming to get me as quickly as you did,' he said, 'He doesn't look so good. Let's operate. You can assist me. There is no time to scrub up.'

Rose held Andy's head firmly and steadily, ensuring that his neck was straight, to make it easier for the surgeon to cut into the centre of his trachea. The boy was almost black in the face and in great distress.

Dr Stephenson was about to make the incision when a deafening alarm sounded, the familiar shrieking making Rose jump and momentarily let go of Andy's head. The child groaned.

'What's happening?' she cried. She couldn't hear herself over the horrible wailing sound.

'An air-raid siren,' said the doctor, his face impassive, his eyes on his patient, his hand ready to administer the life-saving incision.

'Do we need to go to a shelter?' she asked.

Were the Japanese bombing the Philippines? It didn't bear thinking about. But didn't David warn her that this was going to happen? He spoke about it like it was a certainty, a matter of *when* not *if*. She didn't want to believe him. A day ago, the enemy had bombed Pearl Harbor. How could they be here so quickly? It made no sense to her as she leaned over the sick child, her eyes filling with tears.

'We need to finish the surgery or we'll lose our patient,' said the doctor. 'It's probably just a trial run.' He shook his head, as if he, too, found it difficult to believe the Japanese were coming to the islands.

Rapidly, like a lightning flash, Dr Stephenson made the incision. There was an intake of air from the boy, and the colour of his face changed, becoming lighter, more natural. The trachea was open and it was just a simple matter of inserting the dilators. Rose realised she had been holding her breath the whole time. Her shoulders were aching from the tension. As a healthier colour returned to the patient, she felt herself relax, even as the air-raid siren continued to scream and she could hear panicked voices and the sound of stomping feet.

Moments later, the surgery was over. Rose marvelled at the doctor's skill, at the speed with which he had performed the surgery, at the steadiness of his hand and his calm demeanour, even in the face of a storm that any time now threatened to break over Manila. He was only human, and yet, like God, in a few simple moves he had saved a life. She wanted to give him a round of applause but knew he wouldn't appreciate it because he was simply doing his job.

Rose put Andy in a warm cot and sat by his side, holding his hand, making sure he didn't pull out his dilators. A moment later, he fell asleep. She took away the steam tent because he no longer needed it. Thanks to Dr Stephenson, he was breathing normally.

As she worked, all she could think was, *when will it stop?* If it was only a trial run, why was the alarm still on, screaming its fury into the early afternoon air with no end in sight?

Moments later, she heard another sound, more terrifying even than the siren. It was alien to Rose's ears and didn't seem to belong in peaceful Manila – the noise of an aircraft engine, followed by whistling and an explosion. Anti-aircraft guns joined in, and Rose froze, listening with horror to the deathly duet. Outside the children's ward, someone shrieked. Somewhere nearby, a door slammed and glass shattered.

The Filipino troops stationed outside opened fire with their machine guns, rifles and .45s at the Japanese planes that were too high for them to reach. The cloudy sky lit up with a pyrotechnic display of tracer bullets.

Not only were the Japanese bombing the islands, they were bombing the hospital, the place of peace and hope where innocent people in need came for help.

Rose couldn't move. She couldn't believe this was happening and didn't know what to do, so she remained by the window, her eyes on the sky, where the enemy planes glided past in a neat formation, releasing deadly explosives. She blinked and closed her eyes because she didn't want to see. Dr Stephenson grabbed her hand. 'We have to go to the shelter, now.'

She pulled away from him. 'We can't go. What about Andy?'

'Get the stretcher ready. We'll take him with us.'

Rose spun around, searching for a stretcher, when something exploded nearby. A part of the wall splintered and collapsed like rocks from a mountain during an avalanche. Rose reached out her hand for the doctor but couldn't find him. When she turned around, she saw that he had disappeared under the rubble, while a cloud of dust engulfed her, and all around the walls of the hospital were crumbling like gingerbread houses.

She thought she heard David calling for her. 'Rose, where are you? Rose!' His frantic voice rose above the din of artillery, becoming more and more desperate. Then all the noise faded away and there was nothing but darkness.

Rose opened her eyes and groaned. Her vision was blurry and her head hurt. As if through a fog, she saw that she was in a hospital bed with a crisp pillow under her head and a sheet over her legs. She could hear no sound of planes, no anti-aircraft guns barking their anger at the sudden invasion, no machine guns singing their chilling song. Outside, the birds whistled peacefully as if all was well in the world. The sun was setting, throwing shadows on the walls, playing on Rose's face. She shielded her eyes and sat up. Had she imagined the horror, the screams, the destruction? She could almost convince herself that it had all been a terrible dream because she desperately wanted to believe it. Except, to her right was a man with bandages on his head, howling in pain. To the left was another man, a blanket covering what was left of his legs, not howling but staring into space in silence. And all around, other patients were shouting, calling for a nurse, for morphine, for relief and to forget. 'Water,' they pleaded. 'Please, Nurse, can I have some water?'

'Water,' whispered Rose. She was so thirsty, it felt like her throat was on fire. She touched her neck and closed her eyes.

A Filipina nurse she had never met before hurried to her side. 'Look who's awake. Welcome back, Nurse Williams. You slept for forty-eight hours.'

Forty-eight hours. Two days and nights. 'What did I miss?' Rose whispered, her voice coming out in an unfamiliar croaking sound, like it belonged to a stranger.

'Nothing good, I'm afraid. If I could sleep through what's been happening, I would.' The nurse, who introduced herself as Dolores, told her that not only had their hospital been attacked but also Camp John Hay, Clark Field and Fort Stotsenberg. It was a nightmare, she said, and no one could believe it.

Rose wanted to ask if there were many casualties but was afraid to. She felt fragile and not ready for bad news. She could hear patients around her groaning in pain – not only on beds but also on the floor, taking up every available space in the ward. She touched her head and blinked, wishing she was someplace else, wishing she had listened to David and returned home earlier. 'What's wrong with me?' she asked. 'Why is my head so sore? And my arm?'

'I'm surprised you still have your head, to be honest. A wall collapsed on you. You had some shrapnel embedded in your left arm. A surgeon removed it under local anaesthetic. Would you like to see it?'

'See what?' asked Rose, raising her confused eyes to the nurse.

'The piece of shrapnel.'

She nodded, in her shock barely able to fathom what Dolores was saying to her. The shrapnel was the size of a grape and looked harmless as it lay in Rose's lap. She stared at it with wonder.

'It could have killed you,' whispered the nurse, her eyes wide.

Rose ran her fingers over it. 'What about Dr Stephenson? Is he all right?'

Dolores perched on the bed next to her. She took Rose's hand. 'I'm sorry, honey. Dr Stephenson was killed. We are all in shock. We all loved him. They are still digging people out. You are lucky. Not even a broken bone. All you have is a slight concussion. God was looking out for you.'

'Yes, but not for Dr Stephenson.' Rose blinked her tears away. How was it possible that she had survived when their chief surgeon was gone? He who saved lives every day, who dedicated his whole existence to running this hospital, while she merely applied dressings and took temperatures. Why was he dead and she barely had a scratch on her? Where was the justice in that? 'Tess, Kate, Elsie,' she whispered. 'Are they …?'

'They're fine,' the nurse reassured her, telling her all the children were safe, including Andy, who was doing much better after his surgery. The boy was on nasal feeding and had been taking sips of fruit juice with glucose. There was no further spread of the dreaded membrane. For a moment, Rose could breathe again. If Dr Stephenson had stopped the surgery and run for shelter, he would still be alive. But Andy wouldn't. Rose cried at the thought of the selfless doctor who had traded his life for that of his patient. At least his sacrifice was not in vain. Andy would make a full recovery.

The nurse smiled. 'I'll bring you something to eat … wait … what are you doing? Where are you going?'

'I need to run. I need to …' She didn't finish. She couldn't think straight, could barely speak. She had to find David and make sure he was safe. One look at his wonderful face and the world would begin to make sense again.

Dizzy and unsteady on her feet, Rose made her way down the long corridor, taking a left, a right and another left, her head and arm a throbbing reminder of the horror she had been through. As she moved from ward to ward, she could hardly believe her eyes. The hospital was bursting with patients, two to a bed, sleeping on stretchers or simply on the floor, making it difficult for the nurses to manoeuvre through the bellowing, quivering human mass. Rose could hear the pitiful cry of ambulance sirens outside, bringing more people in, even though there was no available space and no staff to welcome them.

When Rose reached the ward, where two days earlier Dr Stephenson had operated on Andy, she wanted to turn back and run for her life. Not a wall had been left standing, not a stone. Horrified, she gaped at the rubble – piles of brick and wooden beams destroyed by fire. In the last two months, this hospital had become her home. She was a small part of something magical, a team of people who worked tirelessly to save lives. Day after day, they alleviated suffering and brought hope. This was what they lived for. This was their purpose. Every morning Rose had arrived within these four walls and made someone's life better. And it had all been destroyed in mere seconds, gone like it had never existed.

'You're not allowed here,' said a Filipino worker in protective gear, waving her away. She must have looked distraught because his face relaxed and he smiled at her kindly. 'It's not safe. Any minute now, what's left of these walls will collapse. Last thing you want is to be under it when it happens.'

She wanted to point out that she had already been under these walls, as they were collapsing. 'I was just leaving,' she said. On shaking knees, she turned her back to the destruction, wishing she hadn't come back to see it, knowing that she would never forget the blinding feeling of helplessness that suffocated her at the thought of so many innocent lives lost for no reason at all, through no fault of their own.

She blindly ran down dark, crowded corridors, not knowing where she was. All she knew was that she had to get away from this place of heartbreak as soon as she possibly could.

Overnight, it seemed, the hospital had turned into a beehive of activity. As much as she wanted to rest, Rose couldn't stay in bed and do nothing. She insisted on returning to work right away and did what she could for the stream of patients that continued to arrive.

After twelve hours on her feet tending to the wounded, Rose

asked Elsie for a break and walked outside. The sun was just beginning to rise, taking Rose by surprise. She didn't know what time of day it was. It had all become a blur. The breeze felt cool on Rose's hot skin, the birds cried with joy at the new day and the palms waved their warm greeting, like nothing had changed. And yet, Rose could tell right away that everything was different. The air in Manila no longer carried the aroma of flowers in it, like a sweet perfume. It smelt of fire. She could hear the distant din of artillery and it seemed out of place here, in tropical paradise, like a terrible nightmare that would end with the first rays of sun. And yet, here was morning and Rose's horrifying dream was still reality.

Not only did the city smell alien but it no longer looked the same. The serenity Rose had grown accustomed to was gone, and the natural beauty she loved so much was marred by smoke and the aftermath of shelling. Across the road from the hospital, she saw a large bomb crater, strange and frightening. Everywhere, it seemed, were carabao wagons, buses, pushcarts, motorcycles and cars moving in disarray, disregarding traffic rules in their elusive quest for safety. Crowds of people were coming into Manila on foot, while others were fleeing, hoping to find solace in the countryside. The city was a bubbling cauldron of fear and discontent, a termite nest that had been disturbed, unexpectedly and without warning, by the sudden arrival of Japanese bombers.

Rose crossed the carpark and spoke to an ambulance driver, who agreed to give her a ride to Fort William McKinley. As they made their way slowly through the stream of honking cars, wailing carabao, cyclists weaving in and out of traffic, people shouting, she closed her eyes and felt herself drifting off.

The last time she had spoken to David, he promised he would see her that evening. Then the Mitsubishi Zeros descended on Manila, destroying everything in their wake. She could still hear his voice inside her head, frantically calling her name. If David was safe, if he was still alive, wouldn't he have come looking for her, to make sure she was all right, to see if she needed help? But he hadn't come, and she was afraid to even speculate about what that might mean.

Rose must have fallen asleep because the next thing she knew, the ambulance driver was shaking her gently, telling her they had arrived. She thanked the man and he drove off, leaving her standing in the midst of a human river that was moving swiftly past with a deafening noise, threatening to swallow her alive. For a few moments, she watched the entrance to David's quarters, looking into every face, hoping to see him. It took her a few minutes to muster her courage to cross the road, walk through the small gate and approach the sentry desk.

'Can I help you?' The sentry looked up and she became self-conscious of her torn uniform that was splattered with blood, of the mud on her face and the grease in her hair. But the soldier smiled at her kindly, like he understood. Even though there was no blood on his uniform and no dirt on his face, he looked every bit as tired and lost as she felt.

She tried very hard not to stammer when she spoke. 'I'm looking for Lieutenant David Taylor.'

The sentry glanced at the roster on the wall in front of him. 'He should be on base. I will send someone to fetch him for you.'

Rose thanked him and sank into a metal chair by the door, clasping her cap, twisting it in her nervous hands, watching the young man speak to another soldier and point in her direction. For the first time since she woke up in the hospital bed, she could breathe freely again. David was safe. He was here. In a mere moment, she would see him and everything would be all right. With David by her side, she could face anything.

For ten agonising minutes she watched the hands of the clock as they crawled around the dial like snails, like they had forgotten how to move. The soldier returned, alone, without David. 'He's not here,' she heard him say.

She approached the two soldiers, her hand on her chest. 'Do

you know where he is? I haven't heard from him and I'm worried.'

They watched her with pity. She didn't want to see pity, she wanted them to tell her that David was safe. Fearing the worst, she looked down at the floor under her feet. The sentry said, 'I'm sorry, we don't know. But don't worry. It's been chaos around here since the attack. Just because he's not where he's supposed to be, doesn't mean something bad has happened.'

'If you see him, please tell him Rose was looking for him. Please tell him to come and see me at the hospital.'

She stumbled out into the morning heat, unsteady on her feet, her uniform clinging to her damp back. With her eyes down, lost in thought, barely knowing where she was, she walked for two hours through the mayhem of Manila at war in the direction of Sternberg Hospital until the familiar ambulance driver noticed her on his way back and picked her up.

Gone were the four-hour shifts, the easy mornings and giddy afternoons of adventure with a peaceful blue sky over their heads that didn't rain deadly explosives. After three hours of sleep and eighteen hours of triage, after administering what seemed like a thousand morphine shots, applying a thousand dressings and hearing nothing but screams of pain and suffering, Rose could barely stand on her two feet. Her knees were trembling and her head was spinning like she was drunk, like she was at the Officers' Club and had had too much champagne, only there was no joy or happiness, only horror.

Rose had no idea what was happening in Manila but the sound of war was unabating and it seemed to be getting closer. She tried to ignore it, hoping it would go away if only she buried herself in other people's needs. But there was no blocking it out. As long as there was daylight, machine guns didn't stop singing their deadly song and planes flew over the hospital, their engines growling like bears. When she caught a glimpse of the aircraft, like locusts obscuring the sky, the sight of the red rising sun of the Japanese

Empire painted on their wings made her tremble. She turned away from the window and refused to look again, but she could still hear them as she moved slowly through the ward, trying to reassure her patients, whose haunted eyes followed her every move, while she herself was in desperate need of reassurance.

Injured men continued to arrive at the hospital, even though there were no beds for them. Tired, wet and hungry, some of the wounded had their skin flayed by oil burns and were screaming in pain, while others were injured by bomb splinters or machine-gun fire. Rose removed dirty clothing and cleaned the men as best as she could, while trying to cheer them up with a kind word and a smile that looked sad and forlorn because there was so little to smile about these days.

The nurses no longer kept personal files on their patients. There was no time for records or charts that had been vitally important only a few days ago in peacetime. Rose wrote notes on her patients' foreheads, scribbling in shorthand what drugs had been administered and what their vitals were, while thinking with longing of the time when these wards were almost empty and didn't erupt with human suffering like an angry volcano.

Finally, she was told by Elsie to go and get some rest. Other nurses were sleeping on cardboard next to the patients so that they could get up after a few hours and resume their duties. It was dawn, the sun streaking through the windows, playing on the floor and the patients' faces as they slept or cried or fretted. Rose found a piece of cardboard of her own and was asleep in seconds.

When she reported for her next shift, the nurses were issued dog tags, gas masks and helmets, left over from the Great War. Nurses studied pamphlets telling them how to detect poisonous gasses and care for gassed patients. Rose wanted to know how they could care for someone if they themselves were gassed. Not answering her question, Kate held up her helmet on one finger and spun it in the air. 'It's a shame you weren't wearing one of these when the building collapsed. It would have saved you for sure,' she said to Rose.

'I didn't need saving,' Rose replied. 'I was fine.'

Tess put her dog tags around her neck. 'I'm not taking any chances. Next time the Japanese decide to drop explosives on us, I'll be ready.' She shook her clunky green helmet at the sky in warning.

'You'll be better off if you wear it on your head, Nurse,' said Kate.

Many nurses believed that help was on its way. Every free moment they got, they ran to the windows and glanced outside, hoping to see the Pacific Fleet sailing triumphantly into Manila Harbour or American planes flying to the rescue. All they saw instead were Japanese Mitsubishi Zeros, rumbling with discontent as they flew over the islands on their deadly mission. Rose didn't share the others' enthusiasm. She remembered what David had once told her. President Roosevelt's number one priority was the war in Europe.

Despite the helmet, the gas mask and the pamphlets, Rose felt helpless and unprepared for what was to come.

The hospital couldn't possibly hold any more patients. Nurses and doctors couldn't possibly handle any more work. And yet, injured men, women and children continued to arrive on splintered doors, dirty carpets, blankets, woven bamboo mats and corrugated roofing. There seemed to be no end to the tide of human suffering unleashed by the Japanese bombers.

Sternberg was the biggest and best-equipped medical facility in the Philippines and the wounded arrived from all over but especially from Forts Stotsenberg and McKinley. When the men came from Fort McKinley in ambulances, Rose looked into every face, searching for David. She asked every soldier she tended to if he knew him. She couldn't find an adequate explanation for David's silence, refused to believe the worst, was dreading the news and yet, desperately needed to know. Despite all her efforts, she found out nothing.

Japanese planes filled the sky over Manila, bombing Cavite Naval Shipyard, Nichols Field and, to Rose's horror, Fort McKinley. From the window Rose watched the reddish hues as fires devoured Manila. Night was bright as day as they worked without a break, without sleep. Their existence was no longer divided into day and night but consistent of never-ending hours of staunching blood, bandaging wounds, trying to save lives and often failing.

Once, as she was changing a dressing for a young soldier wounded by shrapnel from an anti-aircraft gun, she saw aircraft adorned with stars and stripes charging the enemy and bringing a Japanese fighter down. A little while later, she learnt from one of the doctors that most American planes had been destroyed during an assault on Clark Field. The news made her pause for a second, shocked and afraid, even though a chorus of voices was calling her name and begging for help.

The nurses divided the patients into three groups. The first consisted of those who required the doctors' immediate attention, the second those with minor injuries, while the third was made up of the unfortunates who could no longer be helped. All the girls could do was relieve their last suffering with morphine. When she wasn't treating the patients, Rose dabbed away sweat from the doctors' foreheads and passed them the instruments they asked for. The nurses walked up and down rows of patients, administering morphine shots and tetanus vaccines. They no longer needed permission from the doctors to do so. In the chaos of war, they had been given more responsibility.

'Bring your bathing suit, they said. And don't forget your evening gown. The Philippines is going to be one big party, they said,' Tess grumbled as she used soap and saline solution to clean dirt and grease from angry wounds and charred burns.

The screaming was deafening but Rose preferred it to the silence. If the patient in pain was silent, it was a bad sign.

Rose was preparing a soldier for surgery, worried that he would lose both his legs, concerned about his heavy breathing and the distant, resigned look on his face. He had been taking cover face down on the ground when a bomb hit, blinding him. Rose took off his bloodied clothes, cleaned dirt and debris off him and did what she could to soothe his damaged skin and blind eyes with a damp towel. There was a chunk of flesh missing from his back and when Rose saw the wound, she wanted to cry.

She stepped away to fetch him a gown for surgery. She was only gone a couple of minutes, but when she returned, he was dead.

For a moment, she stood perfectly still, as if rooted to the spot, unable to take her eyes off him. Then she crouched on the ground next to him and sobbed. What if David was like one of these men, alone in a hospital somewhere, hurt or, worse, dead? She couldn't bear that thought.

She didn't know how long she remained on the floor. Suddenly, she felt a hand on her shoulder. She heard Elsie's voice. 'Dry your tears. This is not the time to cry. Don't worry, the time will come. After it's all over, we can cry as much as we want. But for now, we need to steel our hearts and keep going. Our patients need us.'

Rose wiped her tears away with the back of her hand and looked up into Elsie's face. For the first time she noticed how tired the older woman looked. She seemed to have aged by years in the last few days. 'What's the point? I do my best and they die.'

'The point is that you make their last moments easier. The point is that when they die, they are not alone. Sometimes it's all we can give them and I know it's heartbreaking but trust me, honey, it's better than nothing.'

Rose shook her head. 'I feel like I'm not doing enough, even though I don't have more to give. I have nothing left.'

'If you weep every time someone dies, you'll be weeping forever. You can't be soft-hearted in our line of work. You must stop feeling so much.'

'I don't want to stop. I won't let this war make me less human.' For a moment, she was silent, breathing heavily, overwhelmed by it all. 'How can we cope, when the patients keep coming and we have neither the space, nor the manpower to help them all?'

Elsie squeezed her shoulder and smiled with affection. 'What choice do we have? We are at war. Each of us has a job to do. I know you will do yours well.'

Rose dried her tears and forced herself to get up and return to work. The next morning, when another patient died in front of her, she didn't experience the same raw emotion, the same devastation she had felt the day before. All she felt was a numb helplessness. Had Elsie been right? Was the unthinkable horror becoming easier to witness? Was Rose getting used to it? She didn't want to believe it.

# Chapter 5

## December 1941

In the third week of December, when instead of festive decorations and carols there were air-raid sirens and wards filled with screaming patients, a storm hit the coast of the Philippines. Once upon a time, before the war, Rose had been afraid of tropical storms. She had felt unprotected here, in Manila. The islands seemed so fragile in the face of frantic winds and gigantic waves, as if at any moment they could be swept away and carried off like a lost ship. But this time, the storm meant that the Japanese could no longer fly their bombers and Rose prayed it would last longer.

And yet, to Rose, the sound of the sea hitting the shore, of the wind howling outside and the thunder exploding overhead was eerily familiar. It made her shudder just like the bombs did. They both sounded the same, she realised, the war inflicted by humans and the war inflicted by nature.

One morning, she heard a voice asking for her and another voice replying that she was over there, in operating room number four waiting to assist with an amputation. Rose swung around, hoping for some tidings of David, and saw Anne standing at the entrance, watching her. For a few seconds, both of them were silent, Anne seemingly lost in thought and Rose feeling surprised and a little guilty. She hadn't seen Anne for a couple of weeks and not once had she wondered if she had been safe. 'Hi, Anne,' she said. 'What are you doing here?'

'I need to talk to you,' replied Anne. 'Are you busy?'

'I can talk for a few minutes.' They were waiting for the anaesthesiologist to arrive. The operation couldn't begin until he was there.

They walked out into the corridor, where patients were lying on the floor, groaning, screaming, reaching their arms out to them. It was as alone as they were going to get. 'How are you? Where have you been all this time?' Rose asked.

'They transferred me to the Philippine Women's University a couple of weeks ago. They need all the help they can get. Too many patients.'

'Yes, same here,' Rose said sadly, glancing at the men and women lying at her feet.

'I'm not here for small talk.' Anne's eyes squinted and for a moment she looked displeased, like she was upset at Rose about something. 'I don't have much time.' She seemed to hesitate but only for a moment. 'It's about David. He sent me to find you.'

Rose took a sharp breath. Over the last couple of weeks, she had been listening to whispered conversations, glancing out the window, watching the road outside, hoping to catch a glimpse of him, a word of him. And here was Anne, bringing him up so casually, like he hadn't disappeared off the surface of the earth without a trace, without hope. 'I didn't realise you knew David.'

'Of course I know David.' Anne smiled. A cold smile that made Rose shiver. 'He's my brother.'

Rose's hand flew to her mouth. She trembled. 'Thank God. And he's all right? I thought something bad must have happened because I couldn't find him anywhere and he hasn't been around to see me—'

'That's exactly why I'm here,' Anne interrupted, stepping from foot to foot, looking uncomfortable and a little put out, as if she would rather be anywhere else but standing in front of Rose, listening to her questions. 'He wanted me to tell you he doesn't want to see you anymore.'

'What?' Rose muttered. 'What are you talking about?' It couldn't be. Anne had misunderstood or she was playing a prank on Rose.

'David asked me to tell you that he enjoyed spending time with you very much. But it's over now.'

Rose took a shallow breath. For some reason, her lungs felt empty, like there was no oxygen left in the room. It took a few moments before she could speak again. 'Why didn't he come here and tell me in person? Why did he send you?'

Anne shrugged, rubbed her hands together, looked away. She seemed bored, like she was done with the conversation and wanted to leave. 'He thought it would be easier coming from me. You know men. Most of them are cowards. David was never good at taking responsibility for his actions. It drives our parents crazy.'

'It doesn't make sense. We spoke about the future. We made plans.' Even as she said it, Rose didn't know if any of it was true. *I love you*, David had whispered to her hours before the bombs rained on Sternberg Hospital. But as she stood in front of Anne, feeling small under her indignant gaze, she wondered if he had really said it or if she had imagined the words she longed to hear. He promised to take her to Paris one day. He wanted her to leave the Philippines because he was saving her for himself. Wasn't it what all lovers did? Said things they didn't necessarily mean, made promises they had no intention of keeping?

'I don't know what he told you in the heat of the moment. But he can't be planning his future with you. He's engaged to someone else.'

Rose shook her head. 'No,' she whispered. She didn't want to hear another sound from Anne, didn't want to believe a word coming out of her mouth. She closed her eyes and when she opened them again, a black-and-white photograph had appeared in Anne's hand, while the other hand was reaching for Rose, fingers pointing, mouth sniggering, talking-talking-talking, a barrage of words Rose couldn't comprehend. She didn't want to take the photograph. She knew she wasn't going to like it. She tried to push it away but there was no stopping Anne. The image looked blurry and Rose realised she had been crying. She blinked fast, until she could see clearly again. But as soon as she saw the happy couple on the photograph with their heads close together, looking at each other the way David had once looked at Rose, with love, she squeezed her eyes shut and pushed it away. David looked younger, his hair longer, his face beaming. He seemed enthralled by the beautiful woman on his arm and Rose couldn't bear the look of adoration on his face that was meant for someone else.

The earth moved under Rose's feet. How else to explain that she couldn't stand unsupported any longer and had to lean on the wall behind her? Her ears were ringing as if a deafening blast had gone off nearby. She couldn't speak.

Ignoring Rose's crestfallen face, Anne said, 'David is going to marry my best friend. A girl from a rich, well-respected family. Their wedding date has been set. The invitations have gone out. As soon as we return from the Philippines, he will be a married man.'

Rose let go of the photograph like it was burning her fingers. She whispered, 'He didn't tell me. He never mentioned it.'

'Of course he didn't. All men are liars. They tell you what you want to hear and then they take what they want and leave. David wanted to have some fun before he settled down. I don't approve but I understand. I'll keep his dirty little secret to myself.'

Rose shuddered. Is that what she had been to him, his dirty little secret?

Anne added, a cruel smirk on her lips, 'The last thing I want is to hurt Celia's feelings. She's like a sister to me. I'm sorry to be the bearer of bad news. If you love David like you say you do, you should be happy for him. Celia and David suit each other perfectly. They can't wait to get married and start a family.' Anne took Rose's hand and pressed it gently, smiling her sinister smile. 'You need to forget about David. He's not the one for you.'

With that, Anne walked off, leaving the photograph on the floor for Rose to pick up. Rose reached for it, placing her trembling fingers on David's face and trying to read his feelings in his eyes, in his body language, in the way he leaned towards Celia with his arm placed around her. Once upon a time, before the deadly bombs fell on the islands, he had told Rose she was the only one for him. Was that a lie? While they picnicked by the Marikina River, kissed under their waterfall, played ukulele and danced the night away, was he planning his wedding with someone else? She didn't want to believe it and yet, here was proof, in the smiling faces on the photograph in front of her, in the way they looked at each other, with joy, and in David's inexplicable absence.

*Once upon a time, before the war, before the heartbreak, they were alone together, just the two of them and the great expanse of the ocean in front of them. Her head was on David's shoulder. The ukulele was at his feet. An abandoned game of chess was by their side, the rooks and the knights scattered around the board in surrender.*

*'What are your parents like?' she asked.*

*He appeared to think about it for a moment. 'They are judgemental. They judge people based on what they do for a living, what car they drive, which school they attended.'*

*'They wouldn't like me very much. I'm a simple nurse and I don't own a car.'*

*'They are going to love you. I can't wait for them to meet you. In the meantime, I'll introduce you to my sister. She is a nurse at Sternberg, just like you.' He reached his hand out and pinched her cheek. 'What? What did I say? Why do you suddenly look so scared?'*

*'I've never met anyone's family before.'*

*'I am the one who should be nervous. I've never introduced a girl to my family before.'*

*'Never?' she asked, amazed. 'Why not?'*

*'Because I have never felt like this before,' he whispered and his eyes twinkled.*

With her eyes squeezed shut, Rose listened to the patients' panic-filled voices, the ambulance sirens, the plane engines in the distance, bombs whistling, the dull sound of the anti-aircraft guns. The storm was long gone and the fighting had resumed but war no longer scared her. She barely noticed it because all she could see was Anne's twisted face and the image of David with his arms around another woman, his eyes beaming with happiness.

In the afternoon, Tess came to check on her. She kneeled by her side, placed her hands on her forehead, clucked and fussed. *Do you need anything? Are you ill? Are you hungry? Should I bring you some water? A cup of tea? Why don't you sleep?* Rose didn't reply but waited patiently for her to leave. She wanted to be alone with her thoughts, even though they terrified her.

Elsie came over and shook her shoulder. 'Enough lying around. We have work to do.'

Rose didn't move.

'She hasn't been herself since yesterday,' Rose heard Kate's voice. 'We think it's the bump on her head or she's coming down with something. She needs rest.'

Elsie muttered, 'Don't we all.' But she moved on and left Rose alone.

David's happy black-and-white face haunted her. *Celia.* Why did that name sound familiar? He had mentioned a Celia before and when Rose asked if she was a childhood sweetheart, he laughed and said no, she was just a friend. Was he lying? Or was Anne lying?

Rose felt a hand on her shoulder and looked up. It was Kate. 'Honey, what's wrong? You haven't eaten anything since yesterday. Not feeling well? Do you want me to bring you a bowl of rice?'

The tears came then. Rose clasped Kate's hand as if her life depended on it and cried. Kate crouched next to Rose and gathered her in her arms. 'I know it's hard. I know it's scary. But we'll get through it. The reinforcements are on their way, I'm sure of it.'

'It's David,' Rose whispered.

'Oh, no. He's …?'

Rose shook her head. It took a while before she could speak but once she started, everything came tumbling out of her. 'He's been lying, about everything,' she concluded.

'Wait. It makes no sense. Why would he send Anne to tell you all this? Why didn't he come to see you himself?'

'Anne is his sister.' Rose closed her eyes, unable to take the expression of pity and concern on Kate's face. 'My dad left when I was little. Growing up, I never thought I would be able to trust a man. But I trusted David. I trusted him with all my heart. I thought he was different.'

'Do you trust Anne with all your heart?'

'What?'

'How do you know Anne is telling the truth?'

'Why would she lie?'

'It's Anne we are talking about. She lies out of spite. She lies because she's bored and has nothing else to do. She told Elsie on us. She was probably the one who told everyone about Ida's engagement.'

'We don't know that.'

'If not her, then who? All I'm saying is don't jump to conclusions.'

Rose pulled the photograph out of her pocket and pressed it into Kate's hands. 'It's David with his fiancée. Don't they look happy together?' she whispered, her heart breaking.

Kate looked at the photo and then at Rose again. She shook her head. 'You don't know anything for certain. Don't take Anne's word for it. You need to talk to David. You need to hear it from him.'

Rose clung to Kate's words with everything she had. When

she woke up in the morning and before she fell into exhausted sleep, she repeated to herself, *I don't believe any of it. None of it is true.* But Anne's revelation was like poison eating away at Rose's memories of him. She questioned everything, every moment they had shared, every word he had ever said to her.

Once upon a time, when she was still at school, her mother had told her something that had stayed with her. She had said, 'When your father betrayed me, I never saw it coming. I thought we were so happy.' Rose had vowed then not to make the same mistake. There must have been signs. Her mother was just too blind, too gullible to see them. Rose promised to herself to never be gullible or blind, to not give her trust or her heart away so easily. And yet, here she was, abandoned and confused, and she had not seen it coming.

In the afternoon, there was a compulsory meeting for all hospital personnel. Rose was forced to get up, to make her way into the hot staff room, to sit on a chair and pretend to pay attention to Elsie as she addressed the four dozen nurses sitting nervously in front of her. Rose stared into the distance and thought of the last time she had seen David. It was here, at the hospital, moments before the first bombers flew over Manila. He wanted to make sure she wasn't afraid, wanted to keep her safe, to spare her from what was about to happen. He didn't seem to behave like someone who was about to send his sister to break her heart. What was the meaning of it all?

Elsie's voice increased in volume, breaking through the darkness inside Rose's head. 'I want each and every one of you to remember that you are an American. You are an officer in the United States Army. This is an unusual situation and we don't know what is going to happen or what to expect. You know your duty and responsibility. There may come a time when there is no one to guide you but yourself. I believe your conscience will tell you how to behave honourably. I know you will make our country proud. You will remember the oath you have taken and act accordingly.'

A nurse from infectious diseases, a timid young girl with a voice of a mouse and a pinched face, asked, 'Are the Japanese coming here?'

An explosion was heard outside. The walls of the hospital shook.

'I believe they are,' said Elsie. She surveyed the group, studying their faces, perhaps wondering what was in store for her girls, whom she cared for deeply, despite her strict demeanour. 'And one more thing.' She held up a vial in her hands for everyone to see. 'I need you to keep these on you at all times, in case of an emergency.'

Everyone wanted to know what the vials were and what emergency the chief nurse was referring to.

'It's opium, strong enough to kill a human being within seconds, without unnecessary suffering,' she said, not a trace of emotion on her face, as if she were at a dinner party talking about a recipe for a delicious lamb casserole.

Tess rose her uncomprehending eyes to Elsie. 'You want us to poison the Japanese?'

Rose said, her voice as emotionless as Elsie's, 'It's not for the Japanese. It's for us. These are suicide pills.' She looked into Elsie's face. 'Am I right?'

Colour crept up Elsie's cheeks. She nodded. 'I don't want you to panic. This is only a precaution. The last resort.'

The small nurse from infectious diseases, whose name Rose could never remember, put up her hand again, like she was at school and needed permission to speak. Elsie nodded encouragingly. The girl hesitated for a moment, as if gathering her courage, and said, 'If they are coming here, why aren't we leaving?'

'We are waiting for an order to start evacuating the personnel. I don't know if or when this order will come. Until then, we are staying with our patients.'

The room erupted with questions. For a few moments, all Rose could hear was *when*, *how* and *where*. Were they going to be sent back to the States? Would they still be here when the Japanese arrived? And what would the enemy do to them?

Elsie had no answers, except, 'We will be moving the hospital deeper into the jungle, to Bataan.'

'You don't think the enemy will follow us there?' asked Rose. She had a feeling the Japanese who had been relentlessly bombing Manila for the past few days would not stop at anything until all of the Philippines was in their hands.

'It will gain us time,' said Elsie. 'Now, if you don't have any more questions, we have a job to do. Back to the wards everyone.'

Rose had many questions about what the next few weeks, months and years would bring. She wanted to know if they would be safe, if she would ever see David and her mother again, if she would survive the Philippines. She wanted to know if there was hope. But she suspected that not Elsie, nor even those in command had any answers.

Rose was grateful for her duties because they left her with no time to think or feel or wonder. Little by little, other people's pain swallowed her whole existence and only late at night as she lay on her cardboard after a twenty-four-hour shift did she allow herself to take the photograph out of her pocket and study David's face as he gazed at someone else with love.

'Why do you do this to yourself?' Kate asked one evening. 'Why do you keep looking at that? It makes you so sad. I can see it in your face. Why don't you throw it in the trash?'

'I can't throw it in the trash. It's the only thing I have that reminds me of David. What if I throw it away and never see him again?'

Day after day, Rose did the best she could, bandaging and administering shots, assisting the surgeons as they operated, trying her best to heal her patients so they could go back to the front and fight. Every moment of every day, she felt inadequate to her task. Her best didn't seem good enough, not with everything that was happening around them. Nothing in her previous life had prepared her for the never-ending stream of wounded who had engulfed the hospital. It seemed to her that her skills, her energy and her drive were not up to scratch, and she couldn't measure up in the face of the terrible disaster they were facing. It felt like she was standing in the eye of the storm, holding up her hands helplessly and shouting, 'Stop!' But the storm wouldn't abate because every day and night the Japanese planes descended on Manila, unleashing havoc, death and destruction.

And through it all, her eyes were almost constantly drawn to the door, hoping to see David's face, despite everything. She even went back to the barracks looking for him, trembling with nerves. He had sent his sister to tell her he didn't want to see her again. What was she doing, coming to find him, disrespecting his wishes? And yet, Kate was right. She needed to hear it from him.

When the planes flew overhead and explosives whistled, Rose helped the wounded into the trenches. During raids, the soldiers who were digging them would throw their shovels in the nearby ditch and hide. Rose wanted to hide too. She wanted to disappear, to make herself invisible. Her heart stopped every time she heard the dreaded screeching sound above her head. She couldn't bring herself to look up in the sky that had once been a deep shade of blue, breathtaking and peaceful, but now was grey with smoke. She couldn't bear seeing the swarms of Japanese bombers circling Manila. The shelling felt like it was coming closer every time, as if the enemy were seeking her out and wouldn't stop until she was dead.

Unfortunately, she couldn't take cover because she had a ward of men to move first. They had been told not to stay at the hospital during bombing in case it got a direct hit, so she guided the patients who could walk to the trenches, while those who couldn't hid under their beds. Rose wondered what good it would do if a bomb hit the ward. Would the flimsy hospital bed protect them? She didn't think so. And yet, there was nothing else she could do. There was only one of her and hundreds of men and women in her care.

It couldn't get much worse than this, thought Rose as she crawled into a foxhole, hugging her knees close to her chest, bending her head low under the weight of the bombs falling around her, wondering if she would find the hospital still standing and her patients and other nurses alive when it was over.

But she was wrong. It did get worse.

On 21 December, they heard that the Japanese Imperial Army had sailed into the Lingayen Gulf, only 130 miles north of Manila. The next morning, the enemy took the beaches. Tens of thousands of well-trained, well-equipped and experienced warriors were only a short distance away and no one could stop them, not the handful of American soldiers that still remained, nor the under-trained, underfed Filipino troops who were equipped with old rifles from the Great War and had no uniforms, gas masks or tools to dig trenches. From the beaches at Lingayen, a wide valley formed a natural highway leading straight to the city. The enemy was at the gates and eventually they were heading *here*.

One morning, Rose woke up and saw that there were no soldiers digging trenches outside.

'Haven't you heard?' said Kate. 'General MacArthur ordered a retreat to Corregidor.'

*Corregidor*. The word stirred something in her, a happy memory of her and David in each other's arms, playing their ukulele and planning their future. It seemed like a lifetime ago. His laughing face, only inches away from hers. Her hand on a chess piece, his hand on her knee. The giddy sensation of something enormous unfolding in her life, something she hadn't foreseen that was taking her over by storm.

'And the navy?' Rose was used to the reassuring presence of the US military ships in the harbour. They made her feel safe because she knew they were there to protect her if she needed it.

They made her feel like she was not alone. When she glanced at the harbour that morning, she saw nothing but the large expanse of the ocean and the sky, purple with the rising sun. The ships were gone.

'They sailed to Australia,' Kate said with a stony face.

'They left?'

Kate nodded. 'But before they left, General MacArthur declared Manila an open city. The Hague Conventions prohibit military activity in an open city.'

'Well, if the Hague Conventions prohibit it, then we have nothing to worry about,' muttered Rose as the Japanese planes flew overhead, dropping bombs.

Perhaps David was gone, she thought. While she was searching for him in every face that arrived at the hospital, perhaps he was hiding in Corregidor, safe behind its fortified walls. Or maybe he was sailing to Australia and would soon return home and walk down the aisle with his Celia. Perhaps, while she could think of nothing else, he didn't give her a second thought. Would she prefer it if he was happy with someone else but safe and alive?

Yes, she decided. Yes, she would.

The order to evacuate came on Christmas Day. 'Merry Christmas,' mumbled Kate as she threw her things inside a small trunk.

'Don't forget to pack your bathing suits, girls. And your evening gowns,' said Tess.

No one replied. No one even smiled. They knew that, where they were going, they would have no need for those things. They would only need helmets, gas masks and an iron will.

# Part II

# Bataan Peninsula

# Chapter 6

## December 1941–January 1942

Dressed in white uniforms, stockings and caps, the nurses sat side by side on a bench, waiting for buses to arrive and take them deep into the Bataan Peninsula, away from the invading Japanese troops, to safety. Manila Hotel beamed in the sun like a jewel. When Rose glanced at the trees swaying peacefully in the wind, the topaz sky and the waves gently kissing the white sand, she could pretend there was no war and no enemy soldiers marching towards Manila, unstoppable and terrifying in their determination. Except, if she turned her head slightly, she could see buildings damaged by shelling and trenches the soldiers had been digging that now stood empty and abandoned. She could smell the smoke. And the majestic hotel was eerily silent. No limousines slipped through its gilded gates, no couples dressed in their Sunday best filtered in and out with festive drinks in their hands. There was no laughter or cheerful voices, as if the city was holding its breath, fearing for its very existence. Rose knew the silence wouldn't last. In a couple of hours, the pristine tropical sky would fill with enemy planes that would tear up the air with the sound of war.

'Remember how we danced that night at the Officers' Club?' asked Kate. 'Can you believe it was only three weeks ago?'

Rose shook her head. It felt like she had been living like this – under Japanese fire – for many long and miserable years.

'It was the last carefree night that we had,' said Tess.

'If someone told me then that we would be sitting here, waiting for buses to take us away because the Japanese were here, I wouldn't have believed it,' said Kate.

Rose nodded. David had told her from the start that the enemy was coming to Manila. And she hadn't believed him.

'Will we ever dance again?' asked Kate. Her face looked gaunt in the early morning light.

'Will we ever see Manila again?' whispered Rose. *What if the war is over but we remain in the jungle, never to be found again?* she wanted to ask. *What if we don't make it?* She didn't say any of it, of course, because she didn't want to upset her friends.

When the buses finally arrived and whisked them away through the bleeding streets, Rose looked at the places she had fallen in love with, the places she had visited with David, and wept. It felt like she was saying goodbye to more than just the city. She was saying goodbye to the memories these streets held and to any hope of ever seeing him again. As she sat next to Kate, her face glued to the window, her eyes wide at the damage the Japanese planes had wreaked in such a short period of time, she thought of her mother, of her laughing face, of her warm arms and kind smile, and wondered if the Americans back home were told anything about the Pacific, if her mother knew what was happening, if she was praying for her daughter, if she was afraid.

Rose was afraid as the bus carried her towards her unknown future.

Through the open sides of the bus, Rose could feel wind on her face. The warm air did nothing to cool her down, to soothe her burning skin. She needed water but didn't think she had packed enough and was rationing what little she had left.

As their convoy neared the town of San Fernando, the distant din of artillery fire sounded to the east. Somewhere nearby, the American troops were fighting to give the Allied forces time to retreat. For a moment, Rose felt a little less alone.

'I don't understand why they couldn't give us a proper vehicle. Not even glass in the bus windows. If we get strafed by the Japanese, we are done for,' muttered Kate.

'I don't think glass is any good against bullets, Kate,' said Rose.

As they continued on their way, a small dot appeared in the sky, gradually growing in size until it became the dreaded Mitsubishi Zero. When the familiar whistling sound was heard, the buses stopped and the nurses jumped out, grateful for the open sides and the lack of glass. The girls took cover. Terrified, Rose listened to the bombs exploding nearby, drumming the seconds on her knees, praying for it to stop, wondering if it ever would, if there would come a day when she would look up and see a peaceful sky over her head once more.

When it was over, they boarded the buses and continued on their way like nothing had happened. Reaching Layac Junction at the base of the Bataan Peninsula, the convoy turned south. Rice paddies gave way to coconut groves, tall weepy palm trees stretched towards the sky as if in prayer, and soon Rose could see nothing but the dense jungle of acacia trees, their green canopies linked together like arms. It felt like they were a million miles away from civilisation, alone and lost in the wilderness. How could the Japanese ever find them here? Rose's heart stopped beating so violently inside her chest and she breathed easier. As if reading her mind, Kate said, 'We're lucky to escape with our lives. Some nurses from Sternberg are not evacuating. Imagine staying in Manila and waiting for the enemy to arrive! We'll be safe here at least.'

'I don't think anywhere is safe,' said Rose. 'Not in the long run.'

'I can't wait to get to the hospital,' said Tess. 'And sleep in a real bed tonight. It's been a while. Personally, I think we deserve a few days off, after everything we've been through.'

'Dream on, girls,' said Kate. 'Elsie the slave driver is coming with us. If you wanted time off, we should have left her in Manila.'

'Quiet, she'll hear you,' whispered Tess, widening her eyes and pinching Kate on the arm.

But Tess shouldn't have worried. Elsie was sound asleep a few seats ahead of them. Rose wondered how she did that. How did she remain composed, through enemy bombing and invasion, through retreat and uncertainty? She was glad the level-headed chief nurse was with them. Her reassuring presence calmed her nerves.

Rose decided to follow Elsie's example and closed her eyes but the thoughts inside her head were so loud, she couldn't get even a minute of rest.

On the east coast of the Bataan Peninsula, ninety miles from Manila, lay the village of Limay, a dot on the map, hidden from view by the lush jungle, home to fishermen who left in their boats long before sunrise and didn't come back until nightfall, their nets heavy with fish.

When the buses pulled into the sleepy village, the sun was just beginning to set and the sky was an ominous red. The hospital – a former training camp for Filipino troops – was located among mango and bamboo trees on the edge of the small settlement, concealed under a canopy of mahogany and acacia that provided shade and kept it out of view of Japanese bombers. The nurses stared in silence at the tiny shacks on stilts, made of mud and bamboo with palm-thatch roofs and shutters held open with sticks. 'This is the hospital?' exclaimed Kate. 'Surely this can't be it. We travelled all this way to work here?'

'We travelled all this way to be safe. This is as remote as it gets,' said Rose. 'Just what we need.'

Naked Filipino children surrounded them, jumping around and shouting, seemingly unafraid of the shelling in the far distance. Rose wished she was as brave. Every time she heard the explosions, her hands began to shake. She knew that for as long as she lived, she would never get used to this.

A group of soldiers showed them to the shack where they were to sleep and told them dinner was being prepared for them at the beach.

'Great, because I'm exhausted,' said Rose. Never mind a bed, she was ready to curl up right there, on the grass, in the shade of the mighty acacia.

'And I'm starving,' said Kate.

'Excuse me, sir. Do we sleep on the floor?' Tess asked one of the soldiers.

The soldier took them to a warehouse that stored mattresses, bed frames, footboards and headboards. The nurses dragged the heavy items back to their shack, complaining every step of the way. Some of the girls had no idea what to do with the planks of wood in front of them and Elsie had to demonstrate how to put the pieces together.

'It's a Christmas miracle!' said Tess. 'Real beds.' She stretched out on her mattress and kicked her shoes off. 'It's so peaceful here. Can you hear the ocean? It's like a lullaby.' Closing her eyes, she smiled.

'Of course we can hear the ocean. We can also hear the machine guns,' said Rose. 'Come on, let's go for dinner. We'll unpack later.' She pulled her friend by the hand, while Tess protested and pulled in the opposite direction. The girls fell on the bed, laughing.

On the beach, they had pancakes for dinner (another Christmas miracle, according to Kate, who loved pancakes), watched the waves as they hit the shore and listened to a soldier playing his guitar. The soft sounds transported Rose to another time, another evening, when a handsome man played his ukulele just for her, his eyes never leaving her face.

'We can almost pretend we are on holiday somewhere, in Hawaii perhaps,' said Tess.

At the mention of Hawaii, Kate's face fell. She pushed her plate away.

'We can pretend there is no war and we are not on the run from the most terrifying enemy in the world,' added Tess.

As soon as she said that, an explosion was heard across the bay. It felt to Rose like the earth itself moved under her feet and the island tilted to one side. Smoke filled the air and it became difficult to breathe. Rose could see the flames across the harbour, rising high like skyscrapers. The moon itself seemed to be on fire, large, round and bloody. The night was as bright as day. The soldier put his guitar down long enough to tell the girls the US Navy was blowing up ammunition dumps to make sure they didn't fall into Japanese hands. They were burning millions of gallons of oil. He told them not to worry because he and his regiment were stationed nearby to protect them. Rose smiled and thanked him and said she wasn't worried, hiding her shaking hands behind her back.

'Isn't it funny,' said Kate, 'how this place no longer seems beautiful? The beauty vanished the day the Japanese invaded. Now all I can see is death and destruction. Darkness everywhere I look.'

Rose glanced at the water. 'It will always be beautiful,' she said. 'The war will be over one day but the beauty will remain.'

Before she drifted off to sleep that night, Rose fumbled through her things and found the precious photographs she always carried with her. In dim moonlight, she studied the faces she loved. A man with his arms around a four-year-old girl who was looking at him with eyes filled with love. A woman hugging an adolescent wearing a graduation coat and cape. Her mother and father. She wished she could see them now, wished they were here to tell her that everything would be all right, that she would be safe, no matter what the future held. 'What is going to happen to us?' she whispered to them in the dark, bringing the pictures to her lips, holding them close to her chest. They didn't answer and all she could hear were explosions in the distance and her beating heart.

The next few days were a blur as the nurses set up the hospital. While they waited for the trucks with the hospital equipment to arrive from Manila, the girls looked through the warehouse at what was already available. They found rusty hospital beds, untouched since the Great War, packed away in 1918 newspapers. They cleaned old surgical instruments with ether. They had retreated so fast, pans used for cooking were brought dirty from Sternberg. Rose spent hours scouring them with rocks and sand in a nearby stream. After three days of scrubbing and cleaning, her hands were sore and her back was aching but they had eighteen hospital wards of thirty cots each, ready for the first patients to arrive.

'Not too soon, I hope,' said Tess. 'After the last few weeks from hell, I can barely stand on my two feet.'

'It's too quiet here,' complained Kate. 'What is there to do in the jungle? At least in Manila we could go dancing or to the cinema.'

'Do you want to go back to Manila?' asked Rose, taking a sip of hot tea. What a luxury, to be able to sit down and relax. To have nowhere to be. 'Be my guest.'

'Where are the tennis courts? Where is the golf course? I almost wish for some patients, so we have something to do.'

'Why don't we go swimming?' Rose suggested.

And they did. After the horror of Manila, the water felt magical on their wearied bodies. Kate sang popular songs in her loud alto as they splashed. And the girls groaned and shouted at her to stop but eventually one after another they joined in. The cheerful songs – so out of place now that their lives seemed to teeter on the verge of a disaster they couldn't fathom – filled Rose's heart with a longing for peace and the moments in her not-so-distant past when she had felt true joy. A longing to see David's face again, to hear his voice, to ask the questions that were keeping her up at night. *I will never feel like that again*, she thought sadly. Even if the war was over, she would never be carefree again because she had seen things she would never forget. Somewhere between landing in Manila one scorching afternoon and boarding the bus to escape the burning city, she had lost her innocence.

The water was crystal clear and they could see fish swimming underwater. An eel rubbed its slippery body on Rose's leg, making her shriek. The sky was an unblemished blue over their heads and the sun was bright. It would have been paradise, if it wasn't for the acrid smell of fire, if it wasn't for explosions in the not-so-far distance. Fortunately, the shelling wasn't as close as it had been in Manila. In the jungle of Bataan, far from civilisation, they felt a little safer.

'What do you miss the most about home?' asked Kate when they were on the bank and drying.

'I miss my mama,' said Rose. 'She worked too much but on the weekends she always had something baking in the oven, and I would wake up in the morning to the most amazing smell and wonder what it was. She would wear a red apron around her hips and it would always be stained with flour. There would be flour on her hands too and she would have the biggest smile on her face every time she saw me. No matter what happened that day, my heart would feel lighter at the sight of her.'

'I miss my brother. We are twins, have I told you that?'

Rose shook her head. 'I've never met a twin before. What is it like?'

'Growing up, I never had anything of my own. I had to share everything with my brother. But no one understands me better than he does. When he's not around, I feel like half of me is missing. I want to share everything with him but can't.'

Rose took Kate's hand and squeezed it. 'Your brother will be fine. You'll see.'

'I know he will. I can still feel him out there. Twins can do that, you know. Feel each other. It's like magic.' Kate smiled.

Tess said, 'I miss good coffee. And my nana's apple pie.'

'I miss ice skating. The feeling of freedom, of spinning on the ice, there's nothing else like it. Nowhere to ice skate here, in the tropics,' said Kate.

'Nowhere to ice skate, nowhere to buy coffee. But at least we can swim in tropical waters. Isn't it wonderful?' asked Rose, jumping back in again, closing her eyes, floating on water, all her troubles forgotten for a moment.

After the swim, when she was lying on her back on the sand with the sun warming her face, Rose closed her eyes and felt for David out there, inspired by Kate. What was he doing in that exact instant? Was he safe? Was he thinking of her and wondering what had become of her? She tried to imagine his face, his smile, his kind eyes but all she could see was the black-and-white image of him with his arms around someone else. All she could feel was the bitterness and confusion left by Anne's devastating words.

When the girls arrived at work the next day, they learnt that the Japanese had bombed Mariveles Harbour. Just like before, hundreds of patients stormed their primitive facilities until there were no beds left and no space to move freely across the ward.

'Be careful what you wish for,' Rose whispered to Kate as they tended to the patients in the heat of late morning.

Where the day before there were empty cots and silent wards now were men with burns, concussion and bullet wounds. The familiar sounds of suffering and pain filled the hospital. No more cups of tea, no more swimming under the tropical sun. Kate no longer complained that life in the jungle was too dull.

'You must be proud of yourselves,' Elsie said to them at the end of a gruelling day. 'You are the first US military nurses to be subjected to actual combat.'

'Aren't we the lucky ones?' Kate muttered.

But despite her fear and the fog of exhaustion inside her head, Rose did feel proud. They had been bombed and besieged and pursued by the spectre of death but against all odds, they did not give up. Instead, they were doing what they had come here to do – helping those in need.

# Chapter 7

## February 1942

One morning in the first week of February, Rose was woken by a terrible scream. The piercing sound broke through her dreams and she shot up in bed, her hand flying to her mouth. She squinted in the dark, trying to see.

All was quiet. Had she imagined it?

There it was again, and this time she recognised Kate's panicked voice. 'A rat! It bit me. Where is it? Is it gone?'

Rose found the kerosene lamp and lit it. Then she looked at the bite, which wasn't an easy feat because Kate was so agitated, she refused to sit still and was jumping up and down on her bed. 'It's not so bad,' said Rose. 'You are lucky. It could have been worse.'

'Worse? How?' Kate shook.

'Could have been a snake.' Working in the jungle hospital, venomous creatures were always on Rose's mind. Her nightmares were filled with pit vipers and wolf snakes. The first time she saw a gecko, she screamed. The girls were still teasing her about it. Once, she saw an iguana prowling through the jungle and thought it was a king cobra, the longest venomous snake in the world. She had never run so fast.

'It's probably coming back for more. I might wake up tomorrow and half my face will be missing.' Kate wrung her hands.

'Don't worry. If half your face is missing, chances are you won't be waking up.'

'I didn't sign up for this. Rats trying to eat me alive while I sleep.' There were tears in Kate's eyes.

'I prefer rats to some humans,' said Rose, wondering if the dreaded Japanese were in Manila, if they had occupied the hospital where she had worked, and if they had, what would happen to the nurses and the patients? What would happen to David?

The girls got dressed, Kate slower than usual because her hands were still trembling after her close encounter with the rat. They found Tess in the mess, sitting at the table with the other nurses, a radio in front of them. She waved. 'Look at you two sleepyheads. You almost missed the announcement.'

'What announcement?' asked Rose.

'Haven't you heard? President Roosevelt is going to address the people of the Philippines.'

The radio came to life with the sound of static. Moments later, the commanding voice of the president filled the hall. Lauding their efforts, he promised them, from thousands of miles away, an ocean and half the world away, that their freedom would be redeemed, that the entire resources of the United States would soon be at their disposal. 'The skies will be black with planes over your heads,' he said to the desperate people of the Pacific.

The girls cheered.

From that moment on, every spare moment they got, the nurses gazed at the water, hoping to see the reinforcements as they sailed into the harbour in triumph. But, alas, there was no sign of them. Instead, a bulldozer arrived one morning to clear the jungle for a hospital expansion. So many patients had arrived in the last couple of weeks, there were no more beds available. Most of the wounded slept under the open skies. The only tent they possessed was used to shelter medical records. 'The patients will dry. The medical records will not,' said Elsie when Rose pointed out that the tent could be used for the people instead.

Luckily, they had plenty of space in the jungle. What they didn't have was bandages. Their medical supplies were running low, as were blankets, sheets, pyjamas and pillows. 'Soon we will have to treat our patients with acacia leaves,' Kate joked. 'Already we are using ether for sedation like it's the Great War. Sulfa is almost gone. Morphine too.' What little drugs they had left, they buried in deep trenches to protect them from the shelling and the elements.

At night, under blackout conditions, while air raids unfolded nearby, the nurses held flashlights covered with blue cellophane paper for the doctors so that they could continue to operate. Every time Rose entered a ward, she heard screams for morphia. She gave the wounded their injections, wondering what she was going to do when they ran out. She doubted acacia leaves would make a good alternative. But even after all the injections had been administered, the screams of pain continued. Rose heard them through her days and nights, heard them as she tried to sleep, as she cleaned wounds, applied sulfa powder, changed dressings and brought trays of food, as she fought the never-ending battle with bugs and dirt, as she carried water from the river to wash her patients, and even as she bathed in the stream once every few days, washing off the grime and the blood, and trying to forget for a few moments that death was all around her.

One afternoon, when the breeze was especially hot on her cheeks and she felt her uniform stick to her back with sweat, when the sun shone mercilessly on the patients and the nurses who were working under the open skies, Dr Jack Dunham, the chief surgeon, walked in, accompanying a stretcher that carried an unconscious man. 'We picked him up outside,' said the doctor, a tall man in his fifties with short grey hair and the face of a bulldog whose sad eyes had seen too much. 'He has a concussion and a broken arm. The bone needs to be reset. Kindly prepare him for surgery.'

'Right away, Dr Dunham,' said Rose. She glanced at the patient and stopped in her tracks.

'Is there a problem, Nurse?' Dr Dunham frowned.

'It's an enemy soldier,' Rose exclaimed, not taking her eyes off the Japanese man in front of her. She had never seen the enemy up close before. Her hands started to shake.

'We are a hospital. We treat everyone equally. There are no enemies, only human beings. Didn't you learn that at nursing school?' The doctor looked at Rose like he was deeply disappointed.

'I'm sorry, I didn't mean to ...' she stammered.

But the doctor didn't let her finish. 'Have him ready this afternoon,' he barked, turning on his heels and marching away.

Rose settled the new patient into a bed that had just become available. 'You are lucky to have a bed,' she muttered. 'Many others don't.' But the Japanese soldier couldn't hear her. He was asleep. All morning, Rose tiptoed around him, throwing surreptitious glances his way. He was just a boy, seventeen or eighteen, with not a trace of stubble on his face.

When he finally awoke, Rose approached him, asking if he wanted some water, if he was in pain, if he was hungry, if he needed anything.

'Please, don't kill me,' pleaded the soldier. His English was good but accented. His dark eyes were filled with dread. Rose felt an unexpected twang of pity.

'We are not going to kill you. The doctor will operate on you this afternoon. You broke your arm. The bone needs to be reset.'

The soldier didn't reply but stared at Rose like a frightened animal.

When the stretcher bearers came to take the Japanese boy to the operating theatre, he screamed and begged for his life. And when it was time to sedate him, he fought like a tiger. It took three men to hold him down.

When the patient woke up after the operation, he looked around like he didn't know where he was or what had happened. Tears were running down his cheeks. Rose brought him a glass of water and he grabbed her hand, kissing it. 'I'm still alive. I can't believe I'm still alive. Thank you,' he repeated over and over again. 'You saved my life.'

Rose didn't pull her hand away. 'That's a bit of an exaggeration. All you had was a broken arm.' She wiped the sweat off his forehead. 'Now you need to rest and recover. I'll bring you something to eat.'

'Please, don't send me away. I don't want to go to a prisoner of war camp. They will kill me there.'

Rose shook her head. 'No one is sending you anywhere.'

'I will do anything. I will clean and help carry the stretchers. I will be very useful.'

'Why don't you get better first?' Rose smiled. 'Your arm needs to heal before you lift a stretcher, soldier.' Her sympathy for the boy had taken her by surprise. Days ago, he was fighting against them. Now he was in hospital, afraid for his life, just like the rest of them. Rose realised she had never thought of the Japanese as human beings. Until now.

One particularly loud morning, when the enemy started bombing before the sun was up and didn't seem to have any intention to stop, Rose woke up early, even though the night before she had finished late, having been on her feet for twenty hours without a break.

In the operating room, she assisted a surgeon as he tried to save a hopeless case shot in the neck. The bullet severed the spinal cord and there was every danger that the patient would never walk again. When a bomb landed nearby, the table shook. The doctor paused with a scalpel in his hand for a moment and then continued operating like nothing had happened. But Rose couldn't control her trembling hands.

By ten o'clock, she was barely able to stand on her two feet. She had skipped breakfast and now felt sick to her stomach. Her limbs felt heavy, like she was wading through water. She had a ward of men competing for her attention but she was stuck in the isolation tent with a mask on her face because one of her new patients, Tony, wouldn't stop talking and she didn't know how to tell him politely that she had no time for idle chatter. Tony had acute pulmonary TB. He was admitted following a severe haemorrhage which could prove fatal. He was a handsome man and had chosen Rose as the target for his attentions, although he couldn't talk for long without bursting into an ear-shattering coughing fit that seemed to go on forever.

'You remind me of my sister,' Tony said.

Without a word, Rose placed her hand on his forehead. He was burning up. She knew from the night nurse that his cough was particularly bad, he had severe night sweats and hadn't had any sleep.

'It's your eyes,' Tony was saying. 'Caring and sweet. And your beautiful face.'

'You can't see my face. I'm wearing a mask.'

'Why don't you take it off so I can see you?'

'I can't take it off. I wear it to protect you from infection. And myself.'

'Come on. Just this once.'

Rose laughed and shook her head, adjusting his pillow and trying to make him more comfortable.

'I will never see my sister again,' he whispered. 'I will never see my family.'

Rose sat next to him and took his hand, trying very hard not to cry. Seeing despair in the eyes of the men who realised they were close to death broke her heart every time.

When Tony fell asleep, she returned to the ward, wondering if she could get away to find something to eat, when she saw Dr Dunham leaning over the table with the instruments. 'Have these been sterilised?' he asked. 'It doesn't seem so.'

'I was just about to do it,' said Rose, flustered, her cheeks hot after a brisk walk. She was always rushing, it seemed, and never had a moment to spare. There was always another place to be, another patient to tend to, another chore that had to be done. And another, and another. It never stopped.

'Please, do so immediately. We are going to need them in surgery this afternoon. Also, these sheets look dirty and the table hasn't been wiped properly.'

Rose looked down at her feet, her face burning. 'I'm sorry, Doctor. This is a jungle hospital. We are out in the open. It's hard to keep the dirt and the bugs out.'

'That might be so but it's still a hospital. Hygiene levels must be maintained.'

Rose wanted to point out they were fighting a losing battle. To keep the linen clean, it would have to be changed every couple of hours. She wanted to tell the doctor that the nurses were already working twenty-hour shifts, running on no sleep and often no food. With the number of patients in their care, they hardly had time to do the bare minimum. But all she could do was mutter a barely audible, 'Yes, sir.'

The next morning, she woke up an hour early so she could change the linen before the doctor arrived. Her eyes were hurting from lack of sleep and her body was sore but at least she managed to stop off at the mess for a bite to eat.

While she was changing the linen and wiping the surfaces, her patients called her. 'Nurse, can I have a glass of water?'

'Nurse, can you change my bandages?'

'Nurse, I'm feeling lonely. Can you sit with me?'

She fetched a glass of water and changed the bandages, all the while looking at the clock. The doctor would be here any minute and she still had half a ward to go before all the linen was changed.

'This is ridiculous,' she said to Kate. 'Shouldn't the patients come before the linen?'

'Not just the patients but yourself, too. How much sleep did you get last night?'

'Two hours, I think.'

Kate shook her head. 'Damn the linen. You need your rest. If you are exhausted, you won't be able to do your job properly.' Kate put a hand on her shoulder. 'Ignore him. What is he going to do, fire you?' She laughed. 'You should be so lucky.'

Rose sighed. 'He asked me to assist him in surgery this afternoon. I'd rather swim with sharks.'

'I can take your place if you like.'

As tempting as it was, Rose shook her head. 'You don't have to do that. He'll be as hard on you as he is on me.'

'Yes, but my skin is thicker. I can take it.'

When the doctor finally arrived, all the linen had been changed and Rose was a mess of nerves. Dr Dunham checked on his patients without a glance in her direction. As she stood in the corner, watching him quietly, Rose made a promise to herself that she would stand up to the doctor next time and explain to him that her time was better spent elsewhere. She would be assertive and put her needs and those of her patients first. But when she arrived in the operating theatre to assist in surgery that afternoon, she was so nervous, she couldn't get anything right. She passed the wrong instruments, couldn't suture properly and cut herself with the needle. The doctor glanced at the blood on her finger and without a word walked outside, calling out, 'Can I have another nurse in the operating theatre, please?'

By the time Kate turned up to replace her and Rose was told to go, she was in tears.

Rose was walking through the jungle towards the hospital, carrying a bucket of water, wondering if the bulldozer would return soon to dig up another extension, as they now had more than four thousand wounded, and there was hardly space to breathe. They slept on the ground under the trees, and when it rained, they crawled under a piece of tarpaulin if they were lucky enough to find one.

Exhausted and unable to walk another step with the heavy bucket dragging her down, Rose paused for a moment in the middle of the jungle. She had been feeling so weak lately. She didn't know if it was the lack of food, the long hours she had been working, or a combination of both. A few months ago, she had no problem at all lifting a bucket of water and carrying it from the river to the hospital. Now, every step was agony. She dragged the bucket behind her, telling herself she was almost there, when she heard someone calling her name. Surprised, she turned around and found herself face to face with the young Japanese soldier with a broken arm. After his surgery, he had been moved to a different ward and she hadn't seen much of him. He looked different, more confident than before, not as afraid.

'Let me help you,' he said. 'It must be hard for you.'

'Thank you but I'm fine. Your arm is still in plaster.'

'Fortunately, I have two.'

She let him take the bucket, grateful for the help. On the way to the hospital, the soldier, whose name was Hiroshi, told her about his parents and fiancée, a young girl called Hanae, who was an orphan and lived with his mother and father. 'We were supposed to get married two months ago. Instead, I was called up. I hate this war.'

Rose stumbled and nearly fell. It was the last thing she expected a Japanese soldier to say. She had thought they were all warmongers who had come to the islands to pillage and destroy. It had never occurred to her that many of them didn't have a choice. 'I'm sorry to hear that.'

'Don't be sorry. When it's all over, I will go back and we'll get married. She'll wait for me.' He smiled. A moment later, his smile faded. 'But my mother won't wait. I will probably never see her again.'

'Why? Is she ...'

'Ill. Yes. Here, let me show you some pictures.'

He placed the bucket on the ground. A moment later, half a dozen photographs appeared in his hands. Some of them were yellow with age, and Rose looked with curiosity at a couple in their wedding attire, gazing into each other's eyes. Other images were of a young beautiful girl, playing the piano, riding a bicycle, walking a small dog, smiling at the camera without a care in the world. Hiroshi touched the beloved faces with his finger before putting the pictures away. 'I want to go home,' he said.

'Me too,' Rose replied.

They continued through the jungle, moving branches out of the way with their hands. Hiroshi pointed at two inactive volcanoes that surrounded the Bataan Peninsula, like sleeping giants guarding it from evil, Mount Natib in the north and Mount Mariveles in the south. 'Have you heard the legend?' he asked. 'A young nun called Maria Velez fell in love with a monk. They ran away to elope and hid in this jungle but were soon caught and separated. They were punished, I think. Maybe even killed.' He looked heartbroken when he said it. Rose wondered if he was thinking of his family.

'That's the saddest story I've ever heard.'

'But the girl got the volcano named after her. And look how magnificent it is.' He smiled. 'No matter what happens in life, I try to find something magical around me. It makes everything so much easier to bear. And a view like this, it makes my heart sing, even now.'

As she went about her tasks that day, Rose couldn't stop thinking of the faces on the photographs, of a mother, a father and a young girl somewhere in faraway Japan, desperately wishing the war was over so they could see their son and fiancé again. And she thought of Maria Velez, who had been punished because she dared to fall in love.

# Chapter 8

## February 1942

In late February, it was no longer peaceful on the Bataan Peninsula. The birds were no longer chirping with careless abandon and the nurses could not hear the ocean over the noise of the artillery. Just like in Manila two months previously, the bombs whistled and exploded overhead as if seeking them out, filling Rose's heart with dread. They had run away from war, but war was obstinate and determined to catch them. Rose wondered if they would have to evacuate again. The thought of packing up all the hospital equipment and moving the patients, many of whom couldn't walk, made her tremble. Where would they even go? Where in the Philippines was safe?

'Nowhere is safe,' said Kate, looking despondent. 'What was the point of leaving Manila?'

'Why are they bombing us so much?' Rose wondered. 'We're a hospital.'

'We happen to be situated between two important targets. To the south is the storage and staging base for the army engineers. To the north, the major ordnance storage for the Second Corps.'

One morning, when the shelling felt especially close, Rose hid under a bed. She felt panic rising inside her, making it hard to breathe, just like that day at Sternberg, seconds before the walls collapsed around her. She curled up into a ball under the bed and shook with fear. Any moment she expected a sharp impact and the darkness to swallow her. When she looked up, she saw a patient on one of the beds looking down at her with sad eyes. The man couldn't move. He couldn't hide, couldn't take cover, and here she was, sheltering instead of helping him. Feeling ashamed of herself, she climbed out from under the bed, even though the bombs continued to explode overhead.

Next time there was a bombing, she continued working. Dr Dunham happened to be in the ward with her. He didn't try to hide, either. 'Why didn't you take cover?' he asked her after the attack was over.

'I couldn't, not in front of my patients. I should be helping them, not running for safety at the first sign of trouble.'

The doctor looked at her in silence for a moment. He wasn't smiling but his eyes were warm. 'You can't help everybody. But you can help yourself. The patients need you. Take care of yourself first, so that you can take care of them later. Next time, make sure you find somewhere safe to wait out the shelling.'

Hiroshi appeared in the ward one afternoon, his face red, eyes filled with panic. It was clear that he had been running for a while and was now out of breath. Rose was busy preparing saline drips. As the only nurse across five wards, she could hear voices from every direction, calling her. She could see a forest of arms reaching for her.

'Please come with me,' said Hiroshi. 'I need to show you something.' His hands were shaking and he looked like he was about to be sick.

'I can't leave my patients. Can it wait till after the other nurses come back?'

'It can't wait.'

'Let me finish with the drips,' she said, wondering what could be so urgent and why he kept waving his hands in distress like the world was coming to an end.

He pulled her by the sleeve of her uniform. 'Finish the drips later.'

She saw by the expression on his face that there was no use arguing. He didn't say another word as she followed him outside, barely able to keep up. Side by side they ran through the jungle towards the river. In the distance, Rose could hear the chilling murmur of the artillery. Planes were dogfighting overhead, a terrifying sight. The battle over Bataan Peninsula was underway and the American-Filipino troops were not giving up without a fight.

Hiroshi cleared his throat. 'I was taking some baskets of bandages to the river for the nurses to wash when I came across …' He fell quiet.

'What?' Rose prompted.

'There.' He pointed in the direction of the jungle. 'Look for yourself.'

Rose turned around. Among the greenery, she could make out a body. And another. And another. She felt her stomach drop. 'Are they alive?' she whispered.

'I had a quick check,' he said. 'I couldn't tell for sure if they were wounded or dead, so I came to get you.'

'You did the right thing.'

Rose stood as if rooted to the spot for a few moments, wishing she could turn around and run. Thunder clapped overhead, joining the cacophony of war. A moment later, it started to rain. She took a deep breath and stepped into the jungle, not wanting to see and yet unable to leave if there was a tiny hope that she could still help someone. Trailed by Hiroshi, she walked from man to man, leaning over them to take a closer look. 'They're Americans,' she said. Her chest hurt at the sight of their lifeless faces and staring eyes. The familiar helplessness washed over her. She wished she could do something for them but it was too late and it broke her heart. *What a waste this war is*, she thought. What had these men, so young, with their whole lives ahead of them, given their lives for? What was the point of it all?

'We can't help them,' she said finally.

They stood next to each other without a word – a Japanese soldier and an American nurse in the jungle filled with dead bodies – contemplating the horror of war.

Hiroshi pulled her by the hand. 'I'm sorry I wasted your time. I thought …'

'You have nothing to be sorry about.'

'Let's go,' he said. 'I can't stay here another minute.' With the sun behind him and his face twisted like he was in pain, he looked even younger, a child who belonged with his family, with his mother and father, his aunts and uncles, not here, on war-torn Bataan.

Rose didn't move. She thought she heard a groan. 'What was that?' she asked, listening for more, not hearing anything, wondering if she had imagined it.

Hiroshi shook his head.

Nothing disturbed the tranquillity of this stunning spot but the branches whispering in the breeze. Perhaps it had been an iguana slithering through the jungle. There were so many of them around. Just the other day, one climbed into Kate's bed, making her shriek so loudly, all the nurses came running, thinking they were under attack. Rose turned to leave when she heard another groan, louder this time, coming from the jungle.

'I heard that,' said Hiroshi.

Without a second's delay, the two of them rushed towards the sound. Branches whipped Rose's face but she barely noticed. They forced their way through the wilderness, looking around, waiting for another groan, changing direction, searching the hostile jungle that was determined to fight them, scratching their hands and faces and tripping them up with roots. It took them a while to find the wounded man, who was lying face down on the grass, every few seconds shuddering and crying out like he was having a nightmare. Just like the rest of them, he wore an American uniform. Something in the way his hair curled at the base of his neck tugged at Rose's heart. She stopped in her tracks, for a moment forgetting how to breathe. With Hiroshi's help, she turned the wounded man over.

As thunder burst overhead and Filipino-American troops fought valiantly but vainly to stop the Japanese advance, while enemy planes buzzed in the sky and the rain came down hard on bleeding Bataan, Rose found herself looking into David's face.

Wondering if perhaps she was sleeping and this was all a dream, Rose crouched by David's side, cradling his head. She touched his face, whispered his name, her voice trembling, tears falling on his cheeks, her heart in her throat, pumping blood through her body at twice the normal speed. 'I can't believe it,' she muttered. 'I just can't believe it.' Ever since they said goodbye at Sternberg Hospital in Manila on the day the Japanese attacked the Philippines, she had thought of him every moment of every day. She had thought of what she would say to him, of what he would say to her, of seeing his face again. And yet, she wasn't prepared for what she was feeling.

His skin felt clammy and hot. There was a gash on his head that might need stitches. He groaned but didn't open his eyes.

'I'll go and get help,' said Hiroshi. 'We'll need a couple of orderlies to carry him to the hospital.'

'No,' she cried, surprised at how loud her voice sounded in the jungle being torn apart by war. She didn't find David only to let him stay here, among dead bodies, until Hiroshi returned with help. She had to get him to safety, now. 'There is no time,' she added, quieter. 'We will carry him ourselves.'

'Damn this cast,' said Hiroshi. 'I'll do what I can with my one good arm. What about you? Are you sure you can manage?' He glanced at her small, undernourished body and then at David, who was at least twice her weight.

'Don't worry about me. I will pick him up and carry him.'

It took a superhuman effort for Rose to lift David by the shoulders, while Hiroshi carried his legs with his one good arm. She huffed and puffed and once or twice she thought she would stumble and fall. But she didn't stumble and didn't even slow down because David needed her. She focused on his face, on his eyes that remained closed, on the unhealthy colour of his skin. She had to walk faster so they could get him to hospital and make sure he was all right, even though at every step her whole body seemed to scream with pain. As they made their way through the jungle, she whispered a prayer under her breath. 'Please, God, don't let him die,' over and over again, while her legs trembled under her and only her will propelled her forward.

After ten agonising minutes, Hiroshi asked, 'Do you need a break?'

'No, let's keep going.'

It took twenty minutes to reach the hospital. Unfortunately, there were no beds available. Rose didn't want to leave David on the hard floor or under a palm tree in the rain. She thought for a moment and directed Hiroshi towards the small mattress she slept on sometimes when she had no time or energy to return to her quarters. She didn't mind sleeping on the floor if it meant David was comfortable.

'David, can you hear me?' she whispered frantically when Hiroshi left the two of them alone in the busy ward. He didn't reply. His pulse was racing. 'You are safe now. I will look after you. I won't let anything happen to you.'

His eyes were closed and his lips looked pale in the late afternoon light. For a moment, she had forgotten Anne's heartbreaking words. All she saw before her was the man she loved. She placed his head in her lap and stroked his cheek, crying happy tears because in the midst of war, in the middle of nowhere, when she least expected it, she had found him again. It was a miracle, like God's grace.

Forgetting her other patients, Rose spent all her time by David's side. The wound on his head had been stitched by a doctor and was looking better but his fever spiked. She bandaged him, gave him some quinine and a blanket bath, finally placing a damp cloth on his forehead to cool him down. She watched him obsessively, trying to read the truth in his face. She waited for him to wake up and at the same time, was petrified of facing him. After months of doubt and uncertainty, what if he told her that Anne had been right all along, that he had never loved her, that he belonged to someone else? Until she knew for sure, she still had hope. What if this hope was about to be wrenched away from her?

When she wasn't near David, she was edgy and absent-minded. No one seemed to notice except Kate, who sat her down and said, 'This is the third instrument you've dropped in the last five minutes. Is something wrong? Is Dr Dunham giving you a hard time again?'

'Dr Dunham? No, it's not that. David is here, at the hospital.'

Kate's eyes grew wide. 'David is here! Is he hurt?'

'He's unconscious. I've been looking after him.'

'Is he going to be all right?'

'I hope so. I really do. He doesn't seem to have any life-threatening injuries, just the fever.'

'You must be overjoyed to find him alive after all this time.'

'I am but …' Rose hesitated. She didn't know how to put her feelings into words. 'He's engaged to someone else. I can't let myself get close to him again. I can't let him hurt me, again.'

Kate took her hand and pressed it gently, with affection. 'At the very least, all your questions will be answered. You'll get closure.'

Rose didn't want closure. What she wanted was to hear him say that Anne had lied, that all they had shared was not an illusion, that it had all been real. She knew she had to stay away from him, that her heart couldn't take any more heartbreak. But how could she? Kate was right. She had lived the last few months in doubt and uncertainty. Finally, she would know the truth. He owed her that much.

Like a shark smelling blood, Elsie seemed to sense that Rose's attention was no longer on her work. She followed her on her rounds, watching her through narrowed eyes. 'Did I just see you give quinine to this patient?'

Rose nodded. 'Is that a problem?'

'Hasn't he already had some this morning?'

'He was burning up. He needed more.'

Elsie shook her head in disbelief. 'Every single one of these men needs some. We are under strict instructions to limit the amount of medication we use. Where did you even get quinine? I thought we were out.'

Rose didn't meet Elsie's eyes, looking at the floor under her feet instead. She got quinine from Dr Dunham's secret supply when he wasn't looking. The doctor kept it for emergencies. She believed this qualified as one. It broke her heart to see David suffering. Now, as she watched Elsie storm off, she wondered if she was in trouble. With surprise, she realised she didn't even care. This wasn't pre-war Manila when they could put her on the next ship bound for the United States.

Twenty minutes later, Dr Dunham asked to see her.

'Elsie informs me you are not following protocol,' he said. He didn't look angry, just tired. His eyes were dark with lack of sleep.

'If you are talking about administering quinine to a patient, I believe he needed it.'

'What wouldn't I give to have enough quinine and morphine for the men. What wouldn't I give for enough dressings. We have no medical supplies, almost no food and only rudimentary conditions for our patients.' He was silent for a moment, watching Rose with sad eyes. 'This war makes me feel so helpless. It keeps me up at night. It haunts me.' For the first time, Rose felt pity for the doctor. He carried the whole hospital on his shoulders, four thousand patients on zero resources. And even though he faced terrible odds, he didn't give up, working tirelessly through days and nights to save lives, to make a difference, to make these men's burdens a little more bearable. Sometimes he succeeded. Often, he did not. But he didn't let anything stop him from trying. 'Still, procedure must be followed,' Dr Dunham said. 'Or in a few days, we won't have any quinine left.'

'Yes, sir,' she said to the doctor, but that afternoon, when no one was looking, she gave more quinine to David, whose fever was finally under control.

She paused at the entrance to the ward, watching his face. He looked so peaceful, like he was asleep in his childhood bedroom with not a care in the world. His forehead no longer felt hot. His skin assumed a healthier shade of pink. His lips curled upwards, like he was on the brink of a smile. She wondered what he was dreaming about. She had seen that half-smile so often in the past, every time she ran to him from the hospital in Manila with her hand on her heart, every time she said something amusing or when he told her he loved her. His face was so familiar, it made her ache with longing and forget all her doubts for a moment. When she looked at him, she travelled back in time and her heart filled with joy. It was like magic.

She leaned over him, the tips of her hair touching his face. 'David, can you hear me?'

This time he heard her. He opened his eyes and groaned. 'Where am I?' His voice was thick like butter, like he was recovering from a cold. He didn't sound like himself.

For a few moments, she couldn't speak and looked at him in silence. All these months of not knowing where he was, if he was safe, if he was still alive. Day after day, night after sleepless night of looking for answers and not finding any, of wondering if she would ever see him again, whether he had abandoned her or been separated from her against his will. And here he was, right in front of her. She could hardly believe her eyes, could hardly believe her luck. Finally, she said, 'You are in the jungle hospital on Bataan. You've been hurt. But you are going to be just fine.'

He moved slightly away from her, as if her closeness made him uncomfortable. Then he looked up. There was no recognition in his eyes, as if he were looking at a stranger. 'What did you call me?'

She had been thinking of the promise she had made to him to do her best to keep herself alive so that they could have a future together. She remembered the intensity of her feelings in those early days, unmarred by Anne's revelation. She remembered the look on his face as he watched her walk away the last time they saw each other, so different from the look on his face *now*. She shuddered, like she was waking from a dream. 'What?'

'When you first walked in, you called me something. You asked if I could hear you and called me by a name. What was it?'

'David,' she whispered.

'Why?' Confusion was on his face, like he had never heard the name before, like it belonged to someone else.

Looking in his eyes, she was just as confused. 'Because it's your name. David Taylor.'

He stared at her for a few seconds. Finally, he repeated the name, as if trying the words out on his tongue for the first time. 'David Taylor.'

'What's wrong? You don't remember?'

'I don't know. What happened to me? How did I get here?'

Rose wished she knew the answer to his questions. 'A patient of mine found you not far from here, in the jungle. You were wounded. The two of us carried you to the hospital.'

He glanced at her with surprise. 'You carried me?'

Rose nodded.

'Thank you, Nurse. You saved my life.'

After she brought him something to eat, he fell asleep and she sat by his side for a few minutes, watching him, studying his face like it was a poem she wanted to learn by heart. When she heard Elsie's voice, she rushed off to tend to her other patients but every now and then returned to check on David. Finally, long after midnight, she lay down on the floor next to him, taking his hand and bringing it to her face. He didn't stir. She remained like this, unable to close her eyes or stop the tears from falling, his hand in hers, her hair on his face. Their first meeting, their first date, their first kiss, the ukulele in her hands, his fingers on hers, his voice in her ear, telling her he had never felt like this before – he remembered none of it, as if it had never happened and she had imagined it all, as if it only existed inside her head. But she remembered everything. Every second of it.

# Chapter 9

## February 1942

Before the Japanese had come to the Philippines, Rose could not have imagined the horrors of a war hospital. And now, on Bataan, her reality had become worse than her most terrifying nightmare. Day and night, without a break, the noises in the operating theatre made her want to put her hands over her ears and scream. The buzz of a saw as it cut through bone, the thump of an amputated leg falling into a bucket, the rat-tat-tat of a burr drill boring through a skull, the rasp of a file, the tap-tap-tap of a mallet on a chisel grounding out a shell fragment, the snip of scissors cutting through muscle, it never stopped, not at night, not in the afternoon for lunch, not for a minute. Many years from now, when the world was at peace once more, would she close her eyes and hear the dreaded buzz, the rasp and the tap-tap-tap? Would she hear the men's agonising screaming? Today of all days, she wished her life was different, that it wasn't all about death and decay.

As soon as she arrived for her shift, long before the sun came up and dispersed the darkness, she heard a patient wail in panic and then the sounds of grunting and pushing as he fought off two orderlies and a doctor who were preparing him for surgery. His eyes bulged and his face became red, perspiration mixing with tears on his cheeks. 'Get away from me! Don't take my leg off! Animals! Leave me alone!' The young man, almost a boy, looked like a rabbit backed into a corner, frightened and desperate and ready for anything. His fists flew out like those of a boxer, catching one orderly on his chin and the other on the side of his head. Both men staggered away from the wounded, momentarily stunned.

Her arms outstretched, a kind smile on her face, Rose approached the unfortunate patient. She tried to put her hand on his shoulder but he recoiled as if she had scalded him with boiling water. She said, 'We are not trying to hurt you. We are trying to save your life. If we keep the leg, it will kill you. We won't be able to stop the gangrene. I know you're afraid but this is our only option.'

The man stared at her like she spoke a language he didn't understand. Encouraged by his silence, the orderlies approached once again, ready to conduct him to the operating room. The man growled like a wounded tiger and charged.

All of a sudden, Rose felt a sharp pain under her right eye. She cried out and slid to the floor, her hand on her cheek. It felt like she had been hit with a sledgehammer. The orderlies ran to her side, as did Dr Dunham. Everyone wanted to know if she was all right, if she needed anything. The doctor pressed a bag of ice to her eye. 'Hold it for a few minutes. It will help.' And it did, numbing her until she could touch the flesh under her eye without wincing.

The patient watched her in shocked silence, like he didn't understand what had happened. Finally, as if a switch had been flicked and he was no longer a deranged tiger but a human being, he rushed to her and said, 'I'm very sorry, miss. I didn't realise you were so close to me. It wasn't intentional, I just …' He didn't finish his sentence. Dropping his head into his hands, he started to cry.

'Don't worry, I'll live, I think. The black eye will put fear into my other patients.' Through her own tears, Rose tried to smile.

'I can't lose my leg,' he whispered. 'I'm the only breadwinner in my family. My mother is sick and can't work. And my sister has three little ones and no husband. What will I do with one leg?'

'Your mother and sister would prefer it if you were alive, would they not? They won't love you any less if you have one leg. But if we don't go ahead with the operation, they will never see you again. What do you think they would say to you if they knew it was your leg or your life?'

He seemed to think about it. 'They would tell me to stop being so stubborn and listen to the doctor. They would probably slap me around the head too, to knock some sense into me.' He smiled at the thought of his loved ones, then turned to Dr Dunham, his eyes large like saucers. 'Will it hurt very much?'

'You won't be awake to feel anything,' the doctor assured him.

When the patient woke up from surgery, he wept. Rose did her best to comfort him. He told her his name was Daniel and he had been a mechanic before the war. He showed her a picture of his sweetheart, who was waiting for him to return so they could get married. 'She's not going to want me now, is she?'

'Of course, she will. If she loves you, she will,' said Rose.

'She wants children. Will I still be able to have them?'

'We haven't touched anything above the thigh, soldier.'

Daniel kept asking Rose to remove the bedclothes from his non-existent leg. 'Are you sure it's gone? I can still feel it, you know,' he said with hope.

'You will for a while,' Rose replied, adjusting the bedclothes to make sure the patient couldn't see what was under them.

In the afternoon, Dr Dunham came to check on Rose. He touched her eye. It felt tender and stung a little. 'What you did in there was incredible. Another nurse in your position would have complained but not you.'

'What's the point in complaining? It wouldn't change anything.'

'You put the patient first and didn't even think about yourself.'

'I'm a nurse. That's what I do. What I should have done instead was move out of the way faster. I wouldn't make a very good boxer, would I?' She laughed, even though she felt like crying.

'No, you wouldn't. But you make a very good nurse. Thanks to you, we were able to operate. Your actions today saved the patient's life. You should be proud of yourself.'

For a moment, Rose remained quiet, lost for words. 'Thank you, sir,' she whispered finally.

'No, thank *you*, for all your hard work.' He beamed. 'I've been watching you. You have a way with patients. You are a nurse from God, Rose Williams. It's a rare gift.'

Despite her throbbing eye, she flew back to the ward, a smile on her face.

Next time Rose came to see David, she brought some carabao meat on a tray. If she couldn't give him extra quinine, she could bring extra food, even if it had come out of her ration and meant she would be hungry for the rest of the day. He was sitting up in bed, smiling. He seemed a little more like his old self, even though she saw no recognition in his eyes.

'Why do you have a black eye?' he asked, reaching for the tray of food.

'Oh, that? It's nothing. I was in the ring with Jack Dempsey.' She tried hard not to laugh at the expression on his face.

'Jack Dempsey?'

'The famous boxer.'

'Are you teasing me? Tell me what happened.'

She told him. 'It breaks my heart to see men like Daniel, healthy and young and at the start of their lives, destroyed by war. And for what?'

'I know what you mean,' said David. 'It breaks my heart to see young women like yourself, who should be safely home with their families, in the midst of it all.'

'I'm a nurse. This is where I belong.' Although she would love to be home and safe, to see her mother again, to not know the horrors of war, if she hadn't been here, who would have brought him back from the jungle? Who would look after him? *Everything happens for a reason*, she wanted to tell him. She had been at the right place at the right time and she was grateful for it. She didn't know if they had a future together. She didn't know if he had been lying to her all that time. But she did know that he needed her and he had no one else. And she would be there for him, no matter what. Even if afterwards he went home to his Celia.

He poked the meat with his finger and placed a small bit in his mouth. 'What is it?' he asked. 'It's hard to chew.'

'Carabao.' She looked at it with longing. 'You know what they say. To cook carabao, you put a rock and the meat in a pot and boil them. When the rock is tender, the meat is ready.'

He laughed like it was the funniest thing he had ever heard.

She had a ward of patients waiting for her. She had to be in the operating room in ten minutes to assist with a surgery and hadn't had a bite to eat that morning. Elsie was sniffing around, searching for an opportunity to tell her off. And still she stayed by his side, watching him eat, her eyes on his face.

When all the meat was gone, he said, 'It's not so bad, this carabao. Maybe I'm just hungry. I'll eat the rock too if you have it.'

'You are hungry. It's a good sign. You are recovering.'

His smile vanished. 'If I'm recovering, why can't I remember who I am?'

'You've been through trauma. It's probably your body's way of protecting you. With time you will remember.'

'And what if I don't?'

Wanting to reassure him, she touched his shoulder. 'I spoke to the doctor about it. He said temporary amnesia is very common with these types of injury.'

'He thinks it's temporary?'

'He's quite sure of it. Anything could trigger a memory, anything at all. Familiar songs, scents, even food. Talking to someone about your past.'

'If only I could remember anything about my past.' He closed his eyes. 'When I try to think about it, everything is just …' He fell quiet, as if searching for the right word. 'Blank. I have these disjointed images inside my head but I don't know if they are my past or a dream I am remembering. They are fleeting and when I try to grasp them, they disappear.'

'I can tell you a little bit about yourself,' she said shyly.

'Have we met before?'

Her heart filled with the images of the two of them together, of walking hand in hand through Manila, of dancing under the twinkling lights, lost in each other's arms and unafraid, while the river whispered its quiet song and the mountains looked on. 'We have.'

He looked thrilled. 'What luck, to run into someone I know. Tell me everything.'

She told him where he had been stationed and everything she knew about his parents, his sister and his life before the Philippines but didn't say a word about their relationship or how they had met. When the time came for her to scrub up to assist Dr Dunham in surgery, just before she said goodbye, David asked, 'When you knew me in Manila, did I at least ask you out on a date?'

Rose felt her cheeks start to burn. She smiled, looked away and touched his forehead, not because she needed to check his temperature but because she wanted to feel him, to make sure he was here, that she wasn't imagining him, that he was real. Then she rushed off without another word.

# Chapter 10

## March 1942

As she worked, Rose listened to the silence outside. Where was the regular bombing and the ever-present din of machine guns? The sound of war had become an integral part of her day. Suddenly, it was gone, and it felt like something was missing. While the hospital remained as noisy as ever, with men screaming and groaning and begging, the jungle seemed unusually quiet. 'Is it my imagination or has the fighting stopped? There was no bombing at all yesterday and I can't hear the artillery,' Rose said to Kate, who was busy sterilising the instruments they would need in surgery later that day.

'Who is left to bomb? The Japanese know we are in dire straits. Why would they waste their explosives?'

'You think they've left us alone?' Rose asked with hope. The reprieve was more than welcome. Rose didn't know how they were going to cope if new patients continued to arrive at the hospital at the current rate.

'I have a feeling they'll be back, once they gather their strength for the final attack.'

'Final attack?' Rose whispered, terrified.

She sleepwalked through her days, trying not to think of what the future would bring. The silence terrified her. It was like the calm before the storm, inexplicable and therefore frightening. She lost herself in her patients and spent every moment she could find by David's side, telling him about Anne, about his parents, about all the fun things he would do when the war was over.

The sight of his malnourished body made her want to weep. She remembered how strong he had once been, how safe he had made her feel. This quiet, frightened man was a shadow of the David she knew. This war had robbed him of so much more than just his memory. And yet, he was alive. It was a miracle. It was up to her to bring the old David back to the surface. Instead of taking breaks for much-needed sleep, she read to him. In the balmy tropical evenings, she sat by his side with her precious ukulele in her lap and strummed all the songs he had once taught her.

*California I've been blue*
*Since I've been away from you.*

She would sing the same song over and over again, in her mind miles away from the jungle hospital of Bataan. Sometimes she would look up and see recognition in his eyes, as if he knew this melody and was about to open his mouth and join in. As if in his heart he could recall their first carefree afternoon in Manila together.

Rose's black eye healed gradually. Since the incident, she had been busier than ever. Dr Dunham insisted she assist him in every surgery, giving her more responsibility than any other nurse and even teaching her how to perform simple procedures. After a couple of weeks, she was able to do a tracheotomy all by herself. Dr Dunham praised her efforts and told her she was a quick learner. 'Perhaps, when this war is over, you can go back to medical school, become a doctor.'

Seeing the patient's colour return to normal and his breathing become easier gave her a sense of pride and satisfaction she hadn't known in all her years as a nurse. 'Perhaps,' she replied. She hadn't thought about what she wanted to do after the war. It was hard to imagine peace when day and night they were besieged on Bataan, starving and overworked, while the wounded continued to arrive by the hundreds. She could barely remember her life before the attack. It seemed to Rose that her days had always been like this and could never be any other way, a fight for survival, a life of constant fear.

In the evenings, the girls gathered to listen to the Voice of Freedom, a US military broadcast from Corregidor. Sometimes they managed to catch KGEI San Francisco, faraway voices from home that faded in and out, leaving hope behind. One night they heard that the first American convoy had landed in Northern Ireland. Everyone wanted to know what had happened to the reinforcements they had been promised, the reinforcements they had been expecting every day. It felt like the world had forgotten about them. As her days passed slowly in a blur of septic wounds and infectious diseases, Rose was petrified of things to come, feeling that her life and the lives of her friends were hanging by a thread, with no one there to catch them when that thread finally broke. Was it her imagination or were their rations getting smaller by the day?

One evening at dinner, Tess poked around her plate with a spoon, scooping up a bit of meat and lifting it to see better. 'What is in this soup?' she asked.

'Monkey,' replied Kate, her mouth full.

Looking shocked, Tess pushed her plate away.

'Don't you like it? Yesterday we had lizard. It was delicious. Didn't you notice?'

'I ate it so quickly I didn't have time to. There were maybe two bites.'

'Are you going to stop complaining and finish your monkey or can I have it?'

'I'll finish it.' Tess turned to Rose. 'Teacher's pet,' she whispered, a teasing smile on her face. 'I overheard Dr Dunham talking about you to the other doctors this morning.'

'He told me I could be a doctor one day,' said Rose with her eyes closed, a smile on her face.

Tess said, 'I'm done with medicine. When all this is over, I'm giving up nursing. It's too much.'

'I couldn't live without it,' said Rose, thinking of the way her patients' faces lit up at the sight of her, of the gratitude in their eyes, of the satisfaction she felt every time she helped someone. 'It's the only thing that gets me through the day. Knowing that I'm needed, that what I do matters.'

Rose and David sat close together under an acacia tree with the sun on their faces, their hands on the strings of the ukulele, just like before. Only this time, it was Rose who was showing David what to do. After she explained about the chords and the strings, she said, 'Hold it closer to your chest. That's it.'

He watched her. 'Why are you smiling like that? Like you're a million miles away?'

And she was, miles away in a park in pre-war Manila, dreaming of the perfect sunset with him. 'I'm right here. Why don't you give it a go? Someone once told me that music makes everything better.'

'A sweetheart?' he asked, a teasing smile on his face.

'Perhaps.'

The instrument came alive under his fingers. His body knew what to do, it seemed, even if his mind had forgotten. Rose recognised the intimate sounds of Beethoven's *Für Elise* that David had played for her many times in the past, whenever he felt sad or homesick. He looked at her, then at the instrument, then back at her again. An expression of utter astonishment was on his face. 'I feel like I've done this before.'

'You remember.' Rose clapped with joy. 'Does it bring back memories?' To her, the melody evoked whispers of another life, of happiness and joy and hope for love. But judging by his blank face, the music held no recollections of evenings past, no feelings that were hiding below the surface. 'It will all come back,' she said. 'Just give it time.'

But he wasn't listening. He was too busy strumming and singing quietly to himself.

She found a deck of cards and taught him how to play poker and rummy. He lost every game. She found an old chess set in one of the warehouses. He always won because she could never concentrate on the game.

'Isn't it amazing?' he said. 'I don't remember anything about my life but I remember how to play chess.'

'It's a good sign,' she said. 'Other memories will follow.'

Her eyes ached from lack of sleep and the weight fell off her because what little extra food she got she gave to him. One day, he asked her, 'Why is it that I get so much more meat than the other patients?'

'You don't. Everyone gets an equal ration.'

He watched her with disbelief. 'I spoke to my buddy Kenneth and he has no idea what carabao tastes like.'

Rose glanced at Kenneth, asleep in the bed to the right, a sheet over his head to block out the sun. 'Probably for the best. Tell him it tastes like a rock but not as tender.'

'You haven't been giving me your food, have you?'

'No, of course not. Why would I do that?'

He pretended to believe her but next time she brought him food, he refused to have any until she ate three-quarters of it.

One morning, David accompanied her to the river and helped her carry the bucket of water. From that day on, it became a tradition. He waited for her before the sun was up and together they walked in the dark, talking about nothing and everything, listening to the silence. He didn't want her to lift anything heavy, to hurt herself, to tire herself out, so he went everywhere with her and mopped the floors for her and changed the linen in the wards.

One afternoon, he led her behind the main hospital building, where she saw a workbench and some instruments scattered around. 'I made something for you,' he said.

'A cabinet!' she exclaimed, staring at the beautiful piece of furniture, like something she would buy from a shop before the war. The sun reflected off its shiny surface, blinding her. 'I can't believe you made it.'

'For your surgical instruments. So they are not out in the open anymore.'

'Where did you learn how to do this?'

'I wish I knew,' he replied. 'Now, why are you crying?'

'I wish I knew,' she whispered, feeling dizzy and confused, wondering if perhaps in his heart he could remember his feelings for her, if Anne had been lying after all. There was no way to know for certain. She couldn't ask him directly, couldn't tell him anything, couldn't explain what she was feeling, and so she remained still with her hand on the cabinet, tears running down her cheeks, watching his smiling face.

Rumours swirled around the hospital about the reason behind the inexplicable ceasefire. Most people believed that the Japanese were biding their time, gathering strength for one final push into the Philippines, preparing one last fatal blow to the bleeding islands. Rose tried not to think about what the future would bring, taking it one step at a time, focusing on her job and David and making it through each day, grateful for the peace and quiet.

Without an influx of new wounded and with some of the old patients recovering and returning to the front line, the wards became more manageable. Once again, the staff went to the seaside to swim and relax in the sun. They divided into two teams and played basketball. Kate's eyes twinkled with joy when their team won. They celebrated Dr Dunham's birthday with songs and music. Elsie played her guitar, while the girls danced.

Rose didn't play basketball, nor did she go to the seaside with the others or dance to Elsie's guitar. She wanted to spend every moment with David.

'Tell me, Lieutenant, do you know how to dance?' she asked him one afternoon. They were alone in the corner of the mess.

'Dance? I barely remember how to walk, Nurse Williams.'

'One of the nurses on the ward found an old portable phonograph and a pile of records.'

'Found it? Where?'

'In one of the sheds, wrapped in old newspapers from 1917.' She wanted to tell him what a strange feeling it was, to look at the old papers, to read about a different war, a different time when the world was in its death throes. Rose experienced a mix of foreboding and hope. She couldn't believe it was happening again, only two decades later. Hadn't the world learnt its lesson? But it had come to an end then. Surely one day this war would be over too. 'The nurses keep playing old songs. I've never seen them so happy. I even heard Dr Dunham singing to himself during surgery yesterday.'

'Dr Dunham … singing? As much as I want to, I can't picture it in my mind.'

'I told you, music makes everything better. Yesterday I was twenty minutes late and he didn't tell me off.' She placed her hand on his. 'What do you say? Will you dance with me, Lieutenant Taylor?'

'With pleasure, Nurse Williams.'

When the music filled the air, Rose was no longer on war-torn Bataan. She was in a club in Manila reliving the best moments of her life. She trembled, anticipating his arms around her. And a moment later, he was holding her, spinning her in the air, his face inches away from hers. 'Muscle memory,' whispered Rose. David remembered how to dance.

'Did you say something?'

She looked up into his face and smiled. 'You dance beautifully, Lieutenant.'

Rose was at the nurses' station, frowning at a pressure cooker that was hissing like an angry cat, spitting steam everywhere. Rose and the pressure cooker were having a stand-off. She was attempting to sterilise the surgical instruments they would need that day, while the temperamental machine was determined to oppose her every step of the way. It was easier in Manila where they had an electric steriliser. But here in the jungle hospital on Bataan, this steel-jacketed pressure cooker was all they could use to clean their instruments, operating gowns, towels and swabs. Kate always warned her that it would cause one of them an injury one day. She refused to go anywhere near it, claiming it was more unpredictable and dangerous than the Japanese. 'Florence Nightingale had better equipment in Crimea in the last century,' she joked.

As Rose listened to the grunting and growling of the pressure cooker, she wondered if today was the day the infernal contraption would finally explode. She didn't hear Dr Dunham come in over all the noise. When she raised her head, he was in front of her, a determined smile on his face. 'I'm going to the operating theatre. Walk with me,' he said.

'You need my help?' Rose lowered the scalpel she was holding.

'I need to talk to you.'

She followed the doctor, grateful for the excuse to turn her back on the spitting and hissing monster. Perhaps another nurse could deal with it.

'The ceasefire won't last much longer,' said the doctor as they walked through the ward, past the forest of arms reaching for them.

'I know,' said Rose sadly. She was finally getting used to not being woken up by gun fire and explosions, a terrifying alarm clock there had been no escape from, until recently. She suspected it was only a temporary reprieve and that sooner or later the enemy would be coming back. 'Will we have to evacuate?'

'Perhaps.' The doctor looked calm when he said it. Not a muscle moved on his face.

'Doesn't it scare you?'

The doctor shrugged. 'It is what it is. We will deal with it when it happens.'

'I wish I was brave like you.' Her hands shook every time she thought of the Japanese bombers in the sky, of enemy soldiers marching towards their hiding place on Bataan, closer every day, of bombs falling on the hospital.

'I'm not brave. I have no control over it, so I try not to think about it. I have a job to do. My patients need me. That's all that matters.'

'Perhaps they won't come here.'

'They will. They won't stop until all of the Philippines is under their control.'

Rose shuddered. 'Where can we possibly go? Where on the islands is safe?'

She didn't expect an answer. She knew nowhere was safe. But Dr Dunham slowed down and turned to her, like he was about to say something important. 'That's what I wanted to talk to you about. Next week, a navy ship bound for Australia is making a stop in the harbour not far from here.'

'That's great news. Are we finally getting the reinforcements we've been waiting for?'

'Not exactly. They are evacuating civilians from the Philippines and asked me to choose five nurses to be taken to safety. Straightaway, I thought of you. You have a kindness that can't be taught. You genuinely care about your patients. You always put them first.'

'You want me to leave?' She stopped walking and stared at the doctor, stunned. Only a couple of weeks ago, all she wanted was to run as far away from this place as possible and never look back. Not anymore.

'You can go to Australia, start a new life. You can leave this nightmare behind once and for all.'

'I have a feeling we will never leave this nightmare behind. It will always be with us, no matter where we go.'

'That might be so but, in the meantime, you'll be safe. From Australia, you can go home if you wish.'

She hesitated. 'I can't leave. The patients need me.'

'Good nurses are needed everywhere. In Australia, you can make a difference too. And you won't be risking your life while doing so.'

Rose thought of bombs hurtling towards Sternberg like terrifying hail, of Japanese soldiers descending on beaches of the Philippines, of the horror in her patients' eyes, of their voices pleading for help, for salvation, for a miracle. She touched her hair where she still hid the deadly poison. Every morning, she constructed an elaborate bun out of her hair just so she could place the vial inside, knowing that every day could be her last and trying not to think about it. She thought of the expression on David's face as he gave her gifts. Just this morning, he made a bamboo basket for her. 'For your dressings,' he had said.

Without hesitation, she said, 'Thank you for thinking of me, Doctor, but I can't go.'

'Why not?' Dr Dunham looked surprised.

'Are *you* going?' she asked, watching him. Just like everyone on Bataan, he had lost weight and looked like a shadow of the person he had been when they first met but he never slowed down, never allowed himself a moment's rest.

'I was offered a spot but I turned it down.'

'Then you can understand where I'm coming from. If I leave, I will always feel like I betrayed those who needed me, like I turned my back on my friends and patients. I might be safe in Australia but this knowledge will be with me for the rest of my life. I won't be able to live with myself.'

'I was afraid you might say that. Is it your final decision?'

'Yes, sir.'

A week later, five nurses sailed for the safety of Australia, four of them sick with malaria, one pregnant with her first child. They were not the only ones being evacuated from war-torn islands. General MacArthur and his staff left Corregidor and boarded a ship amidst bewilderment and disbelief of those who remained. 'I shall return,' the general said in his farewell speech to the Filipino-American troops. But no one believed him. A dark cloud fell over the hospital, like a premonition of horrors to come. If their beloved general had abandoned them, leaving them to the mercy of a cruel and relentless enemy, what hope did they have?

But Rose didn't dwell on it too much. She was too busy with her patients, too tired during the day. And in the evenings, there was David, the ukulele in his hands, his fingers strumming her favourite songs, his eyes on her. She invited him to the seaside one afternoon and he gladly accepted. They sat side by side, a picnic blanket in front of them. Unfortunately, unlike their picnics in Manila, there was hardly any food. A footpath zigzagged away from the beach, a mass of barbed-wire entanglement and razor-sharp bamboo poles sunk into the sand, their ends pointing towards the sea. Across the harbour, Rose could see the island of Corregidor, like a hunchback guarding the entrance to a magic cave, reminding her of another time, another wondrous day with him.

'I'll race you to the water!' cried Rose.

But before she had a chance to jump to her feet, David was already by the sea, taking his clothes off, standing in front of her in his trunks. 'That's not fair,' she said, coming closer. 'You didn't wait for me.'

'I thought we were racing. What kind of a race would it be if I waited for you?'

While Rose took off her nurse's uniform, David looked away. She smiled sadly, pushing her helmet with her toes. 'With the war on, I'm glad we can come to the beach and have an hour like this. It's a gift.'

'Me too,' he said. He looked at her and she felt her cheeks burning, suddenly self-conscious in her undergarments.

She followed him into the water, closing her eyes with pleasure when it touched her skin. 'This water is so warm, isn't it?' Rose said. 'Not like a waterfall at all.' Not like the last time they went swimming together.

'A waterfall?'

'Never mind. I bet I can swim faster than you.' She laughed because she knew she would lose. She had never been a strong swimmer, while he swam perfectly well, his strong arms parting water effortlessly and fast. He was ahead of her in no time, while she tried to keep up, laughing, picking up water with her mouth, for the first time in many months feeling free and happy and alive.

'Excuse me, Nurse Williams. You are not swimming at all. You are walking in water. That's against the rules.'

'What rules?' She reached for him and pinched him. 'I'm a lot faster this way, that's all.'

'You said swim. Walking is not swimming.'

He picked her up and threw her in the water. She squealed with delight, doggy paddling back.

Afterwards, they sat side by side on the sandy bank. 'What is my prize as the winner of the swimming challenge, Nurse Williams?' he asked.

'You won fair and square. Anything you want.'

He was looking at her without blinking, his eyes big. 'More than anything in the world, I would like to kiss you right now.'

He was so close, she could reach out and touch his face. Although she wanted to, she didn't. Instead, she moved away from him, shaking her head. 'You don't remember anything about your life. You could have a wife or a fiancée waiting for you back home.' She couldn't continue looking at him as she said it. She lowered her head, staring at the sand, at the waves that rose and fell, oblivious to her pain and fear, oblivious even to war.

'You're right.' He locked his fingers with hers. 'I don't remember anything about my life. I only know what I feel now, in this instant. But this instant might be all we have. We are at war. There is no time to waste.'

She knew by the intensity of his gaze that he was about to kiss her. Her hands trembled, her lips parted, her vision became blurry. She was no longer on Bataan but under their waterfall in Manila, anticipating their first kiss. For a moment, everything ceased to exist: the beach, the merciless sun, the enemy closing in on them, the jungle hospital, her patients. Everything disappeared because all she wanted was him.

But then, out of nowhere, she saw Anne's sneering, hateful face and heard her harsh words. *He will never commit to you. You mean nothing to him at all. Soon he will marry the love of his life and forget all about you.*

How could she let him kiss her when there was every chance he belonged to someone else? She could never break another woman's heart like this, carelessly, without a second thought. And she didn't want to break her own heart either by letting her guard down once again. She took a step back and turned her face away, turned her whole body away, and when she glanced at him, she saw sadness and disappointment in his eyes.

When the Japanese attacked on 22 March, it was like a lightning strike disturbing the perfect night. They knew it was coming and yet, it took them all by surprise. This time, the fighting was no longer distant. It felt to Rose that the enemy was finally here, by the hospital gates. Every time she heard gun shots, she lowered her head and concentrated on her patients but couldn't stop her hands from shaking. It seemed like the bullets were about to fill the ward like a flock of deathly birds. Once again, the sky was black with enemy aircraft and machine guns barked with rage in the jungle. Long range heavy artillery roared from Cavite, aiming at Corregidor. After a short reprieve that felt like an elusive dream, the world was on fire once again and all Rose could smell was acrid smoke.

When the fighting resumed, so did the river of wounded flowing towards the hospital. Infectious diseases swept through the wards. With no fresh water available, soldiers on the front line drank from streams and muddy ponds, showing up dehydrated and sick from bacteria. Rose was in charge of hundreds of men with dreaded malaria. Dysentery and dengue fever were rampant, and so was beriberi, the tropical disease that caused extreme exhaustion, loss of appetite, pain in the limbs and swollen feet. And it wasn't just the men. Most nurses were sick and Rose's workload increased tenfold, leaving her with no time for lunch or sleep or rest. No more games of chess with David, no more reading from *The Great Gatsby* or listening to his heart-wrenching ukulele as it serenaded her with love. She looked forward to her morning walks to the river for water because it was the only time she saw him.

Their ration had been reduced once more, until it was almost non-existent. With so many mouths to feed, even the monkeys and the lizards disappeared, while carabao became a distant memory. Rose had never thought she would miss its strong metallic taste in her mouth, but as she sterilised the instruments, assisted in surgeries and changed dressings, as she woke up in the morning and her head spun from hunger, all she could think of was the hard, almost impossible-to-chew meat and the heaviness it left in her stomach. Day and night, she would imagine her mother's roast turkey, mashed potatoes and meatballs, and apple pie.

As she walked through the wards, the wounded no longer asked for a shot of morphine. They didn't demand to see the doctor so he could take the pain away. They asked for food. In the last week of March, while the tropical sun beat down on them as if it didn't know it was only early spring, Rose started noticing symptoms of protein deficiency in the soldiers' wasting muscles and protruding bones.

After lunch of an unknown green substance that looked like

beans but had no taste, Elsie gathered the nurses together and said, 'From now on, we will have one meal every two days.'

The room filled with cross voices. 'We can't work on one meal every two days. I've just been in surgery for thirty-six hours. We are working around the clock. We need our energy.'

'We do what we need to do. I know you won't complain,' said Elsie.

'I *will* complain,' muttered Kate. 'You know how I know? Because I *am* complaining.'

Elsie opened her arms and shrugged. 'What's the point? It won't make our situation any easier. I wish I could give you food. I wish I could grow vegetables and hunt for meat. But I can't. There is nothing left.'

One morning, when David was filling Rose's buckets with water at the stream, enemy planes flew overhead and the bombing started.

'They're early,' said Rose, glancing at her watch.

'We better take cover,' David said, placing the buckets on the sand. He seemed calm while the unthinkable unfolded before their eyes and deathly explosives blasted through the air above their heads.

Rose couldn't move. Her legs turned to cotton wool and wouldn't obey, and so she stood and stared at the dark shapes floating above, threatening to kill them. David picked her up like she were a doll and weighed nothing, carrying her into the jungle. He placed her on the ground and covered her body with his.

Trembling, she clung to him, while the air around them was alive with sound. His body felt warm under her fingertips, and his arms around her were steady and comforting. She could almost convince herself she was on Boston Common on 31st December and the deafening noise wasn't bombs at all but fireworks cracking with joy, welcoming the New Year.

'Don't be scared,' he said. She could barely hear him over the plane engines and the whistling of the bombs. 'I'm here. I'll protect you.'

'I'm not scared,' she whispered through shaking lips.

Gradually, the din of the engines fell quiet. Nothing was heard but the rustling of the leaves. Even the birds were silent, afraid of the horror humans had unleashed on their peaceful home. Rose and David remained close together for a few moments. She was trying to catch her breath and he was stroking her back as if settling a child. Finally, he said, 'We should go before they come back.'

But they didn't move. She didn't want to return to the turmoil of the hospital. What she wanted was to stay like this forever, safe in his arms. He moved away, leaving his fingers on her knee. 'Sometimes when I look at you, I can sense something,' he said.

'A memory?' She sat up, looking into his face, trying to read his mind.

'Not quite. A feeling. An emotion. I can't quite put my finger on it. A joy the likes of which I've never known. A light.' She blinked, waiting for him to say more. He continued, 'It's almost as if my heart can remember what my mind has forgotten. I loved you, didn't I?'

She nodded. 'You loved me. And I loved you.'

Only when they got back to the ward did it occur to Rose that in their confusion they had forgotten all about their buckets, which remained by the river in the blazing sun. When she returned to collect them later that afternoon, she was shocked to find that they had been pierced by bullets. Rose's blood ran cold. The stream where they washed their dressings and fetched their water was only a ten-minute walk from the hospital. Were the enemy closer than any of them had realised?

# Chapter 11

## April 1942

April came in a flurry of airplanes and bombs. Rose was looking after a patient recovering from open incision treatment on his leg. They had run out of antitoxin for gas gangrene and the doctors improvised. They allowed sunlight and oxygen to penetrate the wound, hoping it would destroy the anaerobic bacteria consuming the flesh. It seemed to be working. Some colour returned to the patient's face and he was no longer staring into space in silence. Instead, every time he saw Rose, he flirted and touched her hand. She was feeding him his breakfast, afraid any moment he would propose marriage, when she got called into a meeting.

The nurses were assembled around the table. Dr Dunham sat in front of them in silence, as if he couldn't quite find the right words to start the conversation. He looked tired, grey and stooped. The last few months in the jungle hadn't been kind to him. He gave his all to the patients and soon there would be nothing left of him. After clearing his throat and adjusting his glasses, he said, 'As you know, the Japanese are getting closer.'

'Are we evacuating?' someone shouted from the back.

The room erupted in questions. Everyone wanted to know

what was about to happen. And they expected the chief surgeon to have all the answers.

Dr Dunham raised his hand. The women fell silent. He said, 'Any day now, the Filipino-American forces are going to surrender. If they don't, they will be risking the worst massacre in history. They are outnumbered ten to one and running out of ammunition. Soon they will have nothing left to fight with except coconuts and bamboo sticks. And we all know bamboo sticks are no match for the Japanese artillery.' The doctor sighed and looked away from them, as if he couldn't bear the expressions on their faces. 'But I have some good news. This morning we have received orders to retreat to Corregidor.'

'That's good news?' Kate wanted to know.

'Of course. The underground tunnels on Corregidor are fortified. The enemy can bomb all they want, they won't be able to do any damage. For the time being, we'll be safe.'

Rose tried to read the doctor's face for clues. Did he really believe what he was saying or was he like the radio, telling them what they wanted to hear? 'For the time being?' she asked in her smallest voice.

'One step at a time, Nurse Williams.'

'It will be hard to move the patients,' said Rose. The doctor didn't reply and he didn't need to. In his tense lips, in his reluctance to look the nurses in the eye, in the way his shoulders hunched, making him look helpless and sad, she had her answer. 'We're not taking the patients, are we?' She felt blood rush to her cheeks.

'Our orders are to leave everyone behind and retreat. Moving the patients is not only impractical but will put all of us in danger.'

'Leave everyone behind to the Japanese?' Rose whispered with disbelief.

For months, they had toiled tirelessly to help these men. They had forgone sleep to bring them relief. They'd saved lives. They'd shared their meals with their patients, listened to their stories and formed friendships. And now they sat in shocked silence and contemplated abandoning them to a fate worse than death. Finally, Dr Dunham said, 'It breaks my heart to leave the patients, as you can imagine. But may I remind you that, when we took our oath, we became part of the US military. Our orders are clear and can't be disobeyed.'

'When I took the oath, I swore to put my patients first, to do everything in my power to help them, to be there for them,' said Elsie, squaring her shoulders, daring the doctor to argue.

'Our superiors are ordering us to retreat, and we have no choice but to do so, even if it goes against everything we believe in. We will have to run, to hide in the jungle. We will never make it to safety if we are transporting thousands of wounded. We'll be discovered and everyone will be lost, patients and staff alike. And even if we make it, which is unlikely, there is no space for four thousand patients on Corregidor. What's going to become of them?'

A hush fell over the room. The nurses weighed up their choices. They searched for a solution but it was like fumbling for a light switch in the dark. There was no light, only terror. 'Those men's faces will haunt us for the rest of our lives,' Tess whispered.

'Don't I know it,' replied the doctor.

They were about to leave when Elsie asked, 'Excuse me, Doctor, why are there only American nurses here? What about our Filipina nurses? They are coming with us, are they not?'

It took a moment for the doctor to reply. 'The order we received was very specific. It said American nurses only.'

All colour drained from the chief nurse's face. 'You're leaving the nurses to the enemy? May I point out that they are women? What do you think the Japanese will do to them? What, there's no space on Corregidor for a dozen Filipina nurses?'

Kate nodded. 'These women have worked alongside us for months, without sleep, without food, tirelessly and selflessly.'

'Unfortunately, it's not up to me.'

Elsie stood up tall. Although only five foot four, she radiated authority. 'It's up to all of us. You will telegraph the authorities and tell them all the nurses are going or none at all. Do you agree, girls?'

Everyone shouted in agreement.

'I'll see what I can do,' the doctor muttered, looking defeated and spent.

Rose couldn't help but feel sorry for him. Whatever he decided, he would carry the weight of his decision on his shoulders like a giant boulder for the rest of his life and, judging by the expression on his face, he knew it only too well.

For the rest of the day, the nurses worked in silence, their eyes to the floor because they couldn't bear to see their patients' eager faces. Even the good news that the Filipina nurses could join them on their retreat to Corregidor did nothing to disperse the dark cloud that seemed to have descended on the jungle hospital. They changed the men's dressings, prepared them for surgery, fed them, listened to their laughter and pretended to smile, knowing that tomorrow no one would come when the patients called, no one would bring them food to eat or water to drink. And eventually, the Japanese would be there. They would march through the hospital, destroying everything in their path.

In the afternoon, the nurses were told to pack their belongings. Rose sat on her bed and watched as the others threw their clothes, diaries and shoes inside their rucksacks, chatting nervously. Kate stood close to her with a pair of stockings in her hands.

'You should start packing. We won't have much time. They gave us half an hour.'

Rose shook her head. Kate dropped the stockings on the floor and perched on the bed next to her. 'I know that look on your face. What are you thinking?'

'I can't go without him. I can't leave him behind.'

Kate took her hand. 'I understand how you feel. I know it's hard. But he broke your heart. He lied to you. If you don't come, you'll be throwing your life away and for what?'

'Didn't you tell me not to believe a word Anne said?'

Kate shrugged. 'I know I said that. But what if she was telling the truth? You need to put yourself first, to think about your safety.'

Rose wiped tears from her eyes with the back of her hand. 'Even if Anne was telling the truth, even if I never had a future with him and it's all been a lie, it doesn't matter. If I leave him to a certain death and run to safety, I will never be able to live with myself.'

'But what are you going to do? What choice do you have? They are coming here, Rose. Any minute now, the enemy soldiers are coming here.' She took Rose's hands in hers and looked at her imploringly. 'Even if Anne lied, he'd want you to go. He'd want you to save yourself.'

Rose didn't know what she was going to do. All she knew without a doubt in her heart was that she could never leave without him. She could never turn her back on him because she loved him.

After the allocated packing time was up and the nurses returned to the hospital, Rose found Dr Dunham in his little office, bent over his papers. When he heard her come in, he looked up and smiled. 'What can I do for you, Nurse Williams?'

She hesitated. 'Remember a few weeks ago you told me my kind heart would be my ruin one day?'

'I remember.'

'Well, my kind heart does not permit me to go. I have decided to stay.'

For a moment, the doctor watched Rose in silence. Finally, he said, 'You know it's not up to you. You are a military nurse and can't disobey the direct order of your superiors.'

'My superiors would have to come down here and carry me against my will. Something tells me they won't. They are quite comfortable behind their desks in the safety of their offices on US soil, away from it all.'

The doctor sighed. 'It's hard for all of us. We have given these men so much of ourselves, abandoning them to the enemy is going to break us. But there comes a time when we have to think of ourselves and our safety. Trust me, on Corregidor there will be wounded men who are going to need us. We can still help *them*.'

Rose squared her shoulders and lifted her head. 'I'm sorry, Doctor. I can't come with you.'

'I don't think you understand what is going to happen after we leave. The Japanese, with their tanks and artillery, will comb through this area. What do you think they will do to an American nurse standing in front of them? At best, you will end up in one of their POW camps. At worst ...' He stopped talking as if he couldn't quite put the horror into words.

'I know, sir. And I'm ready.'

'Does it have anything to do with the young man in ward three you keep running to every chance you get?' She felt herself blushing. He smiled and said, 'Are you romantically involved with one of your patients, Nurse Williams?'

'Yes, sir. And I'm not going without him.'

The doctor shook his head. 'My orders are clear. I am not allowed to leave a nurse behind.'

'You are going to have to because if he stays, I stay.'

'And nothing I say will change your mind?'

She shook her head. 'No, sir.'

'Well, then, you are just going to have to bring him with you.'

At first, she thought she had misheard. She couldn't believe what she was hearing. 'Did you just say I could bring him with us?'

'Like you said, our superiors are safe in their offices on US soil. They can't see what is happening on the ground. They can't even imagine what we are going through. Bring your man. I wish we could bring them all.'

Rose grabbed the doctor's hand and shook it. 'Thank you, Doctor! Thank you for being so kind.'

'You are welcome. And who knows, perhaps if we bring him, the knowledge that I left my patients behind will be a little easier to live with. Not by much. A little bit.'

She wanted to hug the doctor, to dance across the small room with him in her arms, to kiss him on both cheeks. What she did instead was shout out another *thank you* and run out of his office to find David.

'Wait, Nurse Williams,' she heard as she was about to dash through the door. 'Don't tell your patient yet. Don't tell anyone because if word gets out, everyone will want to come. We'll have a mutiny on our hands. We'll never be able to leave. Just have him ready at a moment's notice.'

'Yes, sir!' She flew back to the ward as if she had grown wings and they were carrying her above ground, above war, above pain and loss and sadness. On these wings she would take David to safety. She would not lose him again.

In the morning, as Rose walked through the wards, she noticed the patients were unusually silent, as if they knew something out of the ordinary was happening. It seemed to Rose that they were screaming at her with reproach and resignation. She felt her cheeks grow hot, felt her hands shake, as if she was personally responsible, as if it was her who had brought war and death to the Philippines. These men trusted her to do what was best for them. And she was about to betray them.

A patient smiled at her and said, 'You're leaving, Nurse.'

For a moment, Rose couldn't speak. 'How did you know?'

'People talk. But don't worry. We understand. You girls can't stay here any longer. But we are men. We can face anything.'

'I'm sorry,' she whispered.

'Don't be sorry. You've done so much for us. I will be forever grateful. Promise me to keep yourself safe.' Through her tears, she smiled. The man took a golden ring off his finger and placed it in her hands. 'I want you to have this ring.'

'No,' she said, pushing it back to him. 'I couldn't.'

'Take it and if you ever make it out of here alive, if you ever make it back home, give it to my mother. I want her to have something that belonged to me.'

'I will,' she whispered, staring into the man's face, trying to read the truth in his eyes. Did he think he was about to die? Did he know he would never see home again? The smile on his face, the cheerful demeanour, was it all an act?

By the river, as she washed the soiled linen, Rose touched the ring inside her pocket and cried. She looked at the churning water in front of her and saw the men's faces, the silent knowledge in their eyes, and the forgiveness. It was war. They didn't hold it against her. But she held it against herself that she couldn't save them all. Dr Dunham was right. The helplessness she felt here on war-torn Bataan was like nothing she had ever experienced before.

The shelling seemed so close, it felt like the Japanese were right there, on the other side of the river or perhaps in the jungle behind her. She heard a voice calling her name and turned around. Hiroshi was walking towards her, waving and grinning. 'I was looking for you,' he said. 'I didn't want you to leave without saying goodbye.'

Rose couldn't meet his eye. 'I should have told you we were going.'

'Don't worry. I will be fine. They are my people. Nothing bad will happen to me. I will tell them to be kind to the men.'

Grateful, Rose touched his hand. 'You think they'll listen?'

Hiroshi shrugged. 'I don't know. The Japanese are honourable and just. But it's war.' He hesitated. 'I wanted to thank you. For everything.'

'No, thank *you*. For all the buckets of water you carried for me. For helping me with the patients.'

'Take care of yourself. And remember, the world can still be a good place. There is magic everywhere you look.'

And then he was gone, leaving Rose alone with her thoughts, while the river rustled by her feet and the bullets whizzed nearby.

Rose packed what little belongings she had. A spare uniform, her helmet, the deadly poison in her hair, her precious ukulele. She only had space for one book and was forced to leave the rest behind, reluctantly. What little medicine they had fitted in the doctor's small rucksack. They were hoping they would be able to replenish their supplies on Corregidor. But most of all, they were hoping there would be something to eat. 'I would kill for a morsel of meat, anything, even if it's a lizard,' whispered Kate. Rose nodded, even though she was too nervous to think of food.

'This is it, nurses,' said Elsie. 'You have fifteen minutes.'

The Filipina nurses were sobbing with their arms around each other because they couldn't bear what they were about to do – retreat to safety while their patients perished. Little did they know, they would have been left to the enemy too, if it wasn't for Elsie, who refused to go without them, and Dr Dunham, who had the courage to stand up to his superiors.

Rose had fifteen minutes to explain everything to David and help him get ready. She walked briskly through the ward, nodding to the patients who called her name, ignoring the outstretched arms, the imploring mouths. She could already see him, sitting on his mattress facing away from her, an open book in his lap. Her breath caught at the sight of him, his broad shoulders, his straight back, his dark hair curling just above the collar. The war had painted everything around her grey, as if she could no longer see colour. But David remained vivid, a spark of joy in her otherwise gloomy existence. She was about to call him but decided against it. There were maybe twenty steps still separating them.

And then she heard it. The unmistakeable sound of planes, the dreaded whistling noise of bombs being released, the explosions. They were no longer distant, across the island somewhere. The Japanese were bombing the hospital.

Rose screamed his name, again and again. She could barely hear herself over the shelling but David turned around and their eyes met. His mouth opened, he was saying something to her but she couldn't make out the words. 'David,' she whispered.

Around them, people were shouting. 'The hospital. They hit the hospital.'

And another voice. 'Don't they see the Red Cross insignia on our tents?'

David was on his feet, running to her, shouting something. Suddenly, all the voices faded away and she could hear nothing but the ringing in her ears and the explosions, until they were gone too and there was nothing left.

When Rose opened her eyes, she could no longer hear the sound of war. 'David,' she whispered, her gaze searching for him. All she could see was the emerald green of the jungle and the dark blue of the sky over her head. The sun was setting and the trees in the distance were sparkling. Rose felt like she was bathing in sweat. Her vision was blurry and her throat dry. She would give anything for a sip of water. But first, she had to find David.

Dr Dunham's face appeared in front of her. He looked grey and pale in the waning light. His eyes were worried.

'Where am I?' she croaked.

'You are in the jungle. You have a nasty cut on your forehead and a twisted ankle but we patched you up. You needed some stitches. You were—'

She interrupted him. 'And David? Is he here?' She sat up and looked around. She could see a group of nurses on the grass nearby. There was no sign of him.

'David?' asked the doctor.

'You said he could come with us, you said …' Her eyes filled with tears. She knew by the expression on the doctor's face that David wasn't with them.

'I'm sorry, honey. It was chaos at the hospital when the enemy attacked. We had to leave immediately.'

'We didn't stay to help the wounded in the attack?'

'The Japanese were at the hospital. We were lucky to get away with our lives.'

She cried, her face in her hands, her shoulders shaking. 'You promised you would take him with us. You told me … You said he could come.'

The doctor looked lost for words. 'I know, honey, but the enemy … We are lucky not to have lost a single nurse. It's a miracle we are all here, safely.'

She was no longer listening. She was on her feet, limping through the jungle on her one good leg, not knowing where she was going or where the hospital was. All she knew was that she couldn't stay still, that she had to keep moving until she found David.

In a few long strides, the doctor was by her side. He caught her by the arm. 'We have to stay put. The truck will be here any minute. It will take us to the harbour, where we'll get on a boat to Corregidor.'

'I told you. I'm not going without David.' She pulled her arm away, suddenly angry at the doctor, as if everything was his fault.

'You can't go back there. It's too late. The Japanese …'

Determined to get away from him, she continued to hobble in a random direction. 'I don't care. I can't leave him behind, not again. I'm going back.'

'You can't. The enemy …' He held her tight, not letting her move. 'It's too late.'

She fell to her knees, sobbing. 'What will they do to him? What will the Japanese do to David?' she whispered.

The doctor didn't reply and all she could hear was the jungle weeping in the breeze.

Somewhere nearby, a battle was underway. Rose could hear soldiers calling out to one another in the night and the never-ceasing roar of the artillery. Occasionally, triumphant Japanese voices shouted '*Banzai*!' as shells burst overhead. Dynamite explosions filled the air as US troops demolished weapons, vehicles and ammunition dumps so they wouldn't fall into enemy hands.

American and Filipino troops meandered past with their weapons behind their backs, begging the nurses for food. The women looked away, their cheeks flushed with embarrassment because they couldn't bear to witness their army's defeat, and because they didn't have a morsel to give to the poor souls ravaged by war. 'It breaks my heart,' said Kate. 'Seeing them like this, knowing they will be prisoners of the Japanese tomorrow.'

Rose didn't reply. She couldn't bear thinking about the enemy in their jungle hospital on Bataan, of David standing in front of them with his head held high, while Japanese machine guns were pointed at him.

The truck never turned up but the enemy did, bombing the jungle around the nurses. Rose remained on her stretcher, covering her head with her hands in terror, crying silently, barely breathing. The night was bright as day and in the morning, as the largest blast yet shook the earth, the doctor told two dozen shell-shocked and exhausted nurses under his charge that they would have to walk to the harbour.

The nurses and the doctor took turns carrying Rose's stretcher through the jungle. Kate and Tess were by her side, holding her hand, asking if she needed anything, if she was thirsty, if she was hungry.

'I'm not thirsty. I'm not hungry. I need to find David.' She repeated it time and time again, like a broken record that everyone ignored as they smiled and asked if her headache was better, if her leg still hurt, if she wanted to sleep for a bit. Like it even mattered.

Filipino refugees were hurrying past, carrying what little belongings they had, riding their carabao carts through impassable roads, tearing their way through the jungle, away from the terrifying enemy, in their elusive search for safety. Rose wondered if they had anywhere to go. Was there anywhere left to run? She drifted in and out of sleep, while snippets of conversation reached her.

'Any minute now, our troops are going to surrender.'

'They say it's the biggest US defeat in history.'

'Makes one feel so helpless. All this hard work and sacrifice, for nothing.'

Next time Rose opened her eyes, she saw the Mariveles Harbour docks and the ocean touching the pure white sand. Across the harbour was the island of Corregidor, where once upon a time David had played chess with her and spoke of his past, his hopes and dreams, and of their future together. As she cried for her lost love, the Japanese were bombing Bataan and the Allied forces on Corregidor responded in kind, targeting Cabcaben where the enemy had made a landing. As they waited for a boat to take them across to safety, it seemed to Rose that the world was ending and the day of the apocalypse was finally upon them. When one of the nurses spoke to her, she couldn't hear a word she was saying because her ears were ringing from the explosions.

A US officer came to see them. 'No more crossings today,' he told them. 'The Japanese are bombing the wharf. It makes it dangerous for the boats to dock.'

'We are needed on the island. I'm a doctor and these are my nurses,' said Dr Dunham.

'How many are you?' asked the officer.

'Twenty-five.'

'I'll take you across.'

The sloop bobbed up and down on the waves and it seemed to Rose that any second now it would overturn and throw them in the water. Above them, the horizon lit up in bright colours.

'We are still hoping, aren't we?' said Kate. 'Every few minutes I look at the sea and hope to see a convoy of US Army ships coming to rescue us. I hope to see US planes in the sky.'

'No one is coming, Kate. We are on our own,' said Tess.

Dr Dunham said, 'Don't worry, girls. We'll be safe on Corregidor. The Japanese can't blast through all that rock.'

Elsie said, 'This is the last resort. There is nowhere left to go. When they come to Corregidor, what are we going to do?'

The doctor said, 'If they come, we are lost. No point worrying about it now. Try to get some rest. We've had a rough couple of days.'

'A rough five months, you mean,' said Kate.

Rose was not looking at the water that was shimmering like silver beads in the setting sun. She was not scanning the horizon, searching for reinforcements. With tears in her eyes, she was watching the land as it disappeared from sight, the land that had become her home, where she had laughed and loved and hoped for the best. Somewhere deep in the jungle was the hospital where they had all left a part of their hearts. And somewhere inside that hospital was David. What was going to become of him?

# Part III

# Corregidor Island

# Chapter 12

## April 1942

Rose opened her eyes and blinked, searching for a light, a blot of colour, anything to tell her she was still alive. But there was nothing. In the jungle, stars like diamonds had shimmered in the sky. It had never been dark on Bataan. But here, inside the grey concrete shell of Malinta Tunnel on Corregidor, underneath three hundred feet of rock and soil, darkness surrounded her, like a heavy veil, like death. The bombproof shelter that housed twelve thousand people – seven thousand combat troops, two thousand civilians and three thousand military administrators and medical personnel – had been built in the 1920s using mining equipment and convict labour for this particular reason, to protect Rose and others from an attack. The thought of the occupants' safety came before comfort and so the lights worked only sporadically. Occasionally, like now, the whole place became a dungeon without a glimmer of hope.

Suddenly, torchlight broke through the perfect darkness. Rose winced and closed her eyes. A moment later, she felt a strong hand shaking her. 'Get up, Nurse. It's six in the morning. What do you think this is, a resort? Are you here to rest or work?'

Rose couldn't see beyond the blinding light. The voice sounded angry and impatient. The hands grabbing her felt strong. She tried to wriggle away and couldn't. 'Work?' she mumbled. She felt disoriented and lost. Her eyes ached. Her head was heavy.

The torchlight trembled, throwing shadows on the walls. 'The Japanese bomb the island from dawn to dusk, all day, every day. No time to sit around. We have patients to tend to.'

Rose heard Kate's voice. 'She can't go to work. She was injured.'

'Who wasn't? Yet, here we are, doing what we can.'

'If she stands on her bad leg all day, it will never heal.'

Rose felt a wave of warmth towards her friend. She tried to sit up but couldn't. The torchlight was no longer in her face. A round silhouette dressed in white was hovering over her like a ghoul. 'You two have to come with me to the operating theatre this instant,' said the silhouette. 'We're short of nurses today. They're all getting sick.'

'What about breakfast?' demanded Kate.

'I'm afraid you slept through breakfast. Next time, wake up earlier.'

Angry footsteps were heard, walking away from the girls. The light faded. Rose felt her mattress sag and knew Kate had sat down next to her. She reached out her hand and touched her friend's arm. 'Who was that?' Rose whispered.

'That was the chief nurse of Corregidor. She makes Elsie look like a fluffy, cuddly puppy.'

An explosion was heard outside. The walls shook. 'I don't like it here, Kate,' Rose whispered. 'I don't like closed spaces.'

'Me neither. Once, when I was twelve, my brother and I were home alone. We decided to play hide and seek. I hid in our tiny cellar and the door jammed. I couldn't get out and my brother couldn't get in. He banged and banged on the door but it didn't budge. I had to stay there all day until our parents came home. A whole day without food or water. I never felt so scared, not before or since.'

'Not even during the bombing?'

'Well, yes, the bombing is scary. But that feeling, of being trapped and unable to get out, I've never experienced anything like it. I feel a little bit like that now, in the tunnels. I feel like I can't breathe. Like there's no oxygen here. Why is it so hard to breathe?'

'Every time the Japanese bomb the tunnels, the dust and the dirt become airborne. The ventilation system can't cope.' Rose rubbed her eyes. 'I can't get up, Kate. I don't care what the chief nurse says. I can't go to work today.' It was unthinkable, to have to leave her bed, to put on a uniform and smile for her patients, to plaster a mask over her face and pretend she was whole when she felt so broken, to give comfort to others when there was no comfort inside her.

Kate said, 'Don't go to work. I'll talk to Elsie and she'll talk to the chief nurse. I'll try to find you something to eat. Just sleep and get better.'

For the next six days, that was exactly what Rose did, while Kate, Tess and Dr Dunham took turns to bring her food, to sit by her side, to read to her by the light of a torch. Their voices drifted in and out as Rose remained on her mattress with her eyes closed.

One morning, she opened her eyes and saw Dr Dunham in a chair by her bed. The lights must have been fixed because she could see his face, his skin looking unhealthy and grey, his fingers on the pages of a book. He was blurry in front of her and she realised she had been crying. She wiped her eyes with the back of her hand. 'Dr Dunham,' she said.

'Call me Jack.'

'Jack … What book are you reading?'

'*The Great Gatsby*. I found it in your rucksack.'

*Rose and David sat by the river, their arms touching. They couldn't hear the artillery, only birds chirping with joy. She read to him from his favourite book because the doctor said it might trigger a memory. He listened with his eyes closed, a content smile on his face.*

*After each passage, she would look up and ask, 'Do you remember now?'*

*He would laugh and shake his head.*

*'How about now?'*

*'No, not yet. Keep reading.'*

*'You told me once it was your favourite part. How about now?'*

*He shook his head again, his eyes on her as she continued to read, the expression on his face making her heart hurt.*

'Please, stop,' she whispered to the doctor as he turned the page and adjusted his glasses. 'No more reading.'

Rose would have stayed in bed indefinitely, refusing to eat, thinking of David, blaming herself. But she couldn't. Her body was healing, even as her soul remained fractured and torn, and after a week, she had no choice but to return to work. *It's not my fault*, she told herself as she dressed and splashed her face with water. *It's not my fault*, as she made her way down the dim corridor towards the hospital wards. *It's not my fault.* And yet, here she was, safely hidden away under a tonne of concrete, while David was lost. She couldn't bear to imagine what had become of him once the enemy arrived at the hospital, and yet it was all she could think about.

The hospital lay in a tunnel branch the length of a football field, illuminated by blue mercury vapour lights. One end of the tunnel opened to the outside, wide enough for two ambulances to make their way in. Tram tracks ran from the dock through the tunnel, carrying personnel and supplies. The ground generators provided electricity, a cold-storage depot preserved food and a chlorination plant ensured safe drinking water. Searchlights were mounted on poles to provide illumination in operating rooms. As Rose walked through the tunnel, she took it all in, amazed. The tunnels were a small city that seemed to have everything, even a general store. It was clear they had been designed for a large group of people to live underground for a long period of time. The thought made Rose shudder. She couldn't imagine staying here for another day, let alone a week or a month or a year. Would they have to remain here until the war was over? And how long would it take?

In the operating room, she met the woman behind the torch-light, the chief nurse called Fran. She looked like someone's kindly grandmother, round and grey, but she barked instructions at her team of nurses with a ferocity of someone twice her size. After two hours on the ward, Rose realised there was no pleasing Fran, no matter how hard she tried. But the wounded lifted their hurting eyes to her and thanked her with trembling lips every time she brought them a plate of food, a glass of water or a morphine shot. And there were many wounded, men with their limbs blown off, burns on their bodies, concussion and bullet wounds, just like before.

On her first morning, Fran assigned Rose to look after a young American officer called Brian, who was extremely sick with cerebro-spinal fever. Rose put up black-out curtains around him because of his severe intolerance to light. He had a fever and vomited every few minutes. His neck and back muscles contracted spasmodically so that his body was arched like a bow when lying on his back. Rose talked to him in whispers because loud noises caused him headaches. She told him about the war and the enemy on their heels but his desperate eyes let her know that he had seen it all firsthand. She told him that victory was coming, that it was only a matter of time, but he looked like he didn't believe her.

At lunch, Rose and the other nurses ate their food in the canteen, too tired to talk. Navy officers in shorts, off-duty army officers in shirtsleeves, enlisted men in jeans and convalescents in white pyjamas gathered around tables, listened to the radio, played cards and exchanged rumours.

'What is this meat? It tastes like chicken.' Rose poked her food with a fork.

'I think it *is* chicken.' Kate smiled, having already eaten all her lunch. 'And if it's not, does it matter?'

Tess took a tiny bit of jam and brought it to her mouth. 'For the first time since we left Manila, I'm not missing the cans of food I was forced to leave behind.'

The nurses couldn't believe their eyes when they saw butter and eggs and even bread. It was amazing what a difference a full stomach could make. The girls chatted happily, like they didn't have a care in the world, when suddenly, the walls shook and the earth moved under their feet. A deafening sound was heard. It felt like the tunnel walls were collapsing. A moment later, all was quiet again, and Rose could have pretended she'd imagined it if it wasn't for the acrid smoke and a cloud of dust in the air that made it hard to breathe. All she could smell was sweat, blood, disinfectants, anaesthetics and decomposing flesh.

Each raid sent hundreds of wounded to the hospital that was already full to the brim. They arrived on stretchers and ambulances at the entrance of the tunnel, where nurses met them for triage. Fifteen hundred patients filled the wards meant for five hundred. It took hours to clean them, apply temporary dressings and give them food and drink. Many were shocked through loss of blood and required plasma intravenous drip. Rose compiled operating lists and wondered how the surgeons would manage so many operations without passing out from exhaustion. Hour after long hour she toiled, ready to pass out from exhaustion herself, too tired to think, to fret about the past or worry about the future, and she felt grateful for it.

Only when she lay down on her mattress after eighteen hours on her feet, before she fell into the black oblivion, would she whisper his name to herself. *David.*

In the tunnels, it was impossible to tell if it was day or night. Not that it mattered, because the wounded arrived around the clock and required constant care. Rose was helping a patient who had just had a lumbar puncture, trying to get him comfortable, which was proving to be an impossible feat.

'Please, Nurse, don't move me. I don't want to be touched,' he cried.

'I have to move you every two hours. Doctor's orders. If I don't, you will develop bed sores. Now, if you do what the doctor said, I will feed you.'

He smiled and his eyes sparkled. 'What's for lunch? Some pancakes, perhaps, my favourite? Or a steak? I haven't had a good steak in months.'

She smiled back and didn't reply, preparing a Ryles tube that would be inserted into his stomach for feeding. This man reminded her a little of David. Something in his eyes and the way he looked at her. He begged her to stay with him, to talk to him, to read to him. But she couldn't because hundreds of others just like him needed something from her.

When Rose turned her back to the patient, Tess and Kate waved her over. 'Are you busy? Would you like to go outside and look at the sunset?' said Tess.

'Is it safe?' asked Rose. She could hear the sound of distant shelling.

'We are on an island that is bombed constantly. Of course it's not safe. Let's go anyway. If we don't, I will lose my mind.'

They stepped out of the darkness into the light. The sea sparkled like crystal in front of them and the air was still. There was no sign of Japanese bombers and no explosions shook the island. Instead, the palms bent their heads in the breeze and the waves whispered of joy and peace. With relief, Rose took off the gauze mask she had been wearing to protect herself from the dust and grime of the tunnels. The mask didn't seem to make much difference but she wore it anyway because she was told to. She could breathe again, her lungs filling with oxygen, her chest expanding, her eyes aching from the brightness of it all. After so many days hidden underground, she felt light-headed and giddy. 'Thank

God,' she said. 'I felt like a rat trapped in that tunnel, with no air or light.' The sun was going down and the sky above them lit up with a kaleidoscope of pink and purple, as if nature itself was celebrating something, as if there was no war, only joy.

'When all this is behind us, when I'm old and grey, I will remember the sunsets,' said Kate.

'What about the work and the blood and the fighting?' asked Rose.

'Yes, but the sunsets most of all. They are spectacular, don't you think?'

Fran appeared outside, her hands on her hips making her look like an angry kettle. 'Every time you take a break, a patient needs you. Yes, the sunset is beautiful. But watching it could cost someone's life. Is it really worth it?'

'We were just getting some air, that's all. It's impossible to breathe inside the tunnels. We've been on our feet for twenty hours.' Rose didn't like the pleading tone in her voice. She didn't have to explain herself to this woman. They were entitled to a break.

'I've been on my feet for forty-eight hours,' said Fran. 'Come along now. The sunset will be here tomorrow. The men might not.'

Rose felt angry at the chief nurse for interrupting the first few minutes they had had to themselves in days. She wanted to remain outside, where she could breathe without choking, where she didn't feel like she was being buried alive. But, as they were walking back inside, she heard the engines. Minutes later, bombs fell on the spot where the girls had been sitting, admiring the sun, the sea and the peaceful sky.

During Rose's time at Eastern Maine General Hospital, it was common practice to protect the patients from the various facts of their conditions. Nurses were told not to divulge any information in order not to upset anyone. On Corregidor, the opposite was true. With so many wounded to care for, it was impossible for the nurses and the doctors to keep track of it all, and so they gave each patient a detailed list of their treatment, diet and medication and asked them to remind the overworked staff what needed to be done and when. Elsie called it patient participation.

The bombing was ever-present, through long days and even longer nights, and soon Rose forgot what silence sounded like. As she rested on the concrete floor for a couple of hours at a time, as she moved through the wards in a blur of exhaustion, as she changed dressings and administered morphine shots, as she undressed the men and cleaned their wounded limbs, the earth beneath her feet trembled, the walls around her shook, the dust and dirt rose and never settled.

Days and nights blurred together and became one. Did the sun rise outside? Was the sea still blue? Did the birds still sing? It was impossible to tell. Here, in the dark tunnels, Rose experienced a strange feeling of detachment. All she heard all day were ambulance sirens wailing, amputated limbs falling into buckets, the dreaded sound of the saw as it severed the bone and thousands of wounded crying for help, while war raged outside, threatening to tear her apart. She was a prisoner inside these walls, without air or light or hope, and it felt like it had always been this way. The other life, her happy childhood, the first carefree weeks in the Philippines, before the war, the moments she had spent with David, even her time on Bataan, felt like it had happened to someone else, like it had been a dream that quickly disappeared from memory at the first sign of dawn. The child growing up in Brownville, twirling in a ballet studio, her arms raised above her head with grace, running home from school to help her mother, baking a cake for her mother's birthday, a young woman walking through the streets of Manila hand in hand with a dashing lieutenant, falling madly in love, none of it had been real. But this was real – pain, tears, disease, death and the terrifying sound of shelling outside.

One day in the last week of April, a shell hit close to the entrance of the tunnel where a dozen men gathered for air. Rose was doing her rounds with Dr Dunham when they heard the explosions and the shouting. Exchanging a panicked look, they ran towards the commotion. Rose was still recovering and couldn't move as fast as the doctor. He was fifty paces ahead of her, almost at the gate, when more bombing was heard. She cried out to the doctor to stop but he didn't seem to hear, so intent was he on getting to the men, helping them to safety, doing what he was born to do – save lives. Moments later, another shell hit. As if in a bad dream, Rose watched the doctor go down. The cries for help stopped.

An inferno was unfolding in the tunnels that hid them, like a terrifying dream from which there was no escape. Through smoke and dust, Rose glimpsed the men lying behind the gate without movement, their lifeless eyes staring into space, chunks of flesh and bone scattered on the ground. She wanted to scream in horror. The other nurses were running, opening the gate, reaching for the men, while Rose bent over Dr Dunham and whispered his name, shaking him, checking his pulse, listening to his chest and repeating a prayer.

The doctor was silent. His eyes were closed but she could tell he was still alive because his heart was pounding under her fingertips.

She got an orderly to help her carry the doctor to a bed. When he was settled, she placed a wet cloth on his forehead, bandaged his injured hand and sat next to him. 'Dr Dunham, can you hear me?'

He groaned. 'I thought we agreed you were going to call me Jack.'

She could feel the tension leave her body. 'Jack,' she said.

'What happened to me?' His voice was hoarse. His skin looked yellow in the dim light of the tunnels. His eyes were frightened.

In all the months she had known him, Rose had never seen him afraid, not when the bombs fell on Bataan while he operated, nor even when they ran through the jungle on foot for many hours with the enemy in pursuit. She took his hand. 'You don't remember? An explosive wave hit you because you didn't listen to me. You always put your patients first, Dr Dunham, Jack. You were in such a rush to save lives, you risked your own unnecessarily.' She wagged her finger at him and smiled.

'That's what we doctors do.'

'You are lucky to be alive. Much use you would be to your patients if you died.'

She left him on the mattress and joined the other nurses who were trying to help the wounded. There weren't many survivors, and those who were still alive were in a sorry state. Their charred, groaning, screaming bodies continued to arrive on stretchers and Rose did the best she could to clean them, bandage them and take their pain away. She gave injection after injection of morphine, and after a dozen shots she bent over to give another one only to find a headless body on the stretcher. She screamed with horror and turned to the orderly, her heart beating fast. The man shook his head and spread his arms wide. 'I'm sorry, Nurse. It's dark out there. We feel for the bodies and just roll them onto stretchers.'

Another soldier was brought in, his leg hanging by shreds of skin from his thigh. Rose went to cut his clothes. The soldier tried to stop her. 'Please, don't. Got no underpants on,' he murmured, groaning.

'We're nurses. We've seen it all. All we care about is saving your life.'

'Can you save my leg?'

Rose knew the limb was unsalvageable. But she nodded and smiled. 'I will get a surgeon. You'll be as good as new, just you wait.'

'Thank you,' the man whispered, looking relieved.

When Rose returned with a surgeon, the soldier was dead.

Her heart aching, she wanted to curl into a ball in a corner and not move and not see the horror that unfolded before her. She wanted to close her eyes and cry. But she couldn't stop because these men depended on her, and so she cried as she moved among them, a whirlwind of activity, tightening the tourniquets and treating shock, undressing and cleaning and bandaging and administering morphine. She cried with sorrow for every one of these soldiers, for all the suffering she had witnessed in the Philippines, for the most beautiful place she had ever seen that was being torn apart by war. She had been a nurse for a long time. For the last few months, she had been a military nurse in a war zone. She had seen suffering before. But that night, she felt something inside her soul crack.

When Rose managed to get a short break, she found Kate crouched on the floor, her face in her hands. Rose sat next to her and placed her arm around her. 'Honey, what's wrong? What happened?'

Kate's shoulders sagged. Every now and then, a tiny sob escaped her. She sounded like a small animal in pain. She didn't look up when she said, 'I don't think I can take it anymore. No matter what I do for these men, they die.'

Rose took her friend's hand. 'I know it's hard. You're exhausted. You've just worked for thirty-six hours without a break. And when was the last time you had something to eat?'

'It's not that. It's the fear and the helplessness. How can we go on when everything out there is trying to break us?'

'You used to swim with sharks in the Hudson River. Where is that girl now?'

'There are no sharks in the Hudson River,' whispered Kate.

'You are the strongest person I've ever known.'

'We live underground, like we are already dead. We are struggling every minute of every day. What's the point?'

'The point is that we are still here. We're still alive. We're not giving up. As long as our patients need us, as long as we can make a difference, we have to find a way to go on.'

'I don't know how to do that, Rose. How do we do that?'

*I wish I knew, Kate*, Rose wanted to say. *I wish I knew.* 'We take it one step at a time. Let's get up and find you something to eat. Simon in bed seven was asking for you. He needs his dressing changed. Let's go and do that. Then we'll try to get some sleep. We won't think about the future. We will focus on the little steps, all right?'

Kate blinked. She was no longer crying. 'All right. Little steps.'

'We'll get through this together.'

'There is nowhere left to go, Rose,' whispered Kate. 'This is it. We have nowhere else left to hide. And they're not leaving us alone.'

Rose helped Kate to her feet, all the while whispering that everything was going to be all right. Together they tended to their patients. Soon there were twelve blood transfusions and twenty blood plasmas on the go, and Elsie told them personally what a great job they were doing. Afterwards, Rose took Kate to the mess and found her some food and a hot cup of tea. She spoke to Kate about her brother and all the things they were going to do after the war but all she could hear inside her head was her friend's terrified voice as she repeated, 'They're not leaving us alone and we have nowhere else to go.'

# Chapter 13

## April–May 1942

On 29 April, the Japanese celebrated Emperor Hirohito's birthday with the heaviest bombardment yet to hit the island of Corregidor. Bombers from the air and artillery from Bataan and Cavite pounded the tunnels for twelve hours straight. Rose hid her fear deep inside and threw herself into work. She had a ward of shell shock cases under her care who kept shaking and gibbering, unable to get up or feed themselves. She spoon-fed them and chatted to them, cheerfully telling them all about herself and her life before the war. She couldn't relax for a moment, watching for the unexpected haemorrhage from the wounds, using all her senses to identify the early stages of gangrene.

The men were unpredictable. One moment they were perfectly charming, talking to her like they were at the Officers' Club with flutes of champagne in their hands. The next, they were lashing out and trying to hit her, as if in her face they could see all the horrors of war. Many hurled furniture around in a rage. Even as they threw chairs at her, Rose couldn't help but feel sorry for the boys. The strain and the fear had been too much for them. They had their whole lives ahead of them, and yet, their souls had been irrevocably fractured.

During her rounds, she checked on Dr Dunham as often as she could. His hands were badly burnt and he couldn't hold a glass or a spoon by himself. One morning, she fetched him a plate of fried eggs from the canteen and fed him, then brought a glass of water to his lips. After he took a few sips, he said, 'It's a strange thing about war. One never gets used to it but once it begins, it seems always to have been this way. I can hardly remember my life during peace. Can you?'

She shook her head. 'This war has changed us.' She remembered feeling disappointed a few months ago because she didn't have an evening gown to wear to a dance. And now here she was, her uniform black with dirt and blood, her eyes dark with exhaustion, without food, without sleep, almost without oxygen, and still she continued living as best as she could. But she wasn't the same person anymore. 'We see so much death around us, I'm surprised I am still alive. It seems like a miracle, don't you think?'

'It *is* a miracle. Who knows when our luck will run out.' He took a deep breath and put his burnt hand on Rose's arm. 'Will you write a letter for me? For my little girl? If something happens to me, I want her to know how much I loved her.'

'Nothing is going to happen to you. Not on my watch.'

An explosion shook the tunnel. Mud fell on the doctor's face. His eyes became sombre. 'No one knows what's in store for us. No one knows if we will ever see our loved ones again.'

The hospital had been alive with rumours, terrifying whispers of hunger, surrender, POW camps and death. Rose did her best to ignore them, to not think of the future and only live for the present. It was the only way to survive. But every now and then, in the middle of the night, the fear gripped her hard and she found it difficult to breathe. The ghosts of death and surrender were always at her heels. 'Of course, I'll write your letter for you,' she said.

My darling girl,

If by chance this letter finds you, I want you to know that we are safe and doing well. We still have food and a job to do. Many people depend on us, and as long as that is the case, I have a reason to get up in the morning.

As the enemy is closing in on us, I've been thinking long and hard about my life. Not certain what the future will bring, I've been reliving the past. I wanted to tell you that you have always been my greatest joy and the time I spent with you has been my happiest.

I hope you are well, wherever you are. My greatest regret in life is having missed so much of yours. God willing, we will meet again.

Love always,

Dad

'What a beautiful letter,' said Rose, tears in her eyes. 'How will you send it?'

'Haven't you heard? Nineteen nurses are getting evacuated by sea planes. I will ask one of them to post my letter from Australia.'

Rose tried not to show her astonishment. It felt like the tunnels had become their prison. There was no way out, not unless they could break through the Japanese encirclement, eluding the bombs and the artillery that never slept and was always waiting. To be rescued from the horrifying nightmare, to be safe, to not see death every moment of every day and night, to be able to breathe again, wouldn't it be wonderful? But to leave her patients behind like they had done on Bataan, to abandon them and run for safety, was unthinkable. Fortunately, or unfortunately, she had been spared this choice because she hadn't been offered a spot on one of the planes. 'How did they choose these nineteen nurses?'

'Elsie pulled their names out of a hat. When her name came up, she refused to go, giving up her spot to a pregnant girl.'

'That sounds like Elsie. She has a heart of gold, even if she doesn't always show it. Would you like me to write the address on the envelope for you?'

He was silent for a moment. 'I haven't seen my little girl since she was four. I don't know where she lives. But every couple of months, I send her a letter to the last address that I had for her. Hoping that by some miracle she will read them one day and know I'm thinking of her.'

'I'm sorry to hear that.'

'Don't be sorry. When the war is over, I will find her again. I will try to make things right.'

Another long night under the blinking blue lights, listening to the bombs exploding outside. The men on the ward were snoring, talking, laughing and screaming. One of the patients had had a heart attack the day before but, to Rose's delight, was recovering quickly. He was talking to himself, while walking up and down the ward, wheeling an oxygen cylinder behind him. 'I can't sleep,' he explained to Rose. 'I'm afraid if I close my eyes, I will never wake up.'

'You are safe here, in the tunnels,' said Rose.

'I'm not talking about *that*.' The patient pointed outside, where another explosion was heard. 'I'm talking about my ticker.' He placed his hand on his chest, while the oxygen cylinder squealed with every step he took.

Another patient shouted, 'Stop that racket immediately! People need to sleep. Have you no shame?'

Rose looked at her watch and then at the grouchy man, who turned on his side and placed a pillow over his head. 'You have twenty minutes to sleep, Lieutenant, and then I'm waking you up for your jabs,' she said.

The man grumbled unhappily, while the planes roared outside and the oxygen cylinder continued to screech.

In the morning, Rose sat down to breakfast, which consisted of a tablespoon of cold corned beef hash on a dirty plate. Gone were the days when they had eggs, bread and strawberry jam. She took a sip of her tea and broke into a cough. The tea was salty.

'Haven't you heard?' asked Kate. 'The bombs knocked out the water pump.'

'They are giving us sea water?'

'Mine is flavoured. It tastes like lemonade.' Kate smiled. 'I have some orange juice I'm saving for my patients. Want some?'

Rose took a sip of her salty tea. 'Keep it for the patients. They need it more than we do.'

'We are cut off from the outside world here. Soon we'll have nothing left. No water, no food. What will we do then?'

'We'll be fine,' said Rose, smiling. The smile came out sad, uncertain. Who was she trying to convince, Kate or herself? 'Some of the men go out fishing. They go out hunting. Sometimes we have fish and fresh meat.'

'When was the last time we had fresh meat? They would have to kill a hundred carabaos to feed twelve thousand people on Corregidor. Besides, if the Japanese come to the island, no one will be going out hunting. Rose, they don't even need to waste their explosives on us. This place might be impregnable but all they need to do is wait until we starve to death.'

Rose paled. She had never felt safe inside these tunnels, not with the bombs exploding and the walls collapsing in places. This new danger, of being starved by the Japanese, had never entered her mind, until now. She poked her corned beef with her fork. 'They will get the supplies in somehow, won't they?'

'We will have to surrender or die of hunger,' said Kate. Looking into her plate, not meeting Rose's gaze, her cheeks pink, she added, 'I have something to tell you. I've been offered a spot on one of the seaplanes.'

'Kate, that's fantastic! I'm happy for you.'

But Kate didn't look happy. 'I feel so guilty. How can I leave all of you behind? How can I leave my patients?'

Rose placed her hand on Kate's. 'Nonsense. You are leaving your patients with us. We will take good care of them. In Australia, you will be safe. You will have food and all the fresh air that you need. I wish I could go. I wouldn't give it a second thought.'

'You wouldn't?'

'Not for a moment,' Rose lied.

A group of nurses lined up by the harbour, waiting for the seaplanes to arrive. It was eerily quiet. No sign of enemy aircraft, no sound of battle, no bombs falling on the little island. It was as if the Japanese granted them a reprieve so that the nurses could leave. As Rose stood with her arms around Kate, she watched the skies and hoped the peace would last. She didn't trust the quiet before the storm.

'They are an hour late,' said Kate, trying to spot the seaplanes that would carry her and eighteen others to safety.

'They'll be here,' said Tess, wiping tears off her cheeks.

'They should have been here by now. The Japanese bomb the area relentlessly. Anything could have happened.' Kate's shoulders drooped. 'Perhaps it's for the best. It breaks my heart to leave you girls behind.'

Two small dots appeared in the distance and the girls watched as they grew larger, finally turning into the promised seaplanes.

'Look after my patients,' Kate said. 'Peter in ward two needs his dressing changed every two hours. And I've been bringing Felix my orange juice every morning. He looks forward to my visits.'

'We'll look after your patients. Promise to take care of yourself, all right?' said Tess.

Kate trembled in Rose's arms. 'It's a long way to Australia,' she muttered. 'Are we making a mistake? Are we better off in the tunnels?'

Rose kissed Kate on both cheeks. She tried to muster as much enthusiasm as she possibly could when she said, 'Are you making a mistake leaving for safety, while the rest of us will starve to death or surrender to the enemy? I don't think so.'

Leaning into Rose's shoulder, Kate burst into tears.

Rose said, 'I didn't say it to upset you. I said it to cheer you up. You are lucky, Kate.'

'What if I never see you again?'

'Nonsense. Of course, you will. In better times, we will see each other again. Remember what Elsie always says? Think of good things and good things will happen.'

Kate hiccupped and nodded. Her eyes and the tip of her nose were red.

Early morning sun reflected off the silver surface of the seaplanes, making them shine like a beacon of hope, a miracle in the midst of terror and death. As they glided to landing on the mineswept waters off Corregidor, the nurses cheered.

'Remember to write,' Rose shouted over the sound of the engines. She smiled for Kate's sake, even though her heart was breaking with fear for all of them, for those who were leaving and those who were staying behind. 'Write to my mother's address. That's where I'll go when all this is over.'

Kate nodded. Rose pushed a letter to her mother into Kate's hand. It would be the first communication she had received since war had come to the Philippines.

The doors of the planes opened and the crew appeared. Rose watched the brave Australian pilots who had volunteered to help the stranded people of the Philippines, risking their lives in the process. Like Rose, they were scanning the horizon for signs of enemy bombers.

Her chest aching, Rose watched Kate climb inside a small boat that would carry her across the ocean to board one of the planes. When the nurses were finally onboard, Rose waved with tears in her eyes. The engines came to life and the planes took off, whisking Kate and the others away from the horror of Corregidor towards freedom. Gradually, they turned into tiny dots in the sky, soon disappearing altogether, while Rose and Tess remained by the harbour, their eyes on the horizon. Not only did the seaplanes take their friend away, perhaps forever; they took away any chance of salvation. The enemy was at the gate and there was nowhere left to run.

Rose looked after Kate's patients. She changed Peter's dressing every two hours and brought Felix his orange juice, not just in the morning but at lunch and dinner too, until there was no more orange juice left. Her day felt empty without Kate. The wards grew quiet, despite the multitude of voices, despite the men reaching their arms to her, begging for help. There was no one to talk to because Kate was gone and Tess was no longer speaking, her eyes perpetually swimming in tears.

As Rose went about her day, she wondered where the seaplanes were. How long before they were out of danger? How long before they reached Australia? How long before Kate was safe? As she spoke to her patients and brought them food and tended to their needs, in her mind she saw two silver dots in the sky, fighting their way away from here.

Two days after the planes had left, Rose was cleaning and changing an unconscious man with a fractured skull, when a junior nurse said, 'You're wasting your time, Nurse Williams. He'll never make it.'

Rose's anger took her by surprise. Perhaps it was her helplessness. Hour after hour of hard work, of fighting against the tide of death, of staying up nights and giving these men all she had and more, and still she felt that it was not enough because the wounded continued to die. Her hands shaking, she called the nurse into the corridor and told her to never discuss the patients' chances in front of them. It was unprofessional and disrespectful. But most of all, it was insensitive.

'But he's unconscious. He can't hear us,' said the nurse, batting her long eyelashes, looking stunned.

'You don't know that. Imagine if he could. How terrible to be unable to speak, to be afraid for your life and not know what to expect, and then to hear such cruel words. You should be ashamed of yourself. The patients have feelings.' And so do we, the nurses who sacrifice everything for these men, Rose wanted to add.

The nurse apologised but Rose could barely hear her. She was close to tears, as if the patient was a member of her family. This place was getting to her, she realised. Death stretched its arm over the tunnels of Corregidor and nothing Rose did could stop it.

When they returned, the patient was dead.

Rose felt like she was on the verge of a breakdown. With no Kate to talk to, she went to see Dr Dunham.

At the sight of her, he smiled. 'Did you know that 1.8 million pounds of explosives hit Corregidor in the last five hours? One of the engineers told me,' he said.

'Shouldn't they be fixing the water system instead of counting the explosives?'

'They did. We have water again. Haven't you noticed?'

'No, I haven't. I've been so busy. I wish we had some food.' She fell quiet. She had nothing for him today, not even a spoon of rice. 'Tell me about your little girl.' She needed one moment away from death to remind herself she was still alive.

His face lit up. 'She is clever and beautiful. She looks like her mother but is like me in every other way. She wanted to be a doctor when she was little.'

'You must miss her so much.'

'She is always with me, for as long as my heart is beating. Would you like to see a picture of her?'

'More than anything.'

She found his rucksack under his bed and opened it for him. He fumbled inside, muttering to himself, wondering if the photograph had gone missing, saying it would break his heart because it was the only thing he had left to remind him of his daughter. Finally, he exclaimed, 'Ah, here it is.' And handed a small picture to Rose.

She recognised the man in the photograph immediately, even

though he was thinner, had more hair and the biggest smile on his face. His arm was draped around a little girl, perhaps four or five. The girl's eyes twinkled with joy. She was waving at the camera but looking at her father. 'That's us at the seaside in Boston,' Jack said. 'My little girl always loved the sea. I would buy her an ice cream and we would take our shoes off and race each other on the sand. And she would shout, "Wait for me, Daddy! I can't run, my ice cream is melting".'

As he spoke, his words reached Rose but she couldn't grasp their meaning. The image in front of her became blurry and she could no longer see the father and daughter as they laughed at the camera, anticipating another adventure together. With shock, she realised she was crying.

Jack stopped talking. He must have noticed her tears and her pale face. 'What's wrong? You look like you've seen a ghost.'

'I have to go,' she muttered, jumping to her feet, wiping her face.

She couldn't stay by his side any longer because she had seen this photograph before. It was the same photograph she had carried with her for many years.

# Chapter 14

## May 1942

As Rose walked from patient to patient, from ward to ward, she swayed on her feet because she hadn't slept or eaten. Finally, she asked Elsie for a break and returned to her quarters, where she rummaged inside her rucksack and found the photograph she had treasured since she was a child. She put the two images together. They were identical.

She didn't come to see Jack that day or the day after but every now and then, she would pause her mad rush around the hospital, take a deep breath and pull the two photographs out of her pocket, her hand on her racing heart.

She was in the mess, a spoon of beans on the plate in front of her, when Elsie called them into a meeting. The chief nurse was a shadow of her former self. She was no longer bursting with energy, bossing the hospital staff around with a sharp word and a glare of her eye. She had lost weight and, it seemed, a lot of her ferocity. What she hadn't lost was the desire to help her patients and nurses. 'From today, nurses are required to wear their helmets when on duty,' Elsie said, clasping her hands together.

'Why? Are the Japanese going to bomb us a hundred times a

day instead of fifty?' someone asked.

Nervous laughter followed. Elsie coughed. The nurses fell quiet. 'Not only that but you are required to carry your emergency pills on you every day.'

'Suicide pills, you mean?' asked Tess.

A hush descended over the room. There was no more laughter after that. Fifty expectant pairs of eyes watched Elsie, who stepped from foot to foot, her cheeks red, as if standing in front of them was the last place she wanted to be, and she felt personally responsible for the bad news she was delivering. 'In the next day or so, Corregidor will surrender to the enemy,' she said finally, not looking at the shocked faces around her. Not a muscle moved on her own face but her hands trembled.

Rose felt herself trembling too, from the tips of her fingers to the balls of her feet. She leaned on the table, touching her hair where this morning, like every morning, she had hidden the lethal dose of morphine. Before the sun was up, she brushed her hair, pinned it on top of her head in a tidy bun, until every strand was perfect and not a hair was out of place, like a ballerina taking to the stage in front of an adoring audience. She brushed her teeth with soda and washed her face. And only then, after her face was clean and the teeth brushed, did she hide the deathly pill inside her hair. It had become her ritual and for the past few months she had not given it a second thought. Until now.

'If the Japanese are coming here, what will become of us?' Tess asked.

No one replied. The silence hung in the room like a scream of terror.

'Maybe it's for the best,' said one of the nurses. 'I can't imagine living like this for much longer. We have no food, no water. At least it will all be over.'

'Do you think the enemy will bring you a better life?' asked Elsie. 'Do you think they'll have food for you?'

'Anything is better than this. Even death. I hope it's a quick one.'

As Rose sat in the mess with an empty plate in front of her, as she walked through the corridors, her gauze mask on her face, her helmet on her head, the suicide pill in her hair, as she tended to her patients, she heard whispers. Some were saying the enemy had landed on the beaches of Corregidor and were making their way to the tunnels. Others were convinced that the Japanese were at the gates with their tanks, battle-ready and unafraid. What would happen to their tunnels if the enemy attacked with tanks? Would the whole structure collapse? And what if they poisoned them with gas? No one seemed to know anything for a fact, but everyone had an opinion, a guess or a rumour they were desperate to share.

Rose told herself the helmet on her head and the gas mask over her mouth and the morphine in her hair were just a precaution. She couldn't allow herself to get distracted by silly rumours. She had a job to do.

The nurses didn't speak to one another and avoided looking at each other because they didn't want to see fear on their friends' faces. But they couldn't turn away from their patients. As soon as Rose entered a ward, she was bombarded with questions. *What will become of us? Are the Japanese really here? Will they take us away?* The men held her hand, looked at her imploringly and begged for information. As if she knew anything.

There was a tension in the air, a fearful anticipation of an impending storm. Every morning, Rose wondered what the day would bring. Would they still be alive when the sun set outside?

On 6 May, she heard a bugler play 'Taps' outside Malinta tunnel and saw two grim-faced American officers lowering the Stars and Stripes. Standing still like a mouse, surrounded by other nurses, Rose couldn't believe her eyes. She couldn't fathom that the US had been conquered by the Japanese, the enemy they had all underestimated and dismissed all those months ago, when they thought war would be over in mere days because reinforcements were on the way. If someone had told her when she first arrived in Manila that she would be standing with tears in her eyes as the American flag slid down, she would have laughed and not believed it for a second. She was no longer laughing but wept openly at the sight of the white sheet the officers were rising.

It was one of the worst moments of her life.

Every morning since the day she had arrived, Rose would walk past the tunnel bulletin board and read the sign written in bold letters, 'Corregidor still stands'. It filled her with hope, with desire for life. Yes, they were fighting for their very survival inside the smoke-filled tunnels. Yes, they might be running out of water, food and hope. But they were not giving up. That fateful morning in May, as she made her way to the ward to check on her patients, she saw that the sign had been changed to 'Corregidor still stands … under new management'. Her heart raced and for a moment, she couldn't breathe because it was another reminder that they had finally given up and were no longer fighting. After all these months, Corregidor had fallen.

A hush had descended over the hospital. It was as if nurses, doctors and patients were too afraid to utter a sound, in case the enemy would hear them. There were no customary shouts for help, no one asked for water or something to eat, no one called out her name. On every expectant face, in every tense mouth was fear and uncertainty. She walked from bed to bed, whispering reassuring nothings to the men who knew what was coming and couldn't be reassured.

Rose reached inside her pocket and pulled out the picture of the father and daughter. She couldn't avoid him any longer. Faced with an insurmountable disaster, he was the only person she wanted to talk to.

Dr Dunham was still asleep. He looked nothing like the man on the photograph, his face bloated, eyebrows bushy, skin dull and hair grey. She could swear he had aged since she had last seen him. She couldn't blame him. This war had aged all of them.

He opened his eyes. 'Hey, there's my favourite nurse. Where have you been? I was worried about you.'

She rubbed her face with the back of her hand. Smoke and dust filled the tunnels, making her eyes ache. She realised he didn't know. And she didn't want to be the one to tell him. It took her a moment to find the courage to say, 'The Japanese are here. Corregidor formally surrendered two hours ago.'

He didn't look surprised or frightened, just sad and tired and old beyond his years. Had he been expecting this? 'This is said to be the worst surrender in American military history,' he said.

'Didn't they say that Corregidor was impregnable? That the enemy will never take it?' Rose paced nervously.

'Our supplies are running low. If we didn't surrender, we would be dying of hunger.'

'I feel so helpless. So many lives lost, so much hard work, so much effort from so many. And it was all in vain. I feel guilty and ashamed, like I failed somehow, like it's all my fault.'

'You have nothing to feel guilty or ashamed about.'

'Seeing the flag go down … I can't even put into words what it felt like.'

'You should be proud of everything you've done. From the start, it was an unfair fight. We are outnumbered ten to one. We are facing a better-fed, better-equipped, relentless enemy. We did all we could. That should bring some solace.'

It should but it didn't. Rose felt close to tears. 'What do we do now?'

'We go on as before. We continue to do our job. Our patients need us, no matter what happens.'

Rose watched him for a while, silent and afraid. There was only one question she wanted to ask. She wanted to know why he had left, all those years ago when she was four and loved her father more than life itself. But she couldn't find the right words. 'At least some of us were able to escape. And your little girl might read your letter. How old is she now?'

'She turned twenty-two in October.'

'You don't see her or talk to her?'

His eyes dimmed. He looked past her, into the far distance, like he was a million miles away. 'Her mother, my ex-wife, didn't want us to have a relationship. I tried, of course. I still think about her every single day.'

'You say she's a grown woman now. You didn't try to find her?'

'Many times.'

'And your daughter? She didn't look for you?'

He shrugged. 'God knows what her mother told her about me.'

Rose read regret in his eyes, and pain. Her heart hurt. 'She told her you died,' she said.

'Excuse me?' he whispered.

Rose showed him both photographs. 'It's the only picture I have of my father.'

He raised his hurting eyes to her and watched her for a few tense, numb moments. His eyes were wide, his mouth open. 'Rosaline.' There was wonder on his face, like she was a miracle he never thought he would see before him. He reached for her hand. She let him take it.

At the sound of the long-forgotten name, she wanted to weep. 'No one calls me Rosaline anymore,' she whispered.

'I never thought I would find you again. And here of all places.'

'Growing up, I used to imagine what you might be like. But you are nothing like I expected.'

'What did you expect?'

'Mama always said you were incapable of feeling. But I've been watching you with your patients and I don't see that at all. What I see instead is someone who puts others first, someone who sacrifices everything to help those in need.'

'Incapable of feeling,' he repeated, as if trying the words on for size. He didn't look surprised. 'What else did your mother say about me?'

'She said you didn't want to be a father. That you were not

ready.' She hesitated. 'She said you left because things got tough.'

He sat up in bed. 'All I've ever wanted was to be a father.'

A memory surfaced, of a man pushing her on the swings, her legs dangling in the air, her breath catching, while snow landed on her hat and her flushed cheeks. *Higher, higher, higher*, she cried. And a moment later, *No, Daddy, it's too high*. Squealing with delight, because he was no longer pushing her on the swings but holding her in his arms and spinning her in the air, around and around until everything became a blur and she could barely speak, only giggle. A hazy memory of an ice-cream cone melting through her mittens and the laughter in his eyes as he watched her eat. *Don't tell your mother, she'll say it's too cold for ice cream*.

'Then why did you leave?' she whispered.

'The day after you turned four, I went to Manila for six months. It was my first trip here as a doctor. When I came back, you and your mother were gone. I found strangers living at the house we used to rent. No one knew what had become of you.'

'I don't understand. Why didn't Mama let you know where we were?'

He looked like he didn't want to tell her. 'Because she didn't want me to find you. She took you away, changed her name and yours. I spent years looking for you. I even hired a private investigator. He tracked you to Rhode Island. After that, there was no trace of you.'

'I went to primary school on Rhode Island,' she said. 'Then we moved to Brownville.' She raised her confused eyes to him. She still didn't understand.

He lowered his head, like he was ashamed. 'Days before I left for the Philippines, your mother found out I was involved with one of my nurses.'

'You had an affair?'

He nodded. 'I begged your mother to forgive me. I swore it was over, that I loved only her. But she didn't believe me.'

'Did this nurse go to the Philippines with you?'

'Yes, but by then I had ended it with her. Seeing your mother so heartbroken made me realise how much I stood to lose. And I didn't want to lose my family. I wrote to her almost every day but never received a word back.'

Rose remembered the box of letters her mother hid in her drawer, locked away from prying eyes with a little key she kept under a loose tile in the kitchen. A few times over the years, Rose had walked in from school to find her mother reading the letters. On one occasion, she had seen her crying.

'And when I returned,' he continued, 'the two of you were gone. She never forgave me, I suppose. And she decided to punish me by taking my daughter away from me.'

'She punished both of us,' Rose said softly.

# Chapter 15

## May 1942

In the dark of night, Rose curled up on her mattress, hugging her knees close to her chest as if to protect her from everything she was feeling. Unlike the other nurses, she wasn't listening out for noises, afraid of every shadow, waiting and dreading the enemy's arrival. Yesterday, she was consumed with fear and anxiety, just like everybody else on the island. Tonight, she hadn't thought of the Japanese once. All she could think of was her mother and the choices she had made for herself and for Rose.

In the morning, as she was carrying a jug of water for her patients, an American soldier ran inside the hospital and announced that the enemy had entered the tunnels. The jug fell to the ground, shattering into a thousand pieces. The water spilled over Rose's feet. She stood for a few moments, staring blankly at the mess, without a word, as if frozen to the spot. Then she got a mop and began to clean up, wishing she could close her eyes and not see the pale, panic-stricken faces around her or hear the terrified voices whispering of terrors to come.

'What are they going to do to us?'

'What they did to the women in China four years ago, I

suppose. Haven't you heard? They ...'

Rose lifted her hands to her ears. She wanted to scream.

Elsie's steady voice cut through the noise. 'This is what we do. We stay together and travel in groups. We never go anywhere alone. Our strength is in numbers. When we sleep, one of us must watch over the others at all times, to make sure we are safe. And hide your valuables.'

Tess pulled a bedsheet off her bed and with trembling hands spread it on the table. 'Let's leave something to remember us by. This way, if we disappear, there will be a record of us.' At the top of the sheet, she wrote, 'Members of the Army Nurse Corps and Civilian Women Who Were in Malinta Tunnel When Corregidor Fell.'

Solemnly, silently, sixty-nine women took turns to sign their names. As Rose pressed on the pen as hard as she could so that the letters came out clearly, she thought about the moment seven months ago when she had taken her first step on the soil of the Philippines, the moment that changed her life forever. This felt a little bit like that too, a watershed moment that was going to define her life. There would always be *before* and *after*. Once the enemy marched through the doors, everything would change and there would be no going back.

Signing the bedsheet didn't give Rose peace of mind. It didn't reassure her that they wouldn't be forgotten, that they were leaving something behind, even if it was only a sheet with their names on it. On the contrary, it filled her with dread. As she looked at the letters of her name, her identity scribbled on a piece of fabric in ominous black, it felt like she was saying goodbye to everything she held dear, even to life itself.

Afterwards, the nurses went to work like nothing was happening, like their lives didn't hang on the thinnest of threads. During breaks, they huddled together, whispering in hushed voices to one another, looking around fearfully. They discussed the only thing on their minds – the Japanese on Corregidor, inside their safe haven where they had thought nothing could harm them.

Rose didn't join the other nurses, nor did she listen to the rumours. She spent every free moment with her father. They didn't mention their fears or the unspeakable – the enemy minutes away from their hiding place. They didn't talk about the future or ponder what was in store for them. They had eighteen years of the past to catch up on.

'Mama never talked about you,' she told him. 'I remember wondering if we were at all alike. Wondering what my life would have been like if you hadn't left.'

'What was it like, growing up? Tell me everything.'

She told him everything, about school and friends and the best home a child could wish for, and yet, sometimes feeling like she didn't belong, wishing she had a big family, a sibling or an aunt, someone to talk to besides her mother, who was often too tired from working three jobs to spend time with her. 'I was cooking dinner for mama from the age of eight. She would come home from work and eat in silence, and then she would thank me and ask why I wasn't in bed. And when I woke up in the morning, she would be gone, and I would have to get myself ready and then walk across town to school. I barely saw her.' She was quiet for a bit, lost in memories. 'My dream was to dance. Every evening I would hide outside a ballet studio and watch the little ballerinas as they twirled and pirouetted, and I would twirl and pirouette just like them and feel like I was part of something bigger than me. Rain or snow, I would be outside the studio, watching through the window until one day, the teacher noticed me and took pity on me. She allowed me to attend the lessons for free. It was the happiest day of my entire childhood, I think.'

Jack had tears in his eyes. 'I'm so sorry,' he whispered.

'For what?'

'I'm sorry the stupid thing I did broke our family apart. I wish I could take it all back. I wish I could have been there for you. I would have taken you to every ballet lesson. I would have been there every morning to take you to school. I would have cooked breakfast and dinner for you and packed your lunch. If only I could turn back time.'

Rose cried silently, her hands in his. She had so many questions for him. Everything she had always wanted to know and didn't dare ask her mother. 'You and Mama ... How did you two meet?'

'We met at a dance. Your mother was the love of my life. I knew it the moment I saw her.'

'How old were you?'

'Eighteen and nineteen, I think. She was dancing with another boy. The place was crowded but all I could see was her. I couldn't take my eyes off her.'

'She always said she loved to dance, just like me. But I've never seen her dancing.'

'I remember watching her and thinking I would do anything to get her to come home with me instead of him. And she did.'

'How did you do it?'

'I bought her a drink.' He laughed. 'Later she told me her date was such a bore, she was grateful to be rescued. From that day on, we were inseparable. No other woman had ever made me so happy, before or since.'

'What went wrong?'

'I don't want to sound like I'm making excuses for what I did. But after you were born, she threw herself into being a mother, forgetting all about me. In hindsight, I should have been there for her, should have helped more, focused on my family, given her more time. But I was weak. I was tempted by someone else, not because I had feelings for this woman but because it felt like she was putting me first. I regretted it instantly but it was too late.'

'It's never too late,' she said, while somewhere nearby the Japanese soldiers were marching closer and closer. 'When all this is over, we can be a family again. You and I.'

They heard a commotion outside. Light steps and worried

voices. Finally, the sound of heavy boots clomping through the passageways. *They are here*, Rose thought. The voices quietened down and an expectant silence fell over the ward. She could hear a mosquito in the corner, buzzing loudly with not a care in the world. She could hear the water dripping in the tunnel nearby and her father's laboured breathing. She felt his fingers squeezing hers gently, as if to reassure her. For the last few weeks, she had been imagining this moment. She had thought she would be petrified, that she would be shaking with fear. But she wasn't afraid because she was no longer alone.

A group of Japanese officers barged in, accompanied by two sombre-faced Americans. The enemy rounded the nurses up, walked them to the staffroom and ordered them to line up and face the wall. Before she did as she was told, Rose stole a quick glance at the officers. When she had thought of the Japanese during long days and nights on Bataan and here, on Corregidor, trapped for what seemed like an eternity under all that rock, she always pictured faces disfigured by anger, eyes blazing, noses flaring with rage. What she saw that day was very different. The enemy officers showed no emotion as they paced the room, examining the women. Rose wanted to spit at them and hit them as hard as she could, for coming here, for unleashing death and devastation on the islands of the Philippines for the last seven months, for taking David away from her. Even the swords on their hips and the bayonets in their hands didn't scare her.

'Be brave, girls,' Elsie whispered. 'Remember, you are officers in the US Army. Act accordingly.'

The Japanese men smirked like they were looking at something funny or ridiculous. A moment later, they turned on their heels and left.

The girls remained facing the wall for a few moments, too afraid to move. When they were certain the Japanese were not coming back, they relaxed, looking at one another.

'They didn't say a word to us,' said Tess.

'What did you expect? A welcome speech?' asked Rose.

'They could have told us what was going to happen to us. Instead, they gawked at us like we were animals at a zoo.'

'They are not used to seeing women at war. They don't have nurses, only male medics,' said Elsie. 'Now, what are you standing around for? We have work to do. Our patients are waiting.'

Inside their quarters, behind a door with a sign that read 'Nurses, officers of the United States Army', Rose tried to rest. She kept her uniform on at all times because intrusive eyes followed her every move. With the arrival of the enemy, the nurses had lost their privacy.

Rose felt herself drifting off to sleep when she heard a trill of a bell. It was the signal from Tess, who was standing guard. The Japanese were there. Rose jumped to her feet as the lights went on and found herself face to face with an enemy officer with shifty eyes and a slightly disgusted expression, like she was something dirty stuck to the bottom of his shoe.

Suddenly nervous, she hid her hands behind her back, wishing she had taken her mother's ring off her finger and hidden it somewhere safe.

'Take off your ring,' the officer said, his eyes burning with greed.

'No,' said Rose. She shook her head for emphasis. *No.* Other than the photograph, this ring was all that was left to remind her of Mama.

The man wasn't taking no for an answer. He twisted her hand, making her cry out, and tried to pull the ring off her finger. Rose yanked her hand back, shaking, petrified, unable to move or cry or speak. 'It belonged to my mother,' she said finally in her quietest voice.

The officer reached for his sword.

'Rose, just take it off. It's not worth it,' said Tess.

She took it off. The officer grabbed the ring without a word or a glance in her direction and proceeded down the line of women, searching for more loot. He took fountain pens nurses used for record-keeping and wristwatches that measured their patients' pulse. Finally, he was gone.

Rose was sobbing in her bed when she felt a hand on her shoulder. 'Don't cry,' whispered Tess. 'I know the ring means a lot to you, but the most important thing is that we are still alive and they haven't touched us or hurt us. No one can take your memories away. They are in your heart. Your mother is always with you. The ring doesn't matter.' Tess stroked Rose's back, while she continued to cry. She knew Tess was right but, against all logic, she felt an acute sense of loss, as if not just her mother's ring but a part of her soul had been wrestled away from her that night.

# Chapter 16

## June–July 1942

Days turned into weeks and Rose sleepwalked through her shifts at the hospital, pretending life as she knew it hadn't stopped the moment the American flag descended on Corregidor. The nurses continued to work like nothing had happened, talking in hushed voices, smiling through their tears, trying to hide their fear from their patients, each other and, most importantly, the enemy. Rose couldn't quite put her finger on what it was she was afraid of. She wasn't in any immediate danger and yet, she could never relax. The Japanese were an oppressive presence inside the tunnels, like a dark cloud threatening a storm. They had never addressed the nurses directly and hadn't spoken to them about what awaited them, and that was what made them sinister, almost otherworldly and frightening. Had they talked to the women, even if it was in harsh tones, the way conquerors spoke to their prisoners, they would appear more human. They wouldn't be such an enigma and perhaps the nurses wouldn't be so afraid of them.

'Do you regret coming here?' Rose asked her father one afternoon. Once a day, the Japanese allowed their prisoners outside for some air. Rose and Jack sat on the sand, swatting away flies, looking at the pristine sea, blue like the sky over their head and just as peaceful. The green lawns, the flowers, the lush bushes and trees were gone. What remained after months of shelling was a wasteland of rubble and dust.

Jack had spent all day and night in surgery, fighting for a patient's life and winning it, against all odds, and now he was so exhausted, he could barely hold a cup of water in his trembling hands. He looked like he was about to fall asleep on the sand, with the flies on his face. 'How could I regret finding you again?' he said, forcing a smile.

They had mere moments together. Later that afternoon, the Japanese would be taking thousands of American POWs, including male doctors and orderlies, to a prisoner camp in Manila, while the nurses would remain in the tunnels and await their fate. Turning away from Jack, Rose wiped the tears off her face. She didn't want her father to see her crying. She didn't want him to feel sad in the last few hours they had left.

'Tell me a memory,' she said after a long silence, while seagulls screeched overhead and the light breeze brought the acrid smell of fire.

'Let me tell you the happiest memory of my entire life. The day you were born, I was the first to hold you. You were crying but when you were in my arms, you stopped for a few seconds and glanced at me with those big blue eyes of yours, like you were wondering who I was, like you already loved me. Soon you were screaming again but those two seconds were enough for me to fall in love with you.'

'I love you, Dad,' she whispered.

'Please don't cry,' he said, even though he was crying too. 'And don't be afraid. One way or another, all this will be behind us soon. We will survive this, like we survived Bataan.'

'I know. I'm not afraid.'

'Your turn. Tell me a memory.'

She didn't have many recollections of the two of them together.

She remembered a warm hand on her forehead, loving eyes watching her, kind lips kissing her cheek. The sudden absence that broke her heart. A loneliness, a longing that defined most of her childhood. 'I remember the day you left. I was playing with my dolls in the corner. Mama was still sleeping, I think. You called me over and I dropped my dolls and ran to you. There was a suitcase by your feet. You lifted me in your arms and held me for what felt like forever. I remember asking where you were going. You told me you were going to be a doctor, to help people and that you would be back in a few months. You told me to look after my mother. Moments later, you were gone. It was the last time I saw you.' She was sobbing now, her hair falling over her face, a mess of tangles and curls. 'I don't want to lose you again. I just found you. I don't want to say goodbye.'

Jack held her. 'We knew this day would come. We were expecting it.'

'Doesn't make it any easier. I've only been with you for a short time, but I feel like I've known you my whole life. I have loved you my whole life.'

'I loved you from the moment I laid my eyes on you. We have found each other again. What were the chances? I know where to look for you now. As soon as the war is over, we will be together.'

'What if the war is over and we don't make it?'

'We'll make it. We have to.' He smiled. He seemed to really believe it. 'I have to ask you something.' He took her hand.

'Of course. Anything.'

'Do you forgive me?'

'There is nothing to forgive. You are human. You made a mistake. Who hasn't?'

'Say it.' He watched her with sad eyes. 'Say you forgive me. I need to hear the words so that I can forgive myself.'

'I forgive you, Dad,' she said quietly, looking into his eyes, wanting to touch his face, to pause the clock, to stop the hated guards from taking him away from her.

Two hours later, she watched as her father climbed inside a truck, to be separated from her once again. As he turned and waved, as she waved back, she thought, *What if this is it, what if today was the last day we'll have together*? If she ever made it back home, she knew she would wait for him for the rest of her life. But what if months turned to years, and years turned to decades, and he never returned? The familiar loneliness felt like bricks pressing on her chest and she could barely breathe with the weight of it all. When the truck began to move, she closed her eyes and wept. If Tess hadn't had her arms around her, she would have fallen.

The hospital was a ghost of its former self – dark, quiet and frightening. Where once there had been lots of voices, shouting and even laughter, now silence reigned. Where once there had been movement, and kind faces and smiles, now were empty halls. Like a shadow, Rose walked through the wards, her eyes red from tears, seeing Jack everywhere. His face haunted her during the day, and during the night, for hours she stared into darkness and wondered if she would ever see him again. She thought of David and wondered if he was still alive.

Tess did her best to cheer her up. 'Now we have time for a cup of tea,' she would say every morning, pouring a dark one for Rose and a lighter one for herself. 'We can sit down for a moment.'

But Rose didn't want to sit down. She didn't want time to herself. She wanted to keep busy so she could forget.

A week after Rose had watched her father forced on to a truck and disappear in a cloud of dust, one of the guards told them they could send a short telegram back home. Rose wrote a few sentences to her mother, about her patients and her work and how she hoped to come home soon. She didn't say a word about her father. It was too big to put in a telegram.

'Too many words,' said the guard. 'No more than ten.'

Rose wrote, 'Safe and healthy, miss you, will see you soon.'

The nurses banded together and looked out for one another, surviving inspections, midnight searches and never-ending roll calls. They had become prisoners and now that their patients had been moved and their purpose lost, the days stretched before them with nothing to do but worry about the future. Late into the night, they sat in a circle and told each other stories about their childhoods and families. They reminisced about their first few weeks in Manila, memories bright and happy like tropical sun in the dark of war. Sometimes one of the nurses picked up a guitar and the tunnels filled with melancholy music. Rose never sang, nor did she play her ukulele. She wanted to put her hands over her ears and not hear Elsie as she sang the joyful lyrics of Guy Lombardo in a sad voice. She wanted to weep, to curl into a ball in the corner, close her eyes and sleep through the Japanese occupation, through everything the next months and years would bring.

In the last week of June, Tess became sick with malaria. She was no longer talking or laughing or making tea. Instead, she lay in bed and gazed at the wall, while Rose spoon-fed her rice and read to her from *The Great Gatsby*.

At night, Rose prayed. Fervently she prayed for everyone she loved. For her mother back home, so she would be able to endure their separation and uncertainty. For her father in a prisoner camp somewhere, so he would come back to her. And for David, so he would live. She counted how long it had been since the Japanese invaded their jungle hospital on Bataan. Three months. Ninety long days and nights.

When the Japanese allowed them to go outside, Rose looked at the mighty sea with a hand on her heart. Across the harbour was Manila, where she had lived through some of the happiest days of her life. And somewhere beyond the harbour, across the sea, was America where her mother was crying for her only child, not knowing if she was dead or alive. Home. Rose could barely imagine it now, even as she longed for it. How she wished she could embrace her mother, hold her in her arms and hear her beloved voice. She would forgive her in an instant, for lying to her, for keeping her father from her, if only she could see her again. Nothing mattered, all would be forgotten, as long as her mother was still waiting for her when she went back. *If* she went back.

Finally, on 2 July, the Japanese ordered the nurses on trucks that would take them to the harbour, where a large ship by the name of *Lima Maru* was waiting for them. Rose watched as the tunnels disappeared from view, feeling light-headed from hunger and unsteady on her feet. 'I don't ever want to see this place again,' Tess muttered, her head resting on Rose's shoulder. 'I hate it, hate everything about it.'

'I'd rather stay here,' replied Rose. 'Who knows what our future will bring.' She caught a glimpse of the machine guns as the guards hurried the rest of the nurses along. The first time she had seen the island, she was with David and her heart was filled with joy. Inside these tunnels she had found her father. Corregidor would always hold a special place in her heart.

Small boats took them to the ship and they stared in shock at a rope ladder dangling from the deck.

'They want us to climb?' one of the nurses exclaimed. 'Who do they think we are, Moscow Circus?'

But they had no choice. One after another the nurses climbed the rope, until it was just Rose and Tess left in the boat.

Rose was worried about her friend. Tess was burning up. Her eyes were dull and unfocused. When she spoke, it was with great effort, like every word was agony. 'Where are they taking us, Rose? They're not telling us anything.'

'I don't know, honey. I guess we'll find out soon.'

'Haven't you heard what the other nurses are saying? They think they are going to kill us all. And it makes sense. They don't need extra mouths to feed.' Tess was crying and throwing frantic glances at the guards.

'Nonsense,' replied Rose, making her voice sound steady and

strong, making her face appear convincing, for her friend. 'If they wanted to kill us, they would have done it already. They wouldn't need to take us away.'

'You think so?'

'I know so.'

Tess looked at Rose and then at the rope ladder. 'I can't do it,' she whispered. 'I could never climb that. I'm too weak.'

'You can do it. Just think of all the sharks swimming in the harbour, waiting for their breakfast.'

Rose stood underneath the rope, ready to catch Tess if her arms gave out and she fell. But Tess didn't fall. With a tremendous effort, she pulled herself up on the rope, finally collapsing on deck, breathing heavily. Rose followed, and as the ship began to move, she watched the island of Corregidor as it disappeared from sight. It was supposed to be their refuge, to hold them and keep them safe under a tonne of rock until the end of the war. And here they were, saying goodbye to it like they had said goodbye to so many places they had called home in the past few months, but this time there was nowhere left to run. Their destiny was no longer in their hands. Instead, the hated enemy got to decide if they died or lived to see another sunset.

# Part IV

# The Camp of Santo Tomas

# Chapter 17

## February 1944

Every morning Rose awoke at six o'clock sharp to the sound of the loudspeaker and glanced out the window at machine guns pointing in her direction. She saw barbed wire and iron fences with sharp spikes reaching for the sky. To make sure no one could look in or out, woven bamboo matting called *sawali* obscured the outside world as if it didn't exist. For the last two and a half years, no news reached them inside the camp of Santo Tomas, no tidings from those they loved, no inkling of what was happening in the war. It was hard to imagine that life went on beyond the barbed wire. Once upon a time, the large, three-storey building with a square clock tower, topped with a cupola and a white cross, had been a lively university, a place of learning, not suffering, filled with laughter and hope. Now that the Philippines were in Japanese hands, it had become a prison to 3,000 unfortunate souls trapped for eternity inside its gloomy walls.

Their days were spent standing in one line or another. There was a shower and toilet line, six cubicles shared by two hundred people from Rose's block, the line for the laundry, for packages, and, of course, the longest one of all, the *chow* line for food.

Rose's feet ached from queuing all day. She would rub her hands together and step from foot to foot with boredom, looking at the people in front of her, trying to work out how long it had been since the war had started, since they had been captured, since David had been taken away from her, since she had said goodbye to her father.

When they had first arrived, Rose was assigned to clean the showers with four other nurses. Her usual fearless self, Elsie marched into the commandant's office and demanded that the girls were employed according to their profession. 'Good nurses are needed everywhere,' she had said to the balding man sitting in front of her, appearing ill at ease and uncomfortable with the mission entrusted to him – looking after thousands of detainees. Elsie's bravery and determination paid off. Two days later, the nurses were working four-hour shifts at a small hospital in Santa Catalina Convent that was connected to the main camp by a fenced passageway.

Even when the sun was shining, it seemed to Rose like the camp was shrouded in darkness. To be held captive, to be watched every minute of every day, to rely on her captors for every necessity felt like life itself had been snatched away from her. There was no joy within these walls because there was no freedom.

When they had first arrived, they were given a small allotment and planted a banana and papaya tree, as well as some vegetables. Everyone else had laughed because the trees wouldn't produce anything for a year. No one believed they would stay in the camp for long. Any day now, the US Army would sail into the harbour and rescue them. But weeks turned into months and months turned into years with no help in sight. The girls grew delicious fruit they could eat or barter. When they had cooked corn on the cob on a small charcoal stove, it tasted like heaven and smelt amazing, so much so that the whole camp, it seemed, came running. Rose couldn't continue eating under so many hungry eyes. In the end, she had given her share to a child.

Rose loved gardening while the tropical sun played on her face. It was the only time she felt alive. As she weeded, pruned and laid down compost, she could imagine she was in her small garden in Brownville, under the peaceful American sky, the smell of her mother's baking reaching her from the house.

'Are you coming to the dance class?' asked Tess, standing over Rose, blocking the sun. 'Ruth gets upset if we're late.'

Rose didn't feel like dancing that evening. She had had a long day at the hospital, looking after men, women and children who were sick with various infectious diseases, and now her legs were aching. To spend another hour on her feet, even if it was doing what she loved best, didn't appeal to her at all. She wanted to be alone, just her and the damp soil under her hands, a few precious moments when she could forget she was a prisoner. 'I'd love to but these carrots won't plant themselves.'

The girls had been doing dancing lessons with Ruth for over a year. An hour twice a week when they could lose themselves in the music and feel a spark of joy. In their spare time, the internees of Santo Tomas could play basketball, soccer and volleyball, enjoy lectures on various subjects, as well as attend theatre performances and concerts. Rose became fluent in Spanish after attending classes run by a Spanish woman. Every morning children went to a school set up by a group of teachers. With so many people with various talents and time on their hands, the camp had a lot to offer. Rose could almost pretend she was a student living at a university campus, if it weren't for the machine guns and the barbed wire.

Tess crouched by her side. Seeing the worried expression on her face, Rose looked up from her carrot bed. 'What is it?' she asked. 'What's wrong?'

Tess whispered, 'I keep hearing rumours. Soon our camp will no longer be run by the executive committee.' The executive committee was formed of prisoners who governed the camp under the authority of a Japanese commandant. 'It will be taken over by the Japanese.'

'What will that mean for us?' Rose shivered despite the heat.

'I don't know. But I doubt they will allow dancing classes. We better make the most of it while we still can.'

Rose nodded and put the bag of seeds away. Maybe an hour of dancing was just what she needed to take her mind off the darkness inside her head. And the allotment wasn't going anywhere.

When the two of them arrived at the courtyard where dancing classes usually took place, they found a group of women waiting patiently and no sign of Ruth with her frizzy hair and long dancer's legs. They stood for fifteen minutes, throwing confused glances at one another.

A woman approached them, her long and mournful face making her look like a sad greyhound. Rose had seen her around the camp before. She ran one of the makeshift cafés that had sprung up in the camp, and which the girls dreamt of visiting one day, if only they could scrape enough money together from somewhere. She said, 'Haven't you heard? A group of prisoners escaped last night. Ruth was one of them.'

Rose glanced at the guards and the tall walls. 'Escaped?' she whispered, stunned.

'Apparently they'd been planning it for months.'

'Good for them,' said Rose. The thought of freedom, of waking up and not seeing weapons pointed at her, made her heart race with longing.

'Not if they're caught,' said the woman. 'Where are they going to go, anyway? All of the Philippines is in Japanese hands. What are they going to do, swim to Australia?'

Rose turned away from the woman. With all her heart, she hoped Ruth and the others would find a way to safety, even though it seemed impossible.

The girls were queuing for their breakfast at dawn when they heard metal gates screeching and heavy boots stomping across the cobblestones. The guards marched in, pushing a dozen muddy, unhappy people in front of them. One of them was Ruth, her tall body twitching with fear, her beautiful face red and puffy, as if she had been crying. She wasn't crying now but looked proud and resigned, like she knew what was in store for her and had come to terms with it.

Rose and Tess exchanged a panicked glance and left the queue, joining Elsie in the main courtyard where a crowd gathered, watching in horror as the escapees were told to line up against the wall.

'What are they going to do to them?' Rose whispered, her heart in her throat.

'They'll probably throw them in solitary for a month,' said Elsie.

The girls stood quietly, expecting the Japanese to make one of their famous speeches and take the captured prisoners away. The guards were masters of inspirational speeches. Words like honour, respect and model prisoner behaviour came out of their mouths with astonishing regularity. A fight in the *chow* line? Speech. Someone vandalised the only working shower in block D? Another speech. Someone stole someone else's food? Another twenty-minute speech.

The expression on Ruth's face tugged at Rose's heart. She waved to the woman, trying to send some positive vibes across the courtyard, to convey that she was thinking of her. But Ruth wasn't looking at her. Her horrified eyes were staring at the machine guns pointed at her chest.

What happened next was like a scene from a terrifying nightmare, one Rose would never forget for as long as she lived. Instead of making one of their customary speeches, the guards rose their weapons and took aim. A moment later, a volley of shots rang out. Rose squeezed her eyes shut and turned away, burying her face in Elsie's shoulder, her mouth opening wide with horror, a mute scream dying on her lips. Her body shook and she felt like she was about to collapse, like she had been the one struck by bullets. Elsie's hand was on her back, stroking in small circles, bringing no relief. The older woman didn't speak. There were tears in her eyes. Rose wailed, 'Why did they have to kill them? How cruel, how …' She searched for the right word. 'How inhumane.'

'Do they look like humans to you?' Elsie replied. 'They killed them to teach us a lesson. They killed them to convey a message. Try to escape and this is what's going to happen to you.'

Elsie didn't look at all surprised. But Rose was surprised. Even after two years of being a prisoner, after dark nights and even darker days of living side by side with the enemy, of witnessing injustices big and small, punishments for not bowing in time or not standing in a straight line at roll call, she wasn't expecting the guards to kill ten people in bright daylight, in front of everyone, just because they could.

As she sleepwalked though her days, Rose tried her best not to think of the terror flashing in Ruth's eyes seconds before the bullets hit her. And yet, her face was all Rose could see when she closed her eyes at night.

One morning, before the sun was up, she shivered under the shower, turning away from the line of people behind her, pretending she was someplace else, imagining a meadow, a beautiful river, a room of her own with pretty curtains and a bookshelf. As the cold water hit her freezing body, she imagined she was under the waterfall with David, squealing with delight, her heart bursting with joy. Above her head, someone had scribbled with a sharp rock, 'If you want privacy, close your eyes.' Her face flushed with embarrassment, she did exactly that. There was no place for privacy in the camp of Santo Tomas. Even though undressing in front of strangers and seeing other naked bodies was a norm here, even though she had done it every morning for two years, Rose knew she would never get used to it, that she would always feel the numbing sensation of humiliation and shame.

Afterwards, she dried herself off with a sheet and stepped

outside, covering herself as best she could and looking for her clothes. This morning, like always, she had undressed and folded her nurse's uniform neatly, placing it on a bench. To her surprise, when she stepped out of the shower, she saw that the bench was empty. Rose paused for a second, confused. She looked under the bench, wondering if the clothes had fallen to the ground but all she saw was someone's old shoe. She checked the hooks on the wall, even though she knew for a fact she hadn't hung her uniform there. The hooks had a selection of dresses and shirts, all in various states of deterioration, with holes on elbows and entire sleeves missing, but her uniform was nowhere to be seen.

Unsure what to do next, Rose sat on the bench, hiding inside her sheet. All around her, people were shouting and pushing one another. It was never quiet at Santo Tomas. Even at night, she listened to people's voices and longed for peace. The square outside the main building was especially noisy because packages had arrived for the lucky ones who had loved ones in Manila. Once a week, they received food, clothes and household items, and it allowed some enterprising souls to set themselves up for business, selling fruit and vegetables, cookies, muffins and bread, peanuts, carabao milk, eggs and meat. Coffee shops and restaurants popped up for those who could afford to pay. Rose and the other nurses didn't have any money but sometimes a grateful patient lent them some. Once, Rose had a bar of chocolate sitting under the tree outside the cafeteria. Another time, she had enjoyed a cup of coffee. It was like a magical dream and every time she thought about it, she smiled.

Rose watched sadly as the other internees carried their precious packages away. She knew she wouldn't be able to get a new uniform if her old one had been stolen. Hardly anyone made clothes at the camp because there was no fabric. After two years, everyone's clothing and shoes were wearing out. Most internees wore *bakis* on their feet – wooden soles tied with hemp straps to hold them in place. They were uncomfortable and left feet in a bloody mess of blisters but it was better than going barefoot on the hot cobblestones.

Ten minutes later, Tess found her. 'What are you doing here? They'll run out of rice again. And what in the world are you wearing?'

'A sheet. Does it suit me?'

Tess pulled Rose off the bench by her hands, turned her around and adjusted the sheet. 'It makes you look like a Roman Emperor in a toga.'

Rose sat back down with a sigh. 'Someone stole my uniform.' Her shoulders stooped. Suddenly, she felt like crying.

'Look on the bright side. At least it's warm. If you were in Brownville, you would freeze.'

'If I was in Brownville, I would buy myself new clothes.' Rose shook her head despondently. 'It's not just the uniform. The photographs of my parents were in the pocket. They mean the world to me.' She could get new clothes somehow but the photographs were irreplaceable. 'How could I have been so careless? Leaving it on the bench for anyone to take.'

'What else could you have done? It's not like you can wear your uniform in the shower.' The girls sat in silence for a moment, lost in thought. Finally, Tess said, 'I'm sorry about the photographs. Maybe they will turn up? The thief has no use for them.'

'Maybe,' Rose replied with no enthusiasm. She had a feeling that her precious photographs were in one of the garbage dumps lining the fence.

'You can't wear your toga to work. Your best bet is to have something made. I know someone who could help.'

Tess took Rose to a shantytown across the camp. In one of many huts that seemed to spring up here every day, made of sticks and mud and bits of canvas, they found an old woman called Laura, hunched and grey, her face wrinkled like a prune, a needle in her hands, a piece of cloth by her side. She took one look at Rose and her toga and said, without waiting for her to speak, 'Add your name to the list. I already have two hundred orders.'

'How long does it take you to complete each order?'

'Two or three days. If I had my sewing machine, I'd be faster but the guards took it.' Laura shook her needle in the direction of the entrance, where the guards were lurking with their machine guns and sour faces.

'That means it will take at least two years for my uniform to be ready,' Rose muttered. 'What will I wear in the meantime?'

The woman shrugged. 'Not my problem but I expect payment up front.'

'I can't walk around in a sheet for two years. Besides, who knows where we'll be in two years' time.'

'Everyone needs clothes *now*. That's why there's a queue. If you don't pay, I'm afraid I can't accept your order.'

'I understand,' said Rose, preparing to leave.

'But if you want to speed things up, you can always pay extra.'

'I don't have any money,' Rose stammered. In the camp, money was king. Those who had cash ruled their little world. They could buy extra food at the shops, have their hair styled at a hairdresser's salon and get a bigger plot of land for their vegetables. They could get anyone to do anything for them.

'Do you have any valuables? Jewellery? Furniture? Cigarettes?'

'I have a few books and a ukulele.'

'The ukulele will do. I will have your uniform ready for you by the end of next week.'

Rose thought of the precious instrument hidden away under her mattress. When she played it, she was no longer in the camp. She was no longer a prisoner. The music transported her to another place, another time. It sent her, if only for a moment, into David's arms, where she had been happy. She shook her head, turning away from the old woman and her sewing. 'Don't worry about it,' she said.

Dozens of patients arrived at their makeshift hospital every day, sick with beriberi and malaria, weak and dehydrated, begging the nurses for water and extra food. And every day, their supply of medicine dwindled, until there was nothing left and all they could do was sit with the sick and comfort them. Rose was talking to an old man who had broken his leg falling down a staircase, when a guard came in. She jumped to her feet as quickly as she could. The other nurses did the same. Rose bowed. The guard returned her bow with a solemn expression on his face. A moment later, Tess bowed, struggling to suppress a smile. The guard bowed back. Then five other nurses bowed one after another, forcing the guard to bow five more times. By the end of it, the man looked angry enough to strike someone. The nurses exchanged surreptitious looks. 'Silly pig,' Tess whispered in Rose's ear.

It was the game they had invented. If the Japanese imposed their rules on them, beating them and throwing them into solitary for not bowing in time, the nurses were going to have a little fun. They had a competition running – who could make the guards bow the most.

'Army nurses from Sternberg, you have a visitor,' the guard barked.

'A visitor?' Rose turned to the window, feeling a little dizzy. Often, she had no time to wait in line for her meals because she had so much to do at the hospital. Today was one of those days. 'I wonder who it could be.' In over two years at the camp, no one had come to see them.

Across the road from the main gate, she could see a sleek and shiny black car. Puzzled, she followed Tess and the guard to the visitor's room, and there stood Ida, looking sleek and shiny herself, smiling from ear to ear. Her cheeks had colour in them, her eyes glistened and she was dressed like a princess. The girls cried out, ran to her side and hugged her, showering her with kisses and questions, pinching her hands as if to make sure they were not imagining her. 'Ida, is it really you?'

'Of course it's me. Let me look at you!' Her eyes darted from

Rose to Tess. 'It's been such a long time.'

Rose tried to imagine what they looked like to their visitor. They had lost weight, their faces were an unhealthy colour, their eyes dark from lack of sleep. While Ida radiated health, Rose felt like she had aged forty years, not just two. 'You're not in one of the camps, like the rest of us?' she asked.

Ida shook her head. 'It helps being married to a German. The Japanese don't touch us because the Germans are their allies. We get all sorts of concessions. It's good for my husband's business.'

'Look at you. You are beaming,' said Tess.

'What can I say, I'm happy. It sounds horrible, knowing how many people are suffering. But I had a baby. She is the love of my life. Every minute of my day is filled with joy.' She hesitated. 'I've been searching every camp in Manila for you girls. It's good to finally find you. You've become so thin. It hurts me to see you like this. Back in Sternberg—'

'It was a different life,' Tess interrupted.

'How are you holding up?'

'Great,' said Rose. 'They feed us well. We attend lectures and theatre performances. We take dancing classes.' At the thought of Ruth, of the terror on her face, of her body leaning to one side and finally sliding to the ground, Rose started to cry. She couldn't say another word.

Ida hugged her tight. Her warm lips kissed Rose's cheek. 'I'm sorry, girls. I'm sorry you have to go through all this.' She touched Rose's hand. 'Why are you wrapped in a sheet? You have nothing else to wear? I'll help you. I can get you new clothes. I can get you food. You won't have to worry about anything.' Ida wiped the tears off her face. Her nose looked red. 'I want you to know that I'm thinking of you. Anything you need, you let me know. Look at the goods I have for you today.'

From under the table, Ida pulled out a box. When she opened it, the girls saw cans of meat, pickled tomatoes and cucumbers, silky underwear and socks. 'Great,' said Rose. 'Just what I needed.

I've learnt to knit underwear but I'm not very good. It comes out a funny shape and itches so badly, I haven't been able to wear it.' She picked up a bra and stroked the soft material with wonder. Never in her life had she seen anything like it, not even before the war, when she was free.

'I chose food that will last for you girls. But I will come again next week. I will bring some bread from my favourite bakery. Their croissants are to die for.' From the bottom of the box, she pulled out some chocolates. 'For Elsie.'

Rose looked at Ida's flushed face and smiled. 'After the way she treated you at Sternberg, you bring her chocolates?'

Ida waved her hands in the air dismissively. 'It's all in the past. Water under the bridge. You want me to bring you some mangoes next time? We have a mango tree in our garden.'

The girls nodded, grinning. Seeing Ida was a ray of light in the darkness, an unexpected treat. And it had nothing to do with the presents she brought. 'How can we ever thank you?'

Ida hugged them. 'No thanks necessary. At first, I felt so guilty, for doing well while everyone around me was suffering, for having food and money and options. But now I thank God for that because I can help you girls.'

The guard burst in and shouted that it was time to go. Rose felt so angry, she wanted to hit him. She wanted the clock on the wall to stop so she could stay with Ida a little longer, because her sudden reappearance in their lives brought a burst of fresh air and a whisper of freedom. For the first time in many months, Rose fell asleep that night with a smile on her face, her hand on Ida's presents under the bed. Perhaps their luck was changing. Perhaps God had not forgotten them here, in the POW camp in Manila, after all.

# Chapter 18

## February 1944

Ida was true to her word. The next day, Rose received her first ever package. She carried the precious box to her quarters, her heart slamming against her chest. It felt so good to know that someone on the outside was thinking of her, that she was not alone. Inside the box was a nurse's uniform and a note. 'I hope this fits better than the sheet. Love, Ida.'

The uniform was a little loose on Rose. Ida didn't realise how much weight she had lost. It would have fit perfectly back in Sternberg. Not that it mattered. It was comfortable and new, with no patches. The white fabric felt soft against her skin.

Turning this way and that in front of a dirty mirror, admiring herself in her new uniform, Rose felt an emotion she hadn't felt in a long time. Her heart filled with hope. It was as if the uniform was a reminder that there was life beyond these fences, that there had been a time when Rose was free, that, God willing, she won't be a prisoner forever.

To show off her new uniform, Rose decided to take an early morning stroll through the camp. Just like gardening and playing her ukulele, walking kept her sane. Slowly, she made her way through various shantytowns of Santo Tomas with funny names that never failed to make her smile, past rickety huts made of cardboard, bamboo and tar paper. Foggy Bottom was home to a group of middle-aged men who cleaned during the day and shouted loudly in the evenings. Over Yonder was filled with small children, who were running under everyone's feet, while their parents chased them. They spent their days begging for food but received hugs and kisses instead from their exhausted and teary mothers who had nothing to give them. Shantytown was occupied by older people who ran the camp school and busied themselves with theatre performances.

Whole lives were lived out within the barbed wire, filled with hope and joy and sadness and fear, and Rose saw it all this sunny morning as she ambled through the camp in her new uniform.

When she was walking through Foggy Bottom, marvelling at the brilliant stroke of luck that had brought Ida back into their lives, she saw a girl in front of her, a dustpan and broom in her hands. When the girl noticed Rose, she turned around, dropped the items she had been holding and began to walk away.

There was something familiar about her with her long red hair, her graceful neck, the haughty way she carried herself, like royalty, even though she was a prisoner here, just like everybody else. Rose wondered why she stormed off so suddenly, almost as if she didn't want to be recognised. She increased her pace, then broke into a run, trying to catch up to the girl. They raced through Over Yonder and Shantytown. Outside the main building, Rose, who was out of breath, her feet aching, grabbed the girl's hand. And as she did so, she understood why she had been so desperate to get away. The stranger was wearing Rose's old uniform, with its grey patches over the elbows and a little hole on the collar.

The girl tried to pull away but Rose didn't let her. Squeezing her hand tighter, she said, 'You are wearing my clothes.' When the stranger turned around, her eyes round and innocent, Rose gasped. 'Anne!'

'Hello, Rose.' There was no emotion on Anne's face. She didn't look at all surprised to find Rose at the camp of Santo Tomas, three years after they had seen each other last.

'What are you doing here? Petty thievery, by the looks of it.'

'What are you talking about?'

'The uniform. You stole it.'

'I did no such thing.'

Not letting go of Anne, Rose pointed at the sleeve, where her name was stitched in golden thread.

'What do you want me to do, strip naked in the courtyard?' Anne pulled herself up, trying to make herself appear taller.

Rose let go of Anne's hand and took a closer look at her. She had lost weight, like the rest of them. Her face looked gaunt, her hair limp. There were circles under her eyes. And only the arrogant expression on her face remained unchanged. 'Keep the uniform,' Rose said. 'In the inside pocket, there were photographs of my parents. I want them back.'

'Let me go. I didn't find any photographs.' Anne wrinkled her nose in disgust and tried to pull away.

Rose felt a flush of anger. She looked Anne up and down, wishing she could think of something sharp to say to wipe the smirk off her face. And then she noticed that the uniform was tight around her middle, the buttons straining. Her anger melted away. 'You're pregnant!' she exclaimed.

'That's none of your business.' Anne took a few steps away from Rose and rubbed her hand where she had grabbed her. 'I threw the photographs in the trash. Perhaps they're still there. Why don't you go and look for them?'

One day, when Rose was finishing her shift, anticipating a quick dinner and a few hours of rest, a guard burst into the hospital, asking to see a nurse. With horror, she recognised the man who had given the command to shoot when the escapees were brought back to camp. She blinked fast and her knees trembled. She didn't want to look at his face, didn't want to be reminded he had Ruth's blood on his hands.

In bad English he explained that he needed treatment for his bald spot. He was getting married soon and wanted to look his best on his wedding day. 'My bride, she doesn't like me bald.'

Rose wanted to point out that his bride had agreed to marry him knowing he was bald, but didn't dare. 'I could help you. I know just the thing,' she said, lowering her eyes, afraid that the man would notice the loathing on her face.

The guard perked up. 'Really?'

Tess looked at her with surprise. *Really?* she mouthed. There was no cure for baldness and they both knew it.

'Absolutely. But the Japanese don't give us any medicine. We hardly have anything left. No morphine, no sulfa that our patients need like air.'

'Will sulfa help with baldness?' asked the guard.

Rose shook her head. 'Not sulfa. Medicine called grow-hair. But it's very expensive. You can only get it in America.'

The guard beamed. His face lit up with hope. 'I will spare no expense. I will get morphine and sulfa and grow-hair too,' he said, bowing.

Trying hard not to smile, ignoring Tess who was shaking in silent laughter behind them, Rose bowed in response.

When he left, Tess asked, 'Why did you do that? You know nothing can grow the hair on his head. One of these days you will get us killed.'

Rose shrugged. 'Why? He left happy. He promised us supplies.'

On the way to her quarters, Rose took a detour and walked through Foggy Bottom where she had found Anne the day before. She saw her in the same spot, a broom in her hands, slowly moving down an alley, pushing rubbish around. Rose observed her for a few moments. David's little sister was thin like a stick and only her stomach protruded. Every now and then, she stopped and placed her hand on her back like it was bothering her. She glanced up, saw Rose and turned as if to run.

'Anne, wait,' cried Rose.

'What do you want from me now? I'm not giving you the uniform back. Finders keepers.'

'Keep the uniform. I don't mind.'

'Then what?' Anne's eyes flashed with hostility.

'Why don't you come and work at the hospital with us? We are always short-handed. Elsie will take you.'

'The last place I want to be is a filthy hospital filled with infectious cases. Not in my condition, thank you very much.'

'Then the camp is not the best place for you. Every few weeks, there are outbreaks of one thing or another. You can't escape it.' Rose spoke from experience. In the last few months, she had been sick five times.

'Thank you for letting me know,' said Anne, scoffing. 'I will go to the commandant and ask him nicely to let me go. Do you think he will listen? Perhaps he could charter a boat for me so I could return to America and stay with my parents.'

Rose hesitated. 'Speaking of your family, do you have any news of David?' She felt her hands begin to shake. The only thing that sustained her through these years was her hope that by some miracle David was still alive. What if right now Anne told her he hadn't made it?

The broom froze in Anne's hands. Her wary eyes watched Rose. 'I haven't heard from him since December 1941. I don't know if he's dead or alive.' She looked despondent and for the first time Rose felt warmth towards David's sister.

'He was one of my patients on Bataan in April 1942 but we got separated when the Japanese arrived,' Rose said.

'I know all about Bataan. You nurses left thousands of patients behind to the mercy of the enemy and ran to Corregidor like rats.'

'It wasn't like that ...' Rose stumbled. She didn't know what to say because it had been exactly like Anne was describing and nothing she said could change it. Sometimes she still woke up in the middle of the night screaming because the men's faces haunted her.

Anne glared at her. 'You left your patients to a certain death. You left David to a certain death.'

Rose trembled as she thought of the bombs falling on the hospital on Bataan, of the deafening sound of war, of David's panicked face and his terrified voice as he disappeared in a cloud of dust on that fateful day when she was forced to turn her back on him. She thought of waking up in the jungle without him, of 800 days of not knowing where he was. And here was his sister, her voice sounding just like the voice inside Rose's head, indignant and accusatory. 'It wasn't like that,' she whispered.

But Anne wasn't listening. 'My brother died because of you,' she said, her eyes like two burning coals of hatred. 'And you know that. How do you even live with yourself?'

Rose sat on her bed with a plate of dry rice in her lap and David's favourite book in front of her, open on his favourite page, the words he once loved bringing him back to life and filling her heart with longing. Santo Tomas had a large library with books for every taste and on every subject. She would never run out of reading material, even if she were to stay here for life, but she always returned to *The Great Gatsby*, reading it over and over again because it took her back in time, if only for a little while.

This evening, she couldn't concentrate on the book. The words twirled around the page, refusing to form coherent sentences, trembling in front of her weary eyes until she could no longer take it and had to look away. All she could hear was Anne's voice, all those years ago, telling her that her brother could never love her because he was betrothed to another, and the day before, accusing her of abandoning her brother to a certain death.

Through the window, she could see part of the road, beyond the fence and the barbed wire that separated them from freedom. A truck pulled up by the gate and two guards jumped down, followed by a dozen new detainees. The guards shouted and shook their machine guns, while men, women and children cowered in fear. Why do they always have to shout and threaten with weapons, Rose wondered, as if those poor people weren't frightened enough?

The sun was beginning to set. Rose always loved to watch as it disappeared from sight, the purple haze reminding her of another time, another sunset. In the waning light, she saw the new arrivals stumble across the courtyard. She wondered where they would sleep. The camp was bursting at the seams, and yet, the Japanese kept bringing more prisoners, with little thought of how they were going to house, feed or clothe them.

Most new arrivals disappeared inside the main building and only one young woman, thin and long-legged, with her light hair in a bun on top of her head, milled outside as if unsure what to do. As if she could sense Rose's eyes on her, she lifted her face.

'Kate!' shouted Rose, as she pushed her plate away and jumped off the bed. She ran as fast as she could, almost knocking an old lady off her feet, hastily apologising but not stopping. 'Kate!'

In seconds, Kate was standing in front of her. It was like an optical illusion, a mirage. She waited for Kate to disappear like an early morning dream but instead, she hugged her and whispered, 'Rose.'

Moments passed and still they remained in the middle of the courtyard on a warm February evening, holding each other.

Finally, Rose asked, 'Kate, what are you doing here? I thought you would be home by now or at least in Australia.'

Kate shrugged. 'We never made it to Australia.'

'Come with me,' said Rose. 'You must be hungry. I will feed you and then you can tell me everything.'

She took Kate to their allotment and brought the plate of rice she had left on her bed. They sat at the table next to each other, while Kate ate silently. Rose stroked Kate's arm. 'You are the last person I expected to see here,' she said. 'What happened?'

'After we left, we landed on Lake Lanao in Mindanao, to refuel. We thought we would be safe there because Mindanao was still in Filipino-American hands. Then we found out the Japanese invaded the island that morning. There was the biggest rush. We had to fly in the dark. The other plane took off but ours hit a rock and filled with water. I can't even begin to tell you how scary it was. The plane sinking, water up to my waist. We were all terrified.'

'I can imagine,' said Rose, shuddering.

'I thought, that's it. This is how my life is going to end.'

'Oh, no.'

The two of them sat holding hands, while all around people scurried past. It was dinner, the busiest time at Santo Tomas. 'We had to get off the plane and then the Japanese found us. We've been ferried from camp to camp ever since.'

'I'm so sorry, Kate.'

'Don't be. I'm glad to be here. I heard this camp is very good. I'm glad to see you again. Together, what do we have to fear?'

As she said that, tears ran down her face into the plate of old rice.

# Chapter 19

## March 1944

The monotony of her life at the camp overwhelmed Rose. Sometimes the loudspeaker, which woke them, came alive with angry Japanese voices ordering them to get up and report for roll call, while other times it played music. Once, a few months ago, it burst into *California I've been blue since I've been away from you*. Everyone around her hummed along, while Rose remained on her bed with her eyes closed and cried.

Day after day, roll call after roll call, she spent mindless hours in a queue, holding her enamel cup, plate and spoon. Then she took a cold shower that was observed by a hundred strangers, ate a plate of cold rice and walked to the hospital.

Tending to the sick and the wounded, Rose had seen it all – the jungle rot, funguses, diarrhoea, dengue fever and malaria – but she didn't mind. On the contrary, she was grateful for her patients. When she kept busy, the days flew by faster. At night, she would collapse into her bed made of wooden slats, without a mattress or a pillow, close her eyes and fall into black oblivion. After two and a half years in the camp, the slats were permanently wedged into her back, like tattoos.

The only thing that broke through the darkness, like sun through the cloud, were Ida's weekly visits. Every Monday at noon, she was there with gifts, hugs, smiles and excited chatter. She brought mangoes and cakes and canned meat, bread and pastries from the bakery, soap, clothes and books. Rose would touch the presents with awe, touch Ida's happy face and wonder what life was like on the outside. Somewhere behind the fence, people were baking bread, sewing clothes and making soap. Ida had a home to go to, a husband and a child, a normal life. It was hard to fathom, like a magical kingdom that only existed in fairy tales.

One Monday in mid-March, the girls were by the window, waiting impatiently for Ida's car to pull up outside.

'I wonder what she'll bring us this time,' said Tess. 'I hope it's food. We are down to one can of meat.'

Little by little over the last few weeks, their ration seemed to melt away. If it wasn't for Ida's offerings, Rose didn't know how they would survive.

'I can't wait to see her. It's been too long,' said Kate.

Rose looked at Kate's drawn face and thought how much she had changed since the last time she saw her. It wasn't the same Kate that returned to Manila months after flying for freedom to faraway Australia. Her hair was grey at 24, her face had lines on it, her clothes hung off her. She seemed to have aged two decades in two years. Rose wondered if she looked the same, if the transformation had been as severe. For once, she was grateful there weren't many mirrors in the camp and she didn't have to face her reflection on a daily basis. 'She's running late,' she said, glancing at the clock on the wall. It was fifteen minutes past noon. Ida should have been there by now.

'Don't you know Ida at all? She's always late,' said Tess, and the girls turned back to the window, waiting impatiently for their weekly miracle.

'What if she's not coming?' whispered Rose with dread.

‘There she is!’ exclaimed Kate.

The girls jumped up, their faces so close to the window, Rose could feel its cool surface with her forehead. They watched as the familiar black car stopped outside the gate, the door opened and Ida walked out.

‘She’s pregnant!’ exclaimed Tess with disbelief.

‘Are you sure?’ asked Rose, pushing Tess out of the way to see better. As Ida turned around to get something from the car, the light caught on her and Rose saw the rounded outline of her stomach. ‘She never said anything. Why hasn’t she said anything?’

‘Probably didn’t want to jinx it. She might tell us today.’

‘Today she’ll have no choice. She can hardly hide it,’ said Rose, wondering how their friend could go from not showing at all to looking heavy with child in the space of a week and remembering the loose outfits Ida had been wearing recently.

They watched Ida lift a large box and proceed towards the gates, her gait slow and uncertain. ‘She shouldn’t be carrying that,’ said Rose.

‘Yes, she should. It’s food for us,’ said Tess.

Rose was unable to sit still. She got up and paced between beds, every now and then returning to the window and glancing at Ida’s car. Any moment now, a guard would appear, they would execute their customary bowing ceremony and follow him to the visitors’ room.

But to Rose’s amazement, the door remained closed and no one came to fetch them. Ten minutes of tense silence later, they heard the main gate screech open and ran to the window, just in time to see Ida exiting the camp, looking dishevelled and upset. She was no longer carrying the box and when she turned around to throw one last glance towards the camp, Rose read disappointment in her face. Astonished, the girls watched as Ida stood in one spot for a moment, as if unsure what to do. Then she rubbed her back and lifted her head. The girls waved. Ida’s gaze was on their window but she couldn’t see them because the sun was in her eyes.

A moment later, she got into the driver's seat, started the engine and drove away, back to her safe and happy life, while the girls remained behind the barbed wire, surrounded by angry faces, speechless with regret.

That afternoon, Rose asked the friendlier of the guards if he knew why Ida didn't come to see them, having driven all the way to camp.

'Haven't you heard?' he said. 'No visitors are allowed.'

'Are you sure? She comes to see us every week. She brings food.'

'No food from outside allowed.'

'What do you mean? Everyone has visitors and packages from the outside.'

The guard shook his head. 'No more,' he said. 'Against the rules.'

'How can it be against the rules now when it wasn't last week?'

He nodded. 'A week ago, allowed. Today, not allowed. New commandant. New rules.'

Rose felt the loss intensely, as if something terrible had happened. The following Monday, even though they had little hope, the girls gathered by the window. For twenty minutes they stared at the empty road, at the dust swirling in the wind, at the gates that remained closed to the outside world.

When their worst fears were confirmed, that the change of rules was permanent and they might never see Ida again, Rose, Tess, Kate and Elsie fried the last remaining can of meat, divided it into four parts, a few tiny morsels, and ate it in silence. As she swallowed her last piece of meat, Rose wondered what they were going to do without Ida and the food she brought.

Overnight, it seemed, the camp of Santo Tomas descended into darkness. People hovered around the main square as if in a daze, their gaunt bodies trembling. They held their plates in their hands as they queued for food, with hope in their hearts, only to receive nothing but a handful of rotten rice. The stores, cafés and restaurants stood empty and abandoned. Where once there had been a buzzing trade were now empty walls. Schools closed down, forbidden by the new regime, and hungry children roamed the nooks and crannies of the shantytowns, begging for food with mournful faces. Instead of playing basketball and attending theatre performances, instead of learning Spanish and playing musical instruments, detainees fought one another like brigands over a plate of beans that tasted like wallpaper paste.

The hospital filled with prisoners suffering from malnutrition. Only occasionally they asked if there was any food for them. Most of the time they remained still, staring into space, muttering to themselves, following the nurses with their eyes as they made their way between beds.

Rose had known hunger before, on Bataan just before they escaped the invading enemy and on Corregidor when the Japanese took over. She was used to running on empty, assisting in surgeries, tending to patients while leaning on beds because she felt too weak to stand on her own two feet. But this void inside her was new. More and more each day, she felt like her body was shutting down. Things she used to do without thinking, like walking from her quarters to the hospital, had become an endurance feat. Every step she took required a tremendous effort, as if a tonne of bricks was pulling her down. As she bandaged infected limbs and changed beddings, as she read to sick children and washed her patients' faces with a wet sponge, all she could think of was food. But when she closed her eyes at night, it wasn't the food she saw. Hungry faces haunted her, children with their ribs poking through the skin, pleading for a morsel of bread, anything to take the hunger away.

After work, the girls would gather on their allotment and look with sadness at dry leaves and empty vegetable patches. Something was happening to the soil. It was no longer producing anything. Rose wasn't surprised. Of course, the plants were not growing. There was no life inside Santo Tomas anymore, only death.

They harvested their last eggplant in the fourth week of March and fried it. Even without butter or salt, it looked and smelled delicious.

Tess, Kate and Elsie ate their share quickly, while Rose stared at her plate, lost in thought. 'Eat,' said Kate. 'You need your energy.'

Rose shook her head. 'I will give it to the children at the hospital.'

Kate glanced at Rose's plate. There were maybe five tablespoons. It had been a small eggplant. 'How many children are you hoping to feed with that, Nurse Williams? Eat.'

But before Rose had a chance to eat, an old man stopped by their table, grey, hunched and despondent looking. He wore an eye patch and his one good eye glistened as he looked at the food on Rose's plate. 'Do you suppose there is a little bit for me?' he muttered, his crooked finger shaking in front of his large red nose.

The man looked like he could do with some food. He seemed ready to collapse. As if in a trance, Rose got up and pushed the plate closer to him, while Kate placed a hand on her arm to stop her. 'Move along, my friend,' she said to the man gently. 'There is not enough for us.'

'Not much,' he pleaded. 'Just one bite, to see what it tastes like.'

'No,' said Kate.

The old man started to cry. 'My grandson is sick. He's not getting enough food. He's only five. Please give me some, for him.'

Manoeuvring her body around Kate and her outstretched arms, Rose shoved the plate towards the man, who grabbed it without a word and disappeared.

'Didn't even say thank you,' said Kate, shaking her head. 'You are too kind for your own good. And too gullible.'

'It breaks my heart to see so many people suffering. Especially children.'

'How much do you want to bet that he is around the corner now, eating the eggplant himself? He invented a little boy to extort food from you.' Kate took Rose's hand and squeezed it, as if what she was about to say was of utmost importance and she didn't want her to miss a single word. 'I've seen this before. The camps I've been at …' She fell quiet for a moment, her eyes flashing. 'Let's just say, things can get pretty bad. Hold on to your food. If you want to survive, don't give away a single bite.'

# Chapter 20

## April–May 1944

It was nine in the morning, half an hour after she was supposed to start her shift, and Rose was struggling up the stairs to the hospital, wondering why the steep climb seemed more challenging every day, why her limbs felt heavier than ever before. 'I can't do it,' she thought to herself. 'I can't make it.' She paused in the middle of the staircase, holding on to the wall, looking at the impossible summit in front of her, when she heard a shrill voice.

'I asked for a glass of water twenty minutes ago,' a man was shouting. 'I didn't survive the Bataan Death March to die from thirst in this lousy hospital.'

Bataan Death March! Hearing the words gave Rose the strength she needed to stumble up the remaining steps. She fetched a glass of water from the kitchen and approached the man, her eyes down as she stepped over half a dozen patients who were sleeping on the floor between beds. 'Rose? Rose Williams?' exclaimed the man who moments ago had been screaming for water. His voice was no longer shrill with indignation. It filled with warmth.

She recognised her former patient instantly. The same red face, the same irritated curve to his mouth. How many times had she had to lower her voice or stop playing her ukulele to David to avoid waking the angry man in the bed next to them? The glass shook in her hands. Some water spilled on her uniform. 'Kenneth Andrews,' she said. 'I never thought I'd see you again.'

'After you left us all on Bataan? I never thought I'd see you either. It's good to run into a familiar face in this hellhole.'

She handed him the glass and perched on the edge of his bed, not because she wanted to be closer to him but because her legs were suddenly too weak to hold her. 'How have you been?' she asked. 'I can see you haven't changed a bit.' David's buddy from Bataan was just as loud, just as irritated as he had been at the jungle hospital.

'Lousy. My feet are swollen. My gums too. My teeth feel loose.'

Rose glanced at his chart. 'You have scurvy. Unfortunately, they don't feed us well enough to avoid that sort of thing.'

'Can you give me something for it? A vitamin shot? A fresh orange?' He chuckled. 'I don't suppose you have one of those?'

'No oranges and no vitamin shots, either. I'm sorry.'

'Well, that's unfortunate. I don't want to lose my teeth. No woman will want to marry me.'

'Don't worry, women don't marry for teeth. They marry for personality.' She adjusted his pillow and took his empty glass. 'And you have plenty of that.'

A patient was calling for her from across the ward. She ignored him, hovering over Kenneth's bed.

'You sure are busy around here,' he said.

'Everybody is getting sick.' She hesitated. 'I heard you talk about the Bataan Death March. What did you mean?' She held her breath, waiting for his answer, afraid of what she was about to hear.

'Exactly what is sounds like. The cursed enemy soldiers rounded us up like cattle and made us march for miles across the peninsula, without food, without water. They beat us and shot us and left our bodies by the side of the road. No one survived.'

'You survived.'

'Barely. Look at me.'

Her hands shaking, Rose glanced at his skeletal body, at his arms and face covered in scars, at his sunken eyes and hollow cheeks. She sat back down next to him and took his hand. 'Kenneth, do you remember David?'

'How could I forget? The two of you drove me crazy with your books and music and conversations.'

Rose felt her hands trembling. After two years of starting every morning with a prayer, after many months of waiting for news, was she about to learn what had happened to her lover? She couldn't take it and yet desperately needed to know. Kenneth took his time to reply, as if he was putting off an unpleasant task. As she waited for him to speak, there was only one thought running through her head. 'Please, God, let him be alive.'

'I'm sorry, darling. He didn't make it. I saw with my own two eyes as the guards dragged him away because he was walking too slowly and couldn't keep up. I heard the sound of gun shots.'

Something was happening to her vision. She was looking straight at Kenneth but could no longer see his face. She could hear his voice but couldn't make out the words. Everything was fuzzy in front of her as she stumbled away from him, away from the hospital, towards the bustling courtyard, where men were fighting over a bowl of corned beef hash. It was a sunny morning but all Rose could see was darkness as she sank to the ground, her face in her hands. A former patient sat next to her. He spoke at length about his dizziness and demanded to know if he should check himself into the hospital. 'Are there any beds? Will the nurses have food for me?' She didn't reply and didn't even look at him. After a while, he moved on but she remained on the cobblestones, struggling to breathe.

She didn't know how long she stayed there. It could have been minutes or hours. She heard a kind voice asking what was wrong and a pair of strong hands guiding her back to her quarters and pushing her towards her bed. She tried to argue, to say she didn't need to lie down but couldn't find the right words. When she closed her eyes, she saw Kenneth's face and heard his devastating words inside her head, over and over like a curse. *They took him away. And then they shot him.*

*'You are my first love,' she whispered to him with tears in her eyes as they lay in each other's arms on the sand, days before the Japanese bombs fell on Pearl Harbor, tearing them apart. They had mere moments together but didn't know it yet.*

*'Why do you look so sad? You look like you are about to cry,' he said.*

*'I'm afraid.'*

*'What are you afraid of?'*

*'I don't want to lose you.'*

*'You won't lose me.' He stroked her hand, small reassuring movements that made her tremble. 'I'm not going anywhere.'*

*'You say war is coming. Anything could happen. You might have to go and fight. I couldn't bear that.'*

*He took her face in his hands and turned her towards him. 'I promise, no matter what happens, I will find you. If I'm alive, I will come back to you.'*

*And if you are not? she wanted to ask but couldn't. She couldn't get the words out, couldn't say them out loud in case by some dark magic it would make them real.*

*'I will always be with you because you are my first love too,' he whispered to her when it was still peace, when they still had hope and joy and each other.*

Rose remained in her bed all day and night, eyes wide open, listening to the prisoners shouting as they squabbled and settled to sleep. In the morning, she couldn't get up to go to work.

Tess and Kate clucked over her like a pair of hens, asking what was wrong, offering her food, water and kind words. 'Look, I brought you some rice,' said Kate, breezing in at lunch with a plate and a bright smile.

Rose turned away. The sight of food made her nauseous.

'You don't want it? Rice is a rarity these days. I queued for two hours to get three spoons. I was lucky. After they served me, they ran out. Everyone in the queue behind me left empty-handed.' Kate sighed. 'There was some burnt rice stuck to the bottom of the pot. The cook threw it away and people started fighting over it. One man got a black eye, another a sprained ankle, suddenly there was a knife and all hell broke loose, all because of some burnt rice. And then they scooped it up with their fingers and shoved it in their mouths, dirt and all. It was heartbreaking to see.'

'I'm not hungry,' said Rose. 'Why don't you have it?'

She tried to push the plate away but Kate was having none of it. 'Did you know that four patients died at the hospital yesterday? They weren't sick. They weren't injured. They were just …' For a moment, Kate stopped talking and looked at Rose with gloomy eyes. 'Hungry. They died from starvation. So stop arguing with me and eat your rice.'

Rose shook her head.

'Why are you so sad?' asked Kate. Rose couldn't tell her. To say it out loud, to hear the sentences come out of her mouth was more than she could bear. Kate continued, 'We are not doing too badly. We are still alive. One day, the war will be over. Everything will be all right.'

'How? There's no more food,' Rose whispered, blinking fast because she didn't want Kate to see her cry.

'There's this rice. Remember what you told me on Corregidor when I was having a bad day? We take it one step at a time. We don't think about the future and that's how we survive. Little steps.'

'Did I say that?' Corregidor seemed like a lifetime ago.

'Yes. Now eat and try to get some sleep.'

Rose ate the three spoons of rice but couldn't sleep. In the dark, David's face came to her. His eyes, his smiling mouth, like he was happy to see her, like they were still in Manila and she was running to him from the hospital, dressed in her Sunday best, asking breathlessly, 'Where are we going today? Where are you taking me?' Ready for another adventure, another wonderful day with him.

In the morning, she got up before the sun and went to look for Anne. She found her in the line for showers. Joining her, ignoring half a dozen people shouting at her to move to the end of the queue, she said, 'I need to talk to you.'

'I thought I told you never to speak to me again.' Anne glared at her. Rose was surprised by how unwell she looked. Her skin was sallow and grey. There were empty hollows where her cheeks had once been. Her eyes were dark, as if a light had gone out.

'It's important,' said Rose.

'Can it wait till after my shower? It's almost my turn.'

'It cannot wait.'

'All right. Make it quick.'

But Rose couldn't make it quick. Suddenly, she couldn't speak at all. Despite their differences, she didn't want to be the one to cause Anne unbearable pain. And what if Anne accused her again? What if she told Rose that David's death was her fault, as if she didn't already blame herself? But she was his sister. She deserved to know. 'It's about David,' she whispered, choking on her tears.

The expression on Anne's face softened. She no longer looked at Rose with disgust. They stepped away from the line of people and for a moment stood facing each other in silence. Rose wished she could close her eyes, so she wouldn't see the heartbreak on Anne's face. She leaned on the wall and cried, while the shower line moved past them and people gawked at the two of them with interest.

'I'm sorry, Anne,' Rose said finally, ready to break down. 'I'm so sorry. David didn't make it. He died on Bataan. One of my patients told me the Japanese—'

Anne lifted her hand, interrupting Rose. Her face crumbled. 'Stop,' she whispered, lifting her broken eyes to Rose. 'I can't hear it. I can't take it.'

Without another word she took off in the direction of the main building, while Rose remained, leaning on the wall, sobbing quietly.

Rose looked at her reflection in the mirror, at her long face, her trembling hands, her tense shoulders. Outwardly she seemed like the same person she had been two days ago. She wondered how it was possible, when everything inside her felt irrevocably broken.

Since she had left Bataan, through Corregidor and Santo Tomas, through gloom, death and despair, only one thing sustained her and gave her strength. She was waiting for the war to end so she could find him again. And why not? She had found him once before, against all odds. He made her better because he was the best person she knew. When she was with him, she liked herself more, as if she could see herself through his eyes. He brought her joy and light, but now that he was gone, only darkness remained.

She remembered what her father had said to her once. *As long as others need us, our lives have meaning*. The next morning, she returned to work, even though her heart was aching and she could barely walk. Perhaps if she lost herself in others' pain, she wouldn't hurt so much. It had helped her in the tunnels and in the last two and a half years here, at the camp, but it didn't help her now, even though the patients' needs were great and she barely had a minute to herself.

In the afternoon, she heard a strange noise. A small pebble hit the window of the ward, and then another and another. At first, she thought it was raining. But no, the sun was bright and the sky was clear, just like before. It broke Rose's heart a little to see the beautiful weather outside. She needed it to rain, craved the grey skies over her head and the bitter wind in her hair because she wanted nature to mourn, just like she herself was mourning.

Kenneth said from across the ward, 'It must be for you, Nurse.' When she stepped to the window to check, he added with a crooked smile full of black teeth, 'A secret admirer?'

At first, she didn't see anything. But when she moved away from the window, another pebble hit the glass. She looked down one more time and noticed Anne's stooped silhouette. She opened the window. 'What are you doing here? Come up to the ward.'

'No, you come down.'

When Rose came down, Anne pushed something wrapped in paper into her hands. 'I brought you this.'

Rose unwrapped the small package and saw the photographs she thought she had lost, of her parents and herself when she was four and sixteen. At the sight of their familiar smiles, the ice inside her heart melted a little. She wanted to cover the old pictures with kisses, wanted to touch their beloved faces. Instead, she looked at Anne and asked, 'Why are you giving them back?'

'I want you to have them. I know they mean a lot to you.'

'Thank you,' said Rose, hiding the photographs in her pocket, close to her heart.

'Are you busy? I was hoping we could talk,' said Anne.

'I'm busy. But I can spare a few minutes.'

They sat side by side on the stairwell, not looking at each other. Anne said, 'I don't even know what to say. I just feel so sad. I wanted to be next to someone who loved him too.'

'I'm always here if you need me, if you want to talk or sit in silence.'

Anne curled into a small pretzel, her body trembling a little. 'He was furious with me for joining the Nurses Corps, for coming here. He knew it was dangerous. He always tried to protect me, from everything. And it was him all along who needed protection.' She dropped her head into her hands and cried. 'I feel like I failed him. I wasn't there for him when he needed me. He died all alone.'

'Don't blame yourself. It's not your fault.'

'The last time we saw each other, back in December 1941 at Sternberg, we had an argument. I said such hurtful things to him.

Now I wish I could take every single one of them back.'

'What did you argue about?'

'I can't even remember. It was so silly.' Anne sobbed. 'I told him I never wanted to see him again. Those are the last words my brother ever heard from me.'

Rose resisted the desire to put her arm around Anne's tiny, shaking, grieving body. Something told her she wouldn't appreciate that. 'We all say things we regret sometimes. He knew you didn't mean it. He knew how much you loved him. He spoke about you all the time.'

Anne sniffed and rubbed her eyes, smudging dirt over her face. 'He did?'

Rose nodded. 'He told me he was so proud of you, for becoming a nurse in spite of your parents' wishes, for helping people. He wasn't angry that you came here. He was just afraid for you.'

For a few silent moments, they watched the stream of people flowing past. Then Anne said, her voice croaky, 'When we were children, we had a dog. A little spaniel called Henry. One day we were playing by the river. David and I were throwing a ball to each other, while Henry chased it.'

'How old were you?'

'I was nine and David was twelve. I threw the ball too hard and it landed in the river. Henry jumped in the water. We shouted for him not to go but he didn't listen. He wasn't very obedient. The current was strong that day. Henry lost his footing and started to go under.' Anne fell quiet, looking into the distance, beyond the camp, towards childhood and freedom.

'What happened next?'

'I jumped in. But I wasn't a strong swimmer and before I knew it, I was drowning too, spluttering, struggling for breath.'

'Oh, no,' said Rose.

'David had a fear of water as a child. Never came near it, even when we all went to the seaside for a holiday. But when he saw Henry and me in that river, he jumped in right away, without a second thought.'

'Sounds like him.'

'He saved my life that day, and Henry's. He was a hero. I thought our parents would be proud of him but they were angry we risked our lives over some dog. Only Henry wasn't just some dog. He was our best friend.' Anne's body shook as she cried. 'When David was around, I knew I had nothing to fear. He would never let anything happen to me. What do I do now? What do I do without him?'

Crying herself, her heart aching, Rose held Anne in her arms, stroked her back and said, 'You continue to live, for both of you. It's what he would have wanted.'

When the first patient had died from hunger at the hospital, Rose spent all day crying. The all too familiar helplessness suffocated her. The man hadn't been sick, he hadn't been wounded. His limbs were not infected and he didn't suffer from an incurable disease. He didn't need quinine or morphine or bandages on his body. All he needed was food.

The next day, five people died from starvation. The day after that, it was seven. A week later, a dozen a day were dying. Rose no longer cried. She had no tears left. Only her heart ached because, no matter how hard she tried, she couldn't help them. She couldn't even help herself.

One day at the start of May, Red Cross comfort kits arrived at the camp. The detainees gathered in the yard, beaming with joy, unable to believe their luck. It was the first communication with the US they had had since the war had come to the Philippines. To the thousands of men and women standing in uneven lines under the Japanese machine guns, fearful, emaciated and sad, the comfort kits were more than just boxes of food. They represented hope. The US officials had not forgotten them after all and perhaps help was on the way.

Rose found herself in the first row, her stomach aching. What was inside these boxes? Was there enough for everybody? She wanted to feel full, wanted desperately to forget once and for all the numbing light-headedness and the hungry fog inside her head.

After a short speech commanding the detainees to feel eternal gratitude to the Japanese government that felt charitable enough to allow the comfort kits to be distributed among the prisoners, the guards began to slash the boxes open, while at the back of the queue, someone muttered, 'Charitable? They just can't be bothered to feed us themselves.'

Swish-swish-swish went the Japanese swords as they cut at the boxes.

A woman shouted, her voice shrill with fear, 'Be careful. You will damage the goods.' The human mass quivered.

Cans of salmon and meat rolled out of the boxes into the dirt. The detainees took a collective breath. They hadn't seen fish or meat for many months. People cheered. Some prisoners threw their hats up in the air, like they were greeting royalty. All around her, Rose heard elated voices.

'We'll have a nice meal tonight.'

'Strawberry jam, my favourite!'

'Do you think there's some chocolate in there for me?'

The mountain of food grew taller as the guards opened one box after another. One prisoner reached for the meat and nearly paid for it with his hand, the guard's sword descending on it with lightning speed. A woman grabbed a can of fish and was beaten with a stick. The guards told everyone to take a few steps back. Reluctantly, the prisoners obeyed, staring at the food like it was the only thing standing between them and death.

When everyone fell quiet, the guards took their knives out and began stabbing the cans. Rose watched in horror as juicy morsels of meat and salmon fell in the dust and swarms of flies descended on them. People screamed and howled. Rose covered her ears with her hands, feeling like screaming and howling too.

'What are you doing? Barbarians! People are dying from hunger and you are destroying the food.'

Ignoring the outraged mob, the guards continued to stab the cans with their knives. They broke open packets of prunes and raisins, and Rose watched helplessly, her hand at her mouth, as they spilled all over the cobblestones in a dark sticky puddle. She thought she heard the guard say they were checking for contraband. She might have imagined it.

A moment later, all hell broke loose. People threw themselves on the ground to get to the food. They picked morsels of fish and meat out of the mud and shoved them in their mouths. They pushed each other and trampled all over one another. A small child was screaming because someone stepped on his foot. A woman was crying because someone pulled a packet of dates out of her hands.

Suddenly, a gunshot was heard. The prisoners moved back. The guards ordered everyone to move inside, while they cleared up the mess. From the windows, devastated people watched as the men swept up the food they so desperately needed to survive and placed it in trash cans.

Not all the food had been destroyed, however, and that afternoon, Rose was surprised to receive a small bar of chocolate. She placed it on the table in front of her and sat down, touching it with the tips of her fingers. This chocolate had come all the way from the US. All the way from home. She peeled back the wrapping a little, just enough to be able to see inside. Bringing it to her face, she closed her eyes and inhaled. The chocolate didn't smell of much but she could almost taste the sweetness in her mouth. She took a bite and then another, the long-forgotten taste filling her with memories. She was desperate to finish her chocolate but didn't. With a superhuman effort, she hid what was left of it in her pocket and went in search of Anne.

'I brought you something.' She placed the chocolate in Anne's hands.

Anne lifted the chocolate and stared at it mutely, as if she had never seen anything like it before and didn't know what to do with it. Finally, she looked at Rose and said, 'I can't take your food.'

'Of course, you can. And you will. In your condition, you need every little bit you can get.'

'What about you? You don't want it?'

'Don't worry about me. I don't even like chocolate.'

Anne unwrapped the chocolate and took a small bite. She closed her eyes, an expression of pure joy on her face. Then she took another bite, and another. A small part of Rose hoped that she wouldn't finish it all, that maybe there would be a little bit left for her. But Anne finished every bite. 'You are such a liar,' she said finally, straightening the wrapper and placing it in her pocket for safekeeping. 'You love chocolate. I saw you at mealtimes at Sternberg, always going back for more dessert. Why did you give it to me?'

'You need it more than I do. When is your baby due?'

Anne shrugged, tears in her eyes. 'I'm not even sure anymore. I've lost track of time. I met the baby's father in the other camp. When he found out I was pregnant, he asked me to marry him. He wanted this baby so much.'

'Where is he now?'

Anne's mouth twitched and her eyes filled with pain. 'He was killed. Shot by a guard for taking an extra plate of rice. He wanted me to eat, wanted our baby to be healthy, and he paid for it. I'm petrified, Rose. I don't care what happens to me anymore. All I care about is this baby. What if something goes wrong?'

'Nothing will go wrong. You don't have to worry about anything. You are not alone.' As she said that, Rose thought of herself crouching on the floor of the hospital the previous afternoon, holding a patient's hand as he quietly slipped away. She thought of the ration, reduced to almost nothing, of cans of fish and meat on the ground, covered by flies, and of the guards who cared so little whether the people in their care lived or starved to death. She suspected things were only going to get worse but she did her best to smile, to look unconcerned, for Anne's sake.

'Why are you helping me?' Anne whispered. 'I haven't exactly been nice to you.'

Rose hesitated. 'Because you're right. What happened to David was my fault.'

'I didn't mean … I shouldn't have said it. You are a good person, I can see that now.'

'Every night I lie awake at night and I can't breathe because the guilt is suffocating me. Perhaps if I help you, a little bit of that guilt will leave me. Not all of it. Just a little bit. David would have wanted me to look after his sister. He would have wanted me to be there for you and the baby.' Rose sighed and glanced inside her hands. She couldn't look into Anne's eyes because they were so much like David's. 'See, I'm not as good as you think. I'm helping you out of selfish reasons.'

'You are not selfish at all,' said Anne, hugging Rose. 'Now I understand why David loved you so much.'

Rose trembled in Anne's arms, unable to believe her ears. Did she just say that David had loved her? It went against what she had told her previously, that David's heart belonged to another, that he couldn't wait to start his life with Celia, and that Rose had merely been a distraction, a final fling before he settled down. She wanted to ask Anne about it, to challenge her, to force her to tell the truth, but didn't dare.

# Chapter 21

## June 1944

One day in early June, the sun disappeared behind black clouds, while heavy rain washed away the last remnants of canned meat and the blood on the cobblestones where the prisoners had fought over food. From every window, forlorn faces peeked at the deluge, lost and fearful, as if at any moment they expected to be swept away by the torrent. Rose was not afraid of the tropical storm, even though thunder exploded overhead like bombs, deafening her. She stood in the empty courtyard with her arms outstretched and relished the sensation of cool water on her weary, overheated body. It felt cathartic, like a prayer, like a new beginning.

Suddenly, she heard shouting. The magic of the moment faded away. She spun around.

Across the courtyard from her was Anne, her bare stomach large and round, Rose's old uniform no longer buttoning over it, her hair like seaweed over her face, eyes bulging. In her hands was a bowl of what Rose thought looked like mung beans. She held the bowl close to her chest, while a teenage boy tried to wrestle it from her. It was Anne who had been screaming, while the boy uttered profanities under his breath.

'Leave her alone,' cried Rose, breaking into a run.

Startled, the boy let go, Anne lost her balance and fell, the bowl flying out of her hands, breaking into a dozen pieces on the ground, spilling mung beans everywhere. Anne and the boy paused for a moment, looking under their feet at the precious food. Anne said, 'Now look what you've done.'

Rose helped Anne up. 'Are you all right?'

There were tears in Anne's eyes. 'I'm fine. Don't worry.'

'Are you sure?' asked Rose. Anne's hand was on her back and her face was twisted like she was in pain.

'I'm sure.'

The boy scooped up the beans together with dirt and sand, shoving them inside his mouth. Rose grabbed his hand. 'You should be ashamed of yourself. I know your parents. Wait till I tell them what you get up to in the middle of the day when they aren't watching. Terrorising pregnant ladies, taking their food.'

'Let me go,' cried the boy, pulling hard.

Rose wasn't strong but the boy was weaker than her, his arm like a matchstick under her fingers. Despite feeling sorry for him, she was still angry. 'Or should I tell the guards what you've been doing? What you need is a night in the solitary to teach you some manners.'

Anne placed her hand on Rose's arm. 'He's just hungry, Rose. Hunger makes us do things we wouldn't otherwise do.'

'I'm hungry too. I don't go around attacking vulnerable people.'

'Let him go. I can't even look at him without pity.'

Rose released the boy and he stumbled away, soon disappearing around the corner. She turned to Anne. 'Are you feeling all right? You look so pale.'

'Something is happening. I feel sharp pain here.' Anne pointed to her abdomen.

'Let's get out of the rain. I'll take a look at you. Perhaps he pushed you too hard and you hurt yourself.'

'I don't think it's because he pushed me. It started this morning.

It comes and goes. At first, I thought it was hunger. But it's more than that …' Her hands were trembling. She groaned, bent over and rubbed her back. 'Here it is again. Why does it hurt so much?'

'Sounds like you are having contractions. Perhaps you are in early labour. Let's go to the hospital. We'll need some clean linen and boiled water. We'll try to find you a bed where you can rest. The baby is coming.'

Anne paled, her eyes large and frightened. 'I don't think I can do it. I'm afraid of pain.'

Rose placed her hand on her stomach. 'Try not to think about it. Focus instead on meeting your baby, holding him or her in your arms, kissing him or her for the first time. Can you do that for me?'

Anne nodded, trying to smile. 'I'm desperate to know if it's a boy or a girl.'

'You'll find out soon enough. Which would you prefer?'

'I want a girl so I can braid her hair and teach her everything I know. And Marcus wanted a boy. I'll be happy if it's a boy, for Marcus.' Not moving, Anne stared at Rose with large eyes. 'I'm scared, Rose. What if something goes wrong?'

'Don't be scared. It will be over soon and once it's over, you won't even remember the pain because you will have your precious baby.'

'How do you know? Have you had a baby before?'

'No, but I have delivered dozens of them and I know for a fact that you'll be just fine.'

'I've delivered them too. It's not the same, is it?'

Another contraction made Anne cry out. To distract her, Rose asked, 'Have you thought of names?'

'Not yet. I was too afraid. Didn't want to tempt fate.'

'Perhaps now will be a good time.' She took Anne by the elbow, directing her towards the hospital, helping her up the slippery stairs to the ward and settling her into a bed that by some miracle had become available.

'Should I be in hospital? Is it safe?'

Rose knew Anne had every reason to be worried. In recent weeks, waves of infectious diseases had swept through the camp – chicken pox, whooping cough, measles, diphtheria. There was nowhere to hide, not in their sleeping quarters or the line for showers, nor even outside in the yard, where crowds of people milled around every day, looking for food. What could Rose do? How could she protect Anne and her baby? 'You can't have the baby in the rain. Now, will you be all right here for a minute? I need to boil some water and get everything ready.'

Anne nodded. 'I'll be all right,' she whispered. Putting her hand over Rose's, she added, 'Thank you, for everything. I don't know what I would do without you. And I'm sorry.'

'Sorry for what?'

Anne stared at her for a moment without a word. Her eyes were dark, unblinking, afraid. 'For stealing your uniform,' she said finally.

David Robert Taylor was born in the early hours of the morning, as the sun fought to break through the clouds and thunder roared overhead like a cannon saluting an emperor. And like a true emperor, David Junior had everyone at the hospital at his beck and call. The mother and the nurse who delivered him couldn't take their eyes off him and neither could the patients, who gathered around, desperate to catch a glimpse of the baby. In the end, Rose had to ask everyone to leave. Mother and son needed their rest. What they didn't need was a crowd of sick people breathing over them.

'I can't believe you called him David,' Rose whispered, perching on the edge of Anne's bed, watching the baby who was sleeping soundly in his mother's arms, content and without a care in the world. He didn't know he had been born a prisoner. He didn't know there were fences and barbed wire and machine guns out there, intent on keeping him in. And for now, none of it mattered, as long as his mother was by his side. 'It suits him.'

'Do you think my brother would approve?' asked Anne, her lips pressed to the baby's head, a delighted smile on her face.

'He would be so proud of you. You did great.'

Anne kissed the baby's tiny nose. 'He's perfect,' she whispered. 'Out of all the babies you delivered, isn't he the best?'

'He is the best baby in the whole of the Philippines,' said Rose, and she meant it.

'I wish he could have met his uncle. I wish he could meet the rest of our family.'

'One day he will. One day all this will be behind us, and we'll be allowed to return home. Your little boy will meet his grandparents.'

'But not my brother,' Anne said sadly.

The baby stirred and whimpered, then opened his eyes and started to cry. Anne bent her head to him, whispered something, crooned a song in his ear. The baby cried harder.

'What do I do? Why is he so upset?'

'Perhaps he's hungry. Why don't you try feeding him?'

When David was nursing happily, Anne said, 'This is my biggest achievement, you know? I feel like I've done something with my life. Something worthwhile. If anything happens to me, I will be leaving something behind.'

Anne fell asleep with the baby in her arms but Rose remained in a little chair by her side, watching David's nephew and occasionally touching his tiny face, like she couldn't believe he was real. He was a miracle baby, proof that there was hope for them after all, that light would always triumph over darkness, even at war, even in a gloomy prison where death reigned.

A week after baby David was born, Rose was queuing for food, leaning on a wall for support. Her hands trembled, her knees felt weak, her vision was blurry and she moved at a slow pace like an automaton, a fog inside her head making her dizzy. All her senses were on edge this morning. The sun seemed too bright, the sky too blue, the voices around her too loud. All she could think about was food. When she woke up, she thought about breakfast. And after she finished her few spoons of mungo beans or corn mash, she would get up from the table and feel just as hungry, her stomach just as empty as before she had sat down. She would spend hours thinking of lunch and dinner, counting down the minutes until she received a hundred grams of unidentified gooey mass that smelled and tasted disgusting but would disappear off everyone's plates in mere seconds. When she closed her eyes at night, she saw steel cans bleeding meat all over the cobblestones.

These days at the camp, food only existed in Rose's imagination. She hadn't seen rice for many weeks. There were no eggs, meat or milk, and almost no vegetables. She wondered what they would receive at the canteen this morning. When it was her turn, she saw that they were having *camotes*, a poor-quality sweet potato grown in the Philippines. Not only did it have little nutritional value but it didn't taste of much. It was like chewing dust.

In her hands she held two plates – hers and Anne's. She placed them in front of the server. 'My friend Anne just had a baby. I want to take her food to her.'

The woman shook her head, her eyes darting around like a frightened rabbit's. 'If your friend wants the food, she has to come here herself.'

'She is still recovering. She can't wait in line for two hours with her baby. I want to help her.'

'The guards will shoot me for giving away food. My orders are strict. One bowl per person.'

Rose took the plates, one empty and one with a few spoons of *camotes*, and considered her options. She could watch David while Anne got her food but then she would be late for work. She could ask Tess or Kate to look after the baby but she knew they were on nightshifts that week and would most likely be in bed. There was nothing to do but give her breakfast to Anne and go to work on an empty stomach. It wouldn't be the first time and

Rose knew it wouldn't be the last.

'Look,' she said to Anne when she reached her quarters. 'I picked up your food for you this morning.'

While Rose held little David, Anne ate the *camotes*. 'Is there more?' she asked. 'I feel so hungry all the time. Must be the breastfeeding.'

'I'll try to find something,' said Rose, looking away so Anne wouldn't notice the desperation in her eyes. Every time a patient died from hunger at the hospital, Rose felt helpless and afraid. Helpless because there was nothing she could do to help. Afraid because she wondered if she was going to be next.

Anne looked up at Rose and the spoon shook in her hand. 'How will I look after the baby? There is no food. What if I have no milk for him?'

'You just worry about little David. Let me worry about everything else.'

Rose set out for work, her step heavy. Trembling, she stood before the staircase leading to the hospital. Everything swam before her eyes like that one time, years ago in Manila, when she and David had been dancing for too long and he spun her in the air until she was dizzy and collapsed on top of him in a heap of intoxicated giggles. Now she stood at the bottom of the stairs without David, lost and alone, and didn't know what to do because she couldn't make it up to the wards where she was required to sit by the dying and comfort them in their last moments on this earth.

Slowly, little by little, step by step, she reached the hospital entrance and paused for a moment, wondering what was happening to her. Had she finally contracted the dreaded beriberi? She had no fever and her ankles weren't swollen. No, she decided, it was just hunger.

As soon as she walked into the ward, Elsie was by her side, her face red, her hands flailing. She opened her mouth and closed it like a fish.

'Is everything all right?' asked Rose. She had never seen Elsie so agitated.

'No, everything is not all right,' the chief nurse cried. 'The guards were here. They threatened me.'

'What did they want?' Suddenly, Rose felt so tired, she wanted to fall into one of the hospital beds, close her eyes and escape into oblivion, to not see, to not think.

'They are angry because we are putting starvation as the cause of death on our patients' death certificates.'

'But it's true. Starvation is the reason the patients are dying. What do they want us to say?'

Elsie trembled. 'They want us to put down some infectious disease instead. They want no blame in this.'

'That's preposterous. They don't give us anything to eat. And they expect us to lie on official documents?'

Elsie bowed her head. For the first time since Rose had met her, she looked completely lost. 'Sometimes I wonder if it's all part of their plan. Perhaps they are starving us because they can't manage so many of us. It's a big responsibility, taking care of 4,000 internees. It's costly and time consuming.'

'I wouldn't call it taking care of.'

'Still. They have to spend their resources on us. Food, what little they give us. Men to guard us.'

'Wait, are you saying they are starving us to death so they can get rid of us all?' Rose felt a cold fear running through her veins. She leaned on the table in front of her. 'No, that can't be.'

'We went to the commandant last week and told him of our concerns. Want to know what he said? He said if we want more food, we should grow it ourselves.'

'We can't grow it ourselves. We have no tools and no seeds. The soil is so bad, it doesn't produce anything.'

'They don't care. Dozens of people a day are dying from starvation at the camp. They know about it and do nothing. And it will only get worse.'

The nurses stopped putting down *starvation* on death certificates. Every time Rose wrote the dreaded word, *malaria*, the pen in her hands shook and her lips trembled with indignation. It broke her heart to lie, as if she herself had been responsible for these people's deaths. But the guards' solemn faces, their silent presence in the ward, their weapons pointing in her direction at all times of night and day left her no choice. She signed the misleading documents, even though she knew it wasn't natural causes that were killing her patients. Slowly, one after another, they were being murdered by their captors and there was nothing the nurses could do about it.

# Chapter 22

## August 1944

In July, a dozen people a day were dying from hunger. In August, the number rose to fifty. Rose no longer went on long walks around the camp like she used to. Even if she had the strength to move her weary body, to put one foot in front of the other, she couldn't bear to see what was happening to the inhabitants of Santo Tomas, like shadows gliding through the camp, skeletal and slow, their eyes empty.

One morning, Rose was looking under her bed for shoes when the sun bounced off something shiny, momentarily blinding her. She blinked and felt for the object with her hands, wondering what it was. From behind boxes and a pile of old newspapers, barely able to believe her luck, she extracted one of Ida's cans of meat. 'What are you doing here?' she whispered, stunned. The relic of happier times, it must have been overlooked and forgotten, as if God knew that there would come a day when they would need it desperately.

She looked at the meat the way she had once looked at David's face, with longing. The sleeping quarters were almost empty. Having worked a terrible night with six people dying from dysentery and thirty more from starvation, or infectious disease as the Japanese wanted the world to believe, Rose was planning to spend the morning resting. But as she sat on her bed holding the precious can of meat in her hands, she forgot all about sleep.

She looked around carefully and when she was certain no one was watching her, she hid the can under her uniform. It was no longer safe to walk through Santo Tomas with food. People were desperate and ready for anything. A week ago, a woman had been murdered for a spoon of corn mash.

She found Anne still asleep, little David nestled on her chest. Anne must have heard her steps on the wooden floor because she opened her eyes and smiled. She looked tired.

'Rough night?' asked Rose.

'I think it's getting easier. David slept for three hours without waking.'

'Look what I found! A can of meat from Ida. It was under my bed this whole time.'

Anne took the can, turning it this way and that, her eyes wide. 'Ida brought it?'

Rose nodded, wondering where Ida was, if she had had her new baby yet, if it was a boy or a girl. 'She did, back when we were still allowed visitors.'

'Is she free to come and go as she pleases? She's not in one of the camps?'

'She married her German sweetheart. They have two little ones. She's doing well.'

'Isn't it lucky I told Elsie about her relationship with Karl all those years ago in Manila? If I didn't, she might not have married him and she would be here with us, instead of out there, happy and free.'

Rose was about to leave for the hospital. She was standing in the corridor, ready to wave goodbye to Anne and step through the door. When she heard Anne's words, she sat back down. It was a few seconds before she could speak. 'You were the one who told Elsie? That wasn't a nice thing to do, Anne.'

Anne's hands trembled around the baby's tiny body. 'I know what you must think. But I'm not a horrible person. I was just bitter and resentful. Perhaps I was a little jealous of Ida.'

'What did you have to be bitter and resentful about? You had everything you wanted growing up.' Rose thought of her own childhood, of seeing her friends play with expensive dolls and ride shiny bicycles while she had nothing, of years of missing her father, of lies and a gaping hole in her life that nothing could fill.

Anne's eyes dimmed in the bright light coming through the window. 'After school, I got engaged to my childhood sweetheart. I loved him so much but my parents didn't approve, so they paid him off.'

'They did what?' Rose whispered, horrified.

'They gave him money under the condition that he was never allowed to contact me again. And he agreed! I asked him, how much did they pay you? How much was I worth to you? He didn't tell me.'

'Oh, Anne. I'm so sorry.'

'That's why I left, you see. I wanted to punish them. Mother hated my choice of profession. Girls from good families didn't become nurses. She couldn't believe I would be looking at naked men, emptying bedpans, washing floors, serving people. My parents stopped talking to me. When I became a nurse, I was no longer perfect. They were ashamed of me.'

'There's no shame in helping people. But my mama didn't approve either. She was so afraid for me. She thought hospitals were hotbeds of infection. Now I know she's been right all along. Never in a million years did I think I would end up *here*.' She glanced out the window at the fences and the guards, their miserable eyes always watching, always ready, their hands on their weapons. Inside, people lay in their beds and groaned and cried, even though it was morning and the sun was shining. Many of them no longer had the strength to stand up. Rose knew many more would die from hunger today and the next day and the next. One day it would be her turn. And then it would all be over.

Anne continued, 'When I came here, I didn't know it would be war. I came for adventure, for magic. Remember the first few weeks in Manila? How we danced, how we lived, like every day was a celebration. I wanted to travel, to see the world, to meet the love of my life. And look at us now.'

Rose took Anne's hand. 'We'll get through this, Anne. We'll go home. We'll dance again.' She knew Anne didn't believe it. She couldn't blame her. She no longer believed it either.

Anne opened the can of meat. With her eyes closed, she licked the lid. 'It's delicious. Let's eat it all before the others come back from breakfast. Half for you and half for me.'

Rose pushed the can away. 'I brought it for you.'

'I will only have some if you eat. Look at you. You need it. I insist.'

Rose shook her head. 'Have it all. I can get something at the hospital.' It was a lie. But Anne didn't need to know that. 'You are eating for two now. Little David needs his milk.'

Rose was walking through one of the shantytowns, her eyes to the ground. This morning, she had patients to see in almost every shack. It had been two weeks since she had been here last and she was shocked by how much had changed in such a short period. The settlement was silent like a ghost. No one was shouting or squabbling over food because there wasn't any. The inhabitants sat listlessly outside their little huts, their empty eyes surveying the world around them. When they were forced to move, they did so in slow motion. Apathy had replaced the fight for survival.

Near Foggy Bottom, she was about to enter a small cabin made of straw and bamboo that was leaning to one side. Once upon a time, the inhabitants of the little structure would have tried to fix it. Now it remained as it was, moments from collapse, much like the rest of the camp. She had her foot through the door when she heard someone calling her name. 'Nurse Rose! Nurse Rose.' She stopped in her tracks and turned around. She thought she recognised the voice. It couldn't be?

It was! Half hidden behind another shack was Hiroshi, waving at her, smiling brightly. He looked fresh-faced and healthy, taller than she remembered, dashing in his brand-new guard's uniform. His teeth sparkled. His eyes twinkled at the sight of her. He motioned for her to join him behind the shack and whispered, 'Don't make a noise. If anyone sees us talking to each other, we'll be in trouble.'

'I won't make a noise,' she whispered back. 'I'm happy to see you.'

'And I'm happy to see you!' He pressed her to his chest and a moment later, let her go.

She appraised him. 'You're glowing. What are you doing here?'

'I came here yesterday, as a guard. I didn't expect to find you. You've grown so thin. I hardly recognised you.' He was no longer smiling.

Rose couldn't help it, she started to cry. So many memories came flooding back at the sight of his face, so much pain and regret. She had thought they had had it hard on Bataan but it was nothing compared to this. On Bataan, she was free. She still had hope. She had David. And there was a little food.

Hiroshi became visibly distressed at the sight of her tears. He took her hand. 'Don't cry. I know it's been hard for you. I've seen things in this war I wish I could unsee. I wish I could forget every single one. It breaks my heart to find you like this. Wait here! I'll be right back.'

And just like that, he was gone, leaving Rose leaning on a wall in silence, stunned by his reappearance in her life and his sudden disappearance.

He came back five minutes later, carrying a sack. Placing it in her hands, he said, 'Once upon a time you helped me. Now I will help you. I have some milk for you and some carabao meat. In the evening, I will bring more food. Every day I will bring you something to eat.'

Hearing the words milk and meat made her heart ache. She opened the sack and stared with disbelief at food she hadn't seen for many months. She was so touched, she started to cry again. It was a while before she could speak. 'Hiroshi, that's so kind!' She hugged him. She couldn't wait to see Anne's face when she brought her milk and real meat. 'You have no idea how much it means to me. Everyone around us is dying. There is no food.'

'You don't have to worry anymore. As long as I'm here, I won't let you go hungry. But no one can know about it. If the other guards find out, they will shoot me.'

'I won't tell.'

They stood in silence side by side, a Japanese guard and his American prisoner, tears in their eyes at the sudden and unexpected meeting.

'Have a little bit of meat now. But don't have too much at once. Your stomach is not used to food. Take your time but don't worry about making it last, either. I will bring more.'

'I will never forget your kindness,' Rose whispered.

'And I never forget yours.'

The girls sat outside in the sun. The baby was in Rose's lap, gurgling happily. Anne took a bite of the meat. There was an expression of wonder on her face, as if the food on her plate was a miracle from God she had not expected. 'I'd forgotten what meat tasted like,' she said, reaching for another slice.

'It's been too long.' For the first time in months, Rose didn't feel hungry. She felt more hopeful, a little happier. It was amazing how different life seemed on a full stomach.

'Do you think David is looking too thin? I wonder if he's getting enough milk.'

Rose appraised the baby in her arms. Thankfully, he didn't look malnourished like many children she saw roaming the camp and at the hospital. 'He's perfect,' she replied.

'Can you believe he's three months old already? Sometimes I feel like every day is an eternity in this camp. And yet, three months have flown by since he was born.' Anne took a sip of milk and continued, 'When I first arrived at the camp, I didn't want to live. I don't feel like that anymore. Now I have a reason for living.' She reached for David and held him to her chest, covering his face with kisses. 'Every time I pick him up, he smiles. And not just any old smile. His whole face lights up with happiness, like I'm the most important thing in his life, like I am his everything. It melts my heart.'

'You *are* his everything. You *are* the most important thing in his life.'

'And he is mine. I've never known love like this before.' Anne brushed the tears off her cheeks and smiled, a sad smile that didn't reach her eyes. 'Look at me. I found my true love in the Philippines after all, just like I wanted.'

Rose touched Anne's arm. 'What's wrong? Why are you crying? You have a beautiful healthy baby. Everything will be all right.'

'I worry about him so much. I can't stop horrible thoughts in my mind. What if something happens to him? I couldn't bear it if I lost him, Rose.'

Anne was sobbing now, her head in her hands, while David crooned happily in her lap, pulling her hair. Rose put her arms around Anne. 'You don't have to worry about anything. I can get more food. Things are going to get better.'

'How are you going to get more food?' Anne eyed Rose suspiciously. 'You're not ...? You know?'

'What?'

Anne's voice dropped to a whisper, even though there was no one around. 'Fraternising with one of the guards? I know some of the girls who do that. They always have something extra to eat.'

Rose started to laugh and couldn't stop. 'Anne, don't be silly. Of course not.'

‘Then where did this meat come from? And this milk? You can tell me the truth. I won’t judge you.’

Rose told Anne about Hiroshi. ‘I know it’s hard to believe, but during those months on Bataan we became friends.’

‘Who would have thought? Not all of them are monsters.’

‘Hiroshi is not a monster. He’s just an unfortunate young man who wasn’t given many choices in life. He’d rather be home with his family. I think many of them would.’ She fell quiet, thinking of bombs falling on them on Bataan and of David’s smiling face. ‘Hiroshi was the one who found David. He saved his life.’

‘I want to meet him,’ Anne whispered, cradling her baby. ‘I want to meet the Japanese soldier who saved my brother’s life.’

# Chapter 23

## September 1944

Back home in September, the trees would be adorned in the most striking shades of gold and yellow. Here, in Manila, the sun continued to beat down on them like it did all year round. That was what Rose missed the most about home, besides her mother. The seasons. There were no seasons in the Philippines, just unbearable heat that never seemed to let go, until the rain came and stayed for weeks at a time.

Rose stood in line, waiting to wash her clothes and sheets, turning her head this way and that, looking for Anne. They had agreed to meet by the tap in the wall. Anne needed her to hold David so she could wash her dirty rags. It was almost time for Rose to report to work and there was no sign of Anne or the baby. Another five minutes, and Rose would be late. Despite the food Hiroshi brought, she felt weak and confused these days, and it was taking her twice as long as usual to make her weary way to the hospital and climb the treacherous stairs. She wondered what was keeping Anne. Perhaps David was unsettled and she got delayed.

Sighing, she left the line, a heap of dirty sheets in her hands, and went looking for Anne. Lately she had noticed an inexplicable change in her friend. She had withdrawn into her son to the exclusion of everything around her, as if the outside world no longer existed. Often, she would clasp David to her chest in a desperate embrace, not meeting Rose's eye, hiding her face in his hair as she told him stories of his heroic uncle in a hushed voice. Rose had to physically drag her out of bed for some fresh air, and she practically had to carry her to the shower to wash. Sometimes it seemed to her that Anne was a million miles away. While her body was here, at the camp of Santo Tomas, her mind was somewhere else. She was drifting away and as hard as Rose tried, she couldn't get her to smile anymore. Only David Junior could do that.

A month after their conversation, Rose was yet to introduce Anne to Hiroshi. It never seemed like the right time. As she walked through the camp, she felt eyes on her. The guards were always watching and so were the other detainees, who had nothing else to do and plenty of time for idle gossip. If anyone found out, if anyone saw, this gossip could cost Hiroshi his life. He knew it too, and every time they met at their secret place behind the lopsided hut, he looked like a rabbit caught in a watchtower light, afraid of every shadow, of the smallest noise. In spite of the danger, he waited for her every day with a smile on his face and a sack of food. She knew he was the only reason she was still standing, that she hadn't died from starvation like so many others. Before his miraculous arrival at the camp, she had felt it, the cold breath of death on her face. He was the reason Anne and David were still alive. Every day, she thanked him, while he told her that no thanks were necessary, that he was only doing what anyone would do for a good friend like her.

A few times in the past week, she had caught him feeding small children in the main courtyard. A bucket of meat in front of him, he called them over and they descended like baby birds, chirping and squeaking and begging for more. What surprised her wasn't Hiroshi's kindness. She already knew he had a heart of gold. It came as a shock that the other guards saw what was happening and did nothing. Hiroshi didn't get in trouble and every afternoon, he returned with his bucket and whistled to the children, laughing as they rushed to his side.

Rose found Anne in bed, her eyes closed, the baby curled up next to her. She appeared to be sleeping. Perhaps she had had a disturbed night with David. Rose was about to walk away to let Anne get some rest when she heard a groan. She turned around. It was then that she noticed the unnatural colour of Anne's skin. Her cheeks were burning. She placed her hand on Anne's forehead. It felt hot to the touch.

'Malaria,' said Elsie half an hour later, looking at Anne's frantic face as she thrashed in her sleep. 'There's no getting away from it.'

'We have no quinine,' whispered Rose, holding David close to her heart. 'What do we do? She doesn't look so good.'

'All we can do is keep her comfortable. With luck, she'll feel better soon.'

'She has to. For her child,' said Rose, kissing David on the top of his head.

When Elsie was gone, Rose sat down next to Anne, who woke up and glanced around, her eyes large on her gaunt face, looking confused and not sure where she was. 'What's wrong with me, Rose?' she whispered. 'Why do I feel like I'm going to die?'

'Didn't you hear Elsie? You have a little virus. You'll be good as new in no time.'

'Not a little virus. Malaria.'

'Rest and get your strength back. David needs his mother.'

Anne's voice trembled when she said, 'Will you look after him for me?'

'Of course, I will. For as long as you need.'

Anne's hand searched for Rose's face. 'I didn't mean now. If something happens to me, will you take care of him?'

'Nothing is going to happen to you. Not if I can help it.'

'You love him like your own, don't you?'

Rose nodded. 'I do. He is the only thing that's right in our world. The only thing that brings me joy.'

Anne whispered, 'You've been spending all your time with us. You've been giving us all your food, even though you yourself are starving. Without you, we wouldn't have made it. It makes me happy to see how much he means to you. Even if I die, he will still have a mother.'

Rose shook her head. *No*, she wanted to say. *No, don't talk like that.* 'You are not going to die.'

'Why, do you know a spell to conjure quinine out of thin air? How many people have died from malaria in the last month?'

'I don't know. Not that many. I didn't count.'

'You lost count.' Anne smiled sadly. 'Promise me.' She squeezed Rose's hand with tears in her eyes.

'What?' Rose whispered, her heart hurting.

'Promise me you will never leave David. Promise you will bring him up like your own.'

'I promise,' said Rose, her hand on David's head, like she was taking an oath.

For the next few days, Anne drifted in and out of consciousness. Sometimes she didn't seem to know where she was. Other times, she was her old self, bright and alert. Hour after hour at night, Rose sat by her side and prayed to God to spare her life for the sake of her child. He was only four months old. He couldn't lose his mother. Her heart breaking, she listened to Anne as she told little David how much she loved him.

Rose was curled up in a small bamboo chair next to Anne's bed, drifting off to sleep, when she heard her voice. It didn't sound weak, nor did it tremble when she said, 'I lied to you, Rose.'

'What?' Rose blinked the first shadows of sleep away.

'I lied to you back in Sternberg.'

Rose had been thinking of David's face when she splashed

him with cold water under the waterfall, moments before their first kiss. At the time, it made her laugh but now all she wanted to do was cry. How carefree they had been then, how blissfully unaware of what was to come. Anne's words took her by surprise. She stared at her friend's emaciated face that seemed to glow from within in the light of a candle. 'What are you talking about?' she whispered.

'Remember I told you David was getting married?'

Rose took a deep breath. Her heart hurt. 'I do.'

'It wasn't true.'

It took a few seconds for Rose to collect her thoughts, to remember how to speak. 'Why did you lie to me?'

Anne's face looked mournful in the near darkness. 'It's funny. I despise my parents for being so judgemental. For judging people based on their position in life. They didn't think Anthony was good enough for me, so they got rid of him. But now I realise I acted the same way towards you. I wanted David to marry Celia because she was rich and seemed right for him. Just like my parents, I judged you without getting to know you first.'

Rose didn't know what to say, so she remained quiet, her hands trembling.

Anne closed her eyes. When she spoke again, it was with great effort. 'He saved you, you know. When the hospital got bombed in Manila that first day, he carried you out of the rubble himself, risking his life.'

Tears streamed down Rose's face, falling on the sheet, making everything appear distorted and wrong. 'I didn't know that. What happened afterwards? I looked everywhere for him but he was gone. I searched for weeks.'

'He got injured in the next attack and was brought to the Women's University Hospital where I was a nurse. I looked after him. He couldn't walk unassisted but he was desperate to find you, to let you know he was still alive. He begged me to take him to you, but I said I would bring you to him instead.'

'Was that when you came to see me?'

Anne nodded. 'When I returned, I told him you didn't want to talk to him. That you'd met your childhood sweetheart at the hospital and it was over between you and David.'

'He wouldn't have believed it,' whispered Rose. Would he?

'I don't know if he believed me. He never spoke to me about you again. But as soon as he was able to walk, he rushed to Sternberg to find you. It was too late. By then you had already evacuated.'

After a few moments of silence, Rose said, 'Why, Anne? Why did you do it?'

'I'm sorry,' Anne whispered. 'Do you hear me, Rose? I'm sorry for everything I've done. I was stupid and selfish and unkind. Not just to you but to my brother. I thought I was doing what was best for him but I was wrong. I wish I could take it all back. Nothing would make me happier than you and David getting married. If you did, we would be sisters. And I couldn't wish for a better sister.'

Rose closed her eyes. She couldn't look at Anne's sad, apologetic face. Instead, she imagined the warmth in David's eyes as he told her he loved her, before the war had turned their lives upside down, when she still believed every word he said. Because of Anne, she had lost years to doubt and pain.

War had robbed her of her love, but it was Anne who had snatched away her faith. And without faith, without trust, there was no love, only heartbreak. Anne had taken a thing that was pure and magical and turned it into something dirty. She had taken gold and turned it into gaudy and cheap costume jewellery. And here she was, her eyes large, her hand on Rose's hand, pleading for forgiveness, for understanding. Did she think it was that easy? Did she think she could say sorry and the dark years of despair would fade away to nothing?

'It's a little too late for a blessing, don't you think?' said Rose, turning away from Anne, wishing she was anywhere but here, wishing she could disappear, so she wouldn't have to face her shattered future without him. Not looking at Anne, she got up and made an uncertain step towards the exit, her legs weak.

'Don't leave,' Anne whispered. 'I don't know how long I have left.'

Even now, as she lay on her deathbed, Anne was trying to manipulate Rose. Even though she felt ready to break down, Rose didn't turn back.

# Chapter 24

## September 1944

Rose didn't come to see Anne the next day. She felt conflicted and lost. It was as if two Annes existed, the selfish one of the past who had destroyed Rose's future with David through her cruel lies, and Anne of the present, mother to David's nephew and her beloved friend, someone she would do anything for. And yet, finding out David's love for her was real was a solace and a blessing for Rose, even as she grieved him and cried for him. It was Anne's gift to her, finally telling her that his heart had been true all along, that it hadn't been a lie after all.

Later that evening, Kate told her Anne had been asking for her. 'She doesn't look so good, Rose. I've seen enough dying patients in my life to know she doesn't have much longer.'

Putting their last conversation to the back of her mind, Rose rushed to Anne's side, afraid she would be too late. 'Finally,' said Anne, her voice so weak, Rose could barely hear her. 'I've been waiting all day for you.'

Relief washed over Rose. 'It was a busy day at the hospital. Everyone is sick.'

'Yes,' whispered Anne. 'Everyone is dying.'

Rose touched Anne's hand. 'But not you. You'll start feeling better soon, you'll see.'

Anne shrugged and her eyes filled with tears. 'I don't feel better. I feel like what little life I have left is slipping away from me.' Anne hesitated. 'Could you do me a favour? Could you bring me a pen and paper, please?'

'Of course.' Rose brought pen and paper, placing them on the bed next to Anne. 'Are you writing to your parents?'

Anne shook her head. 'No. I want to write to my brother.' Her gaze was on Rose, and yet, it seemed like she was staring through her, into the darkness.

Rose's heart was beating wildly in her chest, like a bird against its cage, desperate to break free. She took Anne's hand. 'Darling, David is …' And stopped talking. Anne was breathing heavily and her voice came out in raspy bursts. The breathing was too familiar to Rose. She had heard it many times before as she sat by her dying patients. She was not going to break Anne's heart all over again in the few moments she had left. If she wanted to believe her brother was alive, Rose wasn't going to be the one to destroy her with the truth.

'David didn't die, Rose,' said Anne, her eyes flashing. 'I can feel him out there. I can see things much more clearly now.' She thrashed on her bed, visibly distressed.

Rose stroked her hand, trying to console her, to keep her calm. 'Of course, darling. I believe you.'

Anne pulled the paper closer. 'After I'm gone, give him my letter.'

'I promise.'

When Anne tried to write, she couldn't press the pen to paper hard enough. No words came out. 'Can I help you with the letter?' asked Rose. 'I could write it for you, if you like.'

'No, I want to write to my brother myself.'

Rose left Anne alone with her thoughts and the piece of paper in front of her. When she returned half an hour later, the letter was finished and the paper was sealed inside an envelope with David's name scribbled on it in an unsteady hand. Anne lay back on the pillow with her eyes closed. Rose took the envelope, folded it and hid it in her pocket.

'I can't breathe. Why can't I breathe?' whispered Anne.

Rose touched her forehead. She took her hand and brought it to her face. 'You are going to be fine. You are a little bit warm.'

'I'm not afraid of dying. But I'm afraid of leaving my son. What will happen to him when I'm not there to look after him?'

'You don't have to worry. He won't be alone.'

'I want to see him so much, it hurts. Can you bring him to me?'

Rose asked one of Anne's neighbours, an old man called Ronald, to fetch David from Rose's quarters across the courtyard, where Kate was watching him. Ronald could barely walk, his legs weak from starvation, but he happily agreed. 'It might take me a while. I used to be the fastest runner in my hometown. I won medals, you know? Now I'm slower than a snail.'

'Don't be too long,' said Rose quietly, her worried eyes on Anne.

While they waited, Rose told Anne about meeting David and falling in love. She shared the most precious memories with her, things she had never divulged to a living soul. Speaking about David after years of silence filled her heart with warmth. It was nice to say his name out loud to someone who loved him too. Anne smiled and nodded, too weak to respond.

When Ronald brought the baby, Anne sat up in bed, as if seeing her son gave her wings. The expression on her face when she held him in her arms broke Rose's heart. There was so much sadness in her eyes, but also such joy. 'I love you,' she whispered. 'I love you more than anything in this life. You make me so happy. Happier than I've ever been. While all around me was darkness, you were light. I will always be with you, no matter what. You know that, don't you?' David looked up at his mother with his big blue eyes and smiled. Anne started to cry. 'I will never leave you,' she murmured. 'Not in a million years. I will always be part of you because you are everything to me.'

Rose couldn't look at Anne as she covered David with kisses, her lips touching his head, his cheeks, his tiny nose. While the baby giggled, unaware that this might be the last time he was seeing his mother, Rose turned away, crying.

'Remember what you promised me, Rose,' Anne said. 'Love him like your own. Don't let anything happen to him.'

'I promise.'

'I can see why David loved you. I grew to love you myself.'

'And I love you,' said Rose and she meant it.

Rose could see Anne's arms around her baby were getting weaker. As dawn broke through the dark cloud and the candle flickered and died, she took David from Anne and rocked him, her tears falling on his head. All she could hear was Anne's heavy, difficult breathing. And soon, she could hear nothing at all, not a whisper, not a rustle of bedsheets, only heartbreaking, devastating silence. Rose checked Anne's pulse and called her name, begging her not to leave them because she had become like a sister to her, because David needed his mother, because he couldn't grow up without her in his life, but it was too late. Anne was gone.

# Chapter 25

## October–November 1944

Day after day, night after sleepless night, Rose would close her eyes and pray for a way out. As little David screamed in her arms, longing for his mother, she would cry silently and wonder what to do. When Anne was alive, David loved to be picked up by his aunty Rose. Now he hated it. Perhaps he could sense she was trying to take his mother's place and deemed her not good enough. No one could take his mother's place. She had been irreplaceable.

Death walked among them through the alleys and shantytowns of Santo Tomas, an unwanted guest that refused to leave, making its presence known every hour of every day. On the way to the hospital with little David in her arms, Rose would walk through the courtyard and see a dead body laid out on the ground. She would squeeze her eyes shut and turn David away, her breath catching. At the hospital, Elsie would tell her they had lost a dozen patients in just a few hours, men and women who had been healthy only a few months ago, who played basketball and baseball, ran theatre groups, attended lectures on astrophysics and talked about their families back home. Young people like her. Except, she no longer felt young. After everything she had been through, after everything she'd seen, she felt centuries old, empty like a hollow tree.

One balmy October afternoon, after her shift was over, she sat with baby David on the grass, playing peekaboo and rocking him in her arms. She tried to do it the way Anne had done it, as if following Anne's rituals could bring her back, if only for a moment. Every day she told David about his mother, little stories and anecdotes to keep her alive a bit longer. David giggled and reached his chubby arms up to her, wanting to be picked up, thrown in the air, tickled and kissed. She had no strength to do any of it. All she could do was hold him tight and inhale his baby smell that never failed to bring comfort. She paid little attention to the buzzing of bombers and fighter jets over her head. The noise of their engines was ever present, like the sun that rose in the morning and set in the evening, like the sea that kissed the white sand of the harbour. She had seen so many Japanese Mitsubishi Zeros in the sky over Manila in the last few years, even if she had the energy, she wouldn't want to lift her head and spot one more.

But this time, something made her glance up. At first, the sun was in her eye and she didn't understand what it was she was seeing, only that it was at odds with what she had expected. A moment later, she knew: it wasn't the Japanese red sun she had been accustomed to on the wings of the aircraft but white stars in blue circles. Forgetting all about how tired she was, she ran through the camp with the baby in her arms and shouted to anyone who would listen, 'It's our planes! American planes!' More black dots appeared in the sky over her head. She counted seven of them, unable to believe her eyes, afraid it was all a dream.

One moment, the camp was sleepwalking silently through another hungry afternoon. The next, the whole place seemed to erupt like a volcano. All of a sudden, as if a magician had flicked his wand and animated an old black-and-white photograph, people were crying with joy, cheering and throwing their hats up in the air.

The loudspeakers came alive, ordering everyone inside. No one paid them any attention. Quite the opposite, out of every door of every building and hut more people spilled out like beans to see what was happening.

'Are you seeing what I'm seeing? Can you believe it?' exclaimed Tess. The girls were silent for a moment, their eyes on the sky, while all around them pandemonium reigned.

'We've been waiting for this moment since the day Pearl Harbor was attacked. We've waited for this moment for three years,' whispered Rose.

'What do you think it means?' Kate wanted to know.

'It means the end is near.'

The girls looked on with their mouths wide open as the planes circled over Manila and released their bombs. The earth shook under their feet and the air rumbled but no one ran for cover. Every time another explosion sounded, the camp cheered.

'I hope they know there are Americans here,' whispered Kate. 'They won't hit us, will they?'

'Let them bomb,' said Rose. 'The sooner they chase the enemy out, the better.'

For the next few hours, the planes buzzed like angry bees and the bombs exploded overhead like fireworks. Rose wasn't afraid. She had never felt more alive in her life.

The guards appeared, pointing their machine guns at the crowd gathered in the courtyard, at Rose and the baby, at Kate and Tess. No one moved. No one even glanced in their direction. Only when they shot their rifles in the air did people shuffle inside but they did so reluctantly, not willing to miss a single moment of the spectacle they had been praying and hoping for.

Inside their quarters, the girls huddled together on Rose's bed and listened to the raid. Rose peered out of the grimy window at a column of smoke rising above the docks, where US fighters had hit a large Japanese cargo plane, knocking it to the ground.

Soon the planes were gone, leaving an unfamiliar feeling behind – hope.

Suddenly and unexpectedly, after years of relative quiet, war had come to the Philippines once more. Over the next few weeks, American raids became more frequent and the Japanese responded in kind, their anti-aircraft guns blaring from the ground. Every now and then, pieces of shrapnel fell inside the camp, wounding dozens of people, and soon Rose was working around the clock, treating shock, cleaning wounds and applying bandages.

There was no longer any doubt. The Americans were coming to liberate them. And yet, Rose was afraid to let hope inside her heart. Thanksgiving dinner was meagre and consisted of one scoop of rice with vegetable stew and a small serving of *camote* tops. Rose observed the people around her. Their eyes sank deep into their faces. Their shoulders drooped. They moved in slow motion, like they were asleep. She wondered if she looked like them, emaciated, sick, barely alive. A few times she caught a glimpse of herself in the mirror and turned quickly away because she didn't want to see. At this rate, how many would be left standing to welcome the US Army to Santo Tomas?

In the last week of November, two hundred Imperial Army soldiers marched inside the camp and strutted about, armed with bayonets and their barely controlled rage. They forced male prisoners weakened by hunger to build guard shacks, string barbed wire and clear the area by the main fence. Every morning, the guards took a group of detainees away, never to be seen again. Queuing for her spoon of *camotes*, Rose tried not to look at mournful faces around her as women waited in vain for their husbands to return, as children cried for their fathers, as men wondered if they would be next.

Another roll call, another hour standing under the blazing sun, waiting for one of the guards to call her name, fearing she would fall and not be able to get up. 'What do they want from us?' she whispered. 'We can barely move. We are starving and exhausted. We can't do what they want us to do.'

'They are afraid because they know they are losing,' replied Kate. 'And they are getting desperate.'

'Before they lose, they will kill us all,' said Tess. 'Yesterday I saw them rolling large barrels under the main stairs of the camp. They will blow us all up before the Americans arrive.'

Everywhere she turned, Rose heard rumours of terrors to come. The Japanese were not going to give the camp up to the Americans without a fight. Before they surrendered, they were going to destroy Santo Tomas, together with its inhabitants. The salvation was coming, but it was coming at a deadly price. Afraid for their lives, the enemy stopped providing food for the camp. Horror in her heart, Rose walked from shack to shack, checking on her patients, averting her eyes form the dead and the living, like skeletons moving through Santo Tomas with empty eyes and shaking limbs.

Through it all, Hiroshi was her rock. Punctual like a clock, every day he was at the same place at the same time with food for her and David, for Tess and Kate, and Elsie, who never left the hospital anymore, sitting with the patients and holding their hands as they died, barely able to walk herself.

The patients realised they were dying. Rose could see the terrible knowledge in their eyes. One man, his arms and legs like matchsticks, refused to touch the food she brought him. He pushed away the plate of mung beans that he needed desperately to stay alive. 'You must eat,' she implored, feeling helpless. 'If you don't eat, you will die.'

'Give it to my son. He needs it more than I do.'

'Right now, no one needs food more than you.'

'My son is only eight. Give it to him, please.'

'Is that what you've been doing? You've been giving your food to your child?'

'All I want is for my son to live,' the man whispered, before closing his eyes and falling into a sleep.

Rose did as he had asked. She fed his little boy, who sat on the ground in silence, haggard and apathetic, a spoon shaking in his hand. Just like the other children at the camp, he was no longer playing or laughing or running around. Rose no longer heard their happy voices as she walked to work in the mornings.

The next day, the man was dead. Rose stood by his bed that was already occupied by someone else and wiped silent tears off her face, while American planes buzzed overhead, carrying on their wings hope of freedom and liberation. Freedom for everyone in the camp, apart from the hundreds of those who hadn't lived long enough to see it.

# Chapter 26

## December 1944

A show unfolded in the sky every single day. Whenever a bomb dropped near Santo Tomas, sending a huge column of smoke upwards, the internees cheered. Every time an American plane spun in the air and fell down in flames, the Japanese shouted with glee. It was like a terrifying spectator sport, only the stakes were higher.

On Christmas Eve, Rose and Kate were making their slow way to the hospital to start their shift, while Tess watched David. Rose didn't feel like working that day. She had no energy to move between beds, to listen to pleas for food, to find words of solace. Instead, she wanted to lie down, close her eyes and drift away. Rather than helping others, she needed someone to help *her*, to give her strength and whisper a kind word of reassurance in her ear. She needed to hear that everything was going to be all right. Faced with death and destruction everywhere she turned, she no longer believed it.

'I wonder if we will have something extra to celebrate Christmas,' said Kate wistfully.

'Would you like some roast turkey and mashed potato? How

about an apple pie?' Rose tried to smile at her joke but couldn't. Just saying those words out loud made her stomach hurt and her head spin.

They heard a whirr of a plane engine overhead. Rose looked up. 'Our planes are back,' she said. She had no strength to express emotion, to jump for joy or shout with glee.

'I wonder how much longer it will take,' whispered Kate.

'Not too long, I hope,' said Rose. 'We can't hold on for much longer.'

'I've never seen a plane so close before,' said Kate, her eyes on the sky. 'Do you think it's going to bomb the camp?'

Before Rose had a chance to respond, something white fell from the plane, like giant snowflakes drifting to the ground, dancing in the breeze. 'What are those?' exclaimed Rose. The white flakes swirled in the air like butterfly wings, finally landing at their feet. Rose realised they were not snowflakes at all but pieces of paper. 'Leaflets,' she cried.

Picking one up with trembling hands, she read, 'The commander-in-chief, the officers and the men of the American Forces of Liberation in the Pacific wish their gallant Allies, the people of the Philippines, all the blessings of Christmas and the realisation of their fervent hopes for the New Year.'

The girls looked at one another in shocked silence. Other than Ida's visits and the ill-fated Red Cross comfort kits, it was the first communication with the outside world they had received since arriving at the camp two and a half years ago.

'They must be coming here. Do you think they are coming here?' cried Kate. 'Is that what it means?'

'They're coming here,' Rose said quietly.

The internees ran after the pieces of paper, fighting over them, passing them to each other, talking in hushed voices. The guards ordered everyone to turn the leaflets in immediately. Anyone found in possession of one would be thrown into solitary for seven days.

Instead of handing her leaflet in, Rose hid it deep in her pocket. She was no longer afraid. At Christmas, she savoured a teaspoon of jam, a bite of chocolate and a few spoons of rice Hiroshi had brought, placing her hand on the precious piece of paper and smiling. For the first time in many months, she had something to smile about. Help was on its way.

Despite hopes of liberation, the camp was plunged in perpetual darkness. Garbage piled up. Human waste accumulated on the stairs and in the halls. The smell was debilitating. No one could muster the strength to get up, to pick up a mop or a broom or a shovel, to clean the debris and maintain an illusion of life when all around them was death.

Rose was on her way to see Hiroshi, rejoicing at the sight of American planes in the sky, wondering when the US Army would finally get here, if it would be months or weeks, days or hours, when some shrapnel from an anti-aircraft gun fell inside the camp gates, igniting a hut she was walking past.

Rose ran towards the fire, hoping no one was trapped inside. 'Hello,' she shouted. 'Is anyone in there?'

There was no reply but she decided to call for help, just in case. Someone had to put the fire out before it spread. She was turning the corner when she saw Hiroshi with a sack in his hands. She lifted her hand in greeting. Hiroshi waved in response, his eyes darting around, afraid to be seen. Once upon a time, she would have run to their hiding place between the two huts, eager to see a friendly face, to exchange a few words, to look inside the sack at the goods that he brought. Now she moved slowly, each step requiring more energy from her than she possessed, but at the sight of his kind smile her heart filled with warmth and gratitude.

Something shattered nearby, startling Rose. Her hand at her mouth, barely able to breathe, she watched Hiroshi slide to the ground, a piece of shrapnel embedded in his chest. It was like a horrible dream. She wanted to scream but couldn't. She wanted to look away, to turn the time back, to take it all away. She broke into a run, the sight of her friend injured, of his blood pooling on the pavement, of his broken body propelling her forward. She reached him in seconds.

'I've been hit, Nurse Rose,' muttered Hiroshi.

She pulled at his uniform, tearing the buttons off. Rolling it into a ball, she tried to stem the blood flow but it didn't seem to make a difference.

'No,' she whispered. 'No, no, no.'

She crawled around him and placed his head in her lap. His eyes were closed. She said, 'Let me go and get help, all right?'

With difficulty, he said, 'Please, wait.' His eyes pleaded with her to stay. Suddenly he looked like a little boy, lost and afraid.

In her heart, she knew there was nothing anyone could do for Hiroshi, even though she didn't want to admit it to herself. She nodded. 'All right.'

'Where are you? I can't see you?' He groaned.

She moved slightly so that he could see her face. His hands in hers felt cold, like he had placed them in a bucket of ice and kept them there for a few seconds. 'I'm right here,' she whispered.

'Where is the bag? I was bringing you food. I dropped it.'

'Over there.'

'Take it. You will need it. Take it and go. If the other guards see you talking to me, they will beat you.'

Wiping her tears away, she said, 'I don't care.'

'They will throw you into solitary.'

'I don't care.'

'What about little David? He needs you.'

'*You* need me.' She left him for a moment, running inside one of the shanties and fetching some sheets. With shaking hands she bandaged his chest as best she could. The white sheet became red with blood almost instantly. Rose wanted to roar in pain, as if she was the one hit by deathly shrapnel with moments left to live.

'I will never see my family again,' he whispered.

Rose sat with his head in her lap, shaking, helpless, not knowing what to do. What a waste this war was, what a shame. It didn't discriminate, it affected everyone, no matter their age or nationality, no matter their beliefs or what was in their hearts. It was random, like lightning.

His eyes were closed. He was gasping for breath. 'Remember,' he said. 'Look for magic wherever you go.'

'There is no magic left in the world, Hiroshi. Look at us. Look at the way we are living.'

'There is always magic.'

His breathing stopped but she didn't move, sitting on the ground with his head in her lap, staring into space with unseeing eyes. She remained there until the guards came and chased her away. When no one was looking, she picked up the bag of food because it was Hiroshi's last wish. On shaking legs, she stumbled back to her quarters and sat on the floor by her bed, crying for the Japanese guard who had kept her alive all this time, risking his position, perhaps even his life to bring her food. She didn't go to work that day. She couldn't.

And only in the evening, when she held screaming David in her arms, Rose thought about what Hiroshi's death would mean for them. There was no more food left. No more food left at all.

Rose could no longer sleep at night. When she closed her eyes, she saw their faces. David's tormented screams resounded inside her head as he called her name again and again, while bombs rained on their jungle hospital on Bataan. Anne's desperate eyes haunted her as she pleaded to hold her baby one last time. Hiroshi's blood ran like a river down the cobblestones of the camp where he had been a guard. Every evening when it got dark, she sat at her little window, watching the sad-looking moon in the sky, imagining the same moon shining over Brownville in a different life when she was happy. It might be snowing back home right now. Pristine white flakes falling on the streets of her childhood that didn't overflow with rubbish and dead bodies. People strolling hand in hand under festive lights, their eyes twinkling. Her mother waiting for Rose at home with a smile on her face, while their Christmas tree sparkled with joy and the house smelt of baking. Rose would give ten years of her life to see her mother again. She would give anything to feel safe, to not worry about little David every moment of every day while American bombs fell on Manila and everyone around them was dying from hunger.

One scorching morning in late December, water pressure failed on the second and third floors of the main building. Rose waited her turn by the first-floor showers, thinking, *Why do I still bother*? She could barely move anymore and there was no food. What was the point of keeping herself clean, of getting out of bed, of waiting for a miracle? Despite the tropical sun shining down on them like all was well in the world, despite the US bombers buzzing overhead, there was no light in her life, only bleak despair.

An American plane flew so low overhead, she could see the pilot's face, and instantly she perked up. There was a point. The liberators were coming.

That afternoon, to the excited screams of the camp population, more leaflets rained from the sky. Rose read, 'Roll out the barrel, Christmas will be today or tomorrow.'

Stunned, she placed the leaflet in her pocket. Did she understand it correctly? Were the Americans coming to liberate them in the next day or so?

At the hospital, Elsie whispered to Rose as they were doing their rounds, 'I overheard a guard saying diet and disease will take care of Santo Tomas population in due course. Just like I suspected.'

'Don't worry. Help will be here soon. Everything will be all right.'

'We are working harder than ever. We are up all night taking care of these people. And still, it's not enough. We are fighting a losing battle.'

'But we won't stop fighting. Until the end.'

# Chapter 27

## January–February 1945

Rose woke up one morning and realised she couldn't open her eyes. Her eyelids were no longer flesh and blood but made of the heaviest of metals, and her arms and legs felt like they had been chained to the bed.

'I can't move,' she whispered to Kate, with an effort focusing on her face, inches away from her own. Shapes danced in front of her eyes, bright spots of colour that appeared as if out of nowhere only to fade moments later. The room, the walls, the beds were no longer stationary but spinning around in a waltz, getting closer, stepping away. Rose didn't feel hungry anymore. She was past that. Her weakened body no longer demanded food. 'I can't get up for roll call or breakfast.'

'You don't need to. The Japanese have forbidden us to leave our rooms. And there is no food.'

'I don't want to die,' Rose whispered. 'I don't want to die so close to freedom.' She sat up in bed, her unfocused eyes searching for David. There he was, in Tess's arms, chewing on a book. Her sole reason for living, the only light in the darkness.

She tried to think of the last time she had had something to eat. The day before, she was lucky enough to get a few spoons of mouldy rice. Since then, she'd had nothing but water. She avoided looking in the mirror but couldn't pretend that nothing out of the ordinary was happening to her. Her cheeks felt hollow under her fingers. Her body had withered away and her uniform hung on her like a tent.

A burst of gunfire was heard outside. Overhead, planes roared in anger. Rose barely noticed them anymore but they startled little David and he began to scream. Hearing his pitiful yelps propelled Rose out of bed. She was by his side in an instant, cradling him in her arms, whispering in his ear. He continued to cry. It wasn't kind words he needed. It was food. 'I have nothing to give him,' she said, wanting to yelp and shout too.

Kate forced a smile. 'When the Americans get here, they will bring bread and cheese and milk. They will have meat for us and maybe even something sweet. I would kill for some strawberry jam or a bar of chocolate.'

Rose nodded, hiding her face in baby David's head, all the while thinking, *how much longer?*

It felt to Rose like the gunfire was getting closer by the minute, that it was inside the gates, that it was coming for her. Little David shrieked in her arms. 'Everything is fine, everything is going to be all right,' Rose whispered, trying to convince not only the squirming baby but herself. 'You don't have to be afraid. I know it's noisy. It will quieten down soon.'

But it didn't quieten down. Moments later, a strange rumbling sound was heard, followed by a crash. Rose could smell gasoline. All around her, men and women were shouting, shoving one another out of the way, pushing to get to the doors and the windows, while children cowered in fear. 'Where are you going, people?' someone cried. 'Didn't you hear the guards? They are going to shoot you if you step outside.'

But the human tide, once unleashed, became impossible to contain. People spilled out of every door and gathered in the courtyard. They hung from windows at the risk of falling and breaking their limbs.

'The gate,' Rose heard. 'They are breaking the gate.'

Pressing David to her chest, she made her way through the human river to the nearest window. And then she saw it. The iron gate of Santo Tomas that had kept them captive for two and a half years trembled and fell, revealing a large Sherman tank behind it. It was from this tank that the rumbling noise was coming from.

Rose blinked fast, watching the commotion outside. Was it the Japanese, determined to raze the camp to the ground before surrendering to the Americans? Or was it the long-awaited liberators?

There was another tank behind the first, with the words 'Georgia Peach' painted in large letters on its side. Rose saw the Stars and Stripes and started to cry.

Over the din of conversation, the gun fire and the explosions, Rose heard an American voice. 'Hello, folks! Merry Christmas!' The tank's turret flew open and a beaming face appeared, followed by a pair of waving hands.

All hell broke loose. Everyone ran towards the tank, while more American soldiers jumped out. People hugged the liberators, embraced one another, shouted out greetings, threw their hats up in the air. Someone started singing 'God Bless America'. There was no sign of the Japanese guards with their threats and machine guns. Rose stood quiet like a mouse with her hand on her chest, unable to believe that finally, after three years of hell, their prayers had been answered.

And through it all the battle continued in the sky and shells tore through the air above them. Rose barely noticed the sound of war as she fought through the crowd with little David in her arms, wanting to be closer to the tanks that brought freedom, wanting to touch the liberators and make sure she wasn't hallucinating from hunger.

'Nurse, would you like some chocolate? What about some

cheese?' she heard. An American soldier handed her something wrapped in paper, while Rose gawked at him in silence, tears running down her cheeks. The soldier radiated health. He looked strong and glowing next to the prisoners, whose mouths were open in astonishment and gaunt faces sparkled with joy as they moved their skeletal arms in the direction of food.

Rose divided the cheese and the chocolate into four portions and shared them with Tess, Kate and the baby. They ate carefully, in tiny bites, knowing that their stomachs were not used to food. Others weren't so patient. They devoured every morsel that was offered to them, and soon hundreds of detainees were violently sick with cramps and diarrhoea.

More US troops arrived, carrying stretchers. While the rest of the internees celebrated, while the soldiers dug foxholes and set up machine guns, the nurses settled seventeen wounded into hospital beds. Rose was assisting an American doctor named Bernie, who looked new and shiny, his well-nourished body bursting with energy, his smile wide on his face, his eyes and teeth sparkling. *Where did you come from*, Rose wanted to ask him, *that you can still smile with such joy*? It was perplexing to her because she hadn't seen a carefree smile like that for many months, perhaps years.

'You sure need help around here,' said Bernie, observing the hospital where patients occupied every inch of the floor, their bodies twitching in their sleep.

'Yes, what took you so long?'

'We had to break through a wall of Japanese to get to you. They thought they could stop us. They were wrong.'

And then she saw the sadness behind the smile. Just like her, the kind American doctor had seen things that he would never forget. He had experienced things that would haunt him for the rest of his life. While the nurses had been through hell waiting for the Americans to arrive, the liberators had been through hell trying to get to them.

As she helped Bernie with patients new and old, she was struck by how much the outside world had progressed while they had been interned. The doctor asked her to fetch some penicillin. 'Some what?' she asked, rubbing her tired eyes. As she asked a million questions about the medicine she wasn't familiar with, the medicine that was known as a miracle drug because of its potential to save many lives, she couldn't help but think, *If only we'd had some on Bataan and Corregidor*. In her mind she was seeing thousands of patients dying in her arms, while all she could do was weep.

She didn't sleep at all that night, her excitement propelling her through hours of work. 'We'll sleep soon,' Kate reassured her. 'When all this is over, we'll do nothing but sleep.'

'It's almost over,' whispered Rose, listening to the bursts of artillery in the near distance. 'Can you believe it? It's almost over.' She had to repeat it to herself over and over again because it seemed like a magical dream. Even though the Americans were in the camp, even though for the first time in years the detainees didn't have to line up for roll call, even though there was food again, the gate was broken and, in the courtyard, new and unfamiliar vehicles were parked (Jeeps, Kate told her), Rose still waited for the Japanese guards to round everybody up and give one of their famous speeches about loyalty and respect. Her heart had hardened against joy, she realised. After three years of war, she found it impossible to hope.

In the morning, as she walked back to her quarters to catch up on some much-needed sleep, she was overjoyed to see that the camp was slowly returning to life. Crews were cleaning the debris. There were lines for showers and food again. The dark cloud had lifted and the sun was shining.

In the cafeteria, they received some rice and a slice of bread. As they tucked in, the sergeant in charge told them they could send messages back home. 'Tell your loved ones you are coming back. Tell them they are going to see you soon.'

'I can't wait to hug my parents,' said Tess.

'I can't wait to hold my little boy. He won't be so little anymore,' said Elsie.

'Elsie,' exclaimed Rose, her arms around sleeping David. 'I didn't know you had a son. Why didn't you tell us?'

Elsie smiled. She had the kindest smile. Rose couldn't believe there had once been a time when she was afraid of the chief nurse. 'He was ten when I left home. He'll be a teenager now. Will he even recognise me?'

Rose pulled the sergeant by the sleeve of his uniform. 'Excuse me, sir. How many words can we put in our messages?'

The man looked at her with surprise. 'Why would there be a limit?'

She shrugged. 'The Japanese only allowed ten.'

The sergeant seemed confused. 'The enemy let you send messages home?'

'Sometimes, on special occasions. Not often.'

'None of those messages had ever been received. Until yesterday, no one in America had any idea what had become of the nurses in the Philippines. You girls were missing in action, presumed dead. Why don't you tell your family you are still alive? In as many words as you want. You are no longer a prisoner. You are an American. You are free.'

Had her mother believed Rose was dead this whole time? Rose couldn't bear that thought, couldn't bear the spectre of her mother's grief. There was so much she wanted to say to her. So much anguish and fear and hope she wanted to put into words to the one person she loved unconditionally. She wrote, 'Darling Mama, I'm coming home. A lot has happened in the last three years. Through it all, the thought of seeing you again has kept me alive. I love you and miss you and can't wait to hold you in my arms.'

As Rose was finishing her breakfast, she heard the familiar sounds of the national anthem. Pushing her plate away, she walked outside and joined the crowd of cheering people gathered in the main courtyard. Hands trembling, she watched the American flag fly high above the camp. With disbelief she stared at the Stars and Stripes, crying tears of joy and sorrow, for every heartbreaking moment on Bataan and Corregidor, for the bleak years in Santo Tomas, without food, without hope. She thought of the day she had stood just like this next to the other nurses as the American flag slid to the ground inside the grim tunnels, breaking her heart, and of starting every morning with a prayer, *Dear God, if you are out there somewhere, please send help*. What a relief it was to know that after all these years God had finally heard her.

# Chapter 28

## February 1945

Not content to sit back and allow the Americans to take the Philippines, the Japanese began heavy bombardment of Santo Tomas neighbourhood on 7 February. From that day on, Manila turned into Dante's circle of hell, devoured by fire, flattened by explosions. Planes whirred angrily overhead while Rose stood in line for showers. When she looked up, she was shocked to discover the Japanese rising sun on the wings above her. When the Americans had arrived at the camp, she had thought it was over. But the Japanese had different ideas. They were not giving up without a fight.

The queue wasn't moving. For weeks, the showers had stood empty and forgotten. Now, it seemed, the internees were awaking from a long sleep, making up for lost time, spending a long time under water, fighting over their spots in line, shouting to each other to hurry. Rose stood, stepped from foot to foot, rubbed her hands together. She knew David would be crying in Kate's arms, desperate for something to eat.

Throwing a regretful glance at the showers, she left the queue to the joy of those behind her. Slowly she made her way back to her quarters to get her plate and cup when a deafening explosion sounded. She cried out and covered her head. For a moment, she could hear nothing but the ringing in her ears. And then she heard the screaming.

A bomb had exploded in the line for the showers, where she had been waiting her turn only moments earlier. A man who had shouted at her to move along was face down on the ground, half of his torso missing. She could see a dozen other bodies. The survivors were crawling out of the inferno, charred, bloodied, shocked.

'Help,' screamed a man to her left. 'Please, help.'

He was lying on the ground in a pool of blood. His eyes were closed. His voice was shrill. Rose rushed to his side and took his hand. 'Who's this?' he shouted, twitching. 'What's happening?'

'I'm a nurse. I'm here to help you.'

'I need water. Please, a sip of water.'

Rose's flask of water was across the yard where she had dropped it. She could fetch it and come back to him in less than a minute. 'Let me check you first. You're losing blood.'

'My throat is burning. I'm dying from thirst. Please, have pity on me. I need water.'

She pressed his hand to reassure him, to let him know he was not alone. 'I'll be right back.'

All it took was sixty seconds to cross the yard, to grab the flask, to run back. Her hands shook as she pressed the flask to the man's lips, telling him to drink. He was quiet in her arms, his eyes open. She didn't understand at first, even though she had seen death many times before. She tried to rouse him, to wake him up. But it was too late. One moment, he was alive and begging for water. The next, he was gone.

The flask fell to the ground, the water spilled, mixing with blood that ran like a deathly stream into the gutter. Rose's legs no longer supported her and she sank to the ground, sobbing. They had been so close to salvation, surviving three years of war and detention, finally rejoicing at the sight of American tanks breaking through the prison gates, hoping to see home and their loved ones again. It all seemed so pointless now, so surreal.

Other wounded people needed her. All around, there were cries for help, for someone to come and take their pain away. In a moment, she would find the strength to get up, straighten her uniform that was soaked with blood and join the other nurses in their futile battle against death. But not just yet. For now, she remained on her knees, her face in her hands, her shoulders shaking.

She felt someone's hand on her back but didn't look up, thinking it was Kate doing what she had done all these years, trying her best to make it all better. Rose didn't look up because nothing could make this better. She had no energy left. Her cup was empty. And then she heard his voice. 'Rose! Is that you?'

Her tears dried as if by magic and she lifted her head, blinking, wondering if she was imagining it all, his voice, his face, his eyes looking down at her with concern. 'David?' she whispered, reaching out her hand and touching his cheek. He felt real under her fingertips. 'David!' she cried, jumping in his arms, feeling the warmth of his body, the comfort of his arms around her. How many nights had she stayed awake, dreaming of finding him again? And here he was, in front of her, his face hidden behind a beard, his eyes dark and haunted but the smile wide on his face.

Rose felt the earth tilt to one side and shift under her feet. For a moment, everything went dark. She felt his warm body next to her and heard his worried voice asking if she was all right. She wanted to tell him that she was fine, just fine. That she had thought she would never see him again and couldn't believe it was really him. That she was afraid he was a mirage that would soon disappear, like everything good in her life which had disappeared with the onset of war.

And then she cried in his arms. She sobbed like she had never sobbed before, her body shaking, tears streaming down her face, her breathing shallow and raspy. He stroked her back and said, 'It's all right. Everything is going to be all right.'

How could she explain to him what she was feeling? How could she tell him that she had said goodbye to him and it had splintered her soul in two? That she had grieved him for months, had spent years longing to see his face. 'What are you doing here?' she whispered.

'Looking for you,' he replied. 'I looked for you everywhere I went for the last three years.' With the tips of his fingers, he wiped the tears off her cheeks. 'Don't cry. You've been through so much. But it's over now. We can go home soon.'

'It's not over.' She glanced away from him, at the bodies on the ground, at the groaning men and women crawling through the debris, at the nurses rushing past, their uniforms no longer white but dark brown with blood.

'Look at you,' he said, his lips in her hair. 'You've lost so much weight. I can practically see through you.'

'I've always been thin.'

'Not like this. Before the war, you were glowing.'

'Not anymore.' She fell quiet, watching him. 'Wait. You remember?'

He smiled. 'I remember everything.' He held her as she cried. 'I was lucky to fall in love with you twice. Once, when we first met. And again, on Bataan.'

Not all was lost in the world. Seeing him again, alive and unharmed, felt like a new beginning, like a miracle. Perhaps there was hope for her after all. With David by her side, she was able to get up, to join the other nurses, to do what she could for the unfortunates who were writhing on the ground. As long as David was with her, she had the strength to keep going and not fall to the ground in despair.

After the wounded had been taken to the hospital and made to feel as comfortable as possible, the two of them sat side by side at the wooden table inside the nurses' allotment that once upon a time had been bursting with life and colour but now was nothing but grey soil and yellow grass under their feet. Their hands touched, their heads leaned close together.

'Where did you come from?' she asked. He had appeared like an angel before her when she least expected it. She was not prepared for it. Her heart fluttered inside her chest with joy and fear, like a bird trapped in a cage. She had lost him twice before and now, as he sat in front of her, she found it hard to believe that he was real. She was so afraid of losing him again. And yet, when he was near, everything else faded away, even death. She felt drunk with joy, like she had done once in Manila, before the war had laid waste to their lives.

'We arrived with the US troops. They liberated Bilibid prison a few days ago.'

'Is that where you've been all this time?'

He nodded. 'There and a few other camps over the years.' He told her the Japanese had marched the wounded soldiers from Bataan sixty-five miles north to Camp O'Donnell. 'I remember it like a terrible dream. Days under the burning sun, with no food, no water. No rest at night. While the guards changed, we had to continue walking.'

'Oh, no,' she whispered. 'How many of you were there?'

'Hard to say. Maybe a hundred thousand.'

'How many survived?'

He looked away, as if he didn't want to tell her. 'Two out of three didn't make it. The guards shot us for falling behind, stopping to find food, having some water from a creek. Some were beheaded. Others died from wounds or hunger. Many perished in the first months at O'Donnell.'

'Kenneth told me you didn't make it. All this time, I thought you were dead.' She still felt the heartbreak, could still hear the terrible words inside her head. She started to cry. 'He told me the Japanese took you away and shot you.'

He held her. 'They took me away. But they didn't shoot me. How could I die? I promised I would find you after the war, remember?'

'I remember,' she whispered, thinking of their last carefree days in Manila, of his worried face as he told her the enemy was coming to the Philippines, of refusing to believe him because she wanted another joy-filled day with him, unmarred by fear.

'We US officers always keep our word.'

'I'm sorry,' she whispered, touching his face. 'You were supposed to come with us to Corregidor. I had it all arranged. Only it didn't work out that way.'

'You have nothing to be sorry for. When they bombed the hospital, I lost sight of you. Suddenly, all hell broke loose. I was looking everywhere for you and couldn't find you. And when all was quiet again, I must have combed through that hospital a hundred times, searching for you. I had no idea what had happened to you. When the Japanese came, all I prayed for was that you were safe, that you were able to get away. Through my ordeal, the only thing that kept me sane was the thought that you were not at the hospital anymore, that you were gone. I'm so happy that my prayers have been answered. So please, don't apologise. I'm so grateful that you weren't there, that you were able to save yourself for me. Seeing you again, finding you alive, it's God's miracle.'

'Speaking of God's miracles, there is someone I want you to meet. Wait here.' She jumped to her feet and kissed his forehead, such a simple act and yet, it made her heart burst with joy because she thought she would never be able to touch him again. Then she ran across the yard into the main building, finding little David with a neighbour, who had a book in his lap and was trying to read it. The baby had other ideas. He wasn't interested in stories, nor was he interested in pictures. Laughing happily, he pulled the book out of the woman's hands, placing it in his mouth and chewing the spine. Rose wondered if he had started teething. It would explain the crying and the sleepless nights.

She thanked the neighbour, picked up David and the book, because the boy refused to leave without it, and carried him to the allotment, where she placed him in his uncle's lap. 'This is David. Your nephew.'

David Senior held the baby close, looking into his face with amazement. The boy babbled happily, touching his uncle's rough cheeks. 'Hello, big boy,' David said, delight and confusion on his face. 'You are a wonderful surprise!'

'He is six months old and the best baby in the world,' Rose said proudly.

'I didn't know my sister was here. I haven't seen her for three years. When I wrote to my parents, I had no idea what to tell them about Anne.' He must have noticed the heartbreak on her face because he paused for a moment, the baby balanced on his knee. 'Where is Anne, Rose?'

Rose sat next to him, praying for strength. 'I'm so sorry, David. Anne died two months ago.'

His body tensed like she had punched him. His eyes dimmed.

'She died from malaria four months after David was born. She wrote you a letter.'

For two months, she had carried Anne's last words in the front pocket of her uniform, close to her heart. Unlike Anne, she never thought she would see David again. She was keeping the letter for their parents. How she wished she could tell Anne that she had been right all along, that David was alive.

They sat in silence while David opened Anne's note, tears falling on the paper in his hands.

'Would you like to read it?' he asked after he was done.

Rose was about to refuse because the letter was private, meant for his eyes only. But before she got a chance, he pushed the paper into her hands, hiding his stricken face in the little boy's hair.

Dear David,

If you are reading this letter, it means I didn't make it. I have something important to ask you. It's about David Junior. Until he was born, I didn't know love this unselfish, this all-consuming was possible. After he was born, he became my everything. I am not afraid of dying but it breaks my heart to leave him behind. I spend what little time I have left in the world worrying about him. What if something happens to him when I'm not there to protect him? What kind of a man will he become? Will he be happy? Will he be good? It kills me that I won't see him grow up.

Look after him for me. Bring him up to be like yourself, kind, strong and unafraid. Tell him every day how much I loved him. I know you will love him just as much, like your own son. I know he will be safe with you.

I've never said it to you before but you are the best brother in the world and I miss you. You are my best friend and I want what's best for you. Marry Rose. I was wrong about her. I couldn't wish for a better sister-in-law or a better mother for my son.

With all my love,

Anne

The next morning, the sergeant in charge gathered the nurses together. Four dozen women stood side by side in the courtyard, metres away from the spot where the guards had executed Ruth and the other escapees. Rose tried not to think of the fear and the misery. She tried not to think of dead bodies laid out in the dust and children begging for a spoonful of rice with tears in their eyes, while cans of meat and fish rotted away in the mud, discarded by their cruel guards. She knew she wasn't the only one affected by the past. On every face she could see the tension, as if, having been through so much pain, the girls found it difficult to let light into their souls.

'Nurses of the US Army!' said the sergeant, saluting them. 'I have an important announcement to make. I am pleased to tell you that you will be the first to be evacuated from Santo Tomas. Tomorrow, you will board a plane that will take you to Leyte, an island under US control. From there, you will fly to Hawaii. Every single one of you should be proud of yourself. Our country will never forget your dedication and sacrifice, your selflessness and excellent work ethic. Many men, women and children wouldn't be here today if it wasn't for your hard work and bravery. We thank you for everything you have done.'

For a few seconds, the nurses were silent, as if they couldn't find the words to express what was in their hearts. Then someone shouted, 'We're going home?'

'You're going home.'

The women cheered and hugged one another. Kate and Tess jumped up and down and clapped their hands. For the first time since the fateful day three years ago that marked the start of the war in the Pacific, they cried tears of joy, not sorrow.

And only Rose stood to one side, not cheering, her eyes on a lone figure of a man holding a baby, waving to her from across the courtyard. As days had turned into weeks, weeks into months, months into miserable years, she had gone to bed at night praying to God for a miracle, to spare David for her, to bring him back. And God did. How could she say goodbye to him now?

'Do you remember our first night on Bataan?' asked Kate.

'Vaguely,' said Rose. So much had happened since then, the fear and the pain clouded her memory like fog.

'Remember sitting on the beach eating pancakes, wondering what tomorrow would bring, while everything was exploding around us like fireworks? And we were watching the harbour, hoping to see the US Navy sailing to our rescue. Imagine if we'd known back then that it would take them three years?'

'They are here now. And we are still alive. It's a miracle,' said Tess and in her eyes Rose saw the shadows of Bataan and Corregidor, where they had stood shoulder to shoulder in front of death and didn't shy away, even though they were weak, even though they were afraid. Often death won but they never stopped striving, toiling day and night to save another life, to help another human being. They were nurses. This is what they did. They gave their patients everything they had and more, often leaving nothing for themselves.

'Don't cry,' David told her when they were alone together in an abandoned hut that had only three walls and no roof. As they lay in each other's arms, the stars looked down on them, just like they had once done in Manila when they were young and untouched by war. 'I heard they will be evacuating the survivors of Bataan Death March next. We won't be apart for long. Go home and wait for me.'

'What if something happens? The Japanese never stop bombing. What if I wait for you and you never come back?'

He threaded his fingers through hers. 'How could I not? I couldn't possibly disobey my sister's last wish.'

'What wish?'

'She told me to marry you. I have no choice but to do as she said.'

'You don't have to if you don't want to.' She smiled in the dark, her cheeks warm.

'I want to. More than anything,' he whispered, his lips on hers. 'Do you know why we keep finding each other? Against all odds, our paths keep crossing.'

'Why?' She put her head on his shoulder and closed her eyes. She wanted to stay like this forever, just the two of them against the world.

'Because we are meant to be together.'

It was a wonderful feeling, to listen to him talk and believe every word, to know that there were no lies between them. She wanted to explain it to him, to tell him how much it meant to her. *I have lived the last three years doubting you*, she wanted to say. *And now my heart is at peace.* But she knew she would never tell him. She would never do anything to tarnish his memory of Anne. 'I'll be happy to marry you,' she said, pinching him. 'Out of respect for your sister.'

How could there be joy in the midst of so much suffering and loss? And yet, Hiroshi had been right all along. Magic did exist, even in war. She wished she could see his face one more time so that she could tell him about it. *I didn't believe you*, she wanted to say to the man who saved her life day after day, food sack after food sack. *But I do now.* She could feel David's arms around her. She could hear his voice, telling her how much he loved her. She could think of their future together and not be afraid. What was it if not pure magic?

Tomorrow she would leave this place, like she had dreamt of since the day the heavy gates closed behind her. Soon she would set foot on American soil. She would hug her mother and watch her cry happy tears for a daughter she thought she had lost. She would walk through the streets of her childhood, looking into shops, passing carefree people who would raise their hats in greeting. She would smile at the passers-by and watch the snow twirl in front of her frozen face. And she would wait for him. She had lost him twice before. She wasn't going to lose him again.

But tonight, she was in his arms and nothing else mattered.

# Epilogue

## A Year Later

Brownville in December was bleak and cold, with sharp ice falling from the sky like tiny daggers. Rose never left the house without a fur hat and a woolly scarf wrapped firmly around her neck. She dressed her squirming, struggling toddler in jumpers and a coat and placed a hat on his head, even though she knew he would throw it off almost immediately. Though she thought every day of the tropical sunsets, purple sky and pristine ocean stretching as far as the eye could see, the white sand, the burning sun, everything bright and shining, bursting with life, she didn't miss any of it. The sky over her head might be grey and oppressive, threatening snow, but it was peaceful. The colours of home might be subtle and understated but here she didn't have to be afraid.

She could never go on holiday in Hawaii, no matter how much her husband wanted to. If she heard the sea rustling quietly by her feet and the palms whispering in the breeze, she was afraid she would see the angry faces of her captors and the desperate eyes of her patients. Instead, the three of them went skiing in Canada and ice skating in New York. Perhaps one day they would visit Texas, where Ida had moved after the war with her growing family.

This afternoon, Brownville was awash with Christmas lights, almost like Manila all those years ago, days before the Japanese bombers filled the sky and changed their lives forever. Rose shivered as she pushed the stroller down the familiar streets of her childhood, while the little boy slept happily.

She took David Junior to the playground, where she chased after him, ready to catch him when he fell. At eighteen months, he fancied himself somewhat of an explorer. If there was a tree nearby, he had to climb it. If there was a muddy, icy puddle, he had to jump in it, no matter how wet and cold his feet would be on the way home. She cherished every moment with her little one, especially in the last couple of months when she had returned to work at the local hospital and her days once again became an exhausted blur of other people's needs.

Her little boy had tired himself out with puddle jumping, tree climbing and propelling himself down the slide head-first, his favourite activity in the whole world. For once, the long walk home was peaceful and quiet. Rose turned around the corner and paused outside the church where she had married David eleven months ago, while cars and passers-by rushed past. In Brownville, people moved at a speed she was no longer accustomed to. They wore pretty clothes but never slowed down to admire a sunset. They smiled politely but never stopped for a conversation. The buses came to a noisy stop next to her and opened their doors, only to slam them seconds later and speed off. Motorcycles like bullets whizzed by in a cloud of dust. None of it seemed real to Rose. She felt like she were in a cinema in Manila, watching a movie about America.

Everywhere she went, on every busy street, in every crowd, she looked for one face. It had been three and a half years since she had seen her father. Ever since she returned to the States, she had been searching for him everywhere, sending enquiries everywhere, to no avail. When did she stop searching and start grieving? When did she accept that he wasn't coming back? How much longer could she wake up in the morning, hoping that today would be the day she would see him walking down the street towards her? She knew the answer to that question. Never. She would never stop looking for him, for as long as she lived.

Sometimes it all became too much for her, the waiting, the uncertainty, the peaceful life she didn't know how to deal with. Thank God her husband was by her side. David knew exactly what to say to make her load a little lighter, even though he carried his own burden on his shoulders. Without David and her little boy, she would have lost her mind, like Kate who had gone through Bataan, Corregidor and Santo Tomas, only to return home and find that her brother hadn't made it. Like Tess, who came back to learn that her mother had died, believing her only daughter didn't survive the war.

Her eyes fell on a ukulele in a shop display and her heart raced inside her chest. Such a small thing and yet, it stirred up so many memories, so much pain. Some objects and words were like that; they had whole lives attached to them. She wondered if the ukulele would make a good present for David on their first wedding anniversary. She was about to enter the shop when it started to snow. Little David woke up and burst into tears. Rose took him out of his stroller and held him close. 'This is nothing,' she whispered. 'Just a bit of snow. Don't you remember how it used to rain in Manila? Like a wall of water, a deluge.'

It was as if the skies above her head had heard her words. The snow increased in intensity and became a deluge, while David screamed louder. Rose was reaching for her umbrella when her bag of shopping broke and everything spilled on the pavement. Oranges, potatoes and onions dashed away from her towards the road like they possessed a will of their own. A bag of pasta tore open, spilling its contents in the mud. A carton of milk split, dripping white liquid all over the pavement.

Rose brought David closer, shielding him from the snow, kneeled on the ground next to the ruined milk and started to cry. Her shoulders shook as she sobbed, while snow seeped under her scarf, melted on her face and ran down her cheeks like tears.

Distressed, little David pulled away from her and started to run. With horror, Rose realised he was running towards the road.

'David, no!' she shouted. The road wasn't busy but occasionally cars and buses drove by at a frightening speed. She jumped to her feet and chased after him, leaving the shopping and the stroller that was rolling away in the opposite direction, propelled by the wind.

A few moments later, David was on the road and Rose was screaming with despair. Perhaps Anne had been wrong about her after all. Perhaps she wasn't cut out to be a mother.

A man dressed in a long raincoat and a large hat appeared as if out of nowhere in front of David. He kneeled by his side, said something to him and scooped him up.

'Thank you,' Rose cried as she approached the two of them at a gallop, slowing down, trying to catch her breath. 'Thank you so much.'

She didn't look at the man as she took the child from him. All she could see was little David and his scrunched-up face as he voiced his displeasure to the world. Unlike his mother, he wasn't impressed with this stranger for arresting his excellent progress towards the opposite side of the road.

'You're most welcome,' said the man.

A shudder ran through Rose when she heard his voice. She looked up from the crying child. Despite the hat covering half the man's face, she recognised him instantly. 'Dad,' she whispered.

They stood facing each other in the middle of the road, while snow came down hard. And only when they heard the sound of a car engine and a blaring horn did they move to the side. He held her and she kissed his rough cheek. 'What are you doing here, on our street?' she whispered, her nose in his shoulder, her heart bursting with emotion.

'Looking for you. I wasn't expecting to find you so quickly.

This is a nice surprise.'

'Quickly? I've been waiting for you for three and a half years. I've been searching for you everywhere.' The little boy twisted in her arms, trying to get a better look at the newcomer. 'This is your grandson, David. He's been desperate to meet you,' she said, smiling through her tears.

Jack lifted the screaming child, looked into his face and kissed his rosy cheeks. 'What's all this racket about?' he demanded. 'You don't like the snow? I know how you feel. I don't like it either. It's awfully cold.'

As if by magic, the child fell quiet and reached his chubby arms out to touch his grandfather's forehead.

Having collected the shopping and the stroller, they found a quiet table at a café nearby, away from the snow. Jack and the baby sat down, dripping water everywhere, while Rose ordered some tea and croissants at the counter.

When she joined them at the table, she said, 'I walked through dead bodies in the Philippines. Walls collapsed on me and bombs fell on me. Men died in my arms. And here I am, crying over spilt milk.'

'Don't beat yourself up. Sometimes the smallest thing can push us over the edge. I bet it hasn't been easy, adjusting to civilian life.'

Rose thought of their homecoming a year ago. When they landed at Hickam Field in Hawaii, the nurses had knelt and kissed the ground. Speeches, band music and blinding flashbulbs welcomed them back home. They were awarded promotions, battle ribbons and Bronze Stars for valour. In Brownville, twenty-five thousand people gathered to see Rose drive by. Children were given a day off from school to meet her. The mayor handed her the key to the town. Strangers hugged her and everywhere she looked there were American flags waving in the wind. A whirlwind of reporters and attorneys interviewed her, listening with bated breath to her tales of horror and taking notes for war-crime trials. She had become somewhat of a celebrity when all she wanted was to be invisible, to be just like everybody else, to go on with her life.

But she wasn't like everybody else. As she walked through the peaceful streets of her town, her memories haunted her. No amount of awards, no battle ribbons or Bronze Stars could make up for what they had gone through. No matter what they did for them, the US officials couldn't give them those years back.

'It's been all right,' she said sadly. 'It's good to be home. What about you? What happened after we said goodbye?'

Jack explained how the Japanese had put him on a ship bound for Manila. As they were crossing the harbour, the ship was hit by a shell and most of the men were killed. Jack and a few others swam ashore, where they were captured by the enemy. He had spent the last three years in a camp in Japan.

'I arrived in the US yesterday,' he concluded. 'I came to find you right away.'

She couldn't believe he was sitting in front of her in a café in Brownville, sipping tea and eating a croissant. Although she had never stopped searching, in her heart she didn't believe she would find him after all this time. It had seemed impossible. She had witnessed so much horror in her short life but she had seen some true miracles too. This was one of them. 'What are your plans? How long are you staying?' She held her breath.

'I haven't had time to make plans yet. Still trying to catch my breath. I feel a bit lost, still figuring out my place in the world, I suppose.'

'I know the feeling.'

'Remember what we used to say on Corregidor? One step at a time.'

She took his hand. 'Come home, Dad. Come home with me.'

He hesitated. 'What about …?'

'Mama? She'll be fine with it. We spoke about it. From day one, we talked of nothing else. You are family. You belong with us.'

When they finished their tea and croissants, Rose placed the tired child in his stroller and together they pushed him back home. Side by side they meandered through the frozen streets into the rest of their lives, while snow fell between them like a white curtain, obscuring their tear-stained faces.

# A Letter from Lana Kortchik

Dear Reader,

Thank you for choosing Angels of War. As soon as I read about seventy-nine American military nurses held prisoner in a camp in the Philippines during the war, I knew I had to write this book. I am so excited to share this story with you and hope you enjoyed it.

On 8 December 1941, nine hours after the attack on Pearl Harbor, air raid sirens screamed across Manila. Moments later, bombs dropped from planes adorned with the sun of the Japanese Empire. The enemy advance was rapid and in January 1942, the Japanese invaded Luzon. Following the three month long battle of Bataan, between 60,000 and 80,000 Filipino and American prisoners of war were marched through the Philippines in what is known as Bataan Death March. Without food or water, they were forced to walk 65 miles under the tropical sun. Those who fell behind and couldn't keep up were beaten, shot and sometimes beheaded. The Allied forces under General Jonathan M. Wainwright surrendered in May and tens of thousands of prisoners spent three hungry years in POW camps, until the Americans liberated the Philippines in February 1945.

The nurses serving in hospitals around Manila in 1941 never

expected to see combat. They were ordinary women caught up in the horror of war. Thanks to their bravery and sacrifice, they became heroes. As shells exploded and the enemy closed in on them, the nurses held their heads high and didn't give up. Often forgetting about themselves and their own needs, they continued to nurse the wounded and the sick, touching thousands of lives.

As I researched this book, Alice Zwicker's biography by Walter Macdougall made a great impression on me. Alice grew up in Brownville and became a nurse because she wanted to help people. She had the time of her life during the first carefree months in Manila but it all changed when the Japanese invaded the Philippines. Through the dark years on Bataan, Corregidor and in the camp of Santo Tomas, Alice battled hunger, death and disease, while saving many lives. She was a true hero and the inspiration behind Rose, Tess, Kate and the other nurses in Angels of War.

If this story touched your heart like it did mine and you would like to learn more about the brave American nurses in the Philippines, Pure Grit by Mary Cronk Farrell is a great resource.

It's always wonderful to hear from my readers. I would love to know what you thought about the book. Feel free to reach out by leaving a review or contacting me via my website or social media.

Thanks,

Lana Kortchik
Twitter: https://twitter.com/lanakortchik
Facebook: https://www.facebook.com/lanakortchik/
Website: http://www.lanakortchik.com/

# Sisters of War

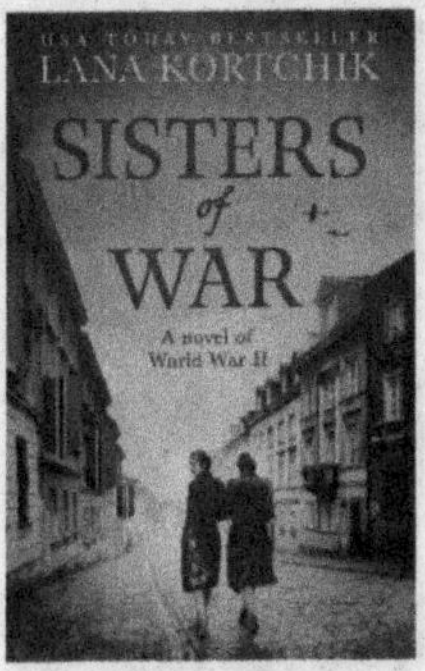


**Can their bond survive under the shadow of occupation?**

**For fans of *The Tattooist of Auschwitz* and *The German Midwife* comes this unforgettable tale of love, loss, family, and the power of hope.**

**Kiev, 1941:** Watching the Red Army withdraw from Ukraine in the face of Hitler's relentless advance, sisters Natasha and Lisa Smirnova realise their lives are about to change forever.

As the German army occupies their beloved city, the sisters are tested in ways they never thought possible. Lisa's fiancé Alexei is taken by the invading army, whilst Natasha falls in love with Mark – a Hungarian soldier, enlisted against all his principles on the side of the Nazis.

But as Natasha and Lisa fight to protect the friends and family they hold dear, they must face up to the dark horrors of war and the pain of betrayal. Will they be strong enough to overcome the forces which threaten to tear their family apart?

## Daughters of the Resistance

**Ukraine, 1943**

On a train from Ukraine to Germany, **Lisa Smirnova** is terrified for her life. The train is under Nazi command, heading for one of Hitler's rumoured labour camps. As she is taken away Lisa wonders if she will ever see her family again.

In Nazi-occupied Kiev, **Irina Antonova** knows she could be arrested at any moment. Trapped in a job registering endless deaths, she risks her life by secretly helping her neighbours.

When Lisa's train is intercepted by the partisans, Irina's husband among them, these women's lives will take an unimaginable turn. As Irina fights to protect her family and Lisa is forced to confront the horrors of war, together they must make an impossible decision: **what would they be willing to lose to save the people they love?**

**Be swept away by this heart-wrenching novel of love, resilience and courage in World War II**

## Sisters of the Sky

**March, 1917**

Petrograd is on the eve of revolution. For **Countess Sophia Orlova**, the city of her childhood – the only home she has ever known – has become her deadly enemy. The mob are ready to get rid of anyone connected to the old regime, including Sophia.

When rebels threaten to shoot Sophia and her husband, they are saved by **Nikolai**, a fervent supporter of the revolution. Determined to help Nikolai's cause, Sophia sets up a hospital wing in the house, nursing injured victims by his side.

Her kindness has captured Nikolai's heart, but their burgeoning romance is forbidden. With battle lines drawn between the new and the old, both their lives are in danger …

**Will their love be strong enough to overcome the horrors of war?**

**From the bestselling author of *Sisters of War* comes a heart-wrenching novel of lovers trapped on the opposite sides of a terrifying political conflict, loss, and sacrifice.**

# Acknowledgements

From the moment I started my research into *Angels of War*, the story of American nurses stationed in the Philippines during the war captured my imagination. It's a dream come true to be able to share this book with readers worldwide and I am grateful to everyone who has made it possible.

Thank you to my amazing agent, Mark Gottlieb, for his guidance and support. Whenever I'm in doubt, you are only a phone call or an email away, and I greatly appreciate it.

Thank you to my fantastic editors, Georgina Green, Sophia Allistone and Audrey Linton, who worked incredibly hard to bring out the best in this story. To Teresa Palmiero and Michelle Bullock for their feedback, to Ellen Rockell for my beautiful cover and to everyone else at HQ and HarperCollins for making this book a reality.

None of this would have been possible without the support of my family. Thank you to my mum for always being there for me, to my husband Joel for holding my hand every step of the way, and to my children for cuddles and unconditional love, and for teaching me something new every day. I am a better person and a better writer because of you. Thank you to Sal for being a role model and an inspiration for the last twenty-four years.

Finally, I would like to thank my readers around the world for buying my books, reading, reviewing and reaching out to share their thoughts. Knowing my story touched someone's heart makes all the hard work worth it.

Dear Reader,
We hope you enjoyed reading this book. If you did, we'd be so appreciative if you left a review. It really helps us and the author to bring more books like this to you.

Here at HQ Digital we are dedicated to publishing fiction that will keep you turning the pages into the early hours. Don't want to miss a thing? To find out more about our books, promotions, discover exclusive content and enter competitions you can keep in touch in the following ways:

JOIN OUR COMMUNITY:
Sign up to our new email newsletter: http://smarturl.it/SignUpHQ
Read our new blog www.hqstories.co.uk

https://twitter.com/HQStories
www.facebook.com/HQStories

BUDDING WRITER?
We're also looking for authors to join the HQ Digital family!
Find out more here:

https://www.hqstories.co.uk/want-to-write-for-us/

Thanks for reading, from the HQ Digital team